# Son of Saint

**The Savage Heirs**

Ruby Vincent

Published by Ruby Vincent, 2021.

# Chapter One

"**B**eams of splintered starlight gathering around you in a blinding halo."

Her whisper gathered around me. Words coming from everywhere at once to sink in my skin—penetrate my bones.

"You're walking through an endless forest. You lost your way miles ago, but you're not afraid. Lost is where you must be."

Leaning in, breath stole from my parted lips.

"One by one, the surrounding beams of light are going out till there are three... two... one left. The final one burns brighter than them all. It does not extinguish. It's growing, growing, grown into the size of a fist."

I lean closer, raising two legs of the stool off the ground.

"That ball of brilliance hovers before you tantalizing, seducing, oh so beautiful, then—"

*Bang!*

"Ah!"

I jerked, pitching off the stool. I barely smothered a shriek as I hit the dirt.

"—it shoots through your chest, leaving a burning hole. Then everything goes black."

"Wh— What does that mean?" the woman asked.

"Death," whispered Sienna. "It means death."

I heaved a sigh as the customer ran out of the tent. Righting the stool, I dusted off my peeling, patchy leather jacket and ducked inside the tent. My sister stared off at nothing—creases wrinkling her forehead.

"Sienna, how many times. People want to hear they're going to meet their soulmate by the next full moon, or that a pile of money is about to drop into their laps. All this death and gloom stuff does not get us repeat customers."

She came to life, blinking at me. "What?"

"You just told that woman a ball of light is going to punch a hole through her chest. That's the very opposite of the positive fortunes we talked about."

"That woman?" Sienna rose from her tattered seat of pillows. Her hands shook as they took mine. "Kenzie, that vision wasn't about her. It was about you."

I quirked a brow. "Oh yeah? What's that make it, the third time this week? Your spirit friends have a hard-on for me all of a sudden."

My expression did not match her mask of worry.

"You know it doesn't work like that. I don't commune with spirits. I don't have that gift."

"Right, of course. How could I forget?"

She shook me. "Kenzie, this is serious. I see people. I touch things, and I get glimpses of their future. Sudden flashes that are easy to interpret. But for the last few weeks, the visions have gotten longer, they haven't made much sense, and they've been about you." Her grip on me tightened. "They also all end one way."

I let out a long breath, softening at the clear panic in her eyes. My belief in her psychic powers was iffy, but Sienna's love for me wasn't. These visions genuinely scared her.

If only her spirit friends would give it a damn rest.

"That I'm going to die isn't news," I said gently. "We've all got a dirt bed in our future. And that mine may be sooner than later isn't news either." I swallowed hard, and the saliva did nothing to ease my gnawing hunger.

I brushed away a smear of dirt on her cheek with fingers that were no cleaner.

"We've got death hanging over us every day," I said softly, "and... after Halloween, this borough's become a dangerous place for me. We've gotta keep our heads down. Can't wander at night. Can't hook up with anyone from the old crew. You're having these visions because your senses are warning us to stay alert at all times."

Her eyes, so much like our mother's, filled. "Do you really believe that's it?"

"Of course, little sister." I injected lightness into my voice. "Trust me, the message is received. So, don't worry about me. Just get ready for the next one. I'm going to hook us another customer."

Her back straightened, smile returning to her lips. It still amazed me she was able to do that. I hadn't given a smile that wasn't faked or rimmed with tears in almost a year.

"How much did we get from the last one?"

Sienna handed me a wrinkled five-dollar bill. It was five more than we got the day before. Or the day before that.

"I saw a stall at the north end of the park selling fruit cups for two dollars," she said. "Preference for strawberry or cantaloupe?"

"Last time we got sick buying fruit from a stall. The guy didn't believe in food sanitation."

"We gotta eat something."

I tugged on my jacket—glad it hid my protruding bones and ribs. The tattered, holey T-shirt beneath didn't do the same job.

"Not fruit," I finally said. "Something cooked. A couple of stalls down from that guy was a lady selling monkey bread. Buy that. It's been a long time since we had a treat."

"That treat is selling for six dollars."

"You've got the kind of face that'll get it for three."

She laughed, and that face lit up, reminding me so much of Mom, my gut twisted.

Sienna's stream of ebony locks was straight where mine was wavy. My nose was a flat bridge between my forehead and nostrils, while hers was a round little button. My lips full and hers heart-shaped. And her hazel eyes upturned and enigmatic, where the dark orbs in my head hid something.

In other words, she was the spitting image of Mom, and I was of Dad. Two people neither one of us wanted to think about, but had to see every day in the reflection of each other.

"It's a deal," she said. "I'll get the monkey bread. You bring me another soul in need of direction." Sienna's eyes glazed. "There are many in this park, Kenzie. They need to know, even if they don't want to."

"Aye, aye."

We split paths in front of the tent, Sienna heading for the carousel of heavenly smells wafting through Mercy Park, me wandering the other way, keeping an eye out for anyone willing to look in my direction.

You read homeless in every inch of me.

The dirt caked under my fingernails and sun baked in my skin. Jeans ripped. Shoes falling apart and held together with duct tape instead of laces. The wild knots and tangles in the thick, wavy hair that used to be my best feature.

One look at me and the majority of polite society averted their gazes. They wouldn't stop to hear my offer of pay-what-you-can-afford psychic readings. Actually, they sped off the second they saw my mouth open—assuming I was on the cusp of begging for cash.

*Isn't that exactly what I'm doing?*

I brushed the thought away.

We weren't scammers. I didn't distract while Sienna snuck behind and stole their wallets. We didn't ask for something in exchange for nothing. We didn't beg favors.

First rule of living on the streets: Don't collect debts or enemies.

For months, that rule kept us on the edge of starvation just as much as it kept us alive. But it did keep us alive.

Encroaching on the wrong territory was how you ended up a broken pile of blood and bones in an alley. Begging money off the guys playing poker in the smoky bar back rooms was how you ended up their bitch, and stealing from the North Quay yuppies got your sketch on a police station corkboard.

That would not be me or Sienna, no matter how desperate it became. For months, we sketched out a half-life on the last of my savings and money from her psychic readings. For *months*, we stuck to the rules.

Then came Halloween.

Laughter, naked flesh, screams, and blood pierced the picture-perfect park scenes.

Grinding my teeth, I pushed back on the memories. Of course Sienna saw dark, grim clouds gathering around me. I saw them too.

I rounded the path, striding past the Duncan memorial. A group of six guys loitered near the tunnel entrance, passing a bottle and blunt around, laughing at something that couldn't possibly be as hilarious as their raucous noise suggested. One of the guys caught my eye and didn't look away.

Lifting my chin, I went up to them. The guy nudged his friends. They all fell silent tracking my approach.

"What's this?" asked the blond one holding the bottle in one hand and his crotch with the other. "Something we can do for you, lovely?"

"Was wondering if you guys would like—"

The lanky, autumn-haired guy cut me off. "Ladies don't come up to us *wondering* if we'd like our needs met till after the park closes. You should come back then." He flashed me a row of crooked teeth. "The answer will be yes."

"—a psychic reading," I finished. "It's 'pay what you can afford,' and it's just in time. You can find out if I'm going to kick your ass for assuming I'm a hooker."

They howled.

"Psychic reading, huh?" said Blondie. "Sounds fun. Max pissed on his chances, but I wouldn't mind finding out if there's a free ride in our future."

I winked. "Come find out."

Their wolf whistles went in one ear and out the other as I turned and led them back to our tiny Founder's Day setup.

Believe it or not, smirking jackals like this group were Sienna's biggest customers. Actual believers had their own psychics on speed dial. So that left skeptics with money to burn and time to kill. Or guys hoping we were denying being hookers just for show, and the readings were cover to take their money legitimately while afterward, we'd sweeten their evenings.

One guy was so convinced of this, he dropped a hundred dollars on Sienna's rickety table for *both of us.* Sienna informed him divorce, split custody, and a shithole Rockchapel bachelor pad were in his future, then we took our money and hauled ass the seven blocks he chased us.

I felt zero ounces of guilt for their delusions. I said up front, plainly, and repeatedly, that no amount of money would get their dicks in my mouth. If they chose to believe otherwise, it was a lesson learned for them, and a meal in my and my sister's belly.

Two kids ran in front of me—giggling at their balloons flying behind, desperate to reach the skies but anchored to their wrists.

Years ago, this was me and Sienna on Founder's Day. Weaving through Cinconites, collecting free kiddie favors, and counting the hours till the sun fell and fireworks lit the sky. It was one of my favorite days of the year.

Now Founder's Day was a convenience. It brought out enough people with their tents, stalls, blankets, and picnics that our little unpermitted psychic setup went unnoticed by the park security that usually chased us away.

Blondie laid a hand on my shoulder. "What else comes with these psychic readings?" He offered a sip from the bottle.

"Insight," I said, ignoring the alcohol. My response set off another round of guffaws.

"And after the reading?" one of them asked. "Say we pay fifty? Each."

My concave stomach tightened at all the meals three hundred dollars would pay for. Enough that there'd be some left over for new shoes and blankets that weren't mere scraps. Winter was coming to Cinco City.

"Is that enough for us to take the party back to our place?"

Blondie slid down my front, fingers grazing over the hollow of my collarbone. Up ahead, our tent and Sienna came into view. She held up the bag of monkey bread triumphantly.

I plucked his hand off with two fingers and flung it away. "Nope."

The group didn't laugh.

"Shame." Blondie passed off the bottle. "Because Digger's really been looking forward to seeing you."

A roaring filled my ears, blocking out the gleeful squeals and laughing parkgoers.

"And he's paying us ten times that to bring you and that crazy bitch back to him in one piece, but two pieces will do if you want to put up a fight."

Four hands gripped my jacket, wrist, and back of the neck. The fifth pressed something hard between my ribs.

"Both of you come quiet and we won't have to—"

My scream shattered the peaceful evening. A woman passing beside us stumbled, dropping her churro in the dirt. Wide eyes flew to us.

"Help," I screamed. "Someone help me. He's got a gun!"

The declaration sounded the bell for chaos. Screams erupted through the crowd. Parents snatched up their balloon-wielding children—the grinning faces of cartoon Junto Trapp marked their escape route as they fled.

The hands on my neck and wrist released me immediately. As fast as that hard object disappeared. I shot through the bodies.

"Hey," Blondie bellowed. "Get after her! Don't let them get away."

I snatched Sienna's arm. The monkey bread fell and crushed beneath our feet. I spared a glance back to mourn the last of our food, and to see where those guys were. Gripping Sienna tight enough to shatter her arm, I ran.

Lungs burning, my weakened body crying out for rest prematurely, I pushed myself faster—dodging sweaty tourists dampened by sun, then terror.

We broke free near the food stalls, hitting the paved path. It would take us to Market Street and the rush of noon-day traffic and pedestrians. All we had to do was dart across the street and blend in. They'd lose us around a corner before they knew what happened.

"Come on, Sienna." The street loomed ahead. "Almost—"

She cried out and slipped from my grip. I skidded to a stop, whipping around to Blondie hauling her back by the hair. He threw her into the arms of the russet-haired pretty boy. So far, they were the only two to catch up to us. The other four were coming through the crowd. One with a gun.

"Just for that, we're going to have some fun with you two before we turn you over!" Blood coated Blondie's lips, from where his nose caught an elbow. "We're not letting three thousand dollars get away." He pressed a blade to Sienna's throat. "Come with us or I fuck up this pretty face."

"No, stop!" People were blind to my fight as they raced to get away as fast as possible. "We'll come!"

I approached them, hands raised.

Blondie dropped the knife a fraction, smiling a terrible red smile. "Good. See? This doesn't have to be difficult."

I flicked behind him as the cane came down, cracking Blondie across the skull. He spun around, missing me as I ran up and punched him in the jaw. Sienna and I took off running.

"Thanks," I shouted over my shoulder.

"This counts as a favor!"

A favor he'd make me repay and then some, but he wasn't the worst person to owe, and for my sister I'd make good.

Sienna and I didn't stop running as the sounds of screams, carnival music, and sirens faded. We caught our breath outside an abandoned firehouse, sharing grave looks as we clung to the bars.

"That answers the question of if Digger has his guys out looking for us," I said.

"And if there's a reward. Three thousand dollars. Our own grandmother would sell us out for three thou. What are we going to do, Kenzie?"

My chest squeezed. "I'm so sorry. This is all my fault."

"Don't say that. Digger had everyone fooled. You didn't see what he was till it was too late."

"Yeah, and I could play that sympathy card if it wasn't the millionth fucking time I let some douchebag manipulate me." I pressed my face against the bars, tears slicking the metal. "Again. The first one took my job and reputation. The second took our home. Now the third wants everything else."

"He's not going to get it." Sienna made me face her. "We'll get it all back, Kenzie. Trust me." She tapped her forehead, smiling. "I've seen it. Soon, everything's going to turn around for us. Won't be long now."

I just shook my head, trudging past.

"You are ten layers of skepticism sprinkled with cynicism." She curled around my arm, laying her head on my bony shoulder. "Life's given you reason to be, but the day's coming that you'll believe in love and people again. I've seen that too."

"Is that before or after I die tragically?"

She whacked me on the backside, nearly pulling a laugh out of me. Nearly.

We continued on in silence, though it wasn't a contented one. Restaurant after restaurant we passed, inhaling fried chicken, Hunan beef, fish tacos, and artisan bread—taunting our aching stomachs.

I stopped as Sienna did—slowing down to a flirting couple sharing a plate of calamari.

"What are we going to do for food?"

I hated that question. Hated it more than "How much for a blow job?" and "What do you think you're doing in here?"

Hated it because unlike the other two, I didn't have an answer.

"We can't go back to the park," Sienna continued. "Digger's guys are going to stake the place out from here on."

"I know." I forced myself to turn from the window, carrying on. "We'll go to the Forty-Second Street shelter."

"That's in Waterford. We don't have money for a bus or cab."

"I know that too. Look, any shelter around here could be watched by Digger's guys. Two homeless girls showing up at a homeless shelter is something even his dumb ass could put together. Nowhere around here is safe," I said. "It's a five-hour walk, but we'll get there in time for dinner. River says they've got good food and they're not shy about second helpings."

The wince at *five-hour walk* washed away at *second helpings*. Our feet would be a mess of blisters we couldn't treat, but at least our bellies would be full.

"Why don't we pack up and move to Waterford? Or any other borough?" she asked. "We could..."

The look on my face silenced her.

"Of course, I'm sorry," she said, rubbing my arm. "We're not going anywhere. Not until all of us can go together."

"We are getting out of here together." We set off for a long walk. "Out of North Quay. Out of Cinco. And we'll be dragging Digger's battered body tied to the bumper the whole way."

"Hmm. I see that getting us pulled over. Let's strap him to the bottom of the car and gag him so no one hears his screams."

I smiled—for the first time in months.

"Even better."

WE LEFT THE SHELTER early the next morning. The director didn't just allow us second helpings. She also offered two empty beds so we wouldn't have to walk the streets late at night.

"It's not as dangerous as it used to be, but this is still Cinco," she said.

She didn't have to repeat herself.

Sienna and I spent the five-hour walk going back and forth on what we were going to do.

"I'll try again to look for work," I said. "Someone somewhere is bound to have a busboy or stock-taking job they can throw my way."

"You'll find something." Despite her doom and gloom predictions, Sienna was definitely the optimistic sister. "Until then... I think we have to go to River."

"We can't," I said before she finished the sentence. "Why do you bring him up when you know that?"

"Because we were just chased out of a park by six gun-toting, knifed-up thugs. Because we're walking five hours to get food. Because the temperature is dropping and a summer breeze rips through our tents like tissue paper. Make that *tent* since mine was trampled."

Shame bit deeper with every word.

"River's got food, beds, a roof, and jobs if we want them—"

"At a cost," I sliced in. "First rule, Sienna. *First rule.* We don't owe debts and we don't make enemies. To get that food, bed, roof, and job, we have to join River's crew. We do what he says, when he says till our debt is square, and if we don't, we'll have an enemy whose reach stretches into every borough."

Sienna gazed back at me with eyes older than her twenty years. "I know the rules, Kenzie. I also know when it's time to break them."

She drew ahead of me, running through the crosswalk as the flashing man counted down. I stopped at the red light, watching Sienna turn the final corner to the *North Quay to Leighbridge* overpass.

Sienna was in this with me one hundred percent—for the mere fact she didn't have a job, home, or money lying around either. She was living with me when the landlord booted us out. Dropping out of college didn't help her employability. Sharing the unfiltered fortunes of every interviewer she met did the rest.

She wouldn't abandon me no matter what, but if I didn't resolve this problem with Digger soon, she'd do even worse and try to protect me. By going to River.

*I didn't get screwed by every man in my life to voluntarily sign up for another to own me.*

Used milk cartons, newspaper scraps, and ground cigarette butts littered my weed-lined path. Over my head, honking horns and the steady drum of rubber on pavement added their own music to the city hum.

Morning crested on the horizon, painting our tiny patch of Cinco pink, orange, and gold. Most overpasses were crowded places. Other down-on-their-luck people gathered beneath for the scant protection from the elements, and the protection in numbers.

Sienna and I used to sleep under the *North Quay to Waterford Express.* Dozens of people, fires, and kind souls willing to share the little they had with us. Until two guys with needle marks on their arms and twitchy noses started eyeing us too often and too long. One night, one of the older women, Judith, woke us up and hissed that we better run. We left without a thought.

A week later, the news hit that those two guys jumped, beat, and stabbed a homeless man for his guitar and the ten dollars he made playing that day. Their faces flashed on the shelter television screen and Sienna and I didn't doubt that was supposed to be us. That was the last day I wore my mother's wedding band in public.

The familiar twinge of sorrow and resignation flooded me at the sight of our tent. Sienna fussed around inside, making room for the two of us to share. Lucky for us, we lost the tent with the pillows instead of the one with the air mattress.

We chose this place because it was tucked away and as secluded as you could get in a bustling city. A different kind of vulnerability, though so far, no one's found a reason to stumble off the sidewalk and come down this far.

"Probably has something to do with you guys."

I stopped beneath the shedding trees, dropping crinkled dusky leaves to make room for the dozens upon dozens of roosting bats. They were on every branch, hanging from nearly every twig. Uncomfortably large brown and black creatures, ducking their sleepy heads beneath their wings.

"You creepy, fascinating little things. One look at the two hundred of you waiting for an excuse to take flight, and anyone thinking of messing with us, turns around to find something better to do."

"Talking to the bats again?"

"If you can see the future, I can talk to bats."

"Those two ideas don't connect."

I cracked a smile. It was gone as quickly as it appeared. "I'm going to make it right, Sienna. We don't need River. We don't need Digger. You've trusted me for a lot longer and further than anyone else would've. I'm just asking you not to give up on me now."

"It's not about giving up on you." Sienna came out of the tent, arms open for me. "It's about—"

A mass of blue and brown fell out of the sky, smashing onto the spot Sienna had just been.

I lunged for her, snapping my sister to me and glanced up out of instinct.

A pale face gazed down on me—twin light pools plumbing the depths of mine. A shiver shot up my spine, rippling goose bumps in time with my blink. I opened my eyes and they were gone.

"Oh my gosh," Sienna breathed. "Kenzie... look."

I closed the distance. Lying in a tangle of nylon, polyester, and fiberglass was a pair of legs. Horror leadened my bones. For a moment, I didn't move or think, refusing to let the truth of what happened and what it meant for the face I'd seen. And that had seen me.

*Murder.*

"Kenzie, what do we do?" Her voice clogged with tears.

Kneeling down, reassurances stuck on my lips. I brushed the fabric aside, sucking in a breath. A perfect, sculpted vision of full lips, thick brows, and a strong jaw that defied his appearance—deceptively soft and smooth under my grazing touch.

This angel fallen on our doorstep would've been perfect in sleep if not for the sweeping seam on his forehead. His lids fluttered as I touched the wound, trying to stanch the blood.

Molten mercury. Swirling smoke. Gathering storm clouds. They flashed in my mind as his shiny gray eyes pierced me.

*Attempted murder.*

He laid his hand over mine—strong. Steady. His soft whisper floated in my ear, sealing my decision.

The beautiful stranger went limp, eyes rolling up in his head.

"What we do is get him somewhere safe," I said. "Whoever did this could be getting off the exit right now to return and make sure he got the job done. Or be looking to get rid of the witness."

"You want to move him? We should call the police," she argued. "Have them waiting here in case the guy comes back."

"We can't." I moved around, slipping my arms under his shoulders. "He said no cops."

# Chapter Two

Sienna brushed his golden-brown locks from his forehead, smile playing on her lips.

She made him as comfortable a bed as we could manage, lining our jackets, clothes, packs, blankets, and leaking air mattress between him and the bitingly cold concrete floor.

The disused bottle factory was a far cry from the hospital he truly needed, but it was the best I could do. On cold or wet nights, or nights we saw groups of guys loitering near our turn for the tent and didn't feel safe letting them notice we slept alone in a dark, deserted part of the city, this factory was where we slept.

This was another dark, deserted part of the city, but it had four walls and a ceiling. We had nowhere else to take him.

"Oh yeah," she whispered—low enough that she probably thought I didn't hear. "You're trouble."

I rooted through a pile of rusted pipes. "Do you recognize him?"

"No."

"Well, you don't get to credit your gift with this one. It's a good bet that anyone who begs you not to call the cops after getting thrown off an overpass, is up to no good themselves."

"I can't credit my gift. So far, no visions. Right now, our friend is on the threshold of living and death. There's nothing for me to see until he makes his choice."

"Not sure how much choice he has in the matter," I muttered.

I carefully stacked the pipes against one door, then the other. It wouldn't do much to keep someone out, but the clanging metal would let us know if someone came in.

"Should we have brought him here?" Sienna called.

"We had nowhere else to take him. Trust me, the last place I want to be"—I peered out the window, taking in the perfect view of Mercy Park—"is this deep in Digger territory."

"There's nothing in his pockets except lint. No wallet. No ID."

"Makes sense. The person who did this waited till early morning to dump him like a pile of trash where he wasn't likely to be found for a good while. There's no upside to helping the police identify his victim. What about his tattoos?" I asked. "Through some incredible foresight, did he tattoo his birth date and mom's name?"

"His tats are a work of art. Seriously, the artist nailed Marilyn Monroe. But I can safely say she isn't his mother."

"It was a long shot."

"How do we take care of him?" Sienna was holding his hand when I returned, tracing the spirals of ink on his fingers. "He was thrown off a bridge onto an air mattress. He could have..."

She waved a hand over his body.

"Internal injuries," I filled in. "I don't think it's a could and more like he *does* have internal injuries." Gnawing on my lips, my stomach twisted. "He wouldn't be unconscious if he was fine. Sienna, if he dies because we didn't get him a doctor, I won't forgive myself."

Sienna peered at me through her lashes. "You're already thinking it, and I love you too much to say it."

I slumped to the floor and took his other hand, lips burning as I forced it out. "I have to go to River. He has a doctor that he takes his people to. A good one, from what I hear. We need him to take a look at our boy. Tonight."

"I'll stay with him. He can't be left alone."

"I know," I said, worrying my poor lip puffy.

"Don't have to be a psychic to know you're asking yourself how you'll get to River without Digger's guys catching up to you."

"They clearly have no problem with snatching me in broad daylight in public places."

"What if you... didn't look like you?"

"What are you talking about?"

She looked me up and down. "We don't have a lot of options in the wardrobe department these days. You're so easy to spot because that's your only jacket and you have to wear it or walk around in flimsy, holey shirts. You'd get around a lot easier without the phoenix on your back telling everyone it's you."

"Suggestions?"

Sienna flicked down. My eyes bugged, picking up what she was saying.

"You want me to strip a dying man and strut around in his clothes?" I hissed.

"If it helps us do something about the *dying* part, I'm pretty sure he won't mind."

I gazed at him, tracing the soft, peaceful lines of that handsome face. "Fair point."

"Help me."

We were gentle, shrugging off his jacket and shirt, unloosing his tie, and slipping off his belt. I let out a low whistle while reading the labels.

"Whoever this guy is, he's definitely not shelter-challenged like us. This outfit is a Camden Caddell. It retails at two thousand. Even the knockoffs are expensive," I said.

"And who said a fashion degree had no practical use?"

I snorted. "My empty bank account would if I had even that anymore. I hope River's got a way to bring him to their doctor, or the doc will come to us. We took a risk moving him. We can't do it again. Will you be okay by yourself?"

"If one of Digger's guys saw us lugging him in, they'd have busted in by now. I'll be fine. Go."

I didn't need her to tell me twice. I wasted enough time. The one thing this guy didn't have.

I stripped off my jacket, rags masquerading as a shirt, and my pants. Our new friend was tall, so his hem hit my knees and turned into a shirt dress. His jacket swallowed me up, filling my nose with cardamom, orange blossom, and nutmeg. Only wealthy people smelled this good.

Perhaps that's how he made enemies. A bitter rival who got crushed on his way to the top, or decided to yank him down before he got there.

"Doesn't explain why you don't like the police."

"You talk to bats and unconscious men now?" Sienna teased.

"Only the ones with a mystery." Gathering up my hair, I secured my wild mane in a bun with his tie. A hat or hair dye would be better to truly disguise myself. If I was willing to steal like half the pickpockets in River's crew, I'd have it. But the cost of getting handed over to the cops by an angry store owner was too great.

"I'll be back with help as soon as I can. Cover the door after I leave."

"Try the Northfleet tunnel," Sienna said. "River's on the move during the day. Recruiting. The tunnel is a good place for it."

I nodded. "I'll hang out there for as long as I can. If he doesn't show, I'll grab one of his people and make them take me to the doc—settle up with River after."

I slipped out of the factory, those probing gray eyes on my mind. The guy was young. Older than me but it couldn't be by more than a few years. I'd place him at twenty-five to my twenty-three.

Who'd want to kill a handsome, young, tatted-up model with money? Who did he piss off so badly this was the death they tried to grant him?

*All questions to be answered when he wakes up. He will not die on me. I won't let it happen.*

Coming out onto Decker Drive, I headed south to the Northfleet tunnel. North Quay was a charming borough for those who could afford to delight in its offerings. This was the home of cat cafés, themed coffee shops, escape rooms, and old-timey bars.

Fairy lights wrapped around the lampposts. Off during the day, they flicked on at night to shimmer their soft glow on the Cinconites deprived of the real thing—stars.

Couples passed me on the cobblestones, gazing at each other to laugh at a joke or catch a smile, instead of avoiding the sight of me. A lanky, red-haired man grinned at me as he passed. A woman loaded down with shopping bags tossed a careless *hello*.

You could—and many people have—argue that a degree in fashion was a waste of my time that left me with an unimpressive résumé and no employable skills. Even so, on the list of things I'd do differently, changing my major to engineering or accounting wasn't one of them. Clothes were as vital to living as food, health, and chocolate.

You know what doesn't get you a job? Showing up to an interview in your underwear. Want that hot guy in apartment 3B to lose interest? Parade around in a Cheeto-dusted muumuu and ratty hair curlers. The difference between a suit and a sundress was the difference between jobless and alone to paid and in love.

With one change of clothes, albeit loose and baggy, I went from the woman no one wanted to see, to a human being again.

No, it wasn't fashion that led to my downfall. It was refusing to see the monster behind the Armani. Clothes give as much as they hide.

I shook the memories away as the tunnel entrance appeared ahead. Counting all the hits I took on the way down wouldn't get me back up. Although, imagining the many revenge scenarios I'd unleash on *him* always worked to turn a bad mood around.

The cute couples, shoppers, and nannies leading their charges on leashes thinned out, then disappeared. No one was hanging around when I strode through the crosswalk to the entrance of the tunnel. Half a dozen pairs of eyes clapped on me through the gloom.

Wadded-up newspapers, blowing plastic bags, and fast-food wrappers littered the tunnel, serving as the only decor accompanying the brick and grime. Claiming their spots on the footpaths, they stared at me from their huddle of sleeping bags and tatty blankets.

A fair number of homeless men and women kept to their own devices. They moved through life with the same principles: have no debts, make no enemies. And for some, make no friends.

Others formed ties, friendships, crews, and sometimes gangs, falling into the natural human instinct of protection through numbers and sharing resources. The Northfleet tunnel wasn't claimed territory, per se. They didn't have a leader, nor did they turn away outsiders. But they were known as the spot for homeless and runaway LGBT youth.

I tread past kids in their teens. One girl looked no more than twelve.

Biting my lip, I forced myself to break eye contact, feeling the rush of pain all the same. This life was unbearable for an adult. The thought of a child sleeping in a bag on the ground ripped my heart in two.

But at least she found this place with people moving closer to protect her, in case the stranger wearing Camden Caddell came to make trouble. She had her crew.

I lit on the broad figure in green, moving from person to person.

*And you used to be mine.*

"River."

He turned, smile playing on his lips like he knew I was coming, all he had to do was wait.

A long, slow breath hissed through my teeth, willing calm into my tightening muscles. I couldn't help it. Something about those wide shoulders, ripped muscles defying years living rough, bright golden eyes, and unblemished dark skin reduced me to a trembling deer who found herself downwind of a stalking panther. My first thought was run. My second was give in and accept my fate.

I was his.

"Mackenzie Blaine."

The seam split, opening into a wide smile that punched me in the gut. It wasn't right for someone so dangerous to be this beautiful. Hang a warning sign on predators, Mother Nature. Give a deer a chance.

He curled around my waist, dropping a kiss on my cheek. "Nice clothes. Not really your size though."

"Got them off a dying man."

River laughed. Why wouldn't he? Even I was having trouble believing everything that happened that morning was real.

"Glad to see you got away from Digger's guys," he continued. "Marty told me he gave you an assist yesterday."

"More than an assist. He cracked the skull of the guy holding a knife to my sister's throat." I wrapped my arm around his waist, resting my head on his shoulder as he led us away for privacy. "Digger's not giving up. Sounds like he put a bounty on my head."

"Five thousand for you and your sister," he rattled off without hesitation. "The price went up since yesterday. Not enough to get the Bowery Boys or Rolling Ninety-Nines after you, but everyone else..." River trailed off, glancing over his shoulder. "You shouldn't be out, borrowed clothes or not."

"I *wouldn't* be out but... I need a favor."

A sound like a moan rumbled from his chest and slipped into mine, turning up the heat. "That's my favorite sentence, Blaine. Name it."

I buried my face in his shoulder, picturing those gray eyes as I said, "A man was thrown off our bridge this morning. My tent broke his fall. He's in bad shape, River. Will your doctor—?"

"Say no more. Where is he?"

"The old Detour factory. Send him over now. I have to get back to Sienna."

River snagged the jacket and towed me back.

"I can tell you right now we'll have to bring your boy to him. A fall from that height, he'll need equipment the doc can't haul in a medical bag."

"It's not safe to keep moving him."

"I'll take care of it. Go back to the factory. We'll be there as soon as we can."

I didn't argue further. River was right, our mystery man needed a full workup to ensure that the world got another glimpse of those star-flecked eyes. It was the hope of that glimpse that made me brave leaving safety, and bind myself to River.

Grasping his chin, I made River look at me. His brows crooked in amusement.

"What do I owe you?"

He curled around my fingers and kissed the tips. "A favor," he said, breath ghosting over my skin. "To be named by me and collected at the time of my choosing. If you don't repay this favor, I'll find out why you came to me instead of bringing this guy to a hospital."

"Understood," I said lightly.

River continued kissing down my palm, rippling bumps over my flesh. "Why won't you come back to me, Kenzie? You know I'd take care of you. Both of you."

My lower belly tightened. The concentrated effort I put into convincing my body I wasn't interested, rattled my brain.

There was a time, shortly after we were kicked out of my apartment, and we were scared, hungry, and bouncing from shelter to shelter, that the offer to be taken care of by this handsome stranger was too irresistible to pass up.

Three months ago, we were a part of his crew, and during that time, the one who taught me the rules of surviving the streets was River.

When a man tells you without irony or guile that you shouldn't trust him—listen.

I walked away from River and the smoldering attraction between us because I didn't need to be a psychic to know the two of us were destined for trouble.

"Because if life's taught me anything, it's that relying on a man to take care of me works out as well as sticking my head in an alligator's gaping maw. Sooner or later, they snap."

"Can't keep making the guy who comes next pay for the guy who came before."

It was my turn to crook a brow. "Is there a price on the unsolicited advice, or can I get going now?"

River's laugh echoed through the tunnel. I heard him as I left, turning the lapels up against curious glances.

"How would you like to drift off in a bed tonight, rubbing your full stomach while serenaded by a crackling fire? I know it sounds too good to be true, but you can have all of that again. If you join my crew..."

River would get a lot of new recruits today, and I hoped that little girl was one of them. It'd be years before the consequences of favors ensnared her. By then, she'd likely decide the safety, protection, and family he offered was worth it. Some days—*that day*—I thought it was worth it too. But the next day I'd wake up and look into the eyes of my true family, and remember what happened the last time protection came at a cost I couldn't pay.

Sienna was meditating when I returned. Legs crossed, eyes closed, low hum emitting from her throat. Our charge lay still and sleeping beside her tangled legs, not rousing when I rested a hand on his forehead.

"Train tracks as far as the eye can see," she whispered. "An endless field of metal and gravel."

I fixed his makeshift bed, tucking the thin blankets in around him. That was Sienna's vision voice.

"You're standing in the midst of pure silence and solitude. No one is coming. No one would ever come."

"By *you're*, I'm assuming you mean me."

"Shh."

I shushed.

"You're confused," she continued. "Like this was where you were told to wait for your train, but you don't see a platform. You turn as the headlights barrel toward you."

Sienna peeled her eyes open. They were rimmed with tears. "I keep seeing it, Kenzie. I keep seeing you die."

I stroked her cheek, reminiscent of my unwise contact with River. "I can't imagine how awful it is to constantly see me like that. It's scaring you, Sienna, but there's one thing stronger than your visions and this fear."

"What?"

"A big sister's promise." I kissed her forehead. "I'm not going anywhere, anytime soon. There are still a lot of fuckers I've got to prove wrong. The universe isn't cruel enough to deny me the satisfaction of seeing their faces when we're back on top. I'd trade my soul if it means being around for that moment."

"I'm holding you to that promise." We locked pinkies.

"River's coming for him," I said. "He's taking him to their doctor."

"What did he want in exchange?"

"A blank check."

Sienna winced. "Wonder what would've happened if you gave in to the ridiculous sexual attraction between you two and banged it out? For one thing, I bet the favors would come free."

"It's not like that between me and River," I said, face heating. "He's slick and charming with everything that moves. I once watched him flirt an eighty-year-old woman into giving us access to her apartment building. I'm pretty sure that's how he holds his crew under his sway. They're all half in love with him."

"Maybe, but there's only one person who has him returning the feeling."

"Help me put his clothes back on."

Sienna cracked up, picking up on my subject change and unkindly not letting it go without notice. I was buttoning up the final button when the pipes clanged their warning.

"Yo, Kenzie. Where are you?"

"Over here," I called.

Marty and Nathan walked around the graffitied pillars carrying a yellow backboard. The two were decked out in the dirty, mismatching clothes that were the fashion of my new world. It didn't conceal the attractive twist of Marty's grin, or the artistry in Nathan's jewel-tone nail designs. Somehow, the best polish and tools always found its way into his pocket.

"How did you get your hands on that?" I asked.

"River called in a favor with a paramedic." Marty set the board down next to him.

"How did he—?"

"We talking or saving this guy's life?"

"Both."

"Ah, Kenzie." He winked at me as we transferred my guy to the board. "I've missed you. When are you coming back? I don't have to tell you Digger is heating up the streets."

"I can take care of myself."

He slid a look to Sienna. If anything was heating up, it was the hearts shooting out of his eyes. Sienna said I was oblivious to River's advances, but I picked up on the fact a guy doesn't charge a knife-wielding banger for just anyone. "What about you?"

"My sister and I stick together."

That mercifully ended the conversation long enough for the four of us to strap him on and carry him to the busted pickup outside. The rattling can was missing a tailgate and a bumper, but it ran.

I stretched out next to him on the truck bed, staying low to avoid Digger's guys, and staying near him. I held him to me, reaching across, I took his hand.

I swore he squeezed back.

*SUNNY*

"*...saving this guy's life...*"

"*...take care of myself...*"

"All of you, wait here." The harsh bark clanged in my skull, sounding the elephants to stampede. My head, neck, chest, and toenails screamed in agony, and that was the only explanation. I was trampled under flat, gray feet.

I peeled an eye open. A cloud of black and brown hovered above me.

"Let me stay with him."

"Absolutely not. Now out of the way. We're wasting precious time."

I didn't know if the voice argued. Darkness stole her away.

I WOKE SOMETIME LATER. How I knew time had passed was simple. My ebony-crowned guardian was nowhere to be seen.

My senses slowly returned to me. Pounding head. Steady beeping in my ears. Dry, aching thirst ravaging my throat. Blank, white ceiling above me.

I dropped my head and landed on the tray of medical tools. I stiffened, fists clenching and brushing against the bandage on my side. A tall figure in white stepped into the room.

"No Name, are you awake—?"

Shooting up, I trapped him in a headlock, stopping the shout in his throat on the tip of the scalpel pressed to his artery.

"Why yes, I am." My voice was a low, chilling rasp. "Awake and bursting with oh so many questions. Who are you and what the fuck did you do to me?"

"I am not the person or persons who tried to kill you."

I was impressed he replied evenly.

"I'm the one who patched up their handiwork."

I was in a small room without much to say for itself other than the cushioned surface I was lying on, a ring of medical equipment, and plastic on the floor.

"You're not our doc," I said, straining to remember the twenty-four, forty-eight, seventy-two hours— How many days had it been? At least one since my last clear memory was of walking into Laser at one in the morning. The sunlight streaming through the slats taunted me.

"Who brought me here?"

"A couple of street kids. Would you mind letting me go?" he asked dryly. "I am perfectly capable of answering these questions without a blade to my throat."

I constricted his neck, hissing in his ear, "What did you do to me?"

"You... ruptured your... liver," he forced. "I stopped the bleeding and... treated your head wound. You'll live... you just... need to... rest."

"What—?"

He twisted. The tiniest pinprick of pain poked my side. The room flipped upside down and faded.

*MACKENZIE*

Sienna and I huddled on the living room couch, making ourselves as small as possible in the immaculate space. When River said he had a doctor on standby, I imagined a ruddy-cheeked grump living in disgrace in an apartment above a pizzeria, sterilizing his tools with leftover tequila.

The private side entrance leading into this mid-century modern space, city prints on the wall, and stew bubbling in the Crock-Pot hadn't entered my mind. I felt bad sitting on his white couches in my dirty clothes. On the other hand, if he ran an illegal surgery catering to men who were allergic to cops, he'd likely had dirtier than me riding these cushions.

"Why is this taking so long?" I said to no one in particular.

For the last two hours, I willed open the door the doctor disappeared through. I couldn't so much as hear a machine beep. This barking, blue-eyed, no-nonsense man in a white coat could be operating on him back there, or he might be harvesting his organs.

"Someone should check on him. Make sure he doesn't need help or something."

Marty held up his hands. "That's what a sterile room needs, my filthy ass."

I rolled my eyes. "Fair enough."

A knock sounded on the front door. All the warning I got before River strode in carrying bags.

"Lunch." River tossed subs at Marty and Nathan. He wedged between me and Sienna, dropping ours on our laps. "Turkey on wheat," he told me. "Just how you like it."

I hesitated.

"No charge. I got these for free."

"Who do you know giving out free subs?" I stopped messing around and unwrapped the fresh treat. "Slathered in the good mustard too."

"The owner's kid ran off with her trash-bag boyfriend. The guy dumped her for someone else and kicked the girl out. I watched her back during the two months she was too ashamed to crawl back to her father." He swept out a hand. "Hence free subs for life."

I tore off a bite, moaning at each flavor hitting my tongue. "Have you ever considered—I don't know—helping without the expectation of something in return?"

"Nope."

Grinning, I bumped his shoulder, taking longer than needed to pull back.

"Just fuck already," Nathan muttered.

"Not on my couch, if you please." The doctor entered the living room, sliding the doors shut behind him. "Your friend is doing well. I stopped the bleeding—"

"Bleeding?" I broke in, jumping up.

He inclined his head. "His liver. A slow bleed, but serious. He'll need to take it easy and come back if there are any problems. I also suspect he sustained a mild concussion. I wasn't able to get very much information when he woke up." The doc rubbed his neck. "But there's nothing else wrong with him that I can see. I'll send you off with painkillers and extra dressings."

"Wait. Did you find out his name or anything about him?"

"As I said, we had little time to chat." He walked off. "You can see him now. Though I ask that you don't wake him..."

I thought I heard him say "for your own safety" at the end of that sentence. I dismissed it and went in to see my charge, River on my heels. He looked nothing but at peace lying on the operating table.

"Thank you for this, River. I can never repay... What's wrong?"

River slowed, stopping dead in the entrance. His natural, affable grin melted as he beheld the man on the table.

"Kenzie... do you know who this guy is?"

I didn't understand the hard edge creeping into his voice, any more than I understood the flinty steel coloring his eyes.

"No. Should I?"

River did not answer. He didn't say anything, do anything for a full minute, meanwhile ignoring my repeated questions.

River closed the distance. He turned his chin toward him, eyes narrowing as if assuring himself he was who he thought he was, and getting pissed the answer was the same.

"Him," River said. "I'll take him."

"Excuse me?"

"We'll settle up right now, Kenzie. I'll take over from here. You and Sienna head out. If you do, I'll consider your favor paid in full and then some."

"No." The request didn't warrant a thought. My reply was automatic.

"No?" he repeated, fixing that hard gaze on me.

"No. I'm not walking off and leaving you alone with anyone when you've got that expression on your face. Especially not without an explanation. Who is this guy?"

"A dangerous man," River said softly.

"Dangerous as in how? I guessed he wasn't a law-abiding citizen going by his request to stay away from the cops. Is he a criminal? Fugitive? Gangbanger?"

"I believe when the level of organized crime becomes as organized as him, you're granted the title mobster."

"He's in the mob?"

"He *is* the mob."

I frowned. "River, stop speaking in riddles and just tell me who he is."

"Shit." He shoved away, going to the door and slamming it shut. "Sunny, Kenzie. He's known on the streets as Sunny. How do you not know who he is? Everyone under and aboveground knows his family. They fucking rule Cinco City."

I stared at him blankly. "I don't know if you've noticed that I've been a bit preoccupied the last twenty-three years."

"Too preoccupied to have heard of the Merchants?"

My expression didn't change.

"Forty years ago, a gang called the Merchants came on the scene. As in one day they didn't exist, and the next they were everywhere. They ripped through Cinco like tissue paper, Kenzie. Murdered the governor and ignited the—"

"Night of Tears," I whispered. "Yes, I remember that much from history class."

"It was chaos. The gangs of the city spilled out of their holes, laying waste to everything in their path between the Merchants and the ledger. Dozens of people died that night. The National Guard had to come in and take control," he said. "You'd think that would be the end of it, but the Merchants weren't done.

"They opened the ledger and dumped its secrets on the internet, going public with every murder, rape, hired hit, bribe, affair, and parking ticket. In the time it took for the warrants to be issued, half the government, police force, and moguls were cowering behind their lawyers. They destroyed everyone powerful enough to stop them, and then grew too big for new players to try."

"What does Sunny have to do with it?" I didn't remember taking Sunny's hand again, but my fingers curled around his. I squeezed him tight. "He didn't exist when all of that went down."

"He's their son, Kenzie. Mommy and Daddies ran their empire for three decades, then up and decided retirement sounded nice. They passed the crowns off to their children, including their youngest son"—he waved a hand over him—"Sole Bellisario."

I considered his words carefully. "So, what's Sunny's deal? Has he done more than simply take over the family business? Has he hurt anyone? Killed anyone?"

"What? Kenzie, are you serious right now? That's what you're asking me?" He flicked to our clasped hands.

My face heated. "You said he's dangerous, but he's getting thrown off bridges, instead of doing the throwing."

"That you know of."

"What have you heard about Sunny specifically? *His* crimes, River. *His* enemies."

"Kenzie, why—? Oh," he said, shaking his head. "I see what's going on here."

"What do you mean?"

A wry smirk twisted his lips. "You clocked the Caddell suit and said to yourself, 'gee, I bet this guy'll be plenty grateful to his rescuer. Grateful enough to float a few thousand bills my way for saving his life.' That's why you won't turn him over to me. You have to be the first face he sees when he wakes up." River snorted. "Wow, Kenzie. Have you ever considered helping without the expectation of something in return?"

"Fuck you." Spitting anger was a sharp reminder of why River and I haven't banged it out. The guy could get under my skin worse than a capillary. "That's not why I'm helping him. I know what it's like to be judged by the sins of my parents. So far, you've told me nothing that explains why I should hand over a broken, helpless man just so *you* can have the son of the Merchant family owe you a favor."

That charming smile returned. "I'm rubbing off on you."

"Get out."

"As you wish." He swept a bow. "I'm taking my guys with me. Don't request another favor until this one is paid up." River looked to Sunny and his mouth twitched, grin vanishing for a second. "Consider if he's worth your name in red in my books."

"You still here?"

"Always a pleasure." River blew me a kiss out the door.

Brushing Sunny's hair back, I sighed. "Son of the Merchants, huh? You are an intriguing mystery."

I GENTLY SHOOK SUNNY'S shoulder. "Hey, wake up. Doc says if you sleep any longer, it's a bad sign."

He groaned deep and long.

"Don't go dying on me after all I've done to keep you alive."

His eyes shot open, reeling me off the edge of the backboard. Oddly silver orbs fixed on me as I straightened.

"Hello," I said, suddenly nervous.

"Angel," he whispered, brushing the back of his fingers down my cheek. "My angel."

"Flatterer."

Sienna was off wandering the factory, eating the last of her sub and humming a song that bounced among the beams, filling the dreary place with a lovely melody.

He let me pull the covers up to his chin. "I'm told your name is Sunny."

"You have me... at a disadvantage. You know my name, but I don't know yours."

"Mackenzie Blaine. Everyone calls me Kenzie."

"Kenzie." He rolled my name on his tongue like he enjoyed the way it tasted. "Was your doctor friend that put out by... the little scalpel to his neck that he downgraded us to... this shithole?"

Sunny grimaced. With consciousness came pain.

"I'm not going to ask about the scalpel. But no, we're in this shithole because it's the only place I could take you. I'm afraid you fell on my home."

"Yes..." His eyes glazed. "I remember... falling."

I sat up straighter. "Do you remember who pushed you? I saw their face for a moment but—"

"You saw their face?" Sunny shot up and cried out, clutching his side.

"Easy." I guided him down. "You were thrown off a bridge and sliced open in the space of a day. Give yourself a minute."

"Not a bad idea." Chest heaving, his eyes opened and closed in preparation of sending him back to sleep.

"It was only a glimpse. Pale face, bald, older, creepy eyes. Ring any bells?"

"No." Sunny slid his hand under mine. "But he could've been hired. Would you recognize him if you saw him again?"

"Absolutely."

Sunny's breaths evened out—soft and slow as he relaxed, shutting his eyes. My pulse had the opposite reaction to his thumb stroking my palm.

"I owe you more than I can repay, Kenzie Blaine. You are gorgeous, by the way. Whatever you want, name it and it's yours."

"Let's focus on getting you on your feet first." I pulled away, holding my hands to my chest where he couldn't reach them. My palm tingled strangely. "How do I reach your family so they can get you home? A disused factory floor isn't the best place to recover."

"Wallet and phone gone?"

"Yes."

"Got money for a pay phone?"

I looked away. "No."

"What's your view on stealing a phone?"

"Dim."

He started to chuckle and quickly cut himself off, groaning. "I'm told asking has been known to work."

"Not when there's dirt in your hair and rags on your body. People give me a wide berth. They're not about to let me use their phone."

"Then don't worry about it. When I can move, I'll take myself home."

"I can get your family here, Sunny. They must be looking for you too. Tell me where they live and I'll bring them."

He was shaking his head before I finished the sentence. "The compound is closed to visitors, Angel. No exceptions. You'll never get in."

*Compound?*

"I could send you to his business, but in the time it'd take for him to vet your story and decide you can be trusted, I'll be river dancing around this place. I can wait, just— Damn, I'm starved."

"I've got half a turkey sub with your name on it."

He hummed, corner of his mouth tugging up as he peered at me through slitted eyes. "Feed me, nurse?"

"You're river dancing on the last of your luck."

Another laugh was cut off by a groan. "Help me sit up?"

A reasonable request. I moved to his head, slowly lifting him by the shoulders and sliding onto the spot, letting Sunny rest on my back. His hairs tickled my cheek, sticking as easily to me as the ridges of his spine against mine. I felt every ridge. Shuddered to each movement.

"Soooo," I drew out. "Sole's an interesting name."

"It means sun."

"It's also a girl name."

"Ah, so my angel is beautiful and brutal. Much like the real thing I imagine."

I giggled for the both of us. "Nothing against your parents. I like Sole. Certainly more unique than Mackenzie."

"Really want to sit around talking about name meanings, or do you want to ask the questions that've been on your mind since you found out who I am?"

I bit my lip. So much for getting him to open up through small talk.

"I've been told you're dangerous. Personally, I like to get to know a man before I dismiss him as a duplicitous liar. Never let it be said I'm prejudiced."

"Great use of duplicitous."

"I'm a college-educated bum, thank you very much."

He shook with mirth, shaking me in turn.

"Anyway," I continued. "I helped you because you're a human being and you needed it. But what my sister and I don't need is trouble. While I get you have no reason to be honest about this, if you're tangled up with dangerous people that make a habit of throwing people off highways, promise that when you're well, you'll go back to your life and leave mine in peace. The last thing I need is more people after me."

"That's all you want? A mutual parting of ways?"

"Yes."

"Can I at least treat you to a dinner that isn't a soggy sandwich?"

"Not necessary."

"Hmm." He was quiet for a long stretch. "You're one of a kind, Mackenzie Blaine."

"I've always thought so."

"Still, I meant it. Whatever you want, if I can, I'll give it to you. I don't take my debts lightly."

"I don't collect debts. Besides..." Her face floated in my mind, so real and beautiful my chest ached. "What I truly want, you can't give me."

"How long you been living rough?"

"Almost a year."

"Mind if I ask how a beautiful, kind, college-educated woman such as yourself ends up on the streets?"

"That's a long story. Mind if I ask how a strapping young mobster ends up flying over a ledge?"

Sunny dropped his head on my shoulder, casual as can be. "Doesn't the mobster part cover it? We tend to pick up enemies."

"Enemies or victims?" I probed. "Was pale-faced baldy avenging the death of his father or something?"

"Couldn't tell you since I don't know who he is. Whatever you heard about me and my family, Kenzie, I can promise you fact became legend long ago."

"I heard you rule the city."

"We keep the peace," he replied smoothly. "No one's fond of the lawmaker. They like the enforcer even less. All the same, we provide the needed service of policing the underworld. The old headlines will tell you what Cinco was like before we stepped in."

The headlines didn't have to tell me. I read the stories, heard the tales. Decades ago, a ledger filled with the deepest secrets of the most dangerous men turned the city on its head. Each new owner filled it with what they knew, then died tragically at the hands of a new owner.

Judges, politicians, wardens, business owners, monsters—everyone with the slightest bit of power found their way into the ledger, and therefore under the control of whoever owned it. Cinco City fell into a dark period. The convicts ran the prison, and no one was policing the fence. For a while, it seemed nothing could stop the spread of evil.

Then, Adeline Redgrave rose from the ashes like a phoenix, turning the city on its spires. We all woke from the worst night in our history to tales of her death and a smoldering fire that claimed the ledger. Until its secrets hit the news.

"I can't do the compare-contrast game since all of this went down long before I was born." I glanced around. "But if this is a better life, I can only imagine the hellscape I would've survived in forty years ago."

"Your life may turn around sooner than you think," Sunny said. "I'd like to hear your long story. What else do we have to do but—? Hello, hello. When the goddess sends a rescue crew, she chooses her best and finest."

I rolled my eyes over Sienna's giggling. How this guy had the energy or inclination to flirt hours after crashing onto a tent and undergoing surgery was beyond me. A picture was beginning to form of Sole Bellisario, and it looked a lot like the rich, self-satisfied high-society folk I once struggled to impress.

"Hello, Sunny."

Sienna greeted him like they'd been friends for years. I twisted as she took his head in her hands, eyes falling shut.

"Hmm." She grimaced for a second, then her face cleared and she nodded. "Return where you are safe and the world is safe from you. Home. There, your enemies cannot reach you.

"You're fine now," Sienna said, dropping her hands. "Out of the woods and a long life ahead of you."

"You a doctor? Damn, I have been out of touch. You guys have gotten younger and more advanced if all you need to do is tap my forehead to check my vitals."

Sienna beamed. "Better. I'm a psychic. I can feel the threads of your life stretching through the years, entwining with those whose importance you haven't begun to understand."

Stiffening, I waited for Sunny's response, and my cue to shut him down. My belief in psychics was iffy, but no one—*no one*—laughed at my sister or called her crazy. Not if they wanted to eat a turkey sub instead of wearing it.

Sunny sat up a little straighter. "No shit? A psychic? That's amazing. What else can you see? Can you see the guy who did this to me?"

Try as I did, I searched his words for a trace of mocking, and found none. Sunny sounded genuinely curious and impressed.

"No, I need closeness, preferably contact, to read a stranger."

"You'd do a better job filling in the blanks," I spoke up. "What do you remember?"

"Do you mind helping me back down? If I was on painkillers, they're starting to wear off."

Sienna helped me ease him onto his back. Beads of sweat collected on his scrunched forehead. Sunny was making an effort to sound fine, but the last twenty-four hours were catching up to him fast.

"Last night, I went to... the club opening."

"Which club?" I asked.

"Laser. The line wrapped around the building twice. All of North Quay came out."

"North Quay." I folded my legs under me, taking his hand out of habit while I thought. "So you weren't driven out of another borough to be dumped here. Whoever did this must know North Quay well too. They knew there are barely any cars on that overpass that early in the morning, and that the area is secluded."

"But they didn't know it so well that they saw we camp there," Sienna added. "We pitched our tents there a while ago. If they scoped the place out recently, they would've seen us."

I bobbed my head, gnawing on my lip in that habit I couldn't break. "You're right, Si. They had the place picked out in advance, which means..."

"He was planning his shot for weeks, maybe months," Sunny finished. "He waited for me to leave the compound, and got me alone."

A shiver climbed my spine. I knew what it was to sense eyes on me everywhere I went. The fear. The paranoia. But for someone to have me in their scope while I walked around blissfully unaware, ill-prepared for the blow meant to end my life. I didn't know which was worse.

At least I knew Digger was coming for me. Sunny skipped out for a good time and ended up thrown over a bridge like garbage. He left his home and family with no idea someone intended to make sure he never saw them again.

"You were alone," I confirmed. "Do you usually go clubbing alone? Did your almost killer know all he had to do was wait for the next grand opening?"

"I see what you're getting at." Sunny closed his eyes, slowly breathing in and out. "No, I usually party with my crew. Usually. Every now and then I'll go out by myself if they're being boring and I'm not about to let that stop me getting some.

"If he's been planning this for a while, I have to assume keeping me under surveillance was part of the package. I left the compound without company or security." He squeezed my hand. "That was his opening, and he took it."

"What happened when you were at the club?"

"Shots. Shots, shots, shots, shots," he sang, bobbing his head back and forth. Sienna laughed while I held back a sigh.

*I guess some of us need humor to get through tragedy.*

"I was in the VIP room with about ten ladies. The last thing I remember was ordering another round for the group." Silver orbs found me, reaching out to drag me into their depths. "Then, there was you."

Heat stained my cheeks. The reaction both surprised and unsettled me. I barely knew this guy, and going from his associations, Sunny Bellisario wasn't someone I wanted to know. Still, holding his hand spread warmth through my bones. Looking into his eyes stirred emotions I thought long dead.

"You were drugged." I gazed at our hands, drawing on my strength to pull away.

It wasn't working.

"That's the only explanation. If anyone's taking my ass anywhere, they're carrying me out."

"Okay, okay," I muttered under my breath. "But no idea who'd want to do this to you?"

"No, I have ideas. I've got plenty, but none of them look like the guy you described. With a hit, I can't hunt down the bastard who paid for it unless their hired dog tells me who they are. I've got nothing without the man only you saw."

I didn't stop myself brushing hair from his sweaty brow. Sunny was warm. Too warm.

"Kenzie can sketch him for you," Sienna said. "She knows his face."

"I'll never forget it."

"When we get our hands on paper and a pencil, you'll have a drawing of your hit man. Next time, get to him before he gets to you," she said. "We're down to one tent now, and Kenzie hogs the blankets. Can't afford to lose another one."

Sunny didn't reply.

"Sunny?" I called. "Sole?"

I lightly shook him. Our mobster was out cold, and good thing. The doc said he needed rest, and with pain and fever creeping up on him, it was much more peaceful in dreamland.

I drew Sienna to a corner of old cardboard boxes and made our bed for the night. We spoke softly while shaking out the critters that had the same idea.

"Someone's been watching and waiting with a patience that freaks me out, Kenzie."

"You said he was safe as long as he locks the doors from now on."

"It's not him I'm worried about," she hissed. "You saw this guy, and *he saw you*. You're a witness. Sunny returns home where he's safe, meanwhile we're as exposed as we've always been. What if he puts the word out about you? What if another bounty hits the streets? I see a long life for Sunny Bellisario, Kenzie. I don't see one for you, except..." Sienna glanced over her shoulder.

"Except what?"

"Can't tell you."

I pulled a face. "Can't tell me? Why?"

"It's dangerous to know too much about your future."

"Since when?" I cried. "Twenty years, and I haven't gotten you to stop."

"Since you're super stubborn and have tried on more than one occasion to prove my visions wrong." She popped a kiss on my cheek. "This one I'm going to let work itself out on its own."

Sienna got the full force of my confusion as she stretched out and rested her head on her arm. She was lights out in minutes. I always envied that about her.

The dankest, most uncomfortable accommodations never got in the way of Sienna and her eight hours. I, on the other hand, couldn't sleep—couldn't settle into the calm I earned after the longest day.

*Not while she's out there.*

I held out for an hour, possibly two. Time ran together for those not chained to it.

Sienna's breaths were soft puffs on my shoulder. I raised her arm and stuck my wadded-up threadbare blanket in my place. Silently, I slipped out of the warehouse.

Surprisingly, I wasn't concerned about Digger's guys searching me out. I know what they got up to at night. I was the last thing on their mind.

I left the warehouses behind. My path lit with color.

The fairy lights dancing up the trees flicked on, showering the sidewalk with its cream and blueberry glow. A memory floated up at the sight, reminding me of mornings sitting on the porch with Sienna, munching on fruit cups topped with whipped cream and blueberries taking the place of sprinkles.

*"The good stuff goes down easier with a side of the bad,"* Dad would say as he squirted more cream.

How much good stuff versus bad stuff made up Sunny Bellisario, and what about him intrigued me to find out? Other than the dramatic way he literally crashed into my life?

I rounded a corner a block away from club street, casting a passing glance at the cars idling on the curb. Did *he* park there? Safe in the shadows of his tinted windows, watching Sunny run into the arms of his perfumed cohort? Was he sitting in one of those cars watching me?

I stopped in my tracks, a shiver rippled goose bumps on my arms. Without another thought, I returned to the top of the street and made for the noise, people, and clubs. The street was closed off this time of night to let drunken coeds stumble from club to club without getting mowed down. The perfect crowd to lose yourself, and a possible tail.

No one could know where I was going. No one could know why. This fact meant more than the risk of Sunny's would-be killer finding me.

Damp bodies bumped me, leaving wet, glittery spots on my jacket. Songs I didn't recognize poured out of every door, in every style there was. Hip-hop, techno, K-pop, R & B, pop, and swing music. The strobe and string lights were alive on Seventh Street, all pulsating to a different beat.

"Kenzie? Mackenzie Blaine, is that you?"

I froze. In the time my mind shouted for me to turn and get out of there, they surrounded me, closing me in a ring of designer dresses, stilettos, clutch bags, and dye jobs. Lyla's smile reached all the way to her eyes. True delight at trapping prey.

"That is you," Lyla purred. "I almost didn't recognize you in those—Heavens, sweetie, what on earth are you wearing?"

My face burned with humiliation. There were three people I prayed every day and night would not see me like this: living at rock bottom. Lyla was number three.

*If I had any doubt the universe hates me, she just kicked sense into my head. She hated me more than anyone.*

Lifting my chin, I said, "Like it? I've been working on this look for months. I call it homeless chic."

Lyla's laugh tinkled above the noise.

The whole crowd was there. Lyla, Madison, Naomi, Skylar, and Brielle—as lovely as their names. On the outside.

Lyla looked like a supermodel in college—time, money, and fancier clothes hadn't changed that. Her kiwi-brown hair flowed past her shoulders and skimmed the waist of her Caddell last-season pants. She looked down her aquiline nose, top-heavy lips tugging up at the side. Her friends/coworkers varied in size, shape, and features, but like last I'd seen them, their haircuts and clothes weren't far off Lyla. Everyone saw her as their image to behold. The goal to aspire to, and then curl into a ball and cry when you inevitably fell short.

Everyone worshipped Lyla Dawson—except for me. No wonder we never hit it off.

"Homeless? You must be joking."

"No, Lyla, I'm not joking." I closed the distance, staring her down. "I sleep in a tent under an overpass now, so take a good look. Snap a picture or two. This is the consequences of your evil, twisted games."

She wrinkled her nose. "Hmm, well, I assume people don't walk around smelling this bad for a gag." Her entourage howled, raising my hackles. "So you fell on hard times and you're blaming me? That's rich. None of this would've happened if you weren't a cheating, scheming liar. But it's not like I expected much more from you. It's in the genes, sweetie. You were cursed from the day Mommy spat you out. How is Mommy Blaine, by the way?" The sickly, sweet tone jarred with the malice etched in that pretty face. "Is she up for parole yet? Or did they grant her the needle? Face it, Kenzie, you're exactly where people like you belong: in the trash."

Lyla straightened, flipping her hair over her shoulder. "This is the part where I shove your shoulder walking off, but I'm sure you don't mind if I skip it. I'd rather roll in that vomit puddle than touch you."

I slid to the side, sweeping out a hand that vibrated with rage. "Please, go ahead. No doubt you've got to rush back to the plastic surgeon and correct that jacked-up nose job. He can't have meant to make one nostril wider than the other."

"Wha—?" She flew to her nose, eyes bugging. "That's not—"

I was already walking off.

"Bitch!"

Middle finger over the shoulder was all Lyla and her buddies got in response. Everything in me ached to go back and jack up her nose job for real, but I saw the outcome playing out in a movie reel. Dozens of witnesses see a raggedy homeless woman punch out the gorgeous, fashionable Lyla Dawson. The cops roar up and receive four sworn statements from Lyla's posse that I attacked completely unprovoked because I was probably off my meds. I'm hauled off to jail, and Lyla shakes her head, smirking through the blood that I'm finally going exactly where I belong.

I couldn't deny her barbs hit home—each and every one. But I would deny her the satisfaction of giving Lyla what she truly wanted: to witness me sink lower.

*As if I could fall any lower.*

Leaving Seventh Street behind, I swipe a stray tear from my cheek, willing the barrier that held my sobs for five months not to break as I turned down a side road, hugging myself tight.

All I'd ever done my whole life was what I thought was right. I worked hard, loved freely, stayed true to myself, and never compromised my beliefs. Why didn't I see in time that there was nothing the phony hated more than the genuine?

My steps slowed on the sidewalk, coming to a stop at the browning lawn's border. Paint chipped off the fading plaster before my eyes—dotting the anemic flower bed with white polka dots. Through the window, she sat in her usual place, conked in front of the television. Her only claim to movement was lifting her hand in and out of the popcorn bowl.

The pressing urge to cry faded under the tide of a stronger, twice-as-scorching swell.

Hatred.

What had goodness and kindness gotten me? What did my rules? Shoes held together with tape and a home beneath the highway with the other discarded trash. All the while, people like Lyla thrived, climbing to the top of the remains of my broken dreams.

Cinco City never was and never would be a city of angels. Only the ruthless survived here. Only the shrewd succeeded. If I was ever going to get back what belonged to me...

I drew the switchblade concealed in the folds of my jacket and crept across the lawn.

...it was time to break the rules.

# Chapter Three

Sienna's eyes snapped open when I tried to swap places with the blanket the next morning.

"Where were you?"

I looked away, lips pressed tight.

"You went to her house again, didn't you." It was phrased like a question, but it wasn't one. Sienna knew exactly where I was. "Oh, Kenzie, that witch said she'd have you arrested if she saw you hanging around again. You can't risk it."

"I didn't hang around." The confession forced out of me. "I broke in."

Sienna shot up. "You did what? Are you insane?"

"When it comes to her, yes."

"What if you had gotten caught?"

"I wasn't caught. Not by her. I was caught by Lyla Dawson, though. I ran into her on Seventh Street."

I expected my sister to jump on the subject change. She did.

"Lyla Dawson? No way." Sienna rubbed my arm. "Are you okay?"

"No. She threw Mom in my face, then stood there licking her bloody chops like Thanksgiving came early and I was the prized turkey. She doesn't feel an ounce of guilt for destroying our lives. Lyla even said I deserved to end up where I did, and this was just the universe putting me in my natural place."

Red splotches stained her cheeks. "I don't approve of this language to describe a fellow passenger on life's journey, but since Lyla is actually a reptile in a skin suit, I have no problem saying I hope that saggy-cunt bitch flips that pretty hair into a wood chipper."

"And that's putting it nicely."

"I can't believe she'd say that to you after all she's done. What kind of sociopath pats herself on the back after ruining someone's life?"

"I was never just someone to Lyla Dawson," I said softly. "From day one, it's been personal between me and her, and last night, she saw without a doubt... that she won."

"She didn't win, Kenzie. One day, we'll get it all back. A home, our family, your job. The only thing Lyla will be licking then is your boots while she's bowing and scraping at your feet."

"You paint the loveliest picture." We hugged. "I hope one day it's more than fantasy."

Untangling myself from her, I crossed the space to check on Sunny.

"Sienna!"

Racing to him, I threw down by his side, taking his face in my hands. Sunny warmed my palms like heat leaking through a tea mug. Sweat soaked his expensive shirt—his jacket long discarded and lying in a pile next to him. He was hot, so hot, but his teeth chattered—clattering in his brain loud enough to drown out my cries. Or that's what it seemed as I screamed for him.

"Sunny? Sunny, what's wrong? Oh, Sunny, I'm so sorry." I rested his head on my lap, stroking his burning forehead like I could brush the fever away. "I shouldn't have left you.

"Sienna, we need ice, medicine—something!"

"There's a pharmacy at the end of the street. I'll make them help me. I don't care if I have to steal the medicine." Sienna ran out the door, and it didn't cross my mind to stop her—warn her to stick to our rules. Sunny would *not* die because I was too broke and useless to buy him proper medicine, give him a real bed to rest, or even a fucking quarter to use a pay phone and call his family to help me.

You could say he wasn't my problem and what happened to him wasn't my responsibility. You could say that, and you'd be dead wrong. I decided the moment he looked up to me on the remains of my tent, that he'd live to gift his jewel tones on the world for another day. I had let down everyone in my life who relied on me. Everyone I swore to protect. Sunny wouldn't be another casualty of my broken promises. He just couldn't.

"Hold on, Sunny," I whispered. I shrugged off my jacket, using the inside cloth to blot his forehead, cheeks, neck. "You're going to be okay. I promise, you're going to make it."

I murmured to him over and over, holding him tight to my chest. Sunny's eyes fluttered open and shut. His mouth worked as if trying to tell me something.

"Don't give up." I stroked his sculpted cheekbones. "You have to find the monster who did this. He doesn't get to win after all the pain he's caused. They don't get to win."

"An... gel..."

"That's me." I pressed a kiss so featherlight to his forehead. My lips burned for more reasons than one. "I'm here, Sunny. I won't leave you."

The warehouse door banged open.

"Sienna, thank goodness. What did you get? I think we have to call the doctor—"

"You don't need a doctor, doll."

My muscles went rigid.

"Not yet."

I gently set Sunny down and scrambled to my feet. He was concealed by conveniently placed pillars and a stack of crates once used for the factory's products. He'd be safe hidden here.

*If I can lead him away.*

Stepping out, my gaze locked on Digger.

"Hello, Luca. It's been a while." I edged closer to him, and away from Sunny. "Why didn't you tell me you were stopping by? I would've cleaned up."

Luca "Digger" Adams grinned, flashing that row of crooked teeth I once thought charming instead of flawed like his fucked-up personality. My knife-wielding friend from the park came in after him, tossing me a wink.

"You're a hard woman to find, Blaine." Luca tossed his head, sweeping his longish sable strands from his eyes. Another move I once thought adorable. "That is until you decided to take a morning stroll down Eighth Street today. What happened? You got tired of our little game of cat and mouse?"

"Fuck you."

"No, thanks," he breezed, "you had your chance. I do know a few gentlemen that would happily accept that offer, though. They got a thing for bony, desperate sluts."

"Then drop your pants and put your ass up."

Luca threw his head back, laughing. "You always did make me laugh, Mackenzie. Remember how we were together?" We circled each other, staring across the divide, daring the other to cross. "Remember how good I was to you?"

"What I remember is dating and falling for a man I thought was sweet and charming until one night, he shows up with a bloody nose and asks me to get him out of a debt by having sex with some random lurking at the end of the hallway. When I said no and kept saying no, the mask dropped and the true loathsome cockroach scuttled out."

Blondie flipped his knife on his palm—waiting.

"You say loathsome cockroach, I say investor," Luca replied, shrugging. "I put time, effort, and money into you, Mackenzie Blaine. I set you and your sister up in my building. I gave you food and money, and when the time came to show how much you loved me, you were too much of a stuck-up bitch to do me one little favor."

"A favor?" I cried. "You manipulated me, Luca. You pretended to love me, so you could groom me into a love-sickened pet. Then when you thought you had me under the spell, you tried to pimp me out like you did all the women forced to work for you!"

"Who was forced?" That easy smile hung on his lips. "I told you that you had a choice between paying off your debt or working it off. Add all the dates, reduced rent, money, clothes, not to mention the emotional damage, that's about ten grand I wasted on you. Either you and that tasty little sister of yours are working for me, or I walk out of here with my money. What's it going to—?"

I bolted for the door. Blondie was on me in two bounds.

"Get off! Get off me!"

Lifting me off my feet, Blondie ran me at the wall. I thrashed in his iron hold, screaming as he ran full speed with no sign of slowing down. My skull bounced off the concrete, killing my screams in my throat. Head lolling, he twisted and shoved my back to the wall, holding me up since I could no longer do it myself. His blade cut a thin, red ribbon beneath my chin.

Through a haze of pain, Luca approached.

"No more running, Mackenzie. The game is over. By the look of you, you're not going with option *B*, so option *A*, it is." Satisfaction oozed off him in waves. "You'll screw the first several johns for free to get back in my good graces. The next fifty, you'll take an eighty-twenty cut—twenty for you. After that, we'll discuss renegotiating your cut so you can buy yourself something nice every now and then. Never let it be said I'm not a generous boss."

"It'll never... happen," I rasped. "I'll bite off every dick that comes near my mouth. I'll break every finger that touches me."

Luca lightly lifted his shoulders. "That's not the threat you think it is, doll. I have a select group of clients that love a woman who... fights."

"You're not hearing me, you limp piece of shit. I'm not going anywhere with—" I struck, punching Blondie in the gut. He doubled over, and I snatched the knife from his grasp. The blade glinted in the streaming beams of light, pouring from the holes in the roof, slicing through the gloom as I did—cutting a graceful arc in the air.

"Stop!"

I slashed across Luca's chest, cutting open shirt and skin. Roaring, he roughly yanked the knife from me, nearly tearing my arm from my socket.

"That is it!" Blondie slammed me against the wall. "I was good to you," Luca bellowed. Blood dripped down his chest and soaked his waistband. "I would've made you one of my top girls. Given you a nice apartment. New clothes and shoes. Gotten your flea-bitten ass off the streets. You would've been my highest earner." Luca slapped the knife on Blondie's palm. "Now you'll be an example. Cut her face, Kingston. Blind one of those doe eyes. I'll let the mutilation-loving freaks pass her around, and work her sister's pussy overtime to make up for the lost revenue."

"Whatever you say, boss." Kingston licked my cheek, then scraped it with the blunt edge. "Let me have a few goes before the freaks mess her up."

"Be my guest."

Kingston brandished the knife. A shot rang out in the factory.

Eyes widening, Kingston opened his mouth to say something, and the knife fell from his grip. His body followed the path.

Luca whipped around. He wasn't fast enough, but I was. I shot out of the way as Sunny seized his collar, throwing him against the spot I was in.

"S-Sunny?" he bleated.

"How ya doin', Luca?" Cheeks flushed and eyes bright with fever, Sunny's hand was perfectly steady, training the gun between his eyes. "How long has it been?"

"I was— I was just—"

I stood pinned to the spot, mind whirling, making sense of the bleeding Kingston at my feet, and the mewling Luca before my eyes. I'd seen Digger angry, impatient, seductive, and falsely sweet. I'd never seen him scared.

"Oh, I remember," Sunny sang. "We chatted a few months ago. During that conversation, I warned you what would happen if I found out you were forcing women to work for you again. Say it with me, Lu-Lu, *I only employ the willing.*"

"She— She was willing!" Luca's eyes rolled in his head, searching for any way out. "That bitch chose to work for me, then she robbed me when my back was turned. You understand, I can't let her get away with that. Everyone would think I'm soft. I'm only getting what's mine."

I found my voice. "That's a lie. Luca posed as my boyfriend, playing the part of Prince Charming so I'd give it up to line his pockets—"

"Sunny, don't listen to a word this bitch says. She—"

"Ah ah." Sunny shoved the muzzle in his mouth. "It's rude to interrupt. I heard your side of the story. Now I'll hear Angel's."

"Mhh!"

"Then what happened?" Sunny prompted me.

I took a deep breath. "When I said no, he threw me and Sienna out on the street. He thought desperation would make me crawl back to him, but when that didn't happen, he had his friends snatch me from a shelter on Halloween and lock me in one of his buildings. Then he sent in a *customer.* I broke the bedpost, smashed it over the guy's head, and made a run for it. Sienna and I hid from him ever since. I knew what would happen if he got his hands on me again."

"Well, you see," Sunny said, swinging back to Luca, "I'm inclined to believe the lady. Her story sounds like ones of coercion and attempted rape I've gotten from other women. The same women we discussed. Is history repeating itself?"

"Mhh hmm hm!"

Sunny clicked his teeth. "I warned you what would happen if I got word you were pulling this shit again. You're just so hardheaded, Digger. Matter of fact, that's how you got the name, isn't it? You keep digging till you're six feet under."

Face streaked with tears, Digger tossed his head, thrashing to get free. Sunny pulled the trigger.

My gasp sounded on the heels of a faint click. Luca's legs gave out. He sunk to the floor, bawling his eyes out.

"Today's your lucky day. I could only get my hands on a single bullet, which I wasted on your friend here. Matter of fact, it's a lucky day for your employees too," Sunny said. "You're going to retire them all with a healthy severance package. If we have to have this conversation again, the gun will be fully loaded. Get the fuck out of here."

Luca tore out of the factory, stomping on his friend's body in his hurry to flee. He nearly took down Sienna on his way out the door.

"Wha— Hey! Digger?! Kenzie, it's Digger."

"Not anymore," I said softly, gazing at Sunny in a new light. "Where did you get that gun?"

"I went out for a midnight trip of my own. Felt naked without some protection." I believe he tried to meet my eyes, but his were crossing. "Got this too."

He stumbled to me, holding a handful of crumpled twenties. I reached for him instead, grabbing Sunny as his knees buckled. The weight dropped us both to the floor.

"411 Dunston St.," he croaked. "Penguin, Angel. Pen..."

His head drooped on my lap. Sunny used the last of his strength wandering streets, and the last of his adrenaline saving me from a fate I refused to imagine.

"You reckless, wonderful fool." I kissed his forehead. "Si, help me carry him. We're going to Dunston Street."

Carrying him out of the factory, and crime scene, was the easy part. The difficulty came in flagging down a cab. Three drivers slowed, took one look at the shabby ladies holding an unconscious man, and sped off. Finally, one woman stopped and we hefted him onto the back seat. I rattled off the address.

"411? Are you sure you should be going there, honey? Nothing but trouble behind those doors."

"Nothing but trouble behind the doors we left behind."

She harrumphed. "Ain't that always the case."

"What happened?" Sienna hissed as the cab sped down Main. She unearthed an ice pack from under her shirt and pressed it to Sunny's temple. "Are you okay? Your head."

I touched it and my fingers came away tacky with blood. "Digger's henchman slammed me against the wall. It looks worse than it is. Or it would've been worse if Sunny wasn't there." I stroked his cheek. "I saved his life, and he saved mine."

Inexplicably, Sienna smiled. "Yes."

I didn't pay attention to where we were going till the cabbie made the turn for the express. The kitschy eateries and yuppy couples disappeared and were replaced by sports cars and skyscrapers. I didn't care about any of them except one.

"409, 410— There! 411." It was an apartment building. It had to be Sunny's home. He'd be safe here.

The car screeched to a stop beside a row of shrubs. Idling by the entrance were two doormen, standing stock-still in solidarity with the Buckingham Palace guards. Sienna got his feet and me his arms. Sidewalk traffic parted for the insane sight in front of their eyes. Gaping at us, the bustle of Cinco halted as we finally neared the end of this horrible event.

"Hey," I called. "We need help."

The doormen broke their staring contest with the opposite building. Frowns marred their neutral expressions.

"This is Sunny Bellisario. I think he lives here. We—"

"On the ground! Don't move!" The guards pulled their guns and shattered the spell. Sidewalk watchers fled in every direction—screaming, pushing, recording. Both men shoved through them, weapons aimed at our heads. "Put him down!"

Sienna dropped Sunny, then herself, falling flat on the pavement.

"No, we didn't do anything," I cried. "We're trying to help him!"

"Release him!" Guard One ripped me from Sunny, kicked the back of my knee, and buckled me to the ground. The world blurred. He shoved my face into the pavement, his weight pinning me down. Sienna cried when Guard Two's muzzle bit into her forehead.

"Who are you?" they demanded. "What did you do to him?"

"Sienna, it's okay. It's going to be okay. I..." Sunny's final word came through the panic. "Penguin," I shouted. "Penguin."

The guard growled, bearing down harder.

"Bring them inside."

*SUNNY*

My next wake-up call, I found myself exactly where I should be. Black textured wallpaper wrapped around the room, breaking up to make room for the eighty-five-inch television, built-in bookshelves, and a wall of windows looking out over my city.

I followed a passing helicopter and landed on the IV beside my bed, next to a series of beeping machines, next to Doctor Hendrix.

"Sunny? Sunny, can you hear me?"

"Receiving you loud and clear, Doctor, and may I say, you're looking good in those scrubs."

She gave me a look. "You may not."

Hendrix popped the stethoscope in her ears and leaned over me. Chanel perfume filled my nose, and wispy red strands tickled my forehead. Thirty-five years old, stylish glasses, and a button nose, I didn't view a potential relationship between us as inappropriate as Hendrix believed it was. The lady was a single mom packing three hundred grand in student loans. Working as my private doctor, she preferred her checks on time and our interactions professional.

That morning—possibly afternoon—taking my shot to convince her of my sexual prowess didn't cross my mind. My first thought was—

"Angel, where is she? And her sister?"

Huge, sad eyes filled my vision, blocking out all thought of patient-doctor sex. It was cheap and shallow compared to the wild-haired deity who held me, her calluses comforting on my skin as she stroked my temple and held my hand. Suffering tried to ravage the beauty of Mackenzie Blaine. Dirt stole her luster. Sorrow dulled her eyes. Worry gnawed on her lips. None of it hid the fact her full mouth was plump and dusky, and her windswept locks were a dark crown on my angel's head.

*She saved my life, though she had nothing to give and expected nothing in return. I've met all types in my line of work, but I've never met an intriguing creature such as Mackenzie Blaine.*

"Ah, yes, would you be speaking of the young ladies that delivered you on the doorstep like an injured bird? What happened to you, Sunny? From your lips."

I grabbed the remote on my nightstand and raised the bed. "It's not going to differ much from what they told you. I went to a club opening where I must've been drugged. Next thing I know, I'm hurling off the 414. The girls took care of me, brought me to an off-the-books doc, and got me here. So I repeat, where are they?"

"Deep breath."

I complied, waiting her out.

"Miss Blaine and her sister were held downstairs by security. They are being taken care of, but despite Miss Blaine's insistence that they be allowed to leave, Thatcher has kept them close until you confirmed their story. He also asked to speak with you the moment you woke up. How do you feel?"

"I feel fine." Actually, I felt like a rhino sat on me, then sat on me again because my shouts made it laugh. "How do I look?"

Hendrix hesitated. "Sunny... the doctor that worked on you did well repairing the bleed, but I assume post-op care was neglected, leading to your infection and fever."

Sinking into the pillows, I fixed on the ceiling. "You assume correctly. What's the damage?"

"The infection has cleared up and your scar is healing nicely."

"That's great. So why do you look like you're about to tell me I'm stage four?"

Bending over, Hendrix retrieved a folder from her bag. "There's something else we have to discuss."

*MACKENZIE*

"Hello?" I banged on the wood. "Hello, is anyone out there? Let us out of here, you trigger-happy wannabe Queen groupies!"

"Kenzie, relax." Sienna stretched out on the couch, sucking down a plate of chocolate chip cookies and a carton of apple juice. "Mr. Thatcher said we'd be released when he's had a chance to talk to Sunny. At least our holding cell is pretty swanky."

I shook my head. It wasn't so much a holding cell as it was a private waiting room complete with couches, coffee table, bland hotel art, a television, and a well-stocked mini-fridge. Thatcher was good enough to bring us lunch, dinner, pillows and blankets, and eventually breakfast as the day bled into the next, and he still waited on that conversation with Sunny. What he did not give me was my knife or my freedom.

"Do you think Sunny's okay? Did we get him here on time?"

"We got him here as fast as we could, considering we stopped for a showdown. Kenzie, what are we going to do?" she asked under her breath. "We can't go back to the underpass in case Sunny's would-be killer ever shows up looking for the witnesses, and now our second go-to place just became a crime scene. Where are we going to go?"

Deflating, I flopped on the couch. "I don't know. Despite Sunny sending Digger running with piss stains on his pants, I have a feeling we don't want to run into him in a dark alley anytime soon. We may have to stay out of North Quay for a while."

Sienna rested a hand on my knee. "I'm sorry. I want to stay in North Quay as badly as you do, but that makes the most sense. We're in Leighbridge now. I'm sure we can find a nice shelter or two, ask the women there about the best spots to sleep and set up for readings."

"Yeah," I said, frustration crushing my chest. "That's what we'll do."

Thatcher came in and gestured to us. "Come with me. Mr. Bellisario has granted you permission to enter his suite."

I didn't move. "Afterward, are we free to go?"

"Yes, ma'am, you can exit the Fairfield whenever you wish, and this should have been said before, thank you for returning Mr. Bellisario to us. You have the gratitude of his family as well as the staff."

*Wow. Sunny is truly loved around here.*

"What... is this place?"

"Fairfield," he said simply. "Mr. Bellisario's home. If you'll follow me."

Thatcher strode off, expecting us to do just that. He led us through the bowels of the staff rooms, into the lobby and elevator. A quick swipe of his badge sent us shooting up.

"Can you imagine what his place looks like?" Sienna said in my ear. "I bet he has a fountain of melted chocolate that he rolls around in with his conquests."

"Who has chocolate fountains in their living room, Si?"

"Rich people, sister mine. Rich people."

The elevator dinged open.

Sunny Bellisario did not have a chocolate fountain, but that was the only thing he didn't own. My mouth fell open walking inside the bachelor's paradise. Arcade games claimed a corner of the apartment and lit the ceiling in multicolor, eager for someone to play. His sunken living room boasted a spread of cushy couches to go with the enviable entertainment system. Chef's kitchen on one side. A random collection of paintings taking up the other—from modernism to surrealism to nude portraits, no two were alike.

*Like Sunny,* I thought. *This is both a showroom and a fantasy indulgence. Sunny is the man flirting and cracking jokes, as well as the man shoving a gun down someone's throat.*

"Ahem." Turning, I faced a tall, sturdy woman with a severe bob and raised brow. "Hello, my name is Bethany Fuller. I'm the house manager. Shoes off, please."

"Oh, right. Sorry." Sienna and I peeled off our tatty sneakers. I tried to hide the holes in my once white, now gray socks as more people emerged from various parts of the apartment. Two women in aprons stuck their heads out of the kitchen. Another dressed in scrubs emerged from a bedroom. I blinked at the figure that stepped out after her.

I flew to my hair, unconsciously brushing back the hopeless mess. He caught the movement and raised a straight, blond brow as if he knew exactly why I did it.

A crisp, stain-defying white dress shirt clung to the dips and mounds of his impressively muscled frame. I used to roll my eyes at guys wearing shirts two sizes too small, showing off their five-times-a-week trips to the gym. Looking at him and the black slacks that left nothing to the imagination, I took back every snarky thought and comment. When you put that much work into looking this deadly gorgeous, it was a crime to hide it.

Honey, almost feline gold eyes traveled over my wide nose and red lips as my gaze caressed his sharp cheekbones and square jaw. In my former line of work, handsome men were a dime a dozen. I built an immunity long ago.

River ignited the symptoms. Sunny set off the fever. This stranger battered my system.

Sunny rolled out in a wheelchair, low-slung cotton pants, and nothing else. He saw me and smiled like Christmas came early.

*Immunity gone.*

"Angel," he said brightly, despite the wheelchair, bandages, and IV rolling behind him. Already his color was returning. "This is everyone. Everyone, Angel."

"Kenzie," I corrected, face heating. I couldn't say why that nickname felt so intimate, but having him introduce me by the name did something to my pulse. "Hello, everyone. Sunny, I'm glad you're on your feet—actually, on your ass. Big improvement from facedown."

He laughed. "You're telling me."

"Really, I'm happy to see you in safe hands. We've got to get going though, so let me draw that sketch for you, and I'll be out of your hair."

"What's the rush?" His study done, the handsome stranger spoke—no sign of his conclusions on his face. "I'm told you rescued Sole, got him medical treatment, and saw his attacker. I'd very much like to hear the entire story from you."

"I told your guard, Thatcher, everything."

His blink was a slow, lazy movement. "Doesn't change what I said."

"I'm sorry, who are you?"

Sunny slung an arm around his waist. "This is my big bro, Liam." He looked to be in his thirties. "Can't you see the resemblance?"

"Uh... no." I wouldn't have pegged these two as brothers even if I saw them come out of the same woman myself. One look at Sunny evoked the rolling Tuscan hills and ancient monuments claimed by his ancestors. In Liam, I saw stone castles and wild, rugged landscapes. The only thing that set them apart from other people and connected them to each other were the waves and coils in their thick hair.

"We get that all the time."

"Where were you when Sunny was thrown?" Liam got straight to the point.

"Two feet away. He came down right in front of me."

"Three seconds sooner he would've come down on *top* of me," Sienna added.

Liam extracted himself from Sunny's hold, approaching me. "And you say you got a good enough look at his face to describe him?"

"I did."

"Even though he was sixteen feet up, it was early in the morning, and he would've ducked out of sight when he noticed you both. In that half a second, you got a clear view of his face?"

I swallowed a few times, heart thumping as he came near, near, nearer. Liam towered over me with hardly an inch between us, dominating two of my senses, and evoking forbidden images of what he could do to the other three.

*Stop lusting over a man who is basically calling you a liar.*

"How many times do you want me to say yes? What? You don't believe me? Give me paper and a pencil, I'll draw him."

"You'll draw a face." His words were as slow and languid as the relaxed aura that cloaked him. Instead of putting me at ease, it made me picture a predator creeping through the high grass—patiently waiting for its moment to strike. "Whether or not it's the attacker's face..."

His unfinished statement stiffened my spine.

"What were you doing under that bridge?"

I held out my hands. "What do you think?"

"Hmm, plausible," he drawled. "Still, it's incredible to me that after the time, effort, and planning that must've gone into Sole's attack, the assassin was suddenly struck stupid and didn't look down to see if there was anyone nearby."

"No one said the assassin was the clever one. For all any of us know, he was the grunt who received the call when the window of opportunity opened up."

"Perhaps you were the clever one, Miss Blaine. The DID play. Damsel in distress. You run in to save the day, and filled with gratitude, Sunny allows you into the place where he's most vulnerable. Where we are all most vulnerable."

My jaw dropped. "Are you fucking with me right now? You're accusing me of orchestrating the attempted murder of a man I didn't know existed three days ago?!"

"So you claim."

I barked a laugh, bobbing my head. "Oh, I see. You're an asshole."

Three gasps and a snort from Sunny broke into our staredown.

"Yes, I am," Liam said smoothly. "Though I prefer cautious."

"I'd prefer to leave. Now. If you don't want the sketch, let's not waste our time."

Liam shrugged and his powerful shoulders lifted his shirt slightly out of his pants. The barest tuft of blond hair peeked through.

"You're staring."

"No, I'm not," I snapped, yanking my attention up. "Don't flatter yourself. I have no interest in over-primped jerks who accuse and call me a liar."

He smirked. "Don't flatter *your*self, sweetheart. I wasn't offering."

"I see a bloody nose in your future, dude," Sienna muttered.

Damn, my sister really was psychic.

"Whoa, slow up." Sunny wheeled between us. "No bad vibes here. This is a happy day. One that'll be marked in history as the day Sole Bellisario was snatched from the grips of Hades and rose from the dead. Angel, don't mind my bro. It's in his nature to be suspicious. If he was in touch with his feelings, he'd hug, kiss, and weep all over you for saving his favorite brother. As it is, this is how close he gets to a thank-you."

"No, it isn't," Liam said, tone smooth. "I can manage a true thank-you. Tonight. Dinner. La Belle's. My treat."

"I'm good," I said.

"What reason do you have to refuse?"

"Is it so hard to believe I have other plans?"

Liam slowly raked me up and down, shrinking me in my ratty clothes and holey socks. "Yes."

"Future amended," Sienna said. "I'm the one who gives you a bloody nose."

Unaware of just how dirty and scrappy a fighter my sister was, he shot her an amused wink. "There's no need to break my nose. I'm leaving," he said, sidestepping me. "I'll be back at seven to escort you to dinner. The invitation is not optional. Bethany, have them ready. Good morning, ladies."

He set off a wave of goodbyes from Sole's staff—all with much sweeter expressions on their faces than mine.

"Bye, Mr. Hunt."

"Have a nice day."

"Ass." I turned on Sunny. "You're his favorite brother, but I'm guessing he's not yours."

"Don't mind him. His bite's worse than his bark."

I frowned. "Isn't that supposed to be the other way around?"

"Not in his case."

"Okay," I drew out. "Well, since he doesn't speak for you, I'm fine with handing you the sketch and being on my way. I won't make it to dinner—"

"Ahem," Bethany interrupted. "Mr. Hunt has requested your presence. I'm afraid not attending isn't an option, as mentioned."

"You can't—"

"She's right, Angel." Sunny kissed my knuckles. "Liam would've sent word to Thatcher by now not to let you out of the building."

Fuller's grip was iron around my wrist, pulling me free and away from Sunny.

"But you can call down and tell him to let us go," I cried.

"I can, but then you would leave. And why would I want that?"

His grin followed me bellowing around the corner. I may be his angel, but Sole Bellisario was not mine.

BETHANY AND TWO OF the house staff deposited me in the bathroom.

"What is wrong with you people? Let me go!"

"We apologize for manhandling you." Fuller was as far from apologetic as you could be. "We'll leave you alone to shower. Just tell me your dress and shoe size. I'll also put a call into the hairstylist and manicurist."

"Like hell you will." I charged the door. Bethany blocked my path.

"Miss Blaine, your anger perplexes me. Everyone from the family to the staff owes you a debt we can't repay for saving Sole and returning him home. All his brother asks is that you allow him to take you to dinner, and you can't get out of here fast enough.

"You say there's something wrong with us for showing you kindness or gratitude. By the looks of you, it's been a while since you received either. If I were you, Miss Blaine, I'd cease with the hysterics and show your fall onto hard times didn't drum out all sense of graciousness."

I jerked back like she struck me. My retort sprang to my lips, hot and scratchy, where it died.

"You're right," I rasped. "Treating me to dinner is the least he can do, and the least I could accept. It's just... I can't afford to pay back new clothes, shoes, haircuts, and manicures."

"No one is asking you to."

"I know." My voice was harsh. "That's the problem. I have an issue with owing favors, Ms. Fuller. In my experience, when it's time to collect, the cost is always more than I can give. And I don't mean money."

Fuller softened—I think she did. Her placid mask slammed into place so fast, I may have imagined it.

"This is not a favor. It is a gift—freely given, without the expectation of something in return. Afterward, you and your sister are free to leave. You have my word."

One of the women turned on the water and bubbles.

"Okay. Thank you." I surrendered to Ms. Fuller's ministrations.

I never regretted an act so swiftly or deeply.

"Ow! Those are attached."

"Stop squirming," Fuller replied. "You're like a squalling infant refusing a diaper change."

"I don't need to be waxed," I forced out. She had a firm hold on my jaw, keeping me still as she plucked my eyebrows. "They're not checking beavers at the door."

My cohort giggled. No less than six women were on me, buffing, polishing, waxing, measuring, and hair-spraying me. Sienna and I were set up in armchairs in a decadent guest room. Sienna sipped iced tea from a lady's hand as hers were occupied by the manicurists. She was looking plenty happy with life right now.

"You have a beautiful aura," she told the woman painting her toes. "It's a soft, lilac-y purple. Prosperity is in your future. It's going to knock into you like a golf ball to the head on your morning jog."

"Ooh, is that golf ball attached to the wealthy, handsome man I'm going to sue?"

"I can dress myself." I was reduced to pleading. "I'll do my own hair, nails, and makeup."

"I'm sure you can dress yourself," said the woman painting my nails. "But we'll dress you right."

"Holding me down and waxing me against my will is listed under torture methods. This is some kind of thank-you."

They all laughed at me and called two women off Sienna to hold my legs apart.

My complaints poured out of my mouth, hit their ears, and bounced off. Slowly but surely, the dirt disappeared from beneath my fingernails. My bushman eyebrows reduced to pencil-thin perfection. My legs were made hairless. My mane washed, trimmed, and styled. Then, they brought in the dress.

My lips parted.

Royal-blue, floor-length evening gown. The sleeveless, off-the-shoulder beauty was the softest velvet, and from across the room, I knew it would sinfully cling to my every inch and curve, transforming me from bony waif to shapely woman.

I didn't have to ask if it was a Caddell. The intricate beadwork on the hip depicted a lotus. That was his signature. I also didn't have to ask if the dress retailed at three thousand dollars.

"I can't wear that," I whispered.

"Can't?" Debra, my hairstylist, repeated. "Honey, you look like you're about to leap out of this chair and rip it out of her hands."

I pressed my lips together. Politeness demanded I refuse the extravagant gift at least once. I did it once. That was all politeness was going to get.

I vibrated as the ladies helped me up, careful of my drying fingers and toes, they helped me step inside. Inch after inch, my ankles, legs, hips, stomach, and new bra were swallowed by the designer gown. I moved to the mirror where Sienna danced in a flowy, knee-length, red chiffon dress. Spotting me, her smile melted away and she moved to the side.

We all stopped—saying nothing, doing nothing as I gazed at myself in the mirror.

"Kenzie," Sienna said softly. "It's…"

"Me."

The reflection touched her cheek, as if checking to see if she was real. Waves of silver teased my dark locks, spreading from the root and growing deeper and bright as they reached my tips.

*It's like they bathed my hair in the color of Sunny's eyes.*

The thought went through my mind too fast for me to stop it and left my cheeks flaming. Sunny Bellisario crashed into my mind that morning and he wasn't leaving.

Following my kohl-lined eyes down, I traveled over my dark espresso lipstick and expertly layered makeup, hiding months of gaping pores and blackheads. The lady in the mirror admired the way the gown hid her dramatic weight loss, leaving behind the girl I knew. Or the one I used to be.

"It's me," I whispered.

"You're beautiful, Miss Blaine," Fuller said. "Both of you."

She squeezed our hands. "You're welcome."

I stood in front of that mirror long after my nails dried and makeup crew left. Long after Sienna kissed my cheek and went off in search of trouble to get into. Long enough that no one was around to see me cry.

This was both the kindest and cruelest thing anyone had done to me. Sunny gave me myself back, only for me to return to the streets and lose Mackenzie Blaine all over again.

Shonda, one of the kitchen staff, stuck her head inside. "Miss Blaine?"

"Please." I hurriedly wiped my eyes and faced her with a smile. "Call me Kenzie."

"Kenzie, Sunny is waiting for you on the balcony, along with drinks. I'll show you the way."

Shonda led me through the maze of hallways into the living room. Sunny's penthouse seemed to go on forever. Hard to believe all of this was just for one man.

"Do you all live here with him?" I asked.

"No, the staff has their own quarters on the bottom floors."

"Quarters. It's like I stepped between the pages into Beast's castle."

She laughed. "Does that make me the French candlestick or the teapot?"

"I'll let you decide," I teased.

"You're a trip." Shonda held out her arm, motioning to the balcony. "I hope we see more of you, Kenzie."

I dropped my gaze. *I wish I could say you will.*

Sunny's wheelchair parked beside the lounger while the man himself stretched out, sipping a beer under shades of red, gold, and blue. A low whistle slipped through my lips, carrying me to the railing and all of Cinco City before me.

My life, my gift, my talent was creating beauty, and still I'd never compare to the master's hand. He painted the world in sweet marmalade and dotted it with marshmallowy clouds. That was the name of a sketch I drew once. A stunning orange and white dress I dubbed marshmallows and marmalade. He chuckled when I showed it to him, caressing me softly with his gaze as he said I was just as sweet.

Memories threatened to pour out. I slammed the door on them, gripping the banister as they battered my shields, fighting to drag me under.

Sunny wrapped his arm around me, holding me to his chest. The memories faded.

"You're gorgeous, Angel."

I hid my smile in the slight *V* exposing his pecs. "Should you be on your feet?"

"I can walk just fine. The wheelchair is my doc overreacting." He pressed a kiss to my forehead. "How do you feel?"

Lifting my chin, I met his eyes. He didn't ask if I liked the clothes or what I thought of his staff's manhandling. Of all the things, he asked how I felt.

"Like me again."

"Good." He kissed between my brows, indulging this brief powerless moment that left me unable to stop him. "I got you something."

"No," I said automatically. "Sunny, seriously, I can't accept anything else."

"This isn't for you, love." Sunny returned to the lounger and picked up a pad and pencil. "It's for me. Sketch this guy while his face is still fresh in your mind."

"Happy to."

The balcony was perfect in its simplicity. Two loungers and the table sandwiched between them. We stretched out, getting comfortable under the warm porch lights.

"Beer?"

"No," I replied, pencil already running across the page. "I don't drink."

"Interesting. There's so much I have to learn about you, Blaine."

"Why?" I grinned at him over the pad. "Will there be a test?"

A slow, sultry, deadly smirk curved his lips. "You tell me."

I flicked away quick. This was a strange sort of flirting. Strange, but effective. I felt the ghost of his kisses like brands on my forehead.

"It's you I'd like to know more about," I said. "You live in this locked-down tower with an army of pretty female servants."

"Is there a question in there?"

"Yes, and you know what it is."

Sunny grinned over the glass rim. "I like to surround myself with beauty. No shame in that."

I looked around. "So, this is the compound."

"Years ago, the Fairfield was outfitted with the best security system in the city. With every year and every upgrade, this place is more secure than the US Mint. So my family bought the building."

"How big is your family?"

He eyed me. "You really don't know anything about us?"

"My whole life's been about protecting my family and giving us a better life. Then it was about hanging on to it when I failed. I wasn't spending a lot of time learning the family trees of the criminal underground."

"You didn't fail."

I gave him a hard look. "My sister was reduced to giving psychic readings in a dirty tent for a couple of dollars because I lost my job, apartment, and pissed off a crazed pimp. What would you call that but failure?"

"I'd call that bad luck and trusting the wrong people. But the thing about life on this spinning ball is, if you wait long enough, the right people come along. They give you a hand up, dust you off, and hand you a piece so you can blow the fucker's brains out."

I cracked a smile. "You're a pretty positive, if violent, guy, aren't you?"

"Why do you think they call me Sunny?"

"I wish I had your rosy view of the world, but I'm guessing that's easy to get when you're in the penthouse, not the gutter."

Sunny didn't lose his smile. "No one's life is perfect, Angel. Need I remind you of our first meeting?"

I winced. *He has a point. Real nice being bitter toward a guy who was thrown off an overpass to die alone.* My pencil slowed. *And this is the guy who did it.*

My teeth clenched, looking into those eyes. I was too good at this. I captured the sharklike emptiness with scary accuracy.

"This is him."

Sunny took the sketch from me, dropping the trickster's grin as he scrutinized the graphite lines. "I can say for certain I don't recognize him. I know my enemies and he's not one of them. I also know more than a few of the people who want me dead can afford a hit man."

"I wish there was more I could do." His hand lay on the table between us. I couldn't resist resting mine over his. "I'm just really happy you're going to be all right. I hope you find the son of a bitch who did this."

Sunny turned his palm up, lacing his fingers through mine. He didn't let go, and neither did I. "Mackenzie, can I talk to you about something?"

"Yeah, of course."

"This... shouldn't have happened. Someone getting close enough to drug and kidnap me. Snatching me the one night I ditch security. The odds of everything coming together so perfectly the night he poised to strike are... infinitesimal."

"He was watching you. For weeks, maybe months, like you said. He saw when you left this place alone."

Sunny was shaking his head before I finished. "I did ditch security and leave the compound alone that night, but I didn't stroll out the front door, Kenzie. North Quay is my turf."

I frowned at the non sequitur. "Your turf?"

"After my parents retired, my brothers, sister, and I split the boroughs, each ruling one. Liam has Leighbridge. Genny has Harlow. Bane's locked up Waterford, and I have North Quay."

"What about Rockchapel?"

"Rockchapel has three times the number of gangs than the other boroughs combined. For the most part, they've existed side by side without needless bloody turf wars. We didn't see the need to kick one off by forcing them to fold into the Merchants. As long as they know who's in charge, we've let them be. Same can't be said for North Quay," he continued. "Whatever they called themselves before, the North Quay crews are now all Merchants. They report to me."

Understanding dawned. I ripped away from him. "Report to you? That's why Luca knows you, and that's how you knew him and the shit he does to women. You let a guy like that run free in North Quay!"

"Whoa, Kenzie, slow up. I run the gangs, love, not the pimps. Not even I want part in the Cinco sex trade. I didn't know about Digger or what he was into until a friend of a friend told me *her* friend was having trouble with the guy. I heard from her and her roommates that he was pressuring them into trading sex and party entertainment for a break on their late rent payments."

That sounded awfully familiar.

"I sat the man down for a chat and told him what would happen if he tried it again. I thought he was a sleezy piece of shit slinging his shot at an easy opportunity. I had no idea then or now that was how he ran his business. Not until I heard the shit he was saying to you."

Tears stung my eyes. "But you had h-him in the factory and you let him go."

"Kenzie." He tried to touch me and I flinched, growling at him. "Hey," he said softly, lacing our fingers together anyway. "I had to let him go. I had him all wrong, Angel. If he built his stable on kidnap and rape, the women he's got working for him are being held against their will. Likely with men guarding to stop them escaping. Killing Digger wouldn't free them. Actually, it'd cut off any chance of me finding them. He's the only lead to where they are."

"Finding them?"

"Yes, gorgeous. First thing I did after waking up was call Liam. He will find out everything there is to know about Luca and his operation. If he doesn't fold up and release those women like I ordered, we'll do it for him. I swear to you, Digger will not get away with this. And those women, they'll get their lives back."

I opened and closed my mouth a few times, trying to speak but unable to push the words through my clogged throat. Against my will, my opinion of Sole and his asshole brother changed.

"Thank you," I whispered.

"You don't have to thank me. This kind of shit's not going down in North Quay. Not while I'm in charge. Not while I'm alive." Sighing, Sunny dropped his head, gazing up to where the stars should be—hidden behind the veil of light pollution. "I figure that's why someone had me taken out."

"To take over North Quay?" I wiped my eyes, smearing my makeup. "Get out from under your rule?"

He nodded. "Over the last few months, there have been attacks on my businesses. My warehouses raided by cops with anonymous tips. My trucks run off the road. A massive shipment that never got to the customer. It just disappeared. It's been costing me money and trust like you wouldn't believe, Angel, and the distrust it's brewing among my guys is worse."

"Why are your guys looking at each other?"

"The locations of my warehouses are a secret I've kept for five years. Suddenly they're blown. The routes too. I randomly change them to stop this from happening, and again it's worked for five years—"

"Until now," I finished. "You have a rat."

"That's what my boys are thinking, but I'm not sure it's that simple."

I sat up, leaning over the table. "Why not?"

"Because it's not just me. Shit's been going wrong for Genny, Liam, and Bane too. We kept our businesses separate, so a rat in my crew wouldn't know anything that affects them too. That's not it, or that's not *only* it. If we all have a rat problem, for this to go down at the same time, someone must've kicked it off. Approached them."

I bobbed along, putting the pieces together. "And this doesn't truly stop until you find the one pulling their strings."

He tapped his nose. "You are an educated bum."

The reply got him a swat across the arm. "So what does that mean for the night you were attacked?"

"You gotta understand, Kenzie. Decades ago, when my parents brought Cinco under their fist, they had trouble from leaders who wouldn't go down easy. By the time the second generation took over, those guys had been put down. My boys know the score. They know who is in charge. I've been working with them for half a decade, if I thought a single one of them would go behind my back..."

He didn't need to finish the sentence. Obviously, if Sunny suspected a rat, they would've been taken care of with the ruthless efficiency that ended Kingston.

"Most of those guys I trust with my life. I decided not to get loud and violent to flush out the rat. Torturing friends tends to put a kink in the relationship." He raised his arms like *who knew*? "Instead, I had them watched. My right-hand men. Everywhere they went. Everyone they talked to.

"Thatcher clocked multiple calls from one of my guys, Xander, to the number for the club, Laser. Before it opened. A little bit of digging and Thatcher turned up the owner was busted for bootlegging in another state," he said. "That wasn't suspicious on its own. I didn't have proof he was resorting to his old ways, or that Xander was trying to start up a side business.

Something my guys are forbidden to do. All rackets run through me. All the cash ends up in my pocket first," he said, voice hard.

I shivered. That was the first Sunny sounded like what he was, a gang leader.

"I went to the club that night to find out."

"Xander knew you were coming."

He shook his head. "He couldn't have, Kenzie. That's what I'm saying. I didn't tell anyone where I was going. Not even Thatcher. That's why I rolled out of here without guards or backup. No one knew I would be at Laser that night, and with it packed for the club opening, I'd get lost in the crowd. It gave me the chance to scope out the place and find out if it was a front."

"Was it?"

Another headshake. "I never got that far. I was in the VIP room, like I said. The drinks were flowing, next thing I know I'm waking up next to you."

"I get it. Drugging you, getting you out unseen, dumping you. How did the rat pull that together so fast when he didn't know you'd be there?"

Sunny tapped his nose and pointed at me. Got it in one.

I chewed my lip, thinking. "What about the owner? Maybe he spotted you, or his bouncers did. He could've called Xander saying he feared you were onto them, and Xander ordered him to put something in the bartender's next round, then he'd send someone to take care of the rest."

"If he did, there's a lot more going on here than bootlegging, and I need to find out what." Sunny leaned in. "That's where you come in."

"Me?"

"Right now, the only people I know for certain don't want me dead, are you and Sienna. Fuck knows, you could've left me to bleed into my lungs if that was the case. I need people I trust around me right now." Flinty silver bore into me. "Someone's coming after my family. Someone's coming after me, and they almost succeeded. Kenzie, if you help me find out who, I'll give you anything you ask."

"Help you find out who?" I cried. "How am I supposed to do that? All I have for you is that sketch, Sunny."

"Hear me out, beautiful. The person who dropped me off that bridge has no reason to believe I survived a fall from that height. I never met or heard of that doctor you took me to, so chances are my crew hasn't either. When we tumbled onto the doorstep, Liam contained the situation. That's why you weren't allowed to leave. It'll hit the news soon: Sole Bellisario is missing and his family is asking anyone with answers to come forward."

"You want your enemies to believe they got away with killing you."

He inclined his head. "If they do, they'll finally make a move. If this was a plot to take over my crew, the rat'll step forward and *offer to lead in this time of crisis*. He doesn't have to hide behind my back any longer. With me out of the way, the path to the throne is clear. And if he has one-fourth of the Merchant business under his control—"

"—that puts him in a strong place to force your brothers and sister into giving him a seat at the table. If not blow the whole fucking table to bits."

We shared a grim look.

"I won't get a chance like this again," Sunny continued. "If I can't trust my guys, then I need someone I can trust who has an incentive to keep me around, scoping out who's sad to see me gone and who's leaking crocodile tears."

"And again, why would that someone be me? I'm a homeless fashion designer who met you three days ago."

"Because once I've got the shit-stain traitor in my hands, I'll send you off with a kiss and half a million dollars. Cash."

I knocked his beer over, jerking back. It crashed to the choked noise strangling my throat. "Half a million?"

"Not enough? Three-quarters of a mill, then."

"Sunny!" *This was not real. What he was saying couldn't be true.*

"Obviously, I won't leave you unprotected on the streets while you're hunting this guy, so you and Sienna will stay here. Rent-free. My cooks are at your disposal. My housekeepers at your beck and call. My cars yours to drive when the mood strikes you. We'll come up with a cover for why you're stepping into my life."

I threw up my hands. "Wait, slow down."

"Unfortunately, my place is a one-bedroom," Sunny mused, turning his face to the sky. "This means we'll have to share, but I'm down to snuggle if you are."

My withering look would've burned the smirk off a lesser man. That man wasn't Sunny.

"You have *four* bedrooms," I said. "I got the tour."

"Oops. I must've miscounted."

Heaving a sigh, I slowed my racing mind, sorting through panic, surprise, disbelief, and amazement flooding me at once. "Sunny, I want to help you. Truly. But I can't do what you're asking. Infiltrating a gang? Mixing with dirty money and illegal activity? You have no idea..." My nails pierced my palm. "No idea what I'll lose if the next anonymous tip leads to me ambushed and arrested. My family depends on me.

"I can't do it," I said, meaning it with every fiber of my being. "No."

"Angel—"

"I'm starting to pick up on you getting free with the pet names when you want something."

His grin was wolfish. "Just imagine what I'll call you when I get it."

"Do you honestly think this is the best time to flirt with me?" I asked, though my cheeks were boiling, conjuring up all the possible things he could want from me, and the naughty things he'll whisper in my ear as he got them.

Sunny fell serious. "Three-quarters of a million, Kenzie. A roof over your head. Sleeping with both eyes closed. And you wouldn't be alone. My family and I will have your back every minute of every day."

"Why can't one of your brothers or your sister do it?" I tried. "Why does anyone have to? All they have to do is wait, right? The guy who tries to step in your place is the guy who did it."

"It sounds that simple, but it isn't. There's still a chance it's not one of my guys, and eventually, someone will have to step up either way. You can find out which it is. You've got good instincts about people."

My lips trembled. "How can you say that after meeting my ex-boyfriend?"

"Because you didn't give in to him, Kenzie, and you got away. For all the women who've told him no, there are women who've said yes, believing they're helping out the man they love. He wouldn't continue running that con if there wasn't a strong success rate. But not you." He stroked my cheek. "When he peeled back the mask, you shoved that cunt out of your life. Some time with my crew, you'll see who is real and who's fake—and you won't have history with them clouding your judgment.

"The sooner we can cross our gangs off the lists, the sooner we can move on to the real leak." Sunny glanced over his shoulder. "Even if it's closer to home."

I followed his gaze. "Is it possible one of your staff or guards is behind this?"

"Possible," he admitted, "but not likely. Most of our staff have been around since Mom and Dads were in charge. They're well-paid, given free room and board, and they know if there's trouble, they can come to us. One of my staff had a daughter who got deep into gambling—ended up sixty thousand dollars in debt to dangerous people. I paid off her bill and got her into a program, no questions asked. I mean, they wouldn't be skipping through my fucking house if I didn't trust them."

"I'm sure you do, and I'm sure no one here wants to hurt you. But the one thing that can break loyalty is fear. What if this guy threatened their family if they didn't give up yours?"

"That is also... possible." Sunny's handsome features twisted like he was in physical pain. This was killing him worse than that fall ever could. "I'm too close to this, Angel. Too close to these people. I can't be objective. All I know now is that my enemy has graduated to killing, I can't afford to sit around while he picks which one of my family to take out next. My next step is firing everyone in the building and questioning each one of my guys—the hard way."

"That's your next step if I say no," I clarified. "It's not fair to put this kind of pressure on me. I can't do it, Sunny. There has to be someone else."

Shifting back, he observed me. "You say you can't because Sienna needs you."

I nodded.

"Then, let me ask you this. Before I crashed into your life, how was that going? Was Sienna safe? Was she fed, happy, and looking at a bright future?

Were you a day or two away from the turn of fortune that would've gotten you off the streets?"

Stiffening, I forced through my teeth, "Careful."

"I'm not trying to piss you off, Angel," he said, expressionless. "I'm floating you a thought experiment. You never meet me and continue holding to your rule to never get caught up with the dirty side of Cinco. Meanwhile, Digger's got his guys looking for you day and night. Your home is a tent under a bridge. And you don't have enough money to replace your taped-up rags, let alone buy a pantsuit for a job interview. How long before the story you were writing ended up in tragedy?

"Or, you stay here. Take the calculated risk of linking up with my Sons of Saint and then walk away with enough money to give yourself and Sienna the life you deserve. Each option could end badly, I won't lie," he said. "But only one promises you food, a home, protection, and seven hundred and fifty thousand dollars. This is your hand up, Kenzie."

He held it out as proof. "It might be stained with blood, but it's attached to someone who owes you everything, and believes in angels."

"Sunny, I—"

"Just think about it," he said gently. "Give me your decision after dinner."

I didn't have to.

"Listen, I want to help you but—"

"Miss Blaine." Fuller stepped out onto the balcony. "Mr. Hunt is on his way down. He asks if you're ready, and I see you're not. Come with me. I'll fix your makeup."

Once again, she wasn't asking. I let her lead me away. My answer would be the same after dinner as it was before. It didn't make a difference when I gave Sunny the news. All I knew was I would leave the Fairfield that night. I had to return to North Quay.

Sunny and Sienna were leaning against the kitchen counter, chatting when I came back. I hurried over in case he was slinging his offer to her.

"—a light, almost neon-blue aura."

"Hmm. Interesting. What does that mean?"

"It means you're trouble, Sole Bellisario."

Sunny beamed at me like she said he was chosen for number one of the sexiest men on earth. "Your sister's the real deal."

"This I know," I replied. "I'm assuming you're not coming to dinner with us."

"You assume correctly."

"Is leaving me at the mercy of Senor Paranoid Pants supposed to seal the deal? 'Cause I'll tell you right now, that man is not a closer."

He chuckled. "Paranoid Pants. I've got to use that. But no, Liam isn't the closer. That would be the lady riding down with him. My girl will take over convincing you."

"Your girl?" Sienna and I said at the same time.

"Oh, yeah. Can't wait for you to meet her." A sweet, shockingly tender smile chased away his natural devil-may-care grin. "She's beautiful, funny, smart. Love of my life."

A thick, sludgy feeling settled in my skin. *Why are you surprised? Rich, handsome, flirty men who surround themselves with "beauty" don't stay single for long.*

A knock sounded on the door.

"Maybe this isn't a good idea," I blurted as Fuller reached for the door-knob. "There's no point since—"

"Uncle Sunny!"

A glittery purple streak shot between us and launched at Sunny. The missile popped him off his feet and dropped Sole laughing on the waiting wheelchair.

"Uncle Sunny, I missed you." The little girl peppered his face with kiss-es, hugging his neck tight enough to strangle.

"I missed you too. Sienna, Kenzie, this is my niece, Tricky."

"I'm his number one girl," she said proudly.

"Actually." The deep, mellow voice drew my attention, as it did every eye in the room.

I swallowed too hard. Stared too long. I couldn't help myself. Liam's blue Caddell suit went down, down, down over his long, sculpted legs, and around his muscled frame, clinging to his arms and stacked shoulders like a happy slut. The oversize pink unicorn under his right arm did nothing to lessen the effect.

"You're my number one girl," he finished.

"Daddy," she said, expression serious as she explained. "I'm your favorite girl *and* Uncle Sunny's *and* Uncle Bane's *and* Aunty Genny's."

*Daddy.*

I would've known without her help. Tricky was the spit of him from the curve of her nose to the way she cocked her brow. Her blonde hair lay straighter than his, but otherwise he succeeded in creating a miniature female clone.

"Nice to meet you, Tricky," I greeted.

"Her name is Elizabeth," Liam corrected.

"Technically, that's true," Sunny said. "If we're going by birth certificates. But my girl here was dubbed her true name, Tricky, when at an early age she displayed an aptitude for getting in and out of trouble. Slipping out of her crib for cookies whenever our backs were turned. Dyeing the family pet pink. A Merchant from birth."

Damned if she didn't look proud of herself too.

"Are you ladies ready to go?"

"I'm ready," Sienna said before I opened my mouth. She lifted Elizabeth in her arms like they'd known each other for years. "That's a beautiful dress."

"Thank you."

"Where did you get it?"

"My daddy bought it for me."

Sienna walked out expecting us to follow—which naturally Liam did, seeing as a complete stranger was strolling off with his kid.

"Bye, Sunny." I leaned over him and whispered, "I'll spend dinner thinking of ways to get you back for letting me think your niece was your girlfriend."

"Then you should know my safe word is pineapple."

Penning in a laugh, I hurried away before it slipped out and encouraged him. Attraction sizzled between us like a live wire. I didn't deny it even though I would not indulge. I got involved with too many men who hid their dark side till they were poised to destroy my life. Only an idiot who learned nothing would get involved with a guy who owned his darkness completely. I'd never be able to say I didn't see the next blow coming.

Liam stood just outside the threshold. It took me a second to realize he waited for me.

"You didn't have to do this. The dinner and..." I waved my hands over my clothes. "Verbal thanks is more than enough."

"It's not a bother." He fixed straight ahead, making for the end of the hall. I fell in step beside him.

"I'm surprised you're letting us meet your daughter after basically accusing me of orchestrating Sunny's attack to get close to all of you."

"The background check came back on you both rather quickly. Spotless records."

"Of course you ran checks on us," I muttered.

"Besides, Elizabeth screamed for ten minutes straight, then held her breath till she passed out at the suggestion she have dinner with Ms. Fuller tonight." Liam dropped this like it was a staple of his life. "She insists I spend all my time when I'm not at work with her."

I snorted, holding back a laugh. "Oh, I see. She's got you wrapped around that little purple-painted pinkie."

A ghost of a smile tugged the corner of his lips. "Not an entirely inaccurate assumption."

We rode the elevator to basement level and were spat out into a parking garage. Two men emerged out of nowhere and joined us. I only jumped a foot in the air.

"Do you ever really get used to bodyguards following you around?" I asked.

"No." Liam pulled ahead and opened the door of a scandalous beauty I clocked as a Rolls-Royce Phantom.

"Sienna's going to sit with me," Elizabeth announced.

The two piled in the back and Liam closed the door behind them. He opened the passenger side and looked at me, waiting.

"There's room for three in the back," I said.

"I'm not a chauffeur."

"But..." I looked around like the guards would help me. The two were busy climbing into individual cars, preparing to trail us.

"Something wrong?" Amusement laced the question. Liam had his own ideas why I was uncomfortable sitting so close to him.

*Don't give him the satisfaction of believing he gets you hot and bothered. He's just like every other attractive man who knows he is. Starve his ego and the cockiness dies like it leaped over a cliff and hit the rocks.*

"Nothing's wrong."

I slid in, keeping my hands firmly in my lap. This was the most expensive thing I'd ever sat on, in, or near. Behind me, Elizabeth dropped the screen embedded in the back of my chair, bringing up an episode of her favorite show for Sienna to watch. Liam slid in next to me, filling the small space with Creed cologne.

His seat pushed all the way back, and still his long, powerful legs and body seemed too small for this car. I counted the fine hairs on his fingers as he shifted gears, carrying us out of the fortress.

I braced myself for the interrogation to start, but no one was getting a word in over Elizabeth. In the span of five minutes, I learned she was six years old. Her mother was a model who lived in Paris. Her favorite color was purple. She liked her tutors, but not her French lessons. Uncle Sunny made the best root beer floats, and Sienna could come up and play with her whenever she wanted.

"What about me?" I teased.

"Sorry." She sounded it. "Daddy says I can't let strangers into our house."

"Miss Sienna is a stranger," Liam reminded.

"No, Daddy. Sienna is my friend."

I covered my smile at the look on his face. I had a feeling he had explained the concept of strangers to her many times, and it went out the window every time someone praised her.

"Don't feel bad." I didn't let my voice carry. "It's a gift to look at people and only see new best friends. We lose that too soon."

"There is truth in that," he replied, "but for some, it's an innocence they can't afford."

Turning away, I gazed at the city zipping by. "There's truth in that too."

"Tell me about yourself, Mackenzie."

Goose bumps popped on my skin. The way he said my name bordered on illicit, and I knew it was out of his control. Every word was rolled around his tongue and shaped by soft lips. The power bowled me over when added to my own name.

I recovered quickly. "You mean fill in the blanks the background check left out."

"That's exactly what I mean."

"What's left to know?" Talking to him gave me an excuse to look—trail down his jaw and study his corded neck muscles. Goodness, there wasn't a part of him I could strike without breaking all the tiny bones in my hand. The man was built.

"You graduated from Cinco University and snagged a coveted internship at Caddell House, designing and working as an assistant to Victoria Webb. You showed great promise from the few designs I dug up, then a year ago, you were terminated and you've been out of work since."

"No," I breathed. "Really? Thanks for letting me know."

"The hard work required to get and keep that internship suggests that it wasn't lack of trying that left you unable to find another job," he went on, breezing over my sarcasm. "Your talent suggests you should've found one. So, what happened?"

My jaw clenched. I'd give Liam Hunt something, the man didn't get this far on just his looks. But tact clearly didn't help him on his way.

"Mr. Hunt, here's a tip. Get some food in a girl before you ask her to spill her life's tragedies."

"Good tip."

We didn't speak for a spell.

"Will I get to know as much about you tonight as you expect to know about me?"

"Depends." Liam didn't skip a beat. "Sunny made you an offer tonight. Do you plan on taking it?"

"Do you... want me to?"

"It'd be a great help to us having someone we trust going where we can't go, asking the questions we can't expect an answer to." His glance pinned me to my seat. "I haven't yet decided if that person is you."

"Well, I have. It's not."

"Better things to do with your time?"

"You don't have to say it like the thought is ridiculous."

A soft chuckle dispersed into the air and disappeared. "Believe it or not, every word out of my mouth is not an insult. The background check revealed everything, Mackenzie. Everything."

I shut my eyes, wishing I could do the same to the world. "I figured," I whispered. "It's not a secret. I have nothing to be ashamed of."

"No, but you do have strong motive to take a payout to get close to Sole. Even stronger to accept a seven-hundred-and-fifty-thousand-dollar bribe."

"I would never—!"

"I believe you," he sliced in.

The hot retort faded.

"In your shoes, I wouldn't hesitate. That you refuse to sink to crime after all you've lost blows my mind. I don't believe I'm exaggerating when I say no one else in your position would make the same call. You are an incredibly strong woman, Mackenzie Blaine. Stronger than anyone knows."

I opened my mouth to say something, I don't know what. His compliments struck me dumb.

"Odd as it is, it's your refusal to have anything to do with my family... that pushes me to trust you."

"It's not that I think you're bad people," I heard myself say. "I can't after Sunny told me all you're doing to stop Luca and free the women under his hold. I just... I can't get my life back if I've got a criminal record."

"I understand."

Funnily enough, I knew he did. We lapsed into a silence that was almost companionable for the rest of the ride. Well, almost silent. Elizabeth kept up a steady string of commentary for the entire trip.

La Belle's rose from the end of the street. The ladies gifted me the most expensive gown to grace my skin, and I was still underdressed. Socialites, models, and trust-fund royalty poured out from the line of cars, each taking their turn at the valet. Liam rolled past it and parked the car himself.

Flicking to the rearview and the happy, excitable girl in the back seat, I forgave him his caution. A single father protecting his little girl. No wonder he was suspicious, and he wasn't always nice about it.

Liam came around to open my car door. Elizabeth got there first. Her long ponytail brushed my wrist as she squeezed my hand, tugging me out. "We can be friends too," she said.

"I'd like that."

She peered around me. "Daddy doesn't like it, but call me Tricky," she whispered. "It's a much better name than *Elizabeth*."

"Tricky it is."

"Do you have a nickname?"

"Everyone calls me Kenzie. It's short for Mackenzie. Not as fun as a name like Tricky."

"You can have a fun nickname too. How about... Angel?"

I blinked down at her, catching her mischievous grin clear as day.

*Oh yeah, Tricky is the right name for you, Sunny's niece.*

"How old are you?" she asked.

"Twenty-three." We stepped onto the velvet carpet. Heavenly smells wafted from the open doors, beckoning us inside.

"Is twenty-three too far from thirty-five?"

"Uhh. What do you mean?"

"Sienna said she can't be my daddy's girlfriend because twenty is too far from thirty-five."

My eyes bugged. When did they have that conversation?

"But if you're twenty-three, then—"

Liam scooped her up, dangling his squealing daughter off his shoulder. "You demanded to have dinner with me, and now you're talking to everyone but me. Did I do something to upset you?"

"No," she said, giggling. Tricky twisted up and smooched his cheek. "I love you, Daddy."

*I love you too, Daddy*, I thought, *for saving me from explaining age gaps to a six-year-old girl.*

"You couldn't have told her twenty-three is too young too?" I asked Sienna out of the corner of my mouth.

"I could, but you don't really think so. You've been eye-boning that guy since you met."

I strode away, leaving her laughing in my wake.

"—Hunt," Liam told the hostess. "Private table, like we discussed."

"Right this way, sir, mesdames."

La Belle's was elegance distilled in a bottle, then sprayed all over this place. Frescos depicted rolling countrysides and the lovers who made it their playground. A web of chandeliers connected to each other, weaving along the ceiling and lighting our way.

The host guided us to a table at the very back, concealed by two pillars and a half-wall. It cloaked us in privacy while letting the soft murmur of the diners wash over us. Liam tucked himself and Tricky on one side of the booth. My sister and I claimed the other. Leaning over the menus saved us another few minutes of forcing small talk.

I was glad Tricky screamed and fainted her way into an invitation. If I was lucky, she'd do all the talking and I wouldn't have to think of something to say to this insightful, enigmatic man who lifted the veil into my life, saw the truth, and instead of judging me, called me the strongest person he knew. How could he see that in me... when I didn't see it in myself?

"Oooh. Black truffle risotto sounds good."

I had a heart attack reading the price tag. "How about two ice cubes and a lettuce leaf? There are two zeros behind that number, Si."

"Please," Liam sliced in. "Order anything you like. It's my treat."

Sienna handed over the menu, her meal decided. I stared at the list of delicious creations, struggling with the sense instilled in me after months on the streets. Beware of men with large watches and even larger wallets. They were trying to lure the homeless waif back to their place to do things their wives wouldn't approve of.

*Well, Liam isn't married and he's already gotten me to his place.*

The waiter arrived with a bottle of wine for the table. You had to be a repeat, valued customer for the staff to have your preferences on hand.

"What can I get you?"

"Caesar salad, please," I said, "and water with lemon."

"Along with the grilled lamb chops and mint sauce," Liam added. "For me as well."

Sienna and Tricky gave their orders. He bowed, promising to return soon with our drinks.

"You know, women don't actually like it when guys order for them."

He swirled his wineglass, examining the rich bouquet in the light. "You tipped me that I had to satisfy your stomach to satisfy my curiosity. I didn't think a salad would cut it."

"You have a comeback for everything, don't you?"

"It's a bad habit of mine." He slid to Sienna. "Do the same rules apply to you, Miss Blaine?"

"Call me Sienna. Miss Blaine is a kindergarten teacher. And no, I'm an open book. It's only right. How can I reveal the mysteries of others' lives and refuse to reveal my own?"

"A refreshing attitude for a psychic."

"Why ask when you clearly know everything about us?" Tricky reached for the knife but I was quicker. I busied myself cutting and buttering her bread roll.

"Words in a report don't tell the whole story. So, Sienna, are you thinking about going back to school?"

She tossed her head. "Higher education isn't for me. I'd like to open a shop. Run my own business."

"Psychic readings?"

"Books," Sienna stated. "Self-help books to be exact. As a psychic, I see so many futures that could be prevented if that person found honesty, assertiveness, or boundaries before it was too late. I do my best to warn them but..." Sienna glanced at me. "The only one who can change your fate is you."

"At what age did you discover you had the gift?"

I searched but couldn't find a trace of mocking in his question. Though he feigned polite interest, I doubted a man like Liam Hunt believed in psychics.

*Then again, I don't know men like Liam Hunt. I only knew the douchebags who admired my attributes, my strength not being one of them. I spent my whole life fighting to stay out of trouble. It's not my fault it kept coming for me.*

"I've always known," Sienna replied. "When I was four, I made my sister wear a helmet on her bike ride to the grocery store. That day, a car jumped the curb, she swerved, and crashed through a glass door."

"If only you told me to wear elbow pads too." I held up my arm and flashed the long, white scar—my permanent reminder of that day.

Liam hissed in sympathy. "Why was a seven-year-old biking around, getting groceries by herself?"

I squeezed Sienna's hand under the table, lest my open-book sister answer that one. Liam knew enough about my past. Some things were mine to share when I was ready.

"We're doing all the talking," I said. "Mr. Hunt—"

"Liam."

"Liam. What do you do?"

Tricky sat up straight. "My dad is a legit-mate businessman. He owns clubs and restaurants. If you have more questions, ask him or our tornies." She beamed up at him, proud she got it all right.

Smiling, Liam flicked her nose. "Well said."

"Perfectly said, Tricky. Though I do have some questions."

"Her name is Elizabeth."

"No, it's Tricky," his daughter protested.

"I'm pretty sure it's not, seeing as I named you and filled out the birth certificate."

Sighing, she shook her head like he was hopeless. Elizabeth popped up and came around to our side, squeezing in to sit next to Sienna. My sister moved over for her and budged up against me, pushing me around the circular booth in turn. My knee knocked into Liam. I snatched it back, he didn't move, barring reaching for his wine. Did anything rattle this man? Or was I presumptuous thinking my proximity had the same effect on him as his did on me?

A thirty-five-year-old *legitimate* businessman with a daughter and over a decade's worth of life and sexual experience didn't get weak-kneed over former fashion designers, whose life experience included eating out of the trash.

His deep voice made me jump.

"Aren't you going to ask?"

"Ask what?"

"You said you have questions." Liam stretched his arm on the booth—close, but not close enough to touch me. I had a wild thought of him tangling in my hair, drawing me close, and tucking me under his arm.

"Yes." I shook my head, chasing the useless fantasies away. "Which clubs and restaurants do you legitimately own?"

He waved a hand. "This one, to start."

"Really?" I looked at La Belle's, and Liam Hunt, in a new light. No wonder this family could drop three-quarters of a mill without a blink. "This place is incredible," I said honestly. "Although, I'm less impressed with your generosity now that I know you're the owner and the meal would've been comped anyway."

Liam's chest thumped, drawing my eye as his laughter boomed through the restaurant. "Do you always say exactly what's on your mind?"

"It's a loveable trait of mine."

His smile—real and true and what I assumed was reserved for his daughter—turned on me, and melted me on my seat. "Forgive me for waiting so long to say what was on mine. You look stunning, Mackenzie. And you, Sienna," he continued, flicking off me so fast, embarrassment killed the silly bubbles popping in my stomach. "The dresses are yours to keep. I hope they stave off the broken nose in my future."

"They're a good start," Sienna lofted.

"Daddy, can I see the fish?"

"Sure."

Elizabeth grabbed Sienna, tugging her along. Just like that, it was the two of us.

I cleared my throat. "So, Elizabeth's mom... can I ask?"

"You can ask. No guarantee I'll answer."

"It's just I figure you're not together if Elizabeth is picking up girlfriends for you."

Liam choked on his sip. He was too dignified a man to spray the table red, but I bet money I brought him close.

"Excuse me?"

"She asked Sienna, and then me, what we thought about taking up the role." I smirked at him. I was both honest and the tiniest bit mischievous. Okay, so maybe I did sometimes go looking for trouble. "She hoped the age difference wouldn't bother me."

He swore. "Forgive her. A misinformed child in her playgroup told her daddies need someone to take care of them or they'll get lonely. I thought we settled this, but it seems I need to speak to her again."

"No, it's okay. I wasn't bothered by it. Actually, I think it's adorable that she's holding auditions for the woman who'll cure your loneliness."

"Adorable is not the word."

I laughed, and our knees bumped again.

"Out of curiosity, did you turn down the audition?"

My grin froze on my face. His widened. I wasn't the only mischievous person at this table.

"Yes," I replied, lifting my chin. "I'm thinking a grown man likes to do his own auditioning."

"I do." Warmth ghosted on my cheeks, igniting sizzling sparks as his fingers glided over my skin, and zinging through my body. "And there's a cut-off age for the role."

He dropped his hand, then our conversation—standing up and moving to join Elizabeth and Sienna at the fish tanks. I half appreciated his walking away from me. He didn't see me sink red-faced into the seat, wishing the cushions would swallow and crush me.

With one sentence, Liam made himself abundantly clear. He was not interested in me, so stop flirting with him.

Groaning, I covered my face. I didn't really mean to. It'd been so long since a man looked at me like I wasn't gum he scraped off his shoe, or an easy ride desperate enough to fuck him for that gum. For the first time in a long time, I felt pretty, sexy, confident... and I acted like a fool.

I didn't blame Liam for shutting me down. The truth was, I didn't think our age difference was too far to overcome. Liam wasn't the first older man I looked twice at, and the last one looked back. He didn't rebuff me. He didn't stop at touching my cheek, and getting involved with him was the worst mistake of my life—worse than Digger.

I peeked at Liam over my fingertips. *Thanks for bringing me back to reality, Hunt. That's the real gift you gave me tonight.*

My man-picker was seriously fucked up. Over and over again, I fell for monsters in human suits. That I was attracted to him was reason enough for me to stay away from Liam Hunt.

*LIAM*

Sienna oohed and aahed over Elizabeth's fish friends. I smiled along as she pointed them out to me, covering my amusement at Mackenzie Blaine's cute attempt to feel me out.

I peeked at her slumped in the booth, hiding her face. Her embarrassment—also cute. On top of blushing every time she bumped my knee and ducking her head at my compliments. Cute was the word for her—except when I walked into Sole's place that night and saw her standing there in that dress, hip jutting out and exposing a long, tanned leg through her slit. Cute was not the word that came to my mind as she brushed her hair back, denying its attempt to cover her ample cleavage.

She was an attractive young woman, anyone with a pulse could see that, but the sticking point was young. The time to date twenty-three-year-olds with a planeload of baggage was seven years and eight months ago, before Hurricane Giselle blew through my life, wrecked everything in her path, and left behind a baby. At this point in my life, any woman I got involved with for longer than an evening had to accept Elizabeth was first, last, and everything in between. And she had to feel the same. Mackenzie Blaine...

My gaze softened on her.

Reading of her past twinged something that felt close to... sympathy. Even if I was willing to meet the sensual woman beneath those blushes and tight dress, she needed to focus on getting her life on track, and I say that without judgment. There were wrongs she had to right. People she had to prove wrong. She couldn't move forward until she did.

*This long list of reasonings is foolish.* I turned my back on her. *I needn't convince myself of the reasons Blaine won't be the one to "cure my loneliness."*

*I never liked brunettes.*

I spotted the waiter heading for our table and carried Elizabeth back. By that time, Blaine had recovered. She sat up straight, chin up, lips moist with beads of lemon water, and ignored me completely. I might as well have vanished from the table, Blaine didn't look past her right shoulder to glance in my direction. She focused solely on her conversation with Sienna and Elizabeth.

"—Daddy buys me a new one every year for my birthday. It's in two months. Want to come?"

"We'd love to," Sienna said.

"Last year, I got Paisley. I put secret notes in her belly," said Elizabeth, the most trusting member of the Merchant clan. "I'll show you. Daddy, where is she?"

"She's in the car."

She held out her hand. "Keys, please."

*She's polite with her demands. Never let it be said my stubborn princess didn't know her manners.*

"You can give up all your secrets after dinner. Speaking of." I slid a look to the back of Blaine's head. "Mackenzie, weren't you going to tell us more about you and your time at Caddell House?"

Blaine replied without sparing me a glance. "Pretty sure I wasn't."

My brow twitched. From daring to call me an asshole to dismissing me for blocking her clumsy advances, this kind of drama was exactly why I didn't date below thirty.

"If you don't wish to talk about the past, how about the future? Where will you go after you leave us?"

I might as well have spoken to the dead lamb on my plate.

Kenzie lifted her shoulders in what could have been a shrug, or she was just picking up her water. "Tricky—"

"Elizabeth."

"—what do you say we upgrade from stuffed animals, and I sew you a leather jacket with a unicorn flying on a cloud of flames and fairy dust?"

Elizabeth gasped. "Really? Yes! Yes, yes, yes."

My daughter climbed over Sienna and threw her arms around her. While I sat there, dropping and lifting my arm on the booth, drumming my fingers on the tabletop. Kenzie ignored me completely, and irritation welled in my chest.

"Don't make promises to my daughter unless you intend to keep them," I said after Elizabeth let her go, not letting her hear. "You claim you're hopping a bus back to your old life tonight. I doubt sewing a leather jacket will be high on your list of priorities."

For the first time in thirty minutes, she faced me. "I'd never tell a child I was going to do something unless I meant it. I was raised on broken promises— Oh, look, you succeeded in getting me to talk about my past, but that's all you're going to get because it's not me who's holding back, it's you.

"I picked it up on the balcony with Sunny and then you confirmed it when you said how much I got to know you depended on if I was accepting Sunny's offer. You admire me for turning down the money and walking away, when it's the easiest decision I've ever made. You don't trust me. Neither one of you has told me what you do, or what you expect *me* to do to flush out the dangerous psychopath that commissioned a murder."

I raised a brow. "This is what has you riled up?"

"Yes. Why? Did you think there was another reason?"

My ego weathered the knockout blow. "You can't expect me to spill my life's story to a stranger with one foot out the door."

"You can't expect me to put my and my sister's life in the hands of a couple of strange men who've proven they're happy to lock me up in their tower when the mood strikes them. If you even want me in your tower. I still haven't gotten a straight answer on if you want me to stay."

"I want you to stay."

Sienna, Elizabeth, and Rico, our waiter, paused and stared at me. I spoke louder than I intended.

"I want you to stay," I said, softer. "Someone tried to kill my youngest brother, and they would've succeeded if not for you. I discovered in the worst way last night that for all my security measures, guards, informants, and men, they're not enough to protect my family from this threat. Sole believes you can help, Blaine. I'm not in a position to refuse."

She studied me for a long time.

"Give me a reason, Hunt."

"We're giving you seven hundred and fifty thousand reasons."

"That's why I should do this for me. Why should I do it for you?"

"Elizabeth."

Blaine softened, smiling at her. "Alright, good answer. But I already trust her. Give me a reason to trust you."

"Because when Lizzie was a baby and she woke up in the middle of the night, I'd turn on the psychic network while I rocked her to sleep. I like expensive cars but only one type, it's a Rolls or it's not worth my money. My father was a carny and he taught me to walk a tightrope at five years old. When I was very young, very drunk, and very stupid, I walked around the compound going from balcony to balcony—on the twentieth floor.

"For thirteen years, that took top spot as my most unwise decision, until I fell in love with Giselle Moreau. She drained my bank account buying out every shop in Leighbridge, disappear for days on a party binge, and dented my skull with a wine bottle the first time I broke up with her. Her final act was to fly home to Paris to visit her family, and forget to book a return trip. Good enough, or should I keep going?"

Blaine sat back, arms folded. "Twentieth floor, huh? That's impressive."

"I'd show you the video, but I was... unclothed."

She giggled—shoulders shaking, almond eyes shiny. It was a light, sweet sound. I liked it more than I should.

"See, the guy you're describing," she began, "he sounds like the kind of guy worth doing a favor for. You should show this side more often. No one likes an asshole."

"I don't know"—I leaned in, brushing my lips over her ear—"I'm partial to rim jobs."

Blaine reeled back, lips parting and nothing coming out.

That was naughty, but what could I do? I wanted to see if I could make her blush again.

She rebounded as quickly, sticking her face in mine. "Mr. Hunt, if you're not accepting auditions, don't read me the script."

"Will you help us?"

"I can't." Regret laced the reply. "You understand why, so this isn't coming as a surprise. But I do want to help you. I have a friend who knows everything that goes on in this city. I'll show him the sketch, ask him if he's heard whispers about the attacks on your family. Hopefully that gets you closer to this guy."

I didn't push it. As she said, I understood why she wasn't about to prioritize my family over hers. Another *legitimate businessman* wouldn't give her the choice. They'd lock her away in the compound and use information in her background to keep her under their thumb. Actually, that's how my fathers met my mother.

*There's no question Elizabeth has changed me. Before her arrival, Blaine's service to the Merchants wouldn't be a question, or an option.*

I reclined against the cushion, pouring myself another glass of wine. I observed pretty little Mackenzie over the rim.

*Changed, but not softened.*

My daughter's safety was paramount. If Sole's plan had the slightest chance of working out, we had to try. Blaine doesn't get to say no, so if three-quarters of a million isn't enough, I'll figure out what is.

Audition held. Cast chosen. Script written.

Mackenzie Blaine's role: Our Savior.

*MACKENZIE*

Liam held the door open for us—the gentleman once again.

His rim job comment tickled my lower belly.

*A gentleman and a rogue. I wonder if that's a book title. If not, it should be.*

"It's a nice night," he announced. "Lumiere Lane isn't far away. Why don't we take a walk? Grab some ice cream."

"Yay," Elizabeth cheered.

I drew in closer. "Liam, I can't. I—"

"Relax." He touched my elbow. "I sent instructions to Fuller to pack your things. There'll be a car waiting when we return. It'll take you wherever you want to go. I'm due at work myself in two hours, so I couldn't keep you."

*Keep me.* He said it without innuendo, but I was humming on nothing but, with the feel of his lips still on my ear.

"I'm simply stealing a little more time with Elizabeth before she has to go to sleep," he said. "I thought you might like to join us. If not, I'll call for the car to pick you up now."

Torn, I checked the time on his wristwatch. Eight thirty.

I couldn't go to her house then even if I wanted. She wouldn't be zonked in front of the television until nine or nine thirty. Asleep by midnight.

"Okay," I gave in. "Although, I couldn't eat another bite. No ice cream for me, but I'll take walking off this meal."

"Ooh, Daddy." Tricky wedged between us, hugging Liam's knees. "Can I bring Paisley, please?"

"Sure. Go ahead and get her."

Elizabeth tugged me along, telling me about the secret pocket in her unicorn's stomach, stuffed with cotton, secrets, and wishes.

"Can you put her on my jacket?" she asked.

"I sure can."

Liam beeped the car to let us in.

"Also, I want—"

*Boom!*

A wall of heat bowled us over, throwing me and Tricky off our feet. I slammed onto the pavement—breath punched out of me once, then again as Tricky fell on top of me.

Wheezing, I couldn't suck in a breath. White spots danced in my vision, and clanging deafened me.

*What... happened? What happened to me?*

The bubble popped.

"Elizabeth!"

"Kenzie!"

Screaming. Shouting. Crying. Horns honking, and a dull roar clear through their chorus.

Shakily, I pushed myself up. Tricky clung to me—little nails breaking my skin, wails battering my bruised eardrums.

"Lizzie." Liam skidded beside us, lost his balance, and shredded his expensive pants on asphalt and the remains of his four-hundred-thousand-dollar car. It didn't register as he patted and tugged on his daughter, bellowing *are you okay?*

Tricky had me in a death grip, bawling her eyes out. Through it all, I watched the inferno swallowing Liam's Royce—flames billowing up to smoke tendrils dissipating in the starless sky.

*A few more feet... and we would have died.* The realization echoed in my still silent mind. *This sweet innocent little girl who'd declared me her friend within an hour of meeting me.*

Liam gave up trying to pull her away and threw his arms around us both. Some of his fevered kisses missed and caught me, dotting my forehead, cheek, and corner of my mouth in salty wetness.

We were supposed to be in that car. Me, Sienna, Elizabeth, Liam. Whoever this guy was, he didn't care who died in his war with the Merchants.

I hugged Tricky, stroking her hair as Sienna hugged and did the same to me.

*He tried to kill Elizabeth.*

I grasped Liam's chin, turning him to face me. Bloodshot rims beheld me, he huffed like his heart burst countless times in the span of minutes.

"I'll do it," I said clearly. "I'll help you take this bastard down. Whatever it takes."

# Chapter Four

Sienna got off the elevator first. She kissed me and Tricky, and waved bye to Liam. Liam and I continued the rest of the way in silence.

Elizabeth refused to let go of me. She cried through most of the wait for another car to come pick us up. She finally fell into an exhausted sleep halfway home. I expected Liam to take her, but he led us into the elevator instead, and lapsed into the quiet that consumed us both. What was there to say after an event so horrible? After facing the truth that you almost lost your daughter?

Liam's place was both what I expected and a surprise at the same time. Unlike Sunny, there wasn't a string of pretty cooks and maids lined up to greet their master. No one awaited when the lights flicked on, beating the shadows from every corner. What did meet my eyes shifted my perspective.

Liam Hunt gave all the appearance of a cold, humorless bachelor. Cold, humorless single men usually had the minimalist, monochrome bachelor pads to go with them. But Liam, he had a home.

Toys littered the plush carpet. An empty snack bowl and juice box mingled with the remotes on the coffee table. In one corner, a pink princess tent clashed with the black and silver of bachelor pads' past. This place was completely taken over by Elizabeth, from the photos on every wall to the drawings covering the fridge.

Liam drew ahead, pulling my attention to the slight hitch in his step. Red seeped through his pant leg's tear. I hadn't noticed he took such a bad scrape. His impassive expression hinted he didn't either.

Down a long hall and to the left, Liam motioned to Tricky's room. I placed her on the unicorn bed, tucking her tight in the sheets. She sported a spot of dirt on her forehead and my blood under her fingernails, but I didn't dare wake her. Cleaning up could come in a new day when sunlight made the world seem less frightening.

"Can you give me a minute?"

"Of course."

Through the closing sliver, Liam dropped to his knees, gently stroking her hair and pressing his forehead to hers. I let the little family have their privacy.

Instead of leaving, I went into the kitchen, opening and closing the cabinets. Liam was the type of guy who took the right precautions. He wouldn't keep medications in the bathroom, so most likely...

I found it by the time he returned. "Sit," I told him, carrying the first aid kit to the couch. "That's bleeding pretty bad."

"I'm fine."

"You're not fine, Liam," I said softly. "You can't be fine."

Maybe he was too tired to argue with me because he sat without another word. I was gentle peeling away the tatters, examining the extent. Half the skin on his left thigh was left behind on the pavement, still it could've been worse. Much, much worse.

"This is going to sting." I doused a cloth in antiseptic. "I'm sorry. I'll try to be quick—"

"Why?" he rasped. "Why did you change your mind? Your situation hasn't."

His leg was warm under my palm—burning heat spreading from him through me as I dabbed the wound.

"Because, Liam... that age when you stop seeing everyone as a new best friend, it's not six. It should never be six."

"Leave that."

"But you're bleeding."

Liam cupped the back of my head. I blinked up at him, pulse rising to his gliding touch behind my ear, along the hollow of my throat, finally to my chin—holding me firm in his piercing eyes' snare.

"I wasn't going to free you," he dropped. "I planned to find a way to bind you to the Merchants and my family for as long as we had need of you."

My heart sank to my stomach.

"But in the end, I didn't need to. Tricks, threats, and broken promises, the tenets my life was built on, aren't necessary with you, Mackenzie Blaine. All you needed to do the hard thing... was hear my daughter cry."

I trembled in his hold. "Why are you telling me this? I agreed to help. I never had to know you intended to force me."

"Because."

His calloused thumb was a whisper caressing my lips. Traitorous, single-minded desire pooled in my middle.

"In exchange for help, you asked for honesty," Liam said, "so that's what I'll give you, Mackenzie. The truth. All of it. More than you'll bear."

My voice was a rasp. "I'm not sure if I should say thank you."

"You shouldn't." Liam pressed a kiss on my forehead. "That's for me to say.

"Thank you, Mackenzie."

Looking in each other's eyes, something passed between us. The air charged with living lightning—standing my hairs on end, rippling beneath my skin, curling my hands on his legs, moving them apart, sliding my body between.

I rose to meet him, and Liam bent for me.

He stood up. The sudden movement knocked me back on my ass.

"You should go. Thatcher will be here in a moment. New measures will have to be put in place. More men hired. I believe Sole has a room, clothes, and everything you need arranged for you." He was talking and moving so fast, I couldn't get a word in. Liam held open the front door, expecting me to walk through it. "Good night, Miss Blaine."

"I... uh... good night, Liam. I'll come by in the morning to see how she's doing."

"There's an intercom in the elevator. Buzz and I'll let you in."

That was something at least. He wanted me out right then, but not out completely.

"There's somewhere I need to be tonight," I admitted. "Despite what happened—actually, because of what happened, I have to go. Will security try to stop me leaving?"

"You're free to come and go as you please. Just be cautious. Take different routes coming and going, and for tonight, take a cab." Liam placed a fifty on my palm. "I believe I know where you're going to go."

The bill crumpled in my fist. I waited for him to tell me I was crazy, stupid, risking everything.

"Don't get caught."

He shut the door, leaving me with those parting words. What else did I expect from a gangster? He was the last one to tell me not to break the law.

THE CAB DROPPED ME off three houses down. I crossed the street, moving through the glow of porch lights. It pushed ten o'clock. She'd be in front of the television by now, volume turned up and drowning out the sound of windows opening and closing.

I stepped around her lawn's sycamore and shot back.

Charlie stood clear and visible from the second-story window, as visible as I would've been if she looked down and spotted me.

Heart yammering, I peered around the bark. Charlie bounced the baby in her arms, cooing a string of soothing nonsense. Burning, acrid hatred swelled in my veins—eroding the rules and morals that guided my life. I went without aching to break another living being until her. A decade embodying and believing in forgiveness, until she came into my life.

I pulled out the knife I rescued during a quick stop in my new bedroom to change. My whole life I never imagined what it'd feel like to bury my blade in someone's chest... until Charlie Mayberry.

My glare bore a hole in her head from where I stood. Considering the kind, peaceful person I used to be, my loathing hatred of Charlie should concern me—push me to seek help. But not this time. There was nothing that made more sense... than I should wish to see this woman rubbed off the face of the earth.

Charlie settled the baby in her crib. I waited for the light to go off. I stilled for the television to turn on. Creeping around the sycamore, she was right where she should be—a floating head over the couch, pinned on *Grey's Anatomy*.

I moved fast. Taking a running leap, I scaled the tree, climbing out on the branch tapping against the nursery window. The baby blinked at the new sight above her mobile.

I wedged the knife between the wood and frame, easing the window up. Silent as a sleeping church mouse, I stepped on the dresser, then dropped to the floor.

Kicking and waving her chubby arms, she sounded the alarm, spreading babble through the baby monitor and into the next room. Charlie kept the monitor in her bedroom, where it couldn't disturb her during her shows.

"You're not going to give our secret away, Laurel."

The babble shifted. Tiny face crumpling, she started crying. I didn't hesitate.

Lifting her out of the crib, I cooed softly to her, kissing her sweet, plump cheeks as I eased onto the rocking chair. My boob was out and in her mouth with the quickness of our secret feedings. My daughter settled instantly, greedily sucking down the only breastmilk on tap.

It had been days since I last held her. Even so, I went through my ritual of inspecting her fingers, toes, nose, ears, and everything. Stroking the thick, curly brown hairs sticking up and out. Smiling into the innocent green eyes looking up at me.

I didn't have much time with Laurel. That bitch foster mother, Charlie, would completely ignore my daughter for another hour to an hour and a half. Then she'd poke her head in to check Laurel was asleep, then head to bed herself. Weeks upon months of watching through the window, then the nights I snuck in. This was her routine, and she had yet to break it. While she was downstairs with the television blasting, I was with my daughter. When she returned to the bedroom and baby monitor, I climbed out the window, leaving another piece of my heart withering with her rosebushes.

"How are you doing, beautiful?" I nuzzled her curls. "Mommy missed you so much. You won't believe what happened since we were last together. I have so much to tell you..."

*SUNNY*

The bullseye glared stark in the middle of the wood, daring me to strike. I chose a knife from my collection—slender, honed, perfection. I didn't have the love affair with blades that my father did, but the satisfaction of hitting the target dead-on was in the blood.

I aimed, ready to throw... and dropped it back on the pile. Rage lit fire under my feet. I raced to the target and ripped it off the wall, flinging it across the room. It struck my armchair and hit the carpet, making a barely audible thud.

*That won't do.*

I grabbed my piece off the nightstand, readying to blow the shit to splinters.

"—you did, didn't you?"

"Shh. Keep your voice down."

My head cocked toward the ajar door. Leaving destruction for another day, I crept to the opening, listening to Kenzie and her sister coming out of her bedroom.

*Her* bedroom. Which it would be until the day we made my room, our bedroom.

"Kens, I know this is killing you, but you can't keep going back there. That woman is rabid. She'll have you arrested, or worse."

*Arrested? Go back where?*

"You don't understand."

"I do—"

"No, you don't," Kenzie hissed. "I tried to stay away, but I can't, okay? I just can't. Look, if we get through this, we'll have the money we need to start over. In the meantime, I won't get caught."

*Get caught doing what exactly, sneaky little Angel?*

Kenzie and Sienna changed the subject, not providing an answer to my internal question. I padded out to join them. If my Angel was out of her room, so was I.

Angel spotted me and flicked away, eyes widening at the floor. She roughly and pointedly cleared her throat. Possibly had something to do with me striding out in nothing but my briefs.

My house—I'd walk around stark naked if I felt like it, and I did on many occasions.

"Kenzie, I heard what happened last night," I began, "and that you're staying to help us because of it." I held her face, capturing a glimpse of her surprise, and kissed her square on the lips.

"Hmmph!"

The sound from my mouth was a wholly different sound. Kenzie's lips were two soft, plump pillows, sweetened with cherry lip gloss. They relaxed for the barest second, releasing a barely audible moan.

I broke away. "Thank you for being there for Tricky. Every time I think I couldn't owe you more, you prove me wrong—and we've only known each other for a few days."

"I— You— You can't—"

"By the end of the week, I bet I'll end up eternally in your debt." I grinned into those owlish eyes. "Then you'll be stuck with me forever."

I left her gaping in the hallway, making for my room and a change of clothes.

"Sunny!"

Sienna followed me to the door. "You just short-circuited my sister's brain. Great as a short-term strategy," she said, swinging on the doorknob, "but long term, if you want Mackenzie Blaine, it takes more than a kiss and cute ass."

"Good to know, Baby Blaine. Good to know."

She paused, narrowing on me. For no good reason, her gaze shifted to the target lying on the carpet.

"Give it time, Sunny."

I tensed. "Are we still talking about your sister?"

"If you want to be." With that, she winked and ducked out.

*MACKENZIE*

I paced the living room, fingers flying to my mouth every other second. Each time they confirmed the spearminty taste of Sunny Bellisario was still on my lips.

*He kissed me. I can't believe he kissed me.*

*I can't believe you let him,* said a treacherous voice.

"Miss Blaine."

I jerked, whirling around to Ms. Fuller.

"You're standing there staring at the couch like you need its permission to sit down. Relax," she said—more like ordered. "This is your home now. Tell me what you'd like for breakfast, I'll get Nadine started on it."

"Nadine doesn't have to trouble herself over us. I'll pour us a bowl of cereal."

"Cereal for one," Sienna announced. "I'll have an avocado and bacon omelet. I'll help if she allows outsiders in her kitchen."

"She does."

Sienna went into the kitchen, hopefully to make me an omelet too. Fuller was still staring at me, so I gave sitting a try.

"Ms. Fuller, what exactly does a house manager do?"

"Everything," she stated. "I handle the day-to-day operations of the Fairfield. Supervising and hiring staff, keeping inventory, paying the bills, and looking after Tricky when both her father and uncle are called away for business."

"You call her Tricky too?"

"She's quite insistent that I do."

"I don't want us to add to your load. I'm sure you have your hands full with Sunny."

I didn't expect a full-belly laugh and I didn't get one. Though, Fuller did crack a smile.

"You two are no trouble at all. Adeline hired me to look after her family while she's away, and right now, you're doing a much better job at it. Whatever you need, I'm at your disposal." Fuller picked a tablet off the end table and handed it to me.

"To start, choose your wardrobe. The family has an account with Caddell House. Send in your measurements, preferences, and needs, your outfits will be here in two weeks at the most. Until then, take this credit card and go shopping. Fashion Ave. is a block down. It's best to walk or take a cab for the time being."

"Hold on," I cut in. "I can't take Sunny's credit card or leave him footing a Caddell House bill. They charge three hundred dollars for a scarf."

"What you can't do is walk around in this"—she pinched my jacket lapel—"for a second longer. One of Sole's fathers invested in Camden Caddell years ago, granting him the start-up to launch his own line. As a thank-you, his company designs exclusively for the family at a heavy discount. Take it." She closed my hand over the card. "Feeling well is a human right, and you deserve to be comfortable in your skin, Miss Blaine."

"Thank you." I held the card to my chest, pushing back overwhelm. No wonder Adeline left Fuller to be the mother in her stead. "I will buy some new clothes, but not from Caddell House. I'm not quite ready to wear my past."

Sunny came in—fully dressed and fit to knock the unsuspecting on their ass with one look, even from his wheelchair. Fuller went to check on breakfast while he parked next to me.

Warmth pulsed beneath my skin thinking of that kiss. "How long do you need the chair?" I asked, straining to sound normal.

"Not for much longer. I'm healing well. Hendrix gave me this 'cause walking tugs on the sutures. Once that stops being as painful as it sounds, I can ditch the chair."

"You shouldn't be on your feet at all, then. Wait till you're one hundred percent."

The corner of his mouth tugged up. "How else was I supposed to reach?"

I shoved away. Laughing, Sunny tugged me back down, then tangled my legs with his to prevent another escape.

"Storm off after we talk about last night, Angel. In the restaurant, did you notice anything or anyone suspicious? Someone watching you?"

I sobered quickly. "No, nothing like that. But Liam asked for a semi-private table. There were two tables in my line of sight, and those couples never looked at us."

"What about outside before the car blew? Think," he said when I opened my mouth. "Close your eyes, and picture it."

I did as he said. Scene unfolding in my mind, I went back to the four of us stepping out of the restaurant. Liam holding the door. Elizabeth taking my hand. After she did, my gaze was down and my attention on her. The world and people in it were blurs on the edge of my periphery, but before I dropped my head...

I frowned, causing Sunny to speak up.

"What? What did you think of right then?"

"There— There was no one at the valet stand." As I said it, the vision solidified, showing me the empty area under the awning, where the lone stand waited for the young gentleman we drove past. "When we arrived, there was a guy there and a line of cars waiting for him. When we came out, no guy. Maybe he was on a break or—"

"Or maybe someone lured, killed, or paid him to leave a present in the car," Sunny said. "I can guarantee that bomb wasn't there when you guys left the compound, so it was put there while you were inside. He was either a witness to get rid of, or he was an accomplice."

I shuddered, hugging myself tight. "It must be terrible having to look at people in terms of bystander or enemy."

He mouth-shrugged. "This is my every day, love. You've got another reality to compare it to. You tell me if it's terrible."

"Doesn't that... bother you?" I asked, voice soft.

"Nothing and nowhere is ever so dark that you can't find the light." His smile punched me in the gut. "If I hadn't been thrown off that bridge, I wouldn't have landed on you—an extraordinarily beautiful *and* observant woman who just gave us another place to start. We have to find that valet."

"Doesn't the restaurant have cameras? If someone lured him away to plant the bomb, or if he did it himself, we can settle it in the time it takes to hit rewind."

Sunny was shaking his head before I finished the sentence. "No cameras in or around La Belle's. Liam has another business running out of that restaurant. It's not the kind you want on tape."

"Of course," I said, accepting that with an ease that twinged my moral conscience. How quickly did it happen? Falling into their world. "If that's the case, are we thinking the bomber got lucky, or that he knew there were no cameras to give him away?"

That smile leeched away. "No one is that lucky. Two attempts on our lives that damn well nearly succeeded. Both at the right times and in the right place. But how did he know Liam would be at La Belle's?"

I couldn't help myself. I shifted toward the kitchen, where Sienna gabbed away over a bowl of beaten eggs with Ms. Fuller and the cook—among the two who knew where we'd be last night.

"I'm not blind." The serious tone drew me back. "And it's not sentiment," Sunny said, "but I'm not ready to go there yet, Angel."

"What other explanation could there be?"

Sunny held my gaze steadily. "What would it take for you to believe Sienna wanted you dead?"

My muscles tightened. "She'd have to plunge the knife in my chest herself," I replied after a long silence, "and I still wouldn't believe it."

He nodded like that was the right answer. "They're family. Families betray each other—"

A memory ripped through my mind, too fast for me to hold on to, and I didn't try.

"—but if I'm going to believe Fuller tried to blow up the little girl she's taken care of since she was a baby, or that Thatcher tried to kill the guy who used to ride his shoulders during the Founder's Day parade, they better have the knife in their hand."

"I understand." I smoothed the wrinkle between his brow. Sunny wasn't made for that look. My Trouble was meant to smile. "I do. That may be the simplest explanation, but that doesn't make it right. And there is another explanation, that the valet was tipped to give the bomber a heads-up the next time the boss rolled up with his Royce."

"Now that is both simple and much more likely." Sunny shoved out of his chair. "Liam's got to know. This dude will be picked up within the hour."

I guided the tatted avenger back into his seat. "*I* will tell Liam. I'm going up there anyway to see Tricky. Relax and listen to your doctor. I didn't trade a favor with River for you to rip open your sutures and pass out on the bathroom floor."

"River?" Sunny repeated, pulling me up short. "As in River Delaney?"

"Yeah. How did you know?"

"Not many Rivers running around." A smirk I didn't understand curled his lips. "The Rat King himself. Let me guess, he hooked you up with the doctor that saved me."

"He did actually."

"And what did Delaney ask for in return?" I hesitated, and Sunny's smile widened. "Let me guess again... me."

I didn't confirm or deny. Why when Sunny didn't need my yes.

"He knew you," I said, "and you clearly know him. How?"

"Oh, everyone in the underground knows the Rat King," Sunny breezed. "The real surprise is that you know him too. But then, eight months on the street, naturally he sniffed you out."

"I hope that's not a comment on my smell." The crack was my go-to in the face of confusion. These two didn't just know of each other. I sniffed something out: history.

"You were in his crew," Sunny stated, not asked. "No wonder you're so comfortable with morally gray men."

"You have that backward. I left his crew when I found out just how gray those morals were. River is a friend, and I appreciate everything he's done for me, but the guy can doublespeak you into believing he slipped out of English. I respect that he does what he has to do for his crew to survive, but honesty is everything to me. I need to know your promises are binding and your word is truth. So, I'm going to ask you, Sunny"—I gripped his chair arms, leaning in nice and close—"what's the story between you two?"

Sunny popped a kiss on my nose too quick for me to shoot away squawking—though I did, flushing down to my toes. The jerk used his freedom to roll away.

"That story is for another day, Angel," Sunny lofted over his shoulder. "You've got to run up and tell Liam about that valet. Every minute we waste, the bomber slips further away."

It was the truth of that which stopped me from chasing him down and... what? Chew him out? Claim another searing kiss? Tackle him out of that chair, rip off those Caddells, and get another tour of his perfect frame?

At some point in the last four days, we graduated to kissing, and Hera help me if I saw the sign. Sunny was clearly taken with me, and funny things happened in my chest when he looked in my direction. Even so, we went through a traumatic event together. As I saw it, he woke up from certain death and imprinted on the first face he saw. Sunny would be making moon eyes at Sienna if it was her instead of me. I would not read more into his kisses, compliments, praise, or touches than there were.

When he knew the real me—the homeless single mom who lost her baby and carries a sordid, heartbreaking past—his crush would vanish into nothing.

"Sienna, I'm running upstairs for a minute."

"I'll keep your breakfast warm. When you come back, we'll go shopping."

I agreed, grabbed the notepad on the living room table, and headed out. The Fairfield was outfitted with the best security there was to offer, including the call that went out to Liam's apartment when I hit the *open* button for his floor.

"Hello?" A tiny voice poured through the speaker.

I softened. "Tricky, sweetie. It's Kenzie. I came to see how you were doing. Can I come in?"

Her tone brightened. "Kenzie, you can come in. Daddy thinks I don't know the code, but I do." With that, the elevator slid open.

Rounding the corner, I took one look and leaped back, plastering myself against the wall. Holding my breath, their murmured conversation poured over me.

"—doing fine. There isn't a scratch on her, Liam," said Doctor Hendrix. "The scare had the worst effect, and knowing our Elizabeth, she'll bounce back in no time."

"I should send her to someone." Tightness laced his baritone, upsetting the natural lazy calm and squeezing my chest. "A therapist or—"

"What she needs is her daddy to hold her, kiss her, and tell her everything's going to be alright." The buxom, pretty doctor's tone dropped to a purr. "It's you I'm worried about, Liam. Who's going to hold and kiss you—make you feel all right?"

My chest tightened for another reason. Of course this was the explanation for why I turned the corner and found them standing with barely a whisper between them, her fingers stroking his chest. Still, it compounded my embarrassment further. Of course Liam popped my bubble at the restaurant and then pulled away when my dense self rose up, deluded into thinking he was going to kiss me.

Liam had my background check. He knew about Laurel and got an eyeful of me in holey socks and dirt as an accessory. There was no crush to kill.

He'd never in a million years want me when gorgeous, age-appropriate doctors were willing to make house calls.

"What are you doing tonight?" he asked, driving the point home.

"You."

"Kenzie?!"

I jerked, banging my head on the wall.

"Kenzie, where are you?" Elizabeth called. "Daddy, did you see her?"

"Kenzie?"

Lifting my chin, I stepped into the hall, praying my mortification wasn't written all over my face. Liam and Hendrix stood before the doorway, Elizabeth clinging to her dad's leg. The two didn't bother to spring apart at the sight of me or his daughter. This relationship was no secret.

*Why would it be? Unlike if the two of us hooked up, there's nothing scandalous about two single people in their thirties getting naked.*

"I didn't mean to lurk," I said, owning up. "It looked like you two were having a private conversation and I didn't want to interrupt."

"You're not interrupting. You were invited." He raised a brow at his daughter. "It's me who didn't realize I had to change the code again."

Elizabeth grinned unrepentantly. "Kenzie came to have breakfast with me."

"I did," I confirmed, "and I brought a sketchpad so we can get started on that jacket. Still want a unicorn?"

"Yeah!" She bounced up and down, shaking her dad. "Can we make it today?"

I laughed and scooped her up as she ran for me. "It's going to take a little longer than that, but we can for sure draw out leather-jacket-domination today. I'm going shopping after breakfast. I'll pick up everything we need."

"Daddy, can I—?"

"No," Liam slid in. "You can't go shopping with Miss Kenzie. After breakfast, we're going to finish packing, then we're driving up to see Grandma and Grandpas. You're staying with them for a few days."

Elizabeth pouted but didn't argue. Liam wasn't wearing an expression I'd try to mess with either.

I squeezed past him, going inside. This early and the man was fresh and heavenly from a shower, drowning me in a cloud of cypress and the barest tang of roasted coffee beans. He devastated in a thin sweater and loose black jeans, and my heart thumped as my breasts brushed against his arm, leaning in. "I need to talk to you about something," I said under my breath. "About last night. It's important."

He nodded. "Give me a minute. I'll be right there."

Liam shut the door behind me, enclosing himself in a private goodbye with Doctor Hendrix. I told myself this didn't bother me while I carried Elizabeth to the table. An impressive spread was laid out for her.

"That looks yummy."

"Peanut butter–banana pancake, fruit, and a unicorn smoothie." She held up her plate. "Want some?"

"I wouldn't mind a sip of that smoothie. I've always wanted to know what unicorn tastes like."

"It's not real unicorn," she cried, giggling. "Dad blends the strawberries, blueberries, and everything by itself, then he mixes it all together to get the colors."

"Very clever." I relaxed and took a seat next to her. Hendrix was right. As long as this sweet little girl had her smile, Tricky would get through this. "So, first things first. What colors are we thinking? Blue mane? Purple, pink, or rainbow?"

"Hmm. Can she be blue with a rainbow horn? My dad's favorite color is blue."

"She sure can."

"—this later." Liam's voice filled the room as effectively as his larger-than-life presence, demanding my attention. "Thanks again."

I got to my feet. "You keep thinking design," I told Elizabeth. "I need to talk to your dad real quick and then I'll be right back."

"Okay."

Liam intercepted me on the way to him. "Not here," he said, curling an arm around my waist. "In my office."

"I—"

His hold was warm and firm on my hip, leading me away from Tricky, down the hall and to a door on the right. We entered a room that fit the monochrome stereotype down to the glass desk, black laptop, black desk chair, and black bookshelves. Though even in here, Tricky made her mark in the many goofy and adorable photos of her scattered about the place.

"Sit." He motioned to the, of course, black leather couch. "Can I get you a drink?"

"It's eight a.m."

"Which would matter on a regular morning," he replied, pouring himself a scotch. "But this is not a regular morning."

"No, it isn't." I went to him instead of the couch, placing a comforting hand on his back. "You didn't sleep a wink last night, did you?"

He turned, concealing his face in shadows. "Is it obvious?"

"No, it's me, Liam. I'm a parent too, and I haven't had a full night's rest since they put Laurel in another woman's arms. Worrying about our children and drifting off into dreamland aren't in the same sentence."

Liam reached behind and took my hand. We didn't speak.

We didn't have to.

"She'll be safe with my parents for the next few days. Perhaps a week." He released me, moving to the couch. "By then, we'll fucking know something," Liam hissed. "We'll have the son of a bitch and my daughter will be safe at home."

"And I can tell you where to start. The valet," I stated. "He wasn't there when we came out of the restaurant. After the... explosion, people were screaming, rushing away from us and to us. Sirens were going off. It was chaos. But after, during, and before, I didn't see him anywhere. That's something, right?"

"Yes, that's something." He slammed the glass down, hurrying to his desk. "Calvin was on staff last night. His shift was until closing. He should've been exactly where we left him when we came out." Liam snatched the phone off its cradle and jabbed in a number.

"Juan," he answered. "Yes, yes, I'm fine. Did you let Calvin leave early yesterday? You didn't." Liam met my gaze. "Find him. Bring him to Astoria. He and I are due a discussion." He paused to listen to the reply, then hung up.

"Astoria?" I asked.

"One of my clubs."

"Let me guess, one of your properties where you conduct more than one kind of business."

He gave me a wicked smirk that was so Sunny, I saw the resemblance between them clear as day. "All legitimate, if anyone asks."

"Of course." I dropped on the couch. "How is Elizabeth? She seems her usual bright self."

"She is. We talked about it earlier, and I explained as best I could. She understands that she's safe and I'll never let anyone hurt her."

"We believe that," I whispered, drawing my legs to my chest. "We believe it when our daddies say everything's going to be okay—until they stop."

"I won't." Liam claimed the spot next to me. "How is Laurel?"

My smile trembled around the edges. "She's sweet and soft and perfect. My baby's crawling now. And she's got a name for me."

"Mama?"

I blushed. "Uh, no. But we're working on that. Liam, will you do me a favor? Don't tell anyone about her. Especially Sunny."

"Why? You don't imagine he'll judge you."

"I know he won't." As I said it, I knew it was true. Sunny would never fault me my past. "But he'll do what you're doing—ask me about her."

"I didn't mean—"

"No, no," I said quickly, gripping his thigh without thinking. "I'm not upset that you asked. I'm happy you did, which is the problem. I could sit here for days and tell you every move she made and every sound she babbled, then I'd lock myself in a room for twice as long and cry till there was nothing left. I realized around the third time I considered suicide—"

Liam's eyes widened a fraction.

"—that the only way I'd survive being away from her is by compartmentalizing. Even though she's on my mind every minute of every day, I can't give in to talking about her, missing her, wishing I could snatch her out of that crib and run, because if I do, that's exactly what's going to happen. When I'm with her, it's just me and my baby, but when we're apart..."

Liam laid his hand over mine. He caressed his thumb over my index finger, then my middle—slow and deliberate gliding the calloused digit along my skin. My hair stood on end, rising with my rippling flesh, and catching in my stopped breath and hard swallow.

"I understand. She stays between you and me."

I think I opened my mouth to say something. All that went through my mind was his thigh— warm, hardened flesh beneath my palm. He was sending comfort into my bones. One single parent to another—providing understanding I couldn't get from those with even the best of intentions. Liam, like me, was crushed under the knowledge that sometimes the safest place for your kid wasn't next to you.

I knew this. Understood on a logical level that his touch was platonic. The soft smile on his lips—kindness. His touch—pity. Liam wasn't coming on to me then, any more than his naughty joke the night before was an invitation. He had a lovely doctor coming over that night to provide the comfort he was looking for.

*So why is his pinkie curling around mine?* Beads of sweat pinpricked on the nape of my neck, cooling my heated skin as he turned my palm up.

*Why is my breath coming in shallow pants?* He glided along my palm, tracing a pattern on my skin.

*Why can't I look away from his lips?*

Liam closed firm but gentle around my hand and drew me in.

"Kenzie?"

We froze.

"Are you coming back?" Tricky asked. She stood innocently in the doorway, slurping her unicorn smoothie.

Liam tugged me the rest of the way and tucked my chin in the crook of his neck. It took me a second to comprehend... the hug.

He patted me on the back, platonic, friendly, and pitying. "Between us," he repeated. "And thank you, Mackenzie. Calvin and I will have a lot to talk about when I find him." Getting to his feet, Liam released me. "She's all yours, Lizzie. Dad's going to start on the packing."

"How long will I be at Grandma and Grandpas'?"

"Till they fill you with so much sugar I have to bring you home before all your teeth fall out of your head."

She shrieked, laughing. "Daddy, you're silly."

Liam propelled her up by the wrists, smooched her cheek, and dropped her on her feet. I was calm and collected by the time she ran up to me.

"Ready?" I asked. "Let's sketch this beauty. I bet by the time you come back, your jacket will be ready for you." Turning, I flashed the phoenix on mine. "We'll be matching."

Elizabeth "Tricky" Hunt turned out to be ten times more exacting than all of the creative directors of Gucci, Chanel, Armani, Burberry, and Caddell House combined. She sat atop her literal throne—plush, purple, and child-size though it may be—and accepted or rejected bits of my design until it was perfect. Only when she was satisfied did she kiss my cheek, say goodbye, and then rush off to make sure Dad didn't leave the must-have toys from her suitcase.

Liam caught the tail end of her goodbye, coming out to pour himself some coffee.

"It would seem I'm dismissed," I told him, finishing up the shopping list on the back of the sketch. A smile stretched my face, aching the unused muscles, and refusing to go away. So long—it had been so long since I'd done this.

Begin the creation of something beautiful.

"You're kind to do this for her. I assume what she wants isn't going to be easy or quick."

"You assume correctly, but it's nothing I haven't done before. Honestly, I'm gonna love the challenge." I stopped short halfway to the door. "This conversation you're going to have with Calvin, will you tell me what he says? If he did it or was paid by a pale bald man?"

Liam sipped from his cup—his neck rippling with the swallow and reminding me of the tangy, sweet smell of him. "Yes."

"You will?"

He inclined his head. "You were almost killed in that blast too, Mackenzie."

I wasn't sure when he decided he would call me by my full name instead of my nickname. The way it rolled around on his tongue in that deep voice shed the common tinge of Mackenzie and made it feel like another secret between us.

"You have a right to know by who," he finished. "You could even join me."

I blinked, not having heard that right. "Excuse me? Did you say join you?"

"I did. Sunny's going to stick you among his pigeons, see who is first to fly away scared when you reveal you're a cat. If you want a demonstration of how a Merchant handles an interrogation, I'm happy to provide."

My mouth opened and closed—the implication of what he implied sinking in. "As in, I should see a *legitimate businessman* in action."

A glint lit in his jeweled eyes, not dimming even as he moved through the blinds' rippling shadows to get to me. "Precisely."

Pulse picking up speed, I stopped trying to talk.

I agreed to this. Sunny was almost killed. Elizabeth screamed in my arms after nearly facing her death. Sienna, Liam, and I were meant to face ours that night as well. I wanted to see this man stopped. Bringing him to justice was what nature demanded, and no one would shed a tear for an attempted child-murderer.

I *agreed* to this.

But I also made a promise to my daughter that I'd win custody of her again, and soon. What judge would grant her to me if I stood in front of them with that look in my eyes. If I fully embraced the acts and ways of legitimate businesspeople.

"Not today," I rasped. "I'm sure I'll learn on the job, and develop my own methods of questioning."

"Whatever you say." Liam was his usual unfettered smoothness. "As promised, I'll give you an update afterward." Walking around me, he held open the door for me to leave. Now I really was dismissed.

Downstairs, Sienna waited with my cold breakfast, slurping down chamomile tea and messing around on a phone. "Here you go." Sienna slid the new Samsung phone across the terrace table, still wrapped in its box. "Mr. Thatcher picked these up for us this morning."

"He didn't have to do that. We can share that one—which you also should've refused," I said, arching a brow.

"I did, but he insisted, and considering we signed up to put targets on our backs, I wasn't fighting too hard at having a way to call for help if things start blowing up and people get thrown off buildings."

"We didn't sign up for a target on our backs, I did."

She mirrored my raised brow. "If you're doing this, I am too. We're together, Kenzie. Always. In everything. Don't bother to argue with me," she said when I readied to do just that. "As the resident psychic, I can tell you there is no future where you win that fight."

I shook my head, sighing. "Course not, because you always use your abilities to win. Isn't that cheating?"

"If it is, you won't tell on me."

Sunny came out to join us midway through my omelet. It floored me—as in if I wasn't sitting, my wobbly knees would've given out and dropped me—how sinfully handsome Sunny was poured into a pair of trunks. He strode over bare-chested and barefoot, leaning over me to pluck a strawberry off my plate. Pulling back, his chin brushed against my forehead—leaving another in the invisible marks the Merchant brothers were leaving on my skin.

"Shouldn't you be resting?" I asked. I was proud of myself for drifting down to the *V* poking out of his trunks and moving no lower.

"That's exactly what I'm about to do. There's a saltwater hot tub a floor above us. A little soak is just what the doctor ordered. Join me when you come back from shopping."

"That sounds nice, actually. I'll pick up a swimsuit while I'm out."

"Oooh, about that." Sunny pulled a face. "There's a limit on the credit card, so if you're tapped out and can't afford the swimsuit, your birthday suit will work just fine."

I flashed out. Sunny whipped away fast but not fast enough. I kicked him square on the right butt cheek. Yelping, he scurried inside, shouting, "Pineapple! Pineapple!"

Snickering, I shifted to Sienna and the knowing expression on her face. "What?"

"Nothing. It's just... I love the energy of you two together. It's like you've known each other for years and your souls have already begun to mesh as they do with the people we're meant to walk this life with. Plus, he makes you laugh so easily. I missed you laughing, Kenzie."

The whole of her speech was too much for me to handle, except for one part. "I missed laughing too."

After breakfast, we headed down to the lobby where Thatcher programmed his number in our phones, stated and then restated the protocols for if we got in trouble, and finally gave us directions for what the Leighbridgers called Fashion Ave.

"I would assign you both a security detail, but that might have the opposite intent of protecting you. This enemy is unknown to us, but we are not to him. It may draw attention to you two as friends of the family if you're seen with Sunny's usual guards."

"Don't we want that attention? The plan is I step up in Sunny's place."

"Not yet," the imposing man explained. "Right now, Sunny is simply 'not picking up his phone.' A few more days, he's 'missing.' A few more and his associates will conclude something happened to him, and then they'll mobilize to do something about it. It's at that point the traitor, if there is one, will ready his next move."

"Makes sense. He or she can't act like they know Sunny is dead before the rest of the gang does. They've got to sit back and wait for the news the family identified the John Doe tossed off an overpass as Sunny."

"Exactly. Once he sets the rest of his plans in motion, you will step in to disrupt them. If the goal is to take over Sunny's business or poise himself to destroy the entire family, naturally he'll arrange for you to meet an unexpected end too. He won't want an agent of the Merchants in his way." Thatcher dropped this as casually as a meteorologist gave the weather. "When he strikes, this time we'll be ready."

I hummed. "Was it a good idea to tell me the rest of the plan while I still have time to run?"

Amusement wrinkled the lines around his mouth. "I can promise you we'll do everything to ensure your safety, but it should be said, you do have time to run. No one is forcing you."

"I do know that." I held a deep breath and released it slow. "I want to help. I have to. If I walked away now and something happened to Sunny, Liam, Tricky, or even you, my new manhandling friend, I'd always wonder if I could've done something to stop it. There are certain regrets you shouldn't carry with you."

"And you, Miss Sienna?" he asked.

She looked away, eyes glazing. "This is where I'm supposed to be. I couldn't run even if I wanted to."

I'd challenge that notion later, reminding her she had the option to stay plump and pampered in Sunny's penthouse while I dangled myself as bait.

We waved Thatcher out the door, setting off into the busy Leighbridge morning.

"No matter how many times I visit this borough, I still feel like I crossed the North Quay line into another world."

"I know exactly what you're talking about, little sister."

Men and women who lived and breathed designer labels breezed past with their steaming lattes and rapid-fire conversations. They didn't pay a lick of attention to us, for once, it wasn't because we were dressed in rags chic. Fuller tossed the clothes we arrived in—I narrowly rescued my jacket on its way to the incinerator. Shonda loaned us jeans and simple blouses to run around in, so we didn't stick out in all the wrong ways.

No, the pedestrians were plain ole ignoring us because we're random strangers and they didn't give a shit.

It was beautiful.

Sienna and I linked arms, talking and running through our shopping list. "Okay, we're going to Fashion Ave. because Fuller said they have a fabric store, and Tricky's jacket will be as fancy as the little cutie herself. Afterward, we're grabbing a cab and swinging by Green Mart."

"Ugh." Sienna wrinkled her nose. "I'm not trying to run up this guy's credit card bill either, but we're supposed to be a couple of badass queenpins, chosen by the late Sunny Bellisario to rule his kingdom. Walking around in Green Mart's cheap, sweatshop threads is not going to cut it."

I worried my lip. "True."

"You're the one who says your mouth is your second impression, your clothes are the first."

"Also true." I heaved a sigh. "You're right. If his crew is going to believe I'm close enough to Sunny that he'd choose me, they have to believe I run in the same circles as a rich, devilish playboy. We'll go to the boutique."

Squealing, Sienna jumped up and down. "Yay. We haven't been in so long. Marcie's going to be crazy happy to see me."

"We'll give her a heart attack. We haven't visited for over a year. Before that, I was in every week. She probably thinks we're dead." The two of us reached the end of the side street, opening onto Fashion Ave. "Be still, my heart."

Window display after window display, up and down both sides of the street, showcasing the latest masterpieces in silk, satin, and polka dots. If I thought the people walking on Dunston Street were runway-ready, I obviously got the sneak preview before the main event.

Two women brushed past—one carrying a textured faux leather shoulder bag.

"Wow," I breathed, heeding its siren call. "Look at the buckles on that."

Sienna towed me back. "Down, girl. The shop is that way."

Brocade sat in the middle of the street, sandwiched between Louis Vuitton and Fendi. Stepping inside was coming home. The shop was an explosion of color—fabrics in every type and hue, sat neat and folded on their shelves. On the shop floor, the tools of my trade—buttons, clasps, buckles, and thread were artfully arranged on the tables.

A woman emerged from the back room. Her black-and-white trench gown's skirt came out before her, trumpeting her entrance like a slender leg in high heels slips out of the limo first. I put her at early forties, and the twisted lips at disapproving.

She raked us up and down. "Can I help you?"

It's impressive the ability some have to say "can I help you?" and make it come out like "what the hell are you doing here?"

I stepped forward. "Yes, I'm sewing a leather jacket. I need five yards of leather, a yard and a half of lining, a separating zipper, pins..." I rattled off the list, noting her expression change.

"Hmm." Her skirts whispered together as she came around the counter. "And just how are you planning to pay for all of that?"

I showed her my teeth. "I was planning to pay with money. Why? Do you take something else?"

To my surprise, she chuckled. "Feisty little thing," she said, "in hideous clothes. The first makes me like you. The second makes me pray no one sees you walking out of my shop and believes you got that cotton-blend night-mare here." She clapped. "But if you've come to me, you're ready to convert. Look no further, Isla is your savior."

She spun away, descending on the wall of fabric. "You'll need more than a jacket, darling. What are the two of you going to do? Share?" She laughed at her own joke. "I'll start you off with six yards of buhp, buhp, buhp—this." A chiffon wave floated to the cutting table. "And two yards of— Don't just stand there. Get some lace. It's in the back."

"There's been a misunderstanding," I rushed out as she picked up the scissors. "I'm only here for the leather. I'm making a gift for a friend."

"Sweetie, anyone who has the talent to create the jacket you're about to undertake and the money to buy their materials here, has no business walk-ing around in that mess."

I tugged on the peasant blouse. "It's just jeans and a top," I muttered. "Did I sound like that when I worked for Caddell House?" I asked Sienna.

"No," she whispered back. "You were nice and kept your judgment in your eyes. Where everyone can see it but you could deny it if they called you out."

I flicked her forehead, making her run off laughing to the lace. "Swim-ming with the rich playboys now," she called over her shoulder.

"What's it going to be?" Isla asked.

Torn, I gazed at the unicorn jacket sketch, recalling our plan to hit my old friend's boutique in North Quay, where the prices didn't make you cry.

"Maybe— Maybe just a couple more yards of the chiffon," I said. "And two yards of that gray satin. It's practically begging to come home with me."

I bought out half the woman's shop. I couldn't help it. I'd glimpse a yard of fabric and all the outfits I could create out of it—dresses, skirts, blazers, purses, hair bows. The next thing I knew, Isla was ringing it up. I comforted myself with the promise that I'd create outfits for Sunny, Liam, Fuller, and everyone who'd been kind to me the last few days while I hissed and spat to get away like a feral cat.

Isla rang me up with a huge smile. It transformed her face. "What's your address, Kenzie? I offer next-day delivery."

"I just moved into a new place." The doorbell chimed. "Give me a sec to check if the doorman accepts delivery."

I went behind a wool display, ringing up Thatcher.

"Is it okay for me to give the Fairfield's address?"

"No," he confirmed. "Delivery man is a favored role for assassins. Packages are sent to 528 Spruce Lane where they are screened and then sent on after they're cleared."

"528 Spruce Lane it is. Thanks." Ending the call, I stuffed the phone in the pocket.

"—Phenomenal Five. My submissions must be perfect, and perfect is what you provide, Isla."

"This is true."

Dread curdled my insides. *No. No, no, no. A brush with death last night wasn't enough, Universe? You had to ruin this day too.*

"What's this? You're that girl," said the unmistakable Lyla. "Her sister... Sierra or something. What do you think you're doing here?"

I shot out, whirling Lyla's attention on me, and ignored her.

"The address is 528 Spruce Lane," I told Isla. Lyla's clique—Madison, Naomi, Skylar, and Brielle—didn't get a glance from me either. "Thanks for everything."

"Makenzie," Lyla said.

"You're welcome, dear. Stop by after you sew that dress we talked about. Walking in and out of here in that number will be fabulous advertising."

"Mackenzie."

"Deal." I took Sunny's card and sidestepped Lyla like she was a store mannequin.

"Mackenzie, stop—! Isla, call the police," Lyla cried. "I know for a fact that woman is a broke, homeless waste. She can't afford to breathe in here. Whatever card she just paid you with is stolen."

"What?!"

"Excuse me?"

"Saggy-ass bitch," Sienna shouted.

Flushing red, Lyla grabbed her ass automatically, and quickly dropped her hands. "It's true," she said, looking down that nose on me. "She's a street rat. Right, ladies?"

Naomi, Skylar, Madison, and Brielle sounded their agreement.

"She told us herself a few days ago," Skylar said. "Look at her clothes. Couldn't you tell? Call the cops, Isla."

Distress stealing her smile, Isla reached for the phone.

"I didn't steal anything!" I cried. "I *was* homeless—past tense. I'm not anymore—present day."

"Oh, really?" Lyla scoffed. "You found a place to live, scrounged up the rent, and had a little left over to shop here? All in less than a week? She stole that card, Isla. Her name is Mackenzie Blaine, in case she gave you another one. She's a thief." Lyla flashed me a grim smile. "This is what she does."

I bounded across the distance, getting in her face. "Listen, Saggy Ass—"

"My ass isn't saggy!"

"—just because I didn't beat your face in the first time your lies ruined me, doesn't mean you don't have it coming," I hissed. Lyla lurched back. "I didn't steal anything. I got a job and my new boss gave me his card. The fabric is to make clothes for myself and his family." I craned my neck around her, speaking to Isla. "I'll give you the number for his head of security. He'll tell you the same thing."

"I would like that number. I'm sorry, Mackenzie." She was. Discomfort brought out the lines on her forehead. "Just to be on the safe side. You understand."

Stiffly, I gave her my phone. Everyone was silent as the dial tone rang, though Lyla's expression said many things as she gazed back at me. She was not pleased to see me here—clean, clothed, and in my element. Her world would be put right if I was dragged out of here in handcuffs.

*But you won't get the satisfaction.*

"Yes, hello. My name is Isla, owner of Brocade. Who am I speaking to? Yes. Hmm mhh," she said. "I have a woman here, paying for purchases with an Anthony Saint Ark's card."

Yes, Anthony Saint Ark. As in Tony St. Ark.

Tony Stark. Another brazen rich playboy.

I laughed when Sunny gave me the card. I should've spent less time giggling and more time with my butt parked in a chair, online shopping. If I'd known Fashion Ave. was a favorite of Lyla and her bitch crew, that's what I would've done.

"Yes, thank you," Isla said. "That's the address she gave me. I apologize for bothering you with this. Of course I will." Ending the call, Isla handed me the phone. The look she gave Lyla fed an underused, vicious side of me. "In the future, Miss Dawson, I would appreciate it if you didn't burst into my shop, screaming about thieves and accusing my customers."

"But, Isla—"

"Apologize."

"What?"

"Apologize to Miss Blaine for the embarrassment you caused her, or you're no longer welcome in my shop."

Lyla's eyes bugged. Brimming with glee, I couldn't keep it off my face as Isla demanded the one thing Lyla owed me above all else, but would die before she gave me.

"I'm not— Isla, the woman was wearing rags and using dirt as blush less than a week ago. She has a history of theft. Excuse me for trying to help you!"

Isla's expression didn't change. "Apologize."

"Yeah," Sienna said, grinning almost as wide as me. "Apologize."

Cycling through all the stages of rage, Lyla finally settled on distaste, and hitched her bag up her shoulder. "Fine. If this is how you treat long-standing customers, then I am no longer welcome in this dump. You can forget about the five of us as clients. And you can forget about seeing your fabrics featured in the Phenomenal Five spread." She whirled on me. "Mackenzie, drop dead."

I waved. "Nose— I mean, *nice* to see you as always, Lyla. Have a blessed day."

"Bitch."

The five stormed out to the sound of my howling. I didn't get an apology, but watching Lyla turn all those shades of red was Christmas.

"Thank you, Isla. You may have lost them as customers, but you've got me for life."

"You keep ringing up orders like these, and I'll weather the sting. Now, get out of here," she said, smiling to soften the bark. "You're not done shopping for the day. You need to replace those clothes immediately. I suggest Maxfield's at the end of the street."

We didn't hit Maxfield's. Instead, we flagged a cab and hitched a ride to an old friend's boutique in North Quay. She wasn't in that day, but her new clerk pointed us to our sizes and let us loose.

Jasmine Threads was a funky little shop sandwiched between a bank and a café. Back when I was regular old middle class and working for a high-end fashion line, the pressure was on to look runway-ready at all times. Everyone's seen *The Devil Wears Prada*. The way they treated Andrea pre-makeover was a kiss and a parade compared to the hell interns with the wrong haircut are treated in Caddell House. For those with money, it was as easy as picking the latest five-thousand-dollar dress from the catalog. For me, it was a trip to Jasmine's.

Designer brands these were not. High end? No. Expensive? Nothing in here cost more than thirty dollars. Featured in magazines? No again.

This shop held the most random collection of outerwear in one place. Jasmine stocked everything from vintage clothes, to gothic-style threads draped in chains, to canvas-printed shoes in all kinds of designs. It was my fondest pleasure to mix and match my finds, and come up with outfits that shouldn't work, but do. This upset the balance at Caddell House at first. My boss liked my offbeat designs—I wouldn't have gotten the internship otherwise. But my fellow coworkers weren't pleased at the black sheep mingling among the white.

Were they supposed to add some eccentricity to their look? Was that what the director was looking for? Was I a test, a challenge, a goal, or an experiment? When I was first to be promoted to junior designer, that answered the question and sealed Lyla's hatred.

They say there's always someone out there who's better than you. Who jumps higher, works harder, and fucks better. The key to happiness is to accept this and be content with who you are and your abilities.

Lyla Dawson stopped listening before *the key*. All she heard was there's always someone better than you, and her conclusion: destroy them.

*She did a damn good job, and apparently isn't done yet.*

"Stewing?" Sienna held up two lace vintage dresses, shaking her hips at the mirror, holding up each one to her chin.

"The one with the blue bow," I said, "and no, I'm not stewing. Not really. I was thinking back to the first day I met Lyla Dawson, up to today and her helpful suggestion that I drop dead. I keep going over it, and no matter how I look at it, I did nothing to deserve that hell beast selling her soul to the devil in exchange for my eternal torment. I can't be the first person who's beaten her."

"That's the definition of stewing, my favorite sister." She kissed my cheek. "But you do have a point. Reasonable and *unreasonable* people could look at the history between you two and agree she went too far. I've never gotten a good sense of her—that wall she puts up is near enough impenetrable—but I don't doubt that whatever it is that turned her against you, it's personal. It's a good thing she's not a part of your life anymore, because it doesn't look like that hatred is dying."

"Ah, one good thing that came out of losing my job, apartment, daughter, and dignity, I never had to deal with Lyla Dawson again... and then random run-ins went and screwed that up too. You're a psychic, Si, find out why the forces of the universe despise me."

Laughing, she spun me around and pointed me at the shoe racks. "Try on pretty things, that always makes you feel better." I went off grumbling, though my mood did improve with a pair of glittery heels strapped to my feet.

Sienna and I stayed in there for hours—shopping, matching styles, and goofing off. We filled up an entire table with our choices, then we narrowed it down to outfits that'd last us a week, three or four pajamas, and max three pairs of shoes. Considering how buck wild I went in Isla's shop, I convinced Sienna this was all we needed. I'd fill in the rest of our wardrobe with Kenzie Creations.

"Oh, just one more thing." I slid the scraps of fabric across the counter, pointedly looking anywhere but at Sienna. Her cheesing grin bore a hole in the side of my head.

"A bikini?" she said. "I thought Sunny said that wasn't required."

"I'm sorry, does he have a side deal with you? Paying you extra to tease me when he's not around."

"No, but I'd clean up." She tickled me squealing into submission. "I'm the expert."

Breathless, I skipped away from her. "I'm not leaving you two alone from here on."

"But I'll leave you two alone." Sienna winked. "He didn't invite me to join him in the hot tub."

That fact hadn't crossed my mind before then. On the cab ride back, the bikini burned a hole in my bags, taunting me the whole way to slip it on, meet Sunny in the hot tub, and...

My imaginings ended there.

The last guy I was with was a certain sociopathic pimp. Wonder of wonders, guys weren't turned on by my homeless status, so the offers dried up after I escaped Luca. It felt like I was relearning all of this—flirting, attraction, teasing, sex—with an expert. How could I hope to keep up? There was rust on my moves.

Back in Sunny's loft, Ms. Fuller confirmed he took a soak break for lunch and then went back up.

"He's waiting for you, Mackenzie." She said that without smirk, smile, or trace of teasing, and still, I reddened down to my toes. "I'll have cold drinks sent up in a bit. Pineapple mojitos sound good?"

"Yummy. Virgin for me."

And then it happened. A slow smile curved her mouth, turning on a glint in her eyes as she looked me up and down. "Really? I'll send up two. Sunny likes those as well."

My jaw about hit the carpet. She strode off, leaving Sienna cracking up at the expression on my face. "I think I love her."

"I think I'm spending the afternoon with a book instead."

"Don't be silly." Sienna steered me to my new bedroom. "Sunny's waiting for you."

She prodded me inside and shut the door. My feet sank in the plush carpet, inviting me in as the whole room did. Everything was an upgrade from the tent, even so, there was something about the space that made it feel like it was meant for me long before Sunny and I met.

That day at Jasmine Threads I bought canvas sneakers printed with world maps. On the wall above the bed, a massive world map hung in the same place as the tiny one I kept above my bed in my old apartment. Mine was marked with the places I hoped a fashion career would take me. This one was marked by the places I guessed Sunny had been.

I wished the similarities between us ended there. Sunny hung up signed band posters and four out of five of them were my all-time favorites. The soft green bedspread was like lying on my favorite-colored cloud. The furniture pieces were a mix of modern and antique, the kind of mismatch I built a career on. If I had bought this place and designed it with the same unlimited budget, I can't say it'd differ much from this.

Not letting myself think too hard, I changed into my cute, green lotus swimsuit and went off in search of Sunny. The apartment Fuller directed me to was empty, but furnished. A bit of a mellow design. Leather couches, black tables, and hanging plants all over the place, the true personality came in the pops of hot pink with the pillows, ottoman, and curtains.

I peeked around them to the balcony, and Sunny.

He rose out of the bubbling water, droplets racing gleefully down his pecs. Powerful hands gripped the edge of the hot tub, curling over the edge as they would around my thighs, gently pulling them apart—

I tossed my head, slamming the door on the sudden, vivid fantasy. Months without sex was starting to get to me. This was *not* happening today, and if it happened at all, it wouldn't be soon. I believe I mentioned how faulty my man-picker was. The next guy who knocked me up or confessed his love had to prove he wasn't a shape-shifting demon first.

Sunny bent over the rim. A grimace twisted his features, crumpling them in pain.

"Sunny? Are you okay?"

He jerked, head snapping up. His expression smoothed out so fast, I thought I imagined it. "I'm fine, Angel. Are you alright?" he returned. "It's gotta hurt being that gorgeous. It definitely hurts me—forced to look but not touch."

I bit my lip to stop a smile. It would only encourage him. "You're correct, you are restricted to looking. But not me. What's bothering you? I'll give you a massage."

I didn't mean it sexually. Sunny seemed to know that since he missed his window for innuendo, hesitating to give me an answer. "It's... my neck actually. I'm not used to sleeping on my back."

"Just your neck?"

"Yes." He gave me his back, sliding into the water.

I stepped in behind him. The water enveloped me like satin sheets, warm and soothing against my achy legs. Sunny draped them over his shoulder and his arms on either side. He settled his head between my thighs, waiting for the massage I stupidly convinced myself wouldn't be sexual.

His muscled shoulders flexed against my calves, shooting visions in my head of us in the same position, but him facing me, and the bikini bottoms floating in the water. Sole Bellisario was sex. One shot of him and I was a virgin pineapple mojito no more.

"How was shopping?"

The question yanked me to reality. Firming my resolve, I began kneading the base of his neck, ignoring the effect the low moan rumbling out of him was doing to me.

"It was good up until a frigid blast from my past blew in to ruin my day."

"Thatcher mentioned he had to talk a shop owner out of calling the cops on you. Would this frigid wind have anything to do with it?"

"Everything." I sighed. "But she doesn't get to ruin the rest of my day by dominating the conversation. All that needs to be said is she's Echidna, the mother of monsters, and she devours her victims alive. Beware."

Sunny chuckled. "Will do. I was thinking I'd set up a bank account for you and Sienna, so you won't have this problem again. Half the seven hundred and fifty thousand up front. The rest deposits while I'm running naked and covered in war paint through the square, carrying the bastard's head on a spike."

I'm ashamed to say I pictured the scene, and it turned me on more than a little. The naked-with-war-paint part, not the severed head.

"Now that we're on the subject," I began, "Sunny, three-quarters of a mill is too much. We don't need that much money."

He squeezed my knee, breaking the *look but don't touch* rule, and I forgot to care. "You're taking a huge risk for me. For Liam. For Tricky and my entire family. I won't send you off with nothing."

"Well, it doesn't have to be nothing. I have the means now to sew decent clothes to wear on interviews. I've got that sketchpad I've taken off your hands to rebuild my portfolio. What I really need is an address to put on those employment forms. So, that'll be my hazard pay. First's, last's, and the security deposit for an apartment in North Quay."

"Hmm." Sunny dropped his head on the rim, hair brushing my bottoms. "No."

"Excuse me?"

"That would be a no, Angel. How much is that? A few grand? You could get that by walking outside right now. Guys'll fling hundreds at your feet at the sight of you in that bathing suit."

"Bit of an exaggeration," I mumbled.

"No one risks their life, and their sister's life, for something they can get themselves. What do you really want, Mackenzie?"

"All I need is a home and a job—"

"I didn't ask what you needed." Upside down, and his silver orbs pierced me through. "I asked what you wanted."

I tore away, eyes stinging. "Something you can't give me." I swung my legs over the side. "There. I hoped that helped with the pain."

Sunny tracked me climbing in across from him, putting as much distance as the tub allowed. Beautiful, eerie, haunting, clouded with mischief—all of those described his eyes, but an open book into his emotions was not on the list. I couldn't guess what he was thinking as the silence weighed heavier on us, and my guilt at snapping at him burrowed deeper.

It wasn't his fault he almost made me open up about Laurel. I had to keep a separation between my reason for living and my reasons for existing, or I couldn't do either.

"You feel that?" Sunny asked.

"What?"

"That pain between your shoulder blades."

I grasped at my back, twisting. "Between my shoulder blades?"

"That's the awkward silence trying to kill us both."

I barked a laugh before I caught myself. "Well, what can you do? It's times like this you realize we don't really know each other and have nothing to talk about."

"Au contraire, candy thighs. Strangers have the most to talk about. Every topic is uncharted territory. Everything is still there for us to learn

about each other. It's old, weathered couples who run out of things to say."
He took hold of my waist, pulling me across the divide.

"Hey, what are you—"

"Shh, relax." His words were warm honey in my ears. "I'm returning the favor."

Sunny homed in on a knot between my blades that I accepted months ago as my new lifelong companion, and dug in. I melted in his hands.

"Oh, wow..."

"Any time you want to trade massages, I will make myself available."

I tipped my head forward, eyes fluttering shut. "I'll keep that in mind."

I meant that to come out sarcastic. It purred out closer to a moan.

"We'll revisit the subject of your payment, but I'm still going to open an account for you and Sienna. I can't keep a low, dead profile if you're using my aliases around town and calling me up to get you out of trouble."

"I can't fault... that logic," I forced out. "Fine, but don't go overboard. All I need is to eat and buy rolls of lace, and Kenzie's a happy girl."

"What else makes Kenzie happy? Come on," he said when I didn't answer. "Or the awkward silence will get us for good next time."

"Okay. I also love lying out in Mercy Park with a blanket, headphones, and sketchpad. I do my best work under a tree near the statue of Junto Trapp. I love sushi burgers, acoustic albums of The Undisturbed, and camping in Elmshire Woods."

"Camping? My brother's going to love you."

"Who? Liam?"

"Nah. The other one."

*There are more Merchant brothers? Why did that thought come with more interest than was appropriate?*

"How many of you are there?" I asked.

"A lot. My dads hopped on top of Mom and didn't stop spitting them out until they hit upon perfection—me."

"What a lovely image." Sunny's fingers splayed across my shoulders, gently guiding them back and bending me over his knee. "Uhhh," I breathed, feeling all the right muscles stretch and pop. "How did you learn to do this?"

"Porn."

I half snorted, half giggled. "You're the worst."

"But what I do to you isn't."

I smiled at him upside down. "True."

Okay, maybe I didn't completely forget how to flirt.

"Miss Blaine." His husky voice spread over me, tightening my skin as he did the same—lips hovering above mine. "Ready to switch?"

*Ready to put my hands on you again under the guise of being helpful?*

"Yes."

We turned around—Sunny hanging over the tub while my palms climbed up his back, kneading that tanned skin into dough. I wasn't going to sleep with him, or conduct any sort of business beneath my bikini anytime soon. However, the fact remained Sunny was single and interested, and Liam was tangled with a hot doctor and wasn't trying to get anything other than a hug off me. If there were growing feelings I could indulge—and I wasn't saying there were—Sunny was the only Merchant brother interested in exploring them with me.

"So..." My breasts pressed against his back as I rubbed his shoulders. "I heard you and Liam say 'dads' more than once now. I'm guessing that added *s* is supposed to be there."

"Yep. My parents are in what they call a polyamorous relationship. By my dad's description, they all wanted Mom, and it was either share her or kill the others to have her."

"Wow. I've never inspired such devotion. Your mom must be quite a woman."

"Well, you've met me, so you know the one who bore me could be nothing less than flawless."

I poked his good side. "It's amazing how many times you manage to compliment yourself in a conversation."

"You'll learn all of my talents during the course of our relationship."

"Do you mind my asking about your family?"

"No reason I should."

"How many dads do you have?"

Sunny twisted and put me on his lap. I lost my ability to speak as he massaged me from the front, traveling up my shoulders and rubbing slow circles on my temple. Inches from him, there was no hiding my red cheeks. I prayed he blamed it on the steam.

"Four. Killian is Liam's dad. St. John is mine. But that never mattered for more than our last names."

"St. John Bellisario," I repeated. "I like it. Does he ever go by Sinjin?"

Sunny looked at me in surprise. "Yeah. Exclusively, actually. How did you know?"

"I didn't know. I stumbled on St. John in a—" *Baby book.* "In a book," I finished. "The character went by Sinjin, and I always thought that was a cool nickname. Is it weird that I don't know anything about your family? River looked at me like I spent history class eating paste when I blank-stared him."

Sunny laughed. "It's not that weird. Believe it or not, we're not looking to be famous. The underworld knows, fears, and hates us, and as long as they do, pretty designers get to live their lives without hearing a whisper from the dark side of Cinco. That's the future Mom wanted for the city."

"Still," I whispered, brushing a droplet from his lips, and not pulling away. "You're just too... sunny... to be kept in the dark. Somehow, some way, our lives would've intersected. If only you weren't so damn impatient and went by way of bridge."

Sunny curled around my waist, drawing me in. "What do you want me to say? You're not the kind of girl to keep waiting."

I stopped breathing. Stopped moving. Stopped thinking. If I did any of those things, I'd ruin the moment, and the lord strike me down as a fool if I did something to stop Sunny's lips coming toward me.

"Should I come back?"

He stilled, mouth meeting mine in the barest touch.

"I wouldn't want to interrupt," said a smug voice.

"You are a cruel woman, Shonda," Sunny replied. She had the smug smile to match as she held out our drinks. "All because I said your seafood curry tasted like stale milk."

"I forgot about that actually." I was off his lap and shooting across the tub before Sunny grabbed his mojito. "That was for tickling me into dropping a banana soufflé fresh out of the oven. Thanks for reminding me my quest for vengeance isn't over."

I sipped my drink, enjoying their bickering. Sunny was her employee, but if I didn't know that, I'd have thought they were siblings. Suddenly it made sense why he refused to believe his staff betrayed him unless he had proof he couldn't deny.

They were family.

"Sienna said you two didn't eat while you were out," she told me. "Want me to bring you up something or keep it warm downstairs?"

"Bring it up," Sunny answered for me. "We'll be soaking for a while."

"You don't have to. I can go down and make myself—"

"Don't be silly. I've got smoked salmon crepes with your name on it."

Sunny held out his arms after she left. "We got rid of her. Hop back on."

"I'm going to stay right here, thank you. You're very good at luring me in with your sweet talk, bubbles, and half-nakedness, but we need to be halfway to old, weathered couple before we take it any further."

He released a deep, mournful sigh. "I was afraid you'd say that."

"Don't look so sad," I teased. "I've always liked this part. The *before* you find out he's into feet and showtunes is always better than the *after*."

Sunny tossed his head back laughing. "You're quick, Blaine. A guy has to be on alert to keep up with you. Quick—don't think about it, just ask me the most scandalous question that pops into your mind."

"I can't," I cried.

"Whoops. Now I know the expression you make when you're embarrassed." A grin tugged the corner of his mouth. "I'll use that later."

"Okay, okay, nicely done. My turn: have you been to all the places marked on the map?"

"Yes, I have, and one day, you've got to go to Chiang Mai even if I'm not the guy flying in the seat next to you."

"I've always wanted to go. What was it like?"

We talked until my fingers and toes were prunes. Until we finished two plates of crepes and three mojitos. Until Liam came looking for us.

I dropped my smile, holding my breath as Liam took me in, bikini-clad and in a hot tub with his brother.

*Why would he care? He's meeting up with Doctor Hendrix tonight.*

"Did you drop Elizabeth off?" Sunny asked.

"Yes. She and Mom were off to the spa by the time I left."

"She'll be back soon, man."

His jaw ticced—the single sign of his stress. I knew how to read these things. Every parent did.

"I told you I'd share the results of my chat with Calvin, Mackenzie," Liam said, "but since you're both here, we can have this short conversation at one time. He's dead."

"Dead?" Sunny and I said at once.

"Nick called him half a dozen times without an answer. He finally went by his apartment and found Calvin hanging from a beam. He's been dead for hours. Nick estimates he died last night."

I stood. Soak over. "You got a look at him last night, right? The guy parking cars was definitely Calvin and not an impostor in his uniform?"

"It was him. A certain explosion impaired my observation, but before then I was clear enough to note there were only familiar faces among my staff."

"That settles it. Calvin was definitely in on this with someone. If the bomber snuck up on a random valet and killed him, he wouldn't have gone through the risk of dragging the body all the way to his apartment and staging him. I bet someone paid or threatened him to put that bomb under your car, and later that night when Calvin opened the door for him, expecting to collect... he killed the only person who could tell us anything."

Liam gave me a long, level look. "I came to the same conclusion shortly after receiving the call. It was a little while after that I decided we won't be needing you, Miss Blaine."

*Miss Blaine.*

"Sole, pay her whatever you deem fair and send her off. We'll take care of this situation on our own." He made for the door.

"Wait a minute—!"

"Liam, hold up!"

Sole vaulted out of the tub, snatching his towel off the lawn chair. He blocked Liam's path to the door and they dropped into a low, if heated argument. I stayed out of it for as long as it took to dry off and wrap my wrinkly body in a towel.

"—family issue. We'll handle it as a family."

"That's what it is?" I broke in. "You don't want my help because I'm not family? Last night you said you planned to force me. Now that I'm offering, you're kicking me out?"

"I'm not kicking you out. You don't live here."

I reeled like he slapped me.

"And last night, I was possessed to do something I shouldn't. I came to my senses then, and I'm coming to my senses now." Liam finally faced me. "Whoever we're dealing with isn't an opportunist, taking a shot at the king while the palace guards are distracted. This is a patient, methodical, ruthless killer, and you agree, Blaine, because you came to the same result.

"Calvin signed on to help him and was killed without a second thought. Calvin's been in the life since he was fifteen, and he couldn't take this guy. What's a hundred-and-fifteen-pound designer from North Quay going to do if she sniffs out this traitor and we don't make it in time? Other than become another innocent death on my conscience?"

Sole stepped between us. "Liam, listen to what you just said. Calvin was in on it. He *watched* you, Sienna, Kenzie, and Tricky climb out of that car, and he still put a bomb in it. He didn't wait until you came back another night alone. He didn't stone up to warn the man he's worked with for three years. He walked away knowing he sentenced Elizabeth to die."

Sole blocked most of Liam, but not his hands. I saw them tighten into clenched, white-knuckled fists.

"A couple of days ago, we would've said we trusted our employees. Before one of them tried to blow you the fuck up. So, who do we trust now? Who do we ask to root out the traitor when, for all we know, they're working for him too?"

"She's not up for this," Liam snapped. "She can't even handle questioning someone who tried to kill her! How can we expect her to go hard at your crew when she doesn't know if they're guilty?"

My face burned. Part of me hoped he hadn't picked up on the true reason for my refusal. Wishful thinking—Liam saw right through me.

"It doesn't have to be Kenzie," Sole said. "But we need to do something. Now. Someone's eaten away at our business for months, biding his time, and we've discovered the reason. The patient, methodical, ruthless killer weakened our organization, now he's cutting off the heads one by one. Who's next, Liam? Genny? Bane? What if they're not as lucky as we were?"

"I don't need convincing that we're in trouble! I just sent my daughter away!"

I knew Liam for a short time, and I didn't have to ask if hearing him shout was a rarity. He's facing a threat he can't see. Doesn't know how to defend against.

*And the last person he thinks is strong enough to face them is the twenty-three-year-old homeless designer from North Quay.*

"Big bro." Sunny clapped his shoulders—the light breeze in the face of a raging storm. "What I'm trying to convince you is you gotta stop playing this like an old-school gangster and get creative. We've got a rat. Possibly a dozen little rats. We can toss dynamite in their hole—take them out and our own house with it. Or we poison the cheese and let them take it right back to the one in charge."

Liam tilted his chin, looking down on both of us. "I'll put the word out—discreetly. Seven hundred and fifty thousand dollars will give us no end of contract workers willing to infiltrate and get the job done. Do you disagree, Miss Blaine?"

I pulled the towel tighter around me. "I won't beg to put my and my sister's life in danger. If you want us to go, we'll go."

I sidestepped the brothers and walked out. They were arguing before the door shut.

Sienna slipped into my—scratch that, Sunny's guest room that night. Burrowing under the covers, she hugged me and rested her chin on my shoulder. "I could hear you stewing and chewing your lip from across the hall. What's going on?"

"You can't put that on intuition," I grumbled. "You sat through the same awkward, tense dinner with Sunny."

"And I wasn't the cause of it, so yeah, I picked up that something was wrong. Tell me."

I buried my face in the pillow. It smelled like sun-ripened apples, jasmine, and Sunny. "The valet is dead. Committed suicide, but Liam believes it was murder."

"Hmm."

I waited. "That's it? Because Liam had a lot more to say after he heard the news. Including that our services are no longer required. He wants us out."

"Mmm."

"Sienna, I need full sentences from you."

"Why? So I can voice the real reason you're upset?"

"Give it a shot," I bit out.

"Okay. Even though between Sunny's attempted murder, the car bombing, and a valet's suspicious suicide, it becomes more real what a dangerous situation we've gotten mixed up in, you can't run away because, for the first time in eight months, you saw the way forward. We help take down a heartless person, and you'll feel no guilt or charity accepting Sunny's reward. You'll have earned that fat sack of cash. Deserved the apartment and new life we bought with it, and held your head high when you demanded custody of Laurel and had the perfect, put-together life to prove she belonged with you."

I pressed my lips together. It didn't stop them trembling.

"Eight months, no one gave a shit about us. If we lived or died, or ate, or slept with both eyes closed. We were on our own until a silver-eyed devil fell out of the sky and said he needed us. A powerful enough spell, but then he looked at you, and saw what everyone else stopped seeing through the dirt and grime. Sunny wants you to stay with him, and you want to stay too."

I sunk deeper into the pillow.

"If we leave now, what are the chances he'll take a break from saving his family every now and then to grab a cup of coffee with you. Whatever was beginning to spark between you two will fizzle out, and then you'll be left with a pile of money that makes you feel dirty—surrounded by a life gifted from a guy that became a what-could-have-been." Sienna rubbed my shoulder. "So, how did I do?"

"Uncanny," I croaked. "Did you keep your mind-reading abilities from me?"

"It tends to freak people out."

I almost smiled. "Sounds small and petty when it's laid out."

"It's none of those things, sis. Why would you say that?"

Pushing myself up, I dropped against the headboard. "Because that was a story of ego, pride, and silly-little-girl crushes. You know what Lyla said to me?"

"Something poisonous and untrue."

"She said I ended up exactly where I was supposed to be—in the gutter. A version of what people told me my whole life. *The apple doesn't fall far from the tree. The only way you'll ever make money is on your back. Your kind doesn't belong here. You're just another pretty little fool who got herself knocked up.*

"Everyone underestimates me, but for some reason, Sunny looks at me... and sees something else. I saved his life, he saved me from Luca. We're even. Taking money from him now would be pity—plain and simple. I don't want to be the woman he feels sorry for. I want to be..."

"His angel?"

I was glad she couldn't see my embarrassed face in the dark.

"It feels right here, doesn't it?" Sienna snuggled into my side. "It's okay, I feel it too. This is where we're supposed to be, Kenzie. I feel it. I see it. Sunny's family comes out on the other side of this, but they won't do it without you."

"What makes me so important to their future?"

"Because the valet was killed. They don't know who they're fighting, and they can't trust the people they thought were on their side. No one who's alone and surrounded by enemies has much of a future."

The truth of that settled in my bones. "Do you think we can help them find this guy?"

"Yes, because he's already made mistakes." Sienna flicked on the lamp and said it to my face. "Here's what you're thinking but refuse to say out loud. All those visions I had of you dying and in danger, I finally know why.

"What if we don't need to search for the killer because you looked in his eyes... and he looked into yours. The man who threw Sunny off the over-pass is likely behind all of this. If he killed the valet for knowing too much about him, how unsafe did the streets of Cinco just become for you, for me, for Laurel?"

Rage burned my gut at the idea my daughter would cross that beast's mind.

"We have our own reasons for finding and stopping this guy, and we've got a much better chance doing it together." She patted my knee. "So you better get Liam Hunt to look at you and see what Sunny sees, because if I have one more dream about my sister dying, I'm going out there and hunting this guy down myself. I'll take down Digger's ass while I'm at it."

The worst part was, she wasn't joking.

# Chapter Five

Sole and Liam fought it out for a full week. I knew because Sunny disappeared every morning after breakfast and came back before lunch pissed. He couldn't leave the Fairfield on account of being dead, so two guesses where he was and who was making him angry.

Despite Sienna's reasons— Or were they my reasons since she plucked them out of my head? Either way, despite the valid reasons for us to stay and help them find this monster, I stayed out of it and holed up in my room with a sewing machine. The brothers would work it out.

"Gorgeous."

"You know, Kenzie's not that hard a name." I snipped off a stray thread. "Two syllables just like gorgeous. Why don't you give it a try?"

"Beautiful," Sunny corrected.

See? This is why I didn't need to intervene. Sunny was as stubborn as they came. He'd wear Liam down.

"Adjourn with me to the bedroom, please."

"What's happening in your bedroom?" I asked his back. He left, expecting me to follow.

I set down Sienna's new half-finished dress and padded across the hall.

"Kenzie?" Shonda stopped me at his door. "What do you think for dinner? Roast lamb or pumpkin gnocchi?"

"Gnocchi sounds delicious. Let me know if I can help." It's wild how comfortable I'd gotten in Sunny's home in such a short time. Shonda, the girls, Sienna, and I had taken up to chilling on the couch and catching a movie while we ate dessert. Most nights Sunny joined us. Other nights, he tempted me into the hot tub to trade massages.

Sunny stretched out on his black leather chaise. A week of rest, and arguing, did wonders for him. He ditched the wheelchair for good two days before.

"What can I do for you?"

"How do you feel about disembowelment?"

I looked around, then toward the door, wondering if I should leave right then. "Excuse me?"

"Probably too bloody for you. I hear ladies favor poisons. I could hook you up with a few of those, but then comes the issue of how you get them to take it," he said, mostly to himself.

"Sunny, you're frustrating, but I don't want to poison you."

"Cute." I squealed as he tugged me onto his lap, flipped over and encased me between him and the chair. "Liam's still on this contract killer thing, but I'm not on board. Hello, they murder strangers for money. Not the kind of soulful, compassionate beings you entrust with your life."

"Am I in the running for alternate?"

Sunny stroked my cheek. "You're the number one choice."

He wore a simple outfit—jeans and a white tee, and damned if he didn't look like a model. Raven locks tousled and cologne sending my pheromones into overdrive. I was grateful men didn't get that little trick from the animal kingdom, sensing when women were in heat. If Sunny could, he'd know my reasons for saying no were all practical. It had nothing to do with lack of attraction.

"But," Sunny went on, "Liam's not okay with pitting you against my guys without a way to defend yourself. I told him Bane would make the introductions and Genny would have your back, although he's right that for this to work, we can't hang over your shoulder. You need to be able to defend yourself."

I pushed on his chest till he let me up. "I know how to defend myself."

"I'm not talking about the Saturday self-defense classes at the local high school gym."

*Nailed that in one, didn't he?*

"I mean..." Sunny pulled out a case from beneath the chaise. My eyes widened as the collection of sharply lethal knives was placed on my lap. "Defend yourself."

"No," I said slowly. "You mean you need to know I've got the means and the *stomach* to kill if things turn bad."

Sunny granted me one of his rare, serious looks. "I'd never send you or Sienna into danger without protection. Believe me, I've thought about this from every angle, including every tool at my disposal to keep you safe, but... Liam and I use the same tools, and the bastard almost got to us."

I swallowed hard. I hated it when Sunny was serious.

"Doesn't have to be a knife or a gun, but you need something to protect you if I don't make it in time."

Threading my fingers through his, I pressed our clasped hands to my chest. "Promise me you will make it in time."

"Kenzie—"

"Promise me."

His expression changed, melting in an intense, fiery fervor I'd never seen in his eyes before.

"I'll be there when you need me, Kenzie. I promise."

I couldn't say why but... I believed him.

"Okay," I whispered, "then, I'll take a knife. Something small and easy to conceal."

"You will?"

"I'm not naive. I carried a switchblade in my pocket since we almost became the victims of two homicidal crack heads. Not to mention my psychotic ex. I do not have a problem defending myself or my sister."

"Then I'll talk to Liam. It's been over a week and my boys haven't heard from me. They'll buy that I'm good and dead. Now's the time for the bitch piddling on my throne to take his chance and hop up. You have to be there to stop it."

I tugged Sunny down. "It's time I talked to Liam. The decision was never between you two anyway, so I'll go tell him it's been made."

"You're so sexy when you take charge, baby." He growled, snapping his teeth at me. I knew what was coming and took off just as he pounced. "I'm not afraid of a dominant woman."

"Sunny!" I shrieked, racing away from his grasping fingers, fighting giggles and tearing out the door.

"Cuff me to the bed and have your way with me."

Sunny chased me into the hall. I narrowly escaped into my room and locked the door, collapsing on the floor laughing. Sienna read a book on my bed.

"Don't say it."

"I didn't say a thing."

"You're mentally screaming it," I deadpanned. "We're just messing around. Having fun. Don't read into it."

"Again, I said nothing," she sang.

"My last two serious relationships ended like a bag of flaming dog shit, and I've still got poo on my heels."

"Ick."

"I promised myself the next time I'd go slow." I gathered my things off my new worktable, putting them in the bag I bought that morning. "My judgment about men doesn't only affect me now."

"If we're talking about another serious relationship, sure. The same rules don't apply for a hookup."

My eyes bugged. "I can't hook up with the man living down the hall. There's no such thing as a clean break when you have to stare at each other every morning at breakfast."

A gusty sigh turned her pages. "Excuses, excuses."

"Goodbye."

Sienna's laugh followed me into the hall. I rode the elevator up to Liam's floor. It was impossible to surprise the man since he had to input the code to let me out. Liam leaned against the doorframe. I tripped over my feet when I saw him.

Barefoot and bare-shouldered, his tight tank and low-slung pants were the complete opposite of the model outfits I caught him in every day of the week.

*This guy wasn't a businessman. He's a handyman here to teach me the proper way to hold his big wrench.* My lower belly tightened. *Heavens to Hera it's been a long time since I had sex. Coming up here after Sunny filled my head with fantasies of him cuffed to the bed was not my best move.*

*LIAM*

"What can I do for you, Miss Blaine?"

"When did we move off Kenzie?" She ducked under my arm without a by-your-leave.

Amused, I followed her firm ass inside, shutting us in. I felt no shame admiring her assets in that tight, sequined blue skirt. She certainly didn't hold back ogling me as she came down the hall—though I'm sure she believed I didn't notice.

Mackenzie Blaine was night and day the raggedy old mop, trying to melt into the carpet the day I first met her. This woman was classy and confident, wearing the hell out of that skirt, blue sweater, and canvas black sneakers covered in lion heads. A purple gift bag dangled off her fingertips. I was off her shapely back and fixed on her face by the time she turned to me.

"I'm going to help Sunny, and you, find this guy. Whatever it takes."

"Direct approach," I mused, erasing the distance. "Came up here to tell me to my face, leaving no room for argument. I appreciate it. Makes it easy for me to say no."

She cocked her head. "You're a mercurial man. One second you're begging me to stay, the next you're telling me to leave. One minute you're shutting me down, the next you're flirting with me."

"Sweetheart." Our chests bumped. "If I ever flirt with you, you'll know it."

Mackenzie smirked. "When a guy's as indecisive as you, I find it's kinder to put him out of his misery and leave him with one simple choice: mine."

"Indecisive?" I admit it, I was a tad offended. "It's not indecision. It's realizing I'm about to send a girl who gets squeamish at the thought of blood off to get her head blown off for the sake of protecting my daughter. Excuse me for remembering I have a conscience."

"Woman."

"What?"

A strand of hair stuck to her red lips, drawing my gaze to it over and over against my control.

"You're about to send a *woman* who gets squeamish at the thought of blood, off to get her head blown off for the sake of protecting your daughter." She beamed. "Good thing I'm volunteering."

I leaned back, humming. "Interesting. There wasn't mention of psychopathy in your background check. Thatcher didn't do a deep enough dive."

Peals of laughter flowed from her smooth, bronze throat. "Oh, Liam, I'm beginning to love our verbal jousts, but that's enough for one day. I'm doing this and it's not just for you, or Tricky, or Sunny. It's so I don't have to spend the rest of my life looking over my shoulder for pale bald men. If this guy is eliminating people who might lead you to him, who do you think is top of his list?"

"I never liked rhetorical questions, any more than I like questions with only one answer."

"Because we both know what has to happen." Her smile softened around the edges. "Let's stop pretending we can do this another way and get on with it. The sooner I trap you a rat, the sooner he leads you back to the person behind all of this. That's when I'll really be safe."

I considered her words. "Sounded like you were asking for permission there."

"I wasn't."

"Because you're making the decisions around here now."

"That's right. Got a problem with it?"

"That's another one—you'll know when I do." I made a decision. "I'll consider letting you have the job if Bane signs off on you. No arguments," I said over her. "You get the Alexander seal of approval, and I'll believe you can handle anything."

"I can handle you," Mackenzie purred. "What could be more difficult?"

My cock twitched. I wonder if she knew the sexual energy that mixed with her fruity perfume and filled unsuspecting noses, reducing them to drooling cavemen in the span of a heartbeat. I would not be another in her long line of victims. I was twelve years older than her, a father, sleeping with a woman my age, and—

*There I go again, listing the reasons I can't be with her. Why does this keep coming up?*

I plucked the bag from her hands. "What's this?"

"A present for Tricky."

"Elizabeth. As hilarious as she finds the nickname, generally I prefer not to encourage the mischievous side of my six-year-old." I stuck my hand through the tissue paper.

"You know, it's customary to let the giftee open their present first."

Naturally, I ignored this. I trusted Mackenzie—a fact that surprised me. But nothing went to Lizzie that wasn't checked by me or Thatcher first, ever since Lizzie climbed in the car with a *present* the nice man waiting outside her preschool gave her to give to me. That was the end of private school and surprise presents.

I tugged out the jacket, letting the bag fall to the floor. "This is... wow."

I swear, I am an articulate man—just not in her presence it seemed. Mackenzie promised to sew Elizabeth the jacket of her dreams. My daughter would take one look at this and hug her for breaking that promise, and making her something better.

The whole thing was crafted in iridescent leather—blues, purples, and white catching the light and sparkling like my kid's favorite mythical animal. On the back, a unicorn with flaming glitter hooves reared. I traced the intricate thread work that brought it to life.

"Incredible, Mackenzie. Elizabeth's going to love it."

"I'm so glad. It'll put a smile on her face, and it got you to call me Mackenzie again. This little jacket has exceeded all my hopes."

I snorted. Carefully, I draped the jacket on the couch. "I'm envious of those who create such beauty. My father's a painter," I confessed. "He tried to teach me, but you either have the talent or you don't. There's no question that you do."

"All these compliments will make a girl blush."

That wasn't a cute quip. She really was blushing.

*Sexy and adorable.* "You're becoming a problem, Mackenzie."

She blinked. "What?"

"So, I'm putting you and those artist's hands to work. Come with me."

"Putting me to work? Goodness, do I need to tell you my safe word?"

I veered off course, beelining for my room and a change of pants. Something that hid my hardening ridge.

Yes, she was definitely going to be a problem.

*MACKENZIE*

Putting me to work turned out to mean helping him paint fairies, unicorns, and mermaids on Tricky's wall. Liam wanted it to be a surprise for her when she got back, and damn him, it was so sweet, I jumped at the opportunity to help him, forgetting I was angry at his treating me like a child who needed protecting.

Liam held me on his shoulders, lifting me up to paint dancing fairies near the ceiling above her bed. They would watch over her while she slept.

"You don't have to worry, Liam." His head was between my legs. He gave me pants to change into before we started. The shirt was a little short and obviously not his. It exposed my midriff, allowing his hair to tickle me as he tipped his chin. "You're not destroying her childhood. Elizabeth wouldn't be happier with a normal dad or a normal life. All she needs is a family that loves her as much as you guys do."

"That you felt compelled to tell me this makes me wonder if you think I'm overcompensating with all the toys and redecorating?"

My brush halted on the fairy's wing. "Or I'm saying to you what I need to hear."

"I will." Liam traced small circles on my ankle, rippling shivers up my leg. "If you want me to."

"No," I said, voice shaking. "It's okay. I shouldn't have opened that door. But I do have a question and I hope you don't mind me asking. When did you know you were ready to date again?"

Liam hadn't stopped drawing designs on my skin. It was highly distracting. "Who says I ever figured that out?"

"You're with Hendrix. This crop top isn't yours and it's obviously not Lizzie's. She's snuggling with you in the hallway. She's taking her clothes off in your apartment. You're dating."

A laugh rumbled out of his chest. "You shot that off like the evidence at my trial."

"Anyway," I forced out. "Sounds like it was a rough split between you and your daughter's mom. How long did it take for you to get out there again? Accept that you could trust someone and let them into her life?"

"You're asking two questions." Liam made his way down, kneading the arch of my foot. It felt so good my eyes fluttered shut. "When Elizabeth was six months old and started doing this miraculous thing called sleeping through the night, I started dating again—casually. As for when I trusted someone else with her, I'll let you know when that happens."

I smiled wryly. "Nine months or six years. I guess it never gets easier."

"Not for us," Liam confessed, "due to the experiences we've been through. Giselle can abandon me a thousand times. It'd never hurt as much as her abandoning Elizabeth. The day I had to explain to my four-year-old why her mom lived so far away and never visited her..."

I ran my fingers through his hair, trying to soothe him.

"That's tied for the worst day of my life," he rasped. "It's hard—make that impossible—to let a woman get that close to us, and risk having to tell my daughter again why another person she loved was out of her life."

"Thank you." I rubbed the back of my hand down his cheek. "I know that was hard to say, but thank you for sharing it with me. I feel less of a paranoid relationship-sabotaging control freak when I talk to you. Even though I'm probably all of those things."

"You're not, Blaine. He'll wait for you, trust me. For as long as it takes for you to be ready, any man in his right mind will wait."

"He?" My heart thumped. "Were you speaking about a man in particular?"

"Nope, but you're thinking of a man in particular, or you wouldn't have asked the question."

I seriously considered dumping my cup of paint on his head. "You and Sunny are definitely related."

"Did you doubt it?" he asked with a laugh.

"Well, I found the little devil's horns sprouting from his waves around the time he told Shonda I could only have breakfast in bed if he was lying next to me, and I was eating it off his chest. I've been looking for yours." I wiggled my fingers on his scalp for proof. "But apparently they retract."

"They do as it happens."

I giggled. "Luckily, there're other ways to identify the Merchant siblings."

"And you haven't met us all yet. Just wait. You won't have to search for the horns anymore."

"Now that sounds like the beginning of a trial."

He chose to chuckle instead of explain. I wasn't sure what to make of that.

THE NEXT MORNING, SIENNA and I walked into an empty kitchen.

"Shonda? Maggie?" I stuck my head in the butler's pantry. "Ms. Fuller? Where is everyone?"

"It's eight o'clock. Shonda usually has the bacon sizzling by now," Sienna said. "Maybe they have the morning off."

I clapped. "It's all good. We can get the bacon sizzling on our own."

"Morning, ladies," Sunny called.

"Morning, what do you want for— Where are your clothes!"

Sunny paraded into the living room wearing white briefs that left nothing to the imagination. Chest puffed like a peacock, he threw his arms out, doing a little shimmy on the rug. "I gave everyone the day off. We're right on the edge of the perfect window. I've been radio silent long enough that my guys figured something happened to me. Time's right for someone to step up and lead while they find out what. That someone is going to be you"—he bowed—"and the lovely Sienna."

Sienna bowed back. They had a rapport growing that was becoming nothing but trouble.

"I know all of those things," I gritted. "What I don't know is why you're half-naked in the living room?"

"Because it's finally time for introductions, and you won't make it onto the block unless I'm with you."

"Introductions to the Sons of Saint? Won't that defeat the purpose of playing dead?"

"Introductions to the Merchants, baby." His wide, beaming smile reflected the opposite of what I felt. "It's time to meet the fam."

"We're meeting your family? Today?"

"Yep, and that is the answer to your question. I need your help picking out a disguise, designer. No one can recognize me. What do you think?" He did a perfect, sinful rotation—flexing every body part and slicking my palms. "Can you do anything with this? Transform me into someone else?"

"Oh, she can do something with that," Sienna mumbled.

I cleared my throat. "A disguise is a good idea, and if you want invisibility, there's no one better."

Forty-five minutes later, breakfast was still in the fridge, Sienna and I weren't dressed, and a broken underwire in my bra poked me all morning, daring me to rip the damn thing off. I did not accomplish any of those tasks, but I achieved the greatest tragedy known to man, and de-sexied Sole Bellisario.

His sleek, polished shoes were replaced with torn-up sneakers missing their laces. I bathed one of his tight white tees in coffee, then dried it in potting soil. Sienna tore up the new jeans I made him. I ratted his hair. Together we smeared dirt on his face and tucked it under an old hoodie that didn't escape our destruction either. Together, we stepped back to admire our handiwork.

"How'd we do?" Sunny asked.

I mentioned before how drastic a change a little dirt and tears could have. I didn't mention, or know, that they had nowhere close to the power to dismiss those teasing, silver glints, or his full, smiling lips.

"Forget the cloak, this is true invisibility," I said. "People will go out of their way to avoid you, avert eye contact, and run across the street. They'll forget you—the blight to their perfect day—just as fast." I glanced at Sienna. "But what they will notice is two nicely dressed women strolling by your sides. We have to change too."

"I burned my old clothes."

"I know. I was standing next to you, tossing mine on the bonfire. Bring me the white knit dress I made you."

"No, not that one," she cried. "I love that dress."

"I'll make you another, I promise."

Sienna went off to grab clothes for us, leaving me to fuss with Sunny's hoodie, making sure it covered his hair. We tried for regular-person-messy and got cutely-tousled-sexy with Sunny. He drew the line at dirt or scissors going near his head.

"Is it worth the risk?" I asked softly. "Why can't Liam take me to meet your family? Stay here where you're safe."

"Liam left early this morning to pick up Tricky. It'll take him twice as long since he's taking the most twisted, convoluted route—just in case. We can't risk leading this guy to our parents. Not that age has made them less deadly," he added.

"We can wait till tomorrow," I tried.

Sunny shook his head. "We've waited long enough. Bane and Genny need to know exactly what we're dealing with. They have to be prepared."

"Don't they know? Liam isn't playing dead. I assume he took some time over the last week and a half to tell your siblings you both were almost killed."

"You didn't think it was weird neither one came to visit me, Liam, or Tricky? They don't know a thing."

"What? How? Why?"

"They're both a communication black hole." Sunny plopped on the couch, despite the earful he'd get from Fuller for dirtying the upholstery. "For suspicious, paranoid, and practical reasons. If you want to talk to them, you do so in person. Liam tried, but Genny's pissed at him for something or other, and ordered her girls to slam the door in his face. My bro's not known to beg, so he gave her a message to tighten security and left it at that, knowing we'd take this shit out before he got another chance.

"But we need Bane, and to get to Bane, we need Genny." He waved a hand over his rumpled self. "So it's time to send the favorite brother in."

"A communication black hole? I can't think of anything worse when someone's trying to take you out one by one. The last thing you guys should be is isolated."

He stood, expression turning grave. "You're absolutely right, Kenzie, and you'll back me up when I tell them the same thing. It's time for them to come home."

# Chapter Six

S*unny*
The ladies and I snuck out of the Fairfield without incident. An easy thing to do when you slip into the back alley by the dumpsters, and come out onto the street where, yes, the rich Leighbridgers clutched their purses, and double-stepped away from us. We tried to flag down four cabs that rolled on through without slowing down.

"You were right, bubblegum lips," I said. "Totally invisible."

"Running out of the standard pet names, so you're getting creative?"

"That's right, muffin. I'm afraid we're going to Harlow the long way."

Neither Kenzie nor Sienna appeared bothered by this. They set off ahead of me, falling into conversation. They also weren't bothered by the barrier that sprung up between them and the people dodging out of the way to keep from getting too close. I couldn't say the same.

Churning, bitter anger welled in my throat. In the short time I'd known Mackenzie Blaine, I'd come to realize one simple, universal truth: she was perfect.

On the day I met her, she risked herself to save my life. Kenzie thought I was too out of it to know, but when Luca busted into the warehouse, she was with me, then she faced them, running out to lead them away from where I lay fevered and helpless. She was in danger, and still she tried to protect me. She owed me nothing, and still she was here, helping my family.

*For years, she walked among you people,* I thought, lips curling at a man who wrinkled his nose at her. He caught my look and suddenly got busy on his phone. *Lived on the same street, became your friends, worked with you, shopped in your stores, and none of you saw that a literal angel was in your presence. This is why Cinco needed the Merchants' guiding hand on its neck. This was a city of fools.*

Kenzie held her own with me like no one I ever wanted to sleep with. She both shut down my flirting and gave it back just as good, with that cute little smirk on her lips that followed me into my dreams. She was tough, fierce, funny, talented, and good. The last quality meant she had no business getting involved with me.

*But it's too late for that now. Mackenzie is mine. She can fight the attraction all she wants, but I'd sooner throw myself off another bridge than let her walk out of my life. A feeling I know she shares, but damned if she didn't learn to play hard to get from the all-stars.*

By my calculations, we should've had sex twelve times by then. Twice in the hot tub. Three times while I was laid up and needing my Nurse Kenzie to make it all better. The wheelchair sex we were meant to have was going to be nothing short of filthy. It wasn't an exaggeration to say no woman had ever turned me down before. Liam indicated this affected my personality, but if by that he meant I was high on life and had very little to complain about, he was right.

*I met her ex-boyfriend and that was definitely over. So what was holding her back from hopping into bed with me? I'll ask.*

"Kenzie, why haven't we had sex?"

She tripped. Sienna had to grab her, saving Kenzie from an up-close-and-personal look at the sidewalk.

"Excuse me?"

"Why haven't we had sex?" I repeated, and louder. That cute, embarrassed expression shone neon red. I was doubly glad I tucked it away to draw out of Kenzie when the mood struck me.

"Are you seriously asking me this in the middle of the street?" she hissed.

I shrugged. "I'm curious."

"If it helps," Sienna spoke up, "it's not because she doesn't want—" Kenzie clapped her hand over her mouth.

"Do not help," Kenzie ordered. "Sunny, if you want to have an adult conversation about our relationship and if it'll one day change, I'm happy to do that later when we're alone."

"Hmm. Nah, I'm cool with a non-adult convo if it means we do this now. Ballpark the end of this will-they, won't-they dance. Are you waiting until you know me better 'cause I can do Hot Tub Twenty Questions all day, every day if it speeds things along?"

"You are unbelievable."

"Close, but the proper adjective is horny." I slung an arm around her shoulder, drinking her in. Under the grime was the faint scent of peach shampoo. It wasn't fair. Everything about Kenzie made you want to eat her up. "I want you. You want me. We're both single adults. Let's make Shonda, Fuller, and the ladies uncomfortable tonight and have screaming, hot sex that echoes through three floors."

Kenzie's mouth opened and closed, eyes huge. It was clear no guy had ever been this direct with her before. If anyone lived the *life is short, live it fully* motto, it was me—even before the grim reaper swooped down, measured me for a coffin, and tagged me to pick up later.

Why drag your feet on the things you want? If it's that fucking good, chances are someone else will snatch it up while you're plucking up the courage.

Sienna snapped her fingers. "Sunny, you should buy her lilies. They're her favorite."

"Filing that away."

"I told you not to help!"

Her sister skipped off, giggling a laugh that sounded sweet and dreamy to the world, but I now knew was laced with mischief.

Kenzie sucked in an audible breath and let it go. "Look, I'm just not ready for a relationship right now—casual or otherwise. That whole thing with Luca... really shook me. I don't know if I can trust my judgment, and that sounds like it's about you, but it's not. If I can't trust myself, I'll never fully trust any guy I'm with. No matter how sweet, patient, and loving he is. We both deserve more," she said, curling around my fingers. "Do you understand?"

"You want to wait until you're ready. Till you feel safe. I completely understand."

She relaxed. "Thank you."

"If I may, I'd like to throw in evidence in my favor for why when that day comes, I'm the sweet, patient, loving guy you should make a go with."

"Okay. What—?"

I looped around her waist, swinging Kenzie around and catching her leg. She cried out as I dipped her right there on the street, losing my fingers in her sweet-smelling waves. She parted her lips to berate me, and I swallowed the shout—sealing her lips to mine.

The first time I kissed her was a spontaneous indulgence. She was there, I was there, and I wanted to kiss her, so I did.

The second time was a message—pouring everything I felt about her into a single moment in time, before she slapped me. All that I thought she was—beautiful, witty, sexy. All that I wanted us to be—together, trusting, sharing matching rug burns from the carpet sex. I sent it all to my angel as I gained entrance, tangling her tongue with mine.

Kenzie's soft moan did cruel things to my erection. She cupped my cheek, gently pulling me closer as she deepened the kiss. Felt like ages, but was more likely minutes, that I put her back on her feet.

Kenzie blinked up at me, chest heaving. I kissed her nose. "You can take all the time you need, but fair warning, my kisses are poison." She touched her mouth. "That's your second dose. Both combined will eat through your logic, erode your roadblocks, and make it so all you can think about night and day is Sunny, Sunny..." I nipped her bottom lip. "Sunny," I whispered.

"The only cure is becoming mine in every way."

"I..."

I straightened. "But like I said, take your time. No pressure. Won't be long now."

Sidestepping her, I jogged up to Sienna, throwing my arm around her. "The lilies tip is gold. Got any more for me?"

"She loves pralines. Oooh, and the movie nights. Screen *When Harry Met Sally*, *Notting Hill*, *The Notebook*. Just the two of you with a bowl of caramel popcorn. Also..."

Turned out I was keeping Sienna Blaine too. She was a wealth of information, giving me the Kenzie Cheat Book while said sister trailed behind, burning holes in our back. She managed to keep this up for seventeen blocks and two bus rides, which was truly impressive. Every now and then, I'd peeked behind and see her touching her swollen lips.

*Poison, baby.*

She kept up the silent treatment till we stepped off the bus on Archer Avenue.

"Wow."

I just nodded. One look at Archer and they both understood why I risked exposure to escort them to this place.

A group of men loitered at the mouth of a trash-filled alley, passing around a crack pipe in full view of the street. By another alley, a dealer slung his product in between arguing with some guy. The argument looked like it was going south fast. Ladies of the night proved how inaccurate the term was, strolling around in broad daylight, sticking their heads in searching cars to speak to potential johns. Up and down both sides of the street were bar, bar, dive, bar, motel, bar, and bar.

"Stay close," I said. "Don't look at anyone for too long or too hard. But don't avoid eye contact. You act weird and shifty around here and they'll think you're a cop."

The sisters held hands, falling in step with me. Once again it struck me how close these two were. I'd die for my siblings and they'd die for me, but you wouldn't catch Genny and me holding hands and skipping down the street.

"Your sister is here?" Kenzie asked. "Why?"

"Harlow is her turf, like I said."

"Still. Why?"

I jerked a chin at my crack-smoking brothers and got a round of nods in return, along with a "Sup, man."

"How much do you know about Harlow?"

"Before you asked that question, I would've said as much as there was to know about a borough I've lived next to and visited all my life. Tell me what I missed."

"Harlow used to be run by a gang called the Kings."

"That much I knew."

"Did you know they controlled everyone and every business in this borough? Even the cops were on their payroll. Cops that were all fired or arrested after my parents destroyed the Kings. They were replaced by a new force, but after decades of sirens that never came calling after a King hit, or watching officers accept a wad of cash, get back in their cars, and drive away after you called to report the screaming in apartment 3B for the fifth time—the distrust was ingrained.

"Harlownites were free of the Kings. They wanted the police gone too. Neighbors banded together and threw Molotov cocktails at passing police cars. They called bomb threats into the station nearly every day, and more than once tried to attack the officers when they fled outside." I met their shocked expressions. "It was the Wild West out here, my friends. Everyone talks about the Night of Tears, but the National Guard had to come in three times after that to help regain control. Two of those times were for Harlow."

"I was right," Mackenzie muttered. "Saying I knew everything about Harlow would've made a fool out of me."

"Obviously, there are still kitschy restaurants, kiddie parks, art museums, and everything Harlow was known for, but if you know where to go, you'll stumble on streets like this, where the cops and the residents maintain their unspoken agreement to stay away from each other. Red-light streets."

"We did know about the red-light streets," Sienna confessed as we pushed through a group of bikers, parked on the sidewalk and eyeing us like we were in the way. "This is the first we've seen one. I have to ask too, why would your sister be here?"

"According to Genny, if there's trouble, she belongs in the middle of it." I gestured to a bar toward the street's end. "It's that one. Barbarella's."

"Looks like a motorcycle bar," Kenzie noted.

"My sister runs a motorcycle gang."

Kenzie stopped. "Are you for real? What else do I need to know about Genny?"

I whistled. "So much. Unfortunately, my sister likes to do her own introductions."

"Why is that unfortunate?"

*You'll find out.*

*MACKENZIE*

Sunny lowered his head as we approached the bar, hiding in the depths of his hoodie. "Stay close, Sienna. Sugar tush."

I was tempted to ask why Sienna got to be called by her name and I didn't. I swallowed the retort.

Barbarella's was a decent-sized bar housed in brick. The area in front of it was closed off by a gate, but instead of tables for beer-drinkers to sit and chat, the entire area was filled with motorcycles of all types and designs. More than half were occupied by tough-looking leather-clad women, sizing me up to see if I fit.

Sunny warned not to get shifty-eyed and make it obvious I wasn't comfortable here. Advice I didn't think I'd have so much trouble with. It wasn't that I'd never been to a bar or even that I wasn't familiar with biker gangs. You meet a lot of interesting people when you live on the streets.

It was that every. Single. Eye found us when we stepped inside.

Conversations halted. The bartender stopped mid-pour. A game of pool came to a cue-clattering end.

"They're all women," Sienna remarked loud enough for them to hear and blasé enough to show she didn't mind. "Hi, ladies."

Sunny didn't say anything about her greeting. It wasn't like we were keeping a low profile.

The bartender slammed the bottle down. "Something we can do for you?"

*Translation: Get the hell out of here, bums. You're lost.*

Sunny hunched his shoulders. "We, uh... We don't want no trouble." Sunny adopted a slow, halting speech, swaying on his feet like he was high. "We want the boss." Sunny bumped a wall as though he didn't see it there. "Get the boss."

A voice rang over the falling silence. "Oh, you want the boss, do you?" Blonde hair, ripped top, and high-cut shorts pushed through the pack. Sunny was a tall guy and she met him inch for inch. She confirmed it by getting in his face, bobbing her head comically along with Sunny's attempt to stop her from looking under his hood.

"Come on, man," he drew out, sounding pained. "We don't want no trouble."

"Aw, you don't want twrouble? Then, you walked into the wrong bar." She shoved him into the wall, sending up laughs and jeers.

"Hey, back the fuck off!" I jumped between them and was swiftly sent to the side by Sunny. Our new friend must've noticed the oddly fast and strong reflexes of the supposed junkie bum, because the next thing I knew, there was a gun in her hand.

"Out! The three of you," she shouted. "Or I see how the walls look in red."

The situation changed so fast. In the half a second it took to shove Sienna behind me, half the bar had their weapons trained on us.

"Picked the wrong one today."

"Fuck the guy and leave the little one for me."

"Shoot him, Bugsy!"

*What kind of twisted hellhole did Sunny bring us to? Shouting to kill the guy though he didn't lay a hand on her or anyone else?*

I backed Sienna toward the door, calculating both how to shove her outside and grab the gun digging into Sunny's scalp before they opened fire.

*I don't give a shit who his sister is or how she's supposed to help us. I want nothing to do with the leader of this zoo.*

"Everybody relax," Sunny drawled. He was not showing the proper amount of fear for a guy with a gun to his head and twenty more waiting to finish the job. "Your boss and I... are cool. She sent me. Told me to tell you... Shit, what was it again?" Sunny shuffled headfirst into the wall again and was shouted at not to move. "She said... Think she said..."

Bugsy cocked the hammer.

*Dammit, Sunny!* I readied to shove Sienna out. *Do something!*

"Penguins are always dressed for sweater weather."

"You have five seconds to walk out that—"

"Penguins are always dressed for sweater weather," Sunny said clearly. "Your boss said to come here and say that if shit... ever went down and I needed a favor. Call her up and tell her what I said." Force crept into his tone. "I'm guessing she won't be happy if she finds out you sent me away."

Bugsy, so-named I assumed for the ladybug tattoos climbing up her left arm, didn't show an outward reaction, but neither did she count down. I held my breath, heart pounding, waiting for her to speak.

"Penguins are always dressed for sweater weather," Bugsy repeated. "You expect me to believe FGH told you to pour that garbage in our ears? Sounds like the ramblings of a cokehead to me."

Sunny did that slow shrug of his. "If I'm lying, your boss will say the same, won't she?"

Eyes narrowing, Bugsy lowered the gun. "Damn right she will, then she'll give me the order to kill you herself. Ladies, show our friends to a table in the back. Keep an eye on them while I make a phone call."

This wasn't a request. Two women burst in from outside, grabbing me and Sienna, and frog-marching us over the cheap hardwood. I looked back, wincing at Bugsy sweeping his legs and dropping Sunny on his ass. Four biker chicks hauled him up with his arms held out to his sides, patting him down.

I had the idea from the first look at Archer Avenue that the weak didn't set up shop here. All the same, Genny's crew, the Cardinals, didn't mess around. It wasn't hard to learn their name. Half the signs hanging over the bar had the red bird, along with its name splashed on half a dozen ripped shirts. We were almost to the booth when Bugsy Number Two stepped in front of us.

"Hold up." Blonde waves piled on top of her head. A few wispy strands escaped the bun, framing a snarl twice as mean as our welcoming party. "Whoever heard of the boss giving out passphrases like this is some secret girl-party treehouse. If they want to see the boss so badly, let's see them get through me. Toss pretty boy up here."

"What?" I cried. "No, leave him alone."

They dragged me and Sienna shouting and carrying on out of the way. Sunny was thrown at her, running right into her fist. I screamed at her as he went down.

"Get him, Eve!" the ladies hollered.

Eve jumped on him. She aimed a punch at his nose. Sunny dropped the wasted-junkie act quick, blocking her hit and flipping Eve off. They circled each other, Eve looking mighty cocky despite his sudden personality shift. She turned her back, then flashed around, flinging a beer bottle at his head.

Sunny ducked. "Watch out!" I shrieked.

Too late, Eve tackled him. She got him flat on his stomach, knee digging into his back.

"Stop it." I was near tears. "We haven't done anything wrong."

Sunny swung back and smashed her across the temple, snapping her head around. Eve flew off, crashing into a table leg. No one heard my pleas then.

"Bastard!"

"Kill him!"

"Break his neck!"

Sunny shoved up on his feet. He jumped over the first attempt to sweep his legs, dancing out of the way. "Come on, Eve." He ducked another bottle—this one courtesy of Bugsy. That bitch was about to have me coming for her. "Don't let down your fans."

Straightening, Eve rolled her neck. "Worry about yourself. You'll never get through me to the boss with that bitch-ass slap." She held out her hands. "I'm generous. I'll let you have one for free."

Sunny rushed her. She twisted, snatched his arm, and yanked it up his back.

"Arggh!" Sunny's shout ripped my soul to shreds.

"Kill him! Kill him!"

"Nah, bring him and his girlfriends in the back," Eve said. "Let FGH have her fun with them."

Wrenching Sunny by the shoulder, agony twisted his dirt-covered features. She shoved him toward a swinging door and I didn't fight it as we were hauled after them. The three of us were tossed inside an office... with Eve.

I rolled into a massive oak desk, tangling with Sienna. Sunny pushed himself up from where he was thrown against the side bar, not seeing her advance from behind.

"Stay away from him!" I launched at her.

"Whoa." Sunny grabbed me around the middle, lifting me off my feet, and glancing my punch off her chin. "Easy, Angel. I'd like you to meet my sister."

The beautiful blonde menace loosed her hair, letting the silken waterfall trail down her shoulders. Beautiful wasn't me being kind. It was simply the adjective nature demanded, along with gorgeous, stunning, everyone's bad-girl fantasy. A little button nose, blue eyes, and pink cupid lips. Despite this, nothing about her gave off a damsel vibe. She ripped her pink tank at the midriff, leaving just enough room for it to cover her boobs and display the word Cardinals. Ditto the severed shorts' only function was to cover most of her butt cheeks. A simple but expensive look. I clocked the whole outfit as Caddell.

Genny flashed me a smile just as wicked as the younger brother I was going to kill.

"This is Genevieve Hunt. Also known as Genny, Eve, or FGH."

Genny cracked her jaw. "Nice to meet you."

"Fuck you!"

Her grin only widened. "Feisty one, isn't she? Where did you pick this one up?"

"She picked me up actually, and yes, she's feisty like you wouldn't believe." Sunny set me back down, likely assuming I wouldn't attack him or his sister. Faulty assumption on his part.

"This was a trick?" I hissed. "You let me think your life was in danger for what?! Was this some kind of test?!"

Sunny lost his smile quick. "What? No. Kenzie, of course not."

"That show wasn't for you, babe." She crossed the room, swaying with an effortless, hip-jutting swagger that I could try for years to replicate and never get close to matching the confidence. "That was for my girls. Outsiders don't come into my bar. People don't walk in demanding business with me. Ever. Period. They for damn sure don't do it and then walk out looking as pretty as when they came in. Sunny knew whoever came in here, giving the code that we're in trouble, would have to get roughed up to keep my girls thinking everything's normal."

*That's why he risked himself coming with us. To spare me and Sienna being put through the show.*

"Oh," I whispered. "Thank you, Sunny."

"I said I'd have your back. I meant it."

"But are you okay?" I reached for him. "Looked like she hurt your shoulder."

Sunny sidestepped me, shifting out of reach. "I'm fine."

"Course he's fine," Genny scoffed. "I went easy on him and still kicked his ass. What you been doing in that penthouse, baby brother? Besides growing soft."

"Oh, let's see. I've been growing a nice garden of these." He flipped her the middle finger. "And also"—he made a show checking his pockets—"these too," he said, giving her two for two fuck-yous. "Just for you, sis."

Genny barked a laugh. "Nice. So, what's going on? What trouble did you get yourself into now?"

"Me? Trouble? No." Sunny slung his arms around me and Sienna. "I've been living a life of abundance, sister mine. That there's always light in the darkness is the creed woven into my soul. On what should have been my last day on earth, fate brought me an angel, and a new best friend."

Sienna waved, more than pleased with her distinction.

"Last day on earth?"

"I was thrown off an overpass."

Genny didn't have the reaction to this that I expected. Actually, she didn't react at all.

"Ouch," she said simply. "Anybody want a beer?"

"Hell yes," Sunny said.

"I'll take one," Sienna chimed in.

Genny fetched three bottles out of her mini-fridge and popped the caps off with her teeth. Mildly unsanitary, but impressive. She passed them out and offered one to me.

"No, thanks. I don't drink."

Screwing up her face, she said, "Don't drink? Sunny, are you sure about this one?"

I popped up to defend myself.

"Absolutely sure," Sunny replied. "Mackenzie's the most amazing woman I've ever met. I'd pick her if she added pacifism, celibacy, and a vow of poverty to her abstinence list."

Warmth spread through my body. I told Sunny we needed to slow down until I found my good judgment, but there was one contrast I'd make between him and my exes—they never spoke that well of me in private, let alone in public. If Genny had thrown that jab to one of them, they'd laugh in my face, saying they weren't sure about me either and should throw me back—or something along those asshole lines.

I flashed back to our kiss that day and had to stop myself touching my mouth again.

*"My kisses are poison."*

That might've been the truest thing Sunny ever said to me.

"Alright." Despite her desk chair, couch, and pink beanbag in the corner, Genny stretched out on her desk, propped on her elbow like a pinup model. "Someone threw you off a bridge, what's that got to do with me?"

Sienna and I shared a look. I didn't know about visions from the other dimension, but when you were as close as us two, you learned to read each other's minds.

*What a sweet, loving family,* I thought.

*I envisioned this going differently,* she returned.

"This all has to do with what we talked about months ago. Someone's coming after us, Genny. Ambushing my routes, raiding my warehouses. The natural next move was to try and take me out. It's only luck and Kenzie that I'm standing before you."

"Dressed like a hood rat," she rebounded. "The Sons of Saint have fallen on hard times. Sorry to see it, but I'm still not hearing how this is my problem. You're a big boy, Sunny. Swore up, down, and sideways that you were ready to run North Quay. On your own. Without help. You got someone in your borough that you can't control, you find them and put them down. End of."

"Thanks for stopping by for your quarterly dose of sisterly advice and an ass-kicking. If that's all, my ladies will soon be wondering why they're not hearing screams. Go out through the back."

"I'm not going anywhere." Sunny reclined against the mini-fridge, proving his point. "This isn't just my problem and you know it. Need I remind you of the meth lab explosion? What about the bank heist?"

The corners of her eyes tightened.

"What explosion?" I asked. "What bank heist?"

"Six months ago, one of Genny's warehouses went up in flames. Police concluded meth heads were conducting business in there, which would mean Genny's girls who were working that operation were dirty." He swung to his sister. "But you never believed it, did you?"

She didn't answer for a long while.

"No," Genny finally said. "Frenchie had been in my crew since she was sixteen. More than that, she watched her mom, brother, and uncle waste away on drugs. She wouldn't get involved in that shit for millions. But the police got there first. I showed up as they were hauling away crates of the stuff, and I couldn't prove it was a lie."

"But you know," Sunny said. "That explosion wasn't what it seemed, and Frenchie, Missy, and Cub died for it. If there's even a chance we're going after the same guy, you want in on this, Gen. You want to take him down with your bare hands."

"It's not the same guy coming after you," she snapped. "I... know who killed Frenchie and the others."

"What?" Sunny rose up. "Who?"

"Vito." She spat the name. "Grandson of a former King. He wants Harlow and the fool believes he has a right to it. In the beginning, he was a loudmouth idiot begging for a broken nose, but over the years, he's gathered a crew—all of them misogynist pigs chafing at taking orders from a woman. Your people weren't killed during those raids or ambushes, but mine were. That should tell you right there we're not dealing with the same guy.

"My enemy is Vito. If I lose focus to handle problems in your borough, Vito will take advantage and more of my people will die. Not happening, Sunny. Take your angel and your bestie and get yourself thrown out. See you at Christmas."

The siblings locked in an iron stare. I ping-ponged between them, wondering how Sunny's relentlessness fared against Genny's disinterest.

"You know I can't walk away, sis. Bane up and moved again without sending a forwarding. I know you know where he is. Take us to him."

"Hmm." She tapped her chin. "Sorry, can't. Super busy today, tomorrow, and the next time you ask."

"You're going to help me."

"Am I?" She laughed. "And why is that? How exactly do you think you're going to make me?"

Sunny straightened to his full height—imposing even in rags. "If you don't... I'll tell Mom."

Genny howled, nearly falling flat on her desk. "That's the best you got? Do what I say or I'll tell Mommy on you?"

Sunny fished out his phone.

"I'm a grown woman. That doesn't work on me anymore."

*Beep, beep, beep* chimed as he dialed.

"You're embarrassing yourself." She looked at me and rolled her eyes. She didn't have to be my sister for me to read *can you believe this guy?* loud and clear.

No, I could not. I didn't for the life of me know where Sunny was going with this, but I was embarrassed for him.

"Put the phone away."

The call picked up. "Hey, Mom," he answered.

"Seriously, Sunny." Genny stretched out on her desk, breezily sipping her beer. "Hang up."

"Not well, actually," Sunny said. "Someone tried to kill me and Genny won't help."

"That's a lie!" Genny sprung off the desk. Sunny took off running, and she tackled him, pitching them both on the couch.

"She said it's my problem and she couldn't give a shit!"

"He's a liar! Give me the phone!"

I watched the display in disbelief.

"What's that face?" Sienna asked. "That was us a little while ago, and us again in a few weeks when I snatch the television remote and try to run away with it. Some things don't change, no matter how old you get."

Genny got the phone off him. "Mom, it's not like that," she rushed to say. "But— But, Mom! When is Sunny going to take care of himself? Will I be bailing him out when he's fifty?" The two managed to scrap though Genny was one-handed. He tried to tip her off and Genny sat on his head. "No. I'm not giving you attitude!"

Sienna stifled a laugh. I did a better job of holding it in. I had to give Sunny credit. He wasn't above doing whatever it took to get what he wanted.

"Ugh," Genny groaned, slumping over the couch. You knew defeat when you saw it. "Fine. I said I will, gawwwddd. I love you too," she muttered almost too low for me to hear. Genny hung up, and flung the phone at the wall. "Let's see you call your mommy now!" She wrapped her hands around Sunny's throat, throttling him as he guffawed.

*Goodness, this Hunt has a temper.*

"Did... what I had to do," he wheezed. "No regrets."

"Like I have time to tramp through the woods, tracking Bane down. And that's if he hasn't moved again."

Sunny pried her off. "Just get us to him and your part can be over after this. You can protect yourself and your crew, while I take this shit down. It has to be now, Gen. Whoever is coming for me almost got me, Liam, and Elizabeth."

Genny froze. "Wait, what? Almost got Liam and Tricky? What are you talking about?"

"He put a bomb in their car."

"He what?!" The shout brought biker chicks to the door. They banged on it, demanding to know what was going on. "The fucker came after my niece?" Genny shoved off him. We quickly got out of her way, moving aside for her to blow past and snatch keys out of her drawer. "Why didn't you start with that? Move your asses, we're losing daylight."

Genny plowed through the door, barking orders. "Bugsy, you're in charge while I'm gone. Turns out the junkie bum has a problem I do need to take care of. Missy, you're doing collections tonight. Lola..."

I'm not sure what amazed me more, Genny's command over the room or their respect for her. Genevieve Hunt wasn't the tallest, the biggest, or the heaviest tattooed of the bunch—still, the hooting, bloodthirsty ladies became silent, head-bobbing, order-takers in her presence.

Outside, Genny tossed Sole a pair of keys. "Take that blue one in the front." She pointed out the bike while she swung a leg over hers. "Bestie, ride with Sunny. Feisty, you're with me."

"Why?" I asked.

She grinned. "'Cause you seem real protective of the little one. Figured you wouldn't want her on the back of my bike with the way I drive."

"You figure correctly, but now there's the issue of me not wanting to get on the back of your bike either."

"Tough shit." She tossed me a helmet. "Hang on, don't scream, don't break my ribs."

I found all three of those things impossible to do. Genny drove like a maniac with a death wish. She whipped in and out of traffic, two times into *oncoming* traffic because everyone was driving too slow. I clung on for dear life, screaming into her neck while the wind carried her cackling back to me. See? Maniac.

My ride into hell carried us out of Harlow and onto a lone paved road. We were heading into Elmshire Woods. I don't know how long it was till Genny slowed down and parked beside the 101-mile marker. I slipped out of screaming terror and into petrified silence at some point, face buried in her back and praying for it to be over.

"Time to let go." She poked my arms. "I'm not a cuddler, Feisty. I don't make exceptions for my fuck buddies, or for you."

"Tell me," I rasped.

"What?"

"Tell me the sins I committed. Tell me why the devil sent you to torture me." I was shaking untangling myself from her, and fishing my heart from where it shot into my stomach. "I swear I'll find the nearest church and repent."

Genny cracked up. "You're hilarious. I'm starting to see why my brother hasn't shaken you loose yet." She leveled a look on me. "He does this, you know. Pick up strays. If you've been to his place, you've met some of his collection. He's got one he rescued from an abusive ex. One that was left holding the bag—literally—when a friend robbed a dangerous man and then asked if she could *keep something at her place for a few days*. And of course, the one who devoted so much of her life taking care of my family, she never got around to making one of her own." Genny laid a hand on her heart. "Love and appreciate Fuller, though I do. And don't get me started on the guys in his crew. Misfit toys the lot of them."

I climbed off, fixing my hair and straightening my clothes as the sound of an approaching motorcycle reached my ear. "Why are you telling me this?"

"Because I don't know who the hell you are, what you're doing here, or how exactly you got involved—from the CliffsNotes, you saved my brother's life, right?"

I nodded.

"So, here's my way of saying thank you, by giving you advice girl to girl." She propped her arm on the handles, looking so much like a model prepping for her shoot, I fussed with my rat's nest head some more. "Sunny's great— He's amazing when you need him. Stops at nothing to put the world back on tilt for you. But when that happens and he can't play the hero anymore, his interest wanes fast. I've met a lot of new best friends and women basking in his moon eyes."

My chest tightened.

"But the only ones who stick around are those who haven't figured out how to live without him, because once they do, he damn sure can live without them."

Closing the distance, I locked on to her icy lake-blue eyes. "That's one way of looking at it."

"And the other would be...?"

"He can't stand to see people in pain if he can help— No, if it's his job to help. A friend asks him to help a woman pressured into prostitution by her boyfriend, he won't stand by doing nothing. But after she's free of a roach like Luca. After all the people he's helped have found their way, Sunny lets them go without guilt or obligation—expecting them to hang around because he wants them there, instead of letting them start over with their lives."

I leaned on her handles, likely not looking half as sexy as Genevieve. "You strike me as the kind of woman who fought, clawed, and crushed to get where you are. You took no shit and gave it back twice as hard. I can understand why you wouldn't have much respect for people, much less women, who don't do the same. But don't take it out on Sunny. Helping people when they need it should never be seen as a character flaw, especially by a woman who gave a family to a young girl who lost her mother, brother, and uncle to drugs."

Something flashed in her eyes at the mention of Frenchie. I thought I went too far until she said, "Yeah. I can see why he keeps you around."

Sunny parked behind us. He and Sienna hopped off laughing. "That was incredible," my sister said. "Do you have a bike? Will you teach me to ride?"

"Yes and yes." She hugged him, then Sunny landed on us over her head. "Everything cool?"

"Everything's fine," Genny breezed. "Your girl here was just putting me in my place."

"No easy task. Did she kick and scream going in?" he asked me.

Genny flipped him off. "Thanks for growing this for me, but you can have one back." She hopped off, hooking me around the waist and dragging me along. "Let's go. He's about ten miles in."

"Ten?" Sienna and I cried.

"That's right. It gives you three plenty of time to tell me exactly what's going on."

Sunny obliged. We made our trek through the woods, explaining everything that happened over the last couple of weeks. She interrupted a lot—asking us to clarify this or explain how we knew that. At first introduction, I thought Genny didn't care about our problems. I was wrong. The woman raging and cursing while she kept a bewilderingly tight hold on me, cared very much.

"The snake-faced shitcocker. I can't imagine what Liam went through. When I get my hands on that bomber, I'm going to slice him open from shoulder to waist, keeping him alive long enough to watch me rip out his insides. Bastard!"

*Yep, quite a temper.*

"I had a thought while you two were talking earlier," I spoke up. I, and Genny, climbed over a fallen branch. "Is it possible the person coming after the Merchants is who's coming after you, Genny? This Vito guy."

Her brows snapped together, but she didn't confirm. "Keep going, Feisty. Explain your thought."

"Well," I continued. "If he wants to reclaim the glory of his grandpa's old gang, he'll know it wasn't a twentysomething lady with a biker gang that took it away in the first place. If he wants to take Harlow, and keep it, wouldn't it make sense to destabilize your organization, then when the time is right, get rid of all the Merchants?"

Genevieve and Sunny shared a look. "It's possible," Genny said slowly, "but it's not likely. Vito has friends but none with the money or resources to mount the kind of operation you're talking about. Plus, Liam, Bane, and I have dealt with a few possible sabotage attempts over the last several months, but the attacks on Sunny have been relentless."

Sunny inclined his head. "My crew's been the focus. This is all going down in North Quay, North Quay is where it starts."

"North Quay is not where this started," Sienna said, so forcefully we stopped and turned on her. "I can't get a clear picture, but this is bigger, Sunny. So much bigger than you can see."

"What do *you* see?" he asked.

"I see..." Sienna tilted her head to the sky, vision growing unfocused. "A man with... blue hair."

Genny and Sunny moved at the same time, converging on Sienna. "Dad?"

"There are other men too. Blonde, black, brunette." Sienna tossed her head. "So handsome, so beautiful. They shine brighter than the sun... and it does nothing to pierce the darkness surrounding them. They're all there, with a gorgeous woman, loved by them all, but... it's the blue-haired man. He hates him. Oh, he *hates him*!" I jumped at the shout. No matter how many times I experienced my sister's visions, they unsettled the mess out of me. "He would give his life to see everything he loves destroyed. Everything he touched." She dropped her chin, her gaze sticking Sunny through. "Everything he created."

Genny flicked between them, confusion written on her face. In our description of events, we hadn't gotten to my sister's psychic abilities. "Are you trying to say this all started when our mom and dads ran the city? When Sinjin ran the city?" she said. "You think he made an enemy that hates him so much, decades later when he finally set out to get his revenge, he went hardest at Sunny because—"

"I'm the only other Bellisario," Sole finished. "Huh." Sunny did not look put out by this. On the contrary, he bobbed his head, mouth-shrugging, and replied, "Well, that would explain a lot."

With that, it was Sunny and Genevieve tromping in front of us while Sienna and I trailed behind. Pieces of their conversation floated back to us—making me dig my nails deeper in my palms.

"...she's psychic..."

"My ass," Genny snapped. Sunny made an effort to lower his voice. Genny did not. "I now believe in psychics even less than I did an hour ago. Everyone knows about our parents, and everyone knows about Daddy Sin. There's a photo of him grinning with a knife between his teeth next to the word psycho in the dictionary. That this is about some old grudge is almost as obvious. In the end, all things lead back to our family taking over Cinco. And with the number of people our folks have killed, good fucking guess someone somewhere might be mad about it."

"Explain... Give us a place to start..."

"The same place we would've started anyway."

I nudged Sienna's shoulder. "Sorry about this. You're just trying to help."

"It's okay. I'm used to skeptics by now, and honestly, she's right." Sienna frowned. "What I saw wasn't helpful. They could've figured it out on their own. *You* figured it out, suggesting Vito might've done it to avenge the Kings and get back what was taken from them. If their father, Sinjin, was the guy who destroyed his grandfather, it explains why he's going after Sinjin's family. And maybe why he's so twisted with hate, he didn't care if Tricky got caught in the cross fire."

I found myself nodding. "It takes a serious fracture of the soul to order the death of a six-year-old girl, even if she wasn't the main target. He knew she was getting in that car."

"That's Vito."

We snapped up. Sunny and Genny had stopped, clearly overhearing our conversation.

"Fractured soul," Genny continued. "When Frenchie and my girls died, he laughed in my face. Said he jacked off at night imagining their screams as their flesh melted off."

I hissed, disgust twisting my stomach.

"He laughed till I put a fist through his teeth. I would've killed him right then, but he chose his spot well. Taunting me in a crowded bar with two cops drinking beers in the booth next to us."

"I'd believe a man like that would throw someone off an overpass. Is he bald?"

Sunny shook his head. "I've met Vito Bernardi. He's a few years older than me with a full head of hair. He didn't lock eyes with you on that bridge. It's possible he hired someone, but when the Kings went, so did their money. His family is solidly middle class, and it takes serious cash to hire a hit man and pay valets to plant bombs."

"You said he has friends," I pushed. "Friends can have money. Digger would've told everyone I didn't have the means or the backup to get to him, until you put a gun in his mouth."

"The lady has a point." He swung to Genny. "Vito's our strongest lead right now. I say Kenzie talks to him first."

"Excuse me?"

"Me?"

"Yeah, yeah, that's perfect," Sunny said to himself. "Kenzie takes over the Sons of Saint, then she approaches Vito. Tells him since she's in charge now, she's not living under anyone's thumb—least of all the Merchants. She offers to join forces, and while he's getting lost in her inky eyes, he spills all he's already done to break the Merchants' hold on Cinco—including getting rid of her predecessor. If we're lucky, he'll drop that brag quick, thinking it'll get him grateful sex."

"Sunny, there's a whole mess of nonsense spewing out of your mouth right now," Genny said. "Why on earth would Feisty do any of that shit? She's not taking over the Sons of Saint. If something happens to any of us, the family steps up to run the borough. That's how it works. That's how it'll always work. Cinco is ours."

I cocked a brow. "Damn, you're possessive. You can have Cinco if you want, but you should know that unlike your fuckboys, the city does like to cuddle."

She jabbed a finger at me. "I really like her," she said to her brother, "but she better marry you, or marry me, if she wants a seat at the table."

"Gen, relax. We didn't get to the rest of the plan. It all hinges on her."

Genny listened to the rest, brows climbing higher as he described pretending he was dead and sending me in to interrogate his gang, Vito, and any traitors helping avenge an old grudge.

"And Liam agreed to this?"

"With extreme reluctance," Sunny replied. "He agreed to go along if Bane backs it up."

"Oh, hell," she said, screwing up her face. "That's why you want to see Bane? You're making him the tiebreaker? Fucking hell, I leave you boys alone for a second and you get it into your heads that you're equipped to make decisions without me."

"Uh, you dumped your phone in a lake, promised to beat us up if we crashed your bar, and dipped for six months—hardly a second. And yeah, once I learned to use the big-boy potty, I figured I could steer the ship alone from there."

"You were wrong." Genny snapped her fingers. "Feisty, up here with me. I'm handling the vetting from here on out. I'll decide if you can handle playing female Sunny. If not, I'll find someone else to step up."

I readied to argue but, once again, she grabbed me around the waist and marched us through the woods. I overheard Sunny asking Sienna for more details about her visions. I was on my own.

"Alright, Blaine." This close, she smelled faintly of beer and mint soap. Somehow it worked. "Let's cut through the bullshit. Are you fucking my brother? Is that how you got him believing you're superwoman?"

"Wow. That's blunt," I said. "Whether I am or not is private."

"Come on, be serious. You're no blushing virgin. Plus, every chance you both get, you blow each other with your eyes."

Pretty sure I was blushing then.

"He's sliding you some, isn't he?"

"Still private."

Her forehead wrinkled. "Ugh, you're not one of those prissy, prim girls, are you?" Genny placed her finger over her mouth like a mustache, turning her voice up a few octaves. "Oooh, pray chance, milady, mayhap I offend, does doth adjourn to the bedchamber with my brother?"

I giggled. "Okay, even if we did skip back a few centuries, why would you have a mustache?"

"Nah, this is me being the uptight, woman-hater in pantaloons who convinced you women shouldn't talk about sex lest someone have to bust out the fainting couches, milady."

"I don't have a problem talking about sex, I just don't usually do it with people I've known for less than a day, but if it'll let us get past this line of questioning, the answer's no. Sunny doesn't think I can do this because of my bedroom skills. Actually, it's my judgment and observational skills that were mentioned by Sunny and Liam.

"Also, I saw the guy who tried to kill Sunny, and he saw me."

Genny's smile melted away. "He got that good of a look? From the top of the bridge?"

"I got a good look at him. I can only assume he clocked my face too. I can't spend the rest of my life looking over my shoulder. You can say I'm not up for it and find someone else, Genny, but unless they're family, I can promise you they won't be as invested in getting this guy off the street as I am."

"Hmm," she said, looking down her nose at me. "Dedication is a point in your favor."

We talked for most of the trek. The deeper we went, the closer the trees crowded together, raining their leaves on us, leaving the scent of pine on our skin as a gift. It was truly calm, quiet, and remote out here, and Bane must be nuts. What kind of well-adjusted, normal human being cut off contact with most of his family and set up ten miles into the woods with no paths leading the way. That was someone who wanted to be alone with the bodies.

*Liam said he had nothing on his sister and other brother. One day I'll know when he's teasing me, and when he's deadly serious.*

"Why does your brother live all the way out here?"

Genevieve shrugged. "He can't do neighbors. They kept calling the cops to report the noise."

"I'm both curious and scared. Which one should I be?"

"Scared," she replied with her Merchants' smirk.

"That's my fault. I shouldn't have asked. So, while we're on the subject of brothers, can you give me the whole family tree?"

"Sure. There's my mother, Adeline Redgrave, daughter of Oscar Redgrave—you've heard of him, of course." I shook my head. "Ah, you're looking for the entire family history."

Genevieve told me about everyone from her grandparents, parents, aunts, uncles, and carny cousins. "Our oldest sisters, Rosalie and Vanessa, are legit," she explained. "The gang life wasn't for them, and Mom always said it was our choice. Both are married with kids, living out in the suburbs."

"After Vanessa was Liam?" Speaking about him conjured memories of his broad shoulders under my thighs. Was it wrong that I spent most of the time we were painting, imagining what it'd be like if he did something more interesting between my legs?

"Yes, my sainted older brother. He got into more trouble than me, Bane, or Sunny could think of, but nothing calms a man down like a daughter. A daughter is also handy for making him rethink his view that women are a collection of holes waiting to satisfy him. Admit it, you've met him. You got sand in your eyes from the Sahara in his pants, and so uncomfortable from his holier-than-thou act, it gave you a wedgie you're still digging out."

"That's not quite the Liam I met. To be honest, I got the feeling the only time he's completely relaxed is when he's with Tricky. It's sweet."

"Damn." She goggled at me. "You want to fuck him too. Does Sunny know you also want to ride the Liam train?"

I hadn't realized I was smiling until she wiped it off my face. "I never said that," I replied louder than needed, "and it wouldn't happen anyway. He's not interested in a woman twelve years younger than him. Besides, you were wrong about the Sahara in his pants. Liam's not going through a dry spell. Not even close."

"Whew, the jealousy is strong." She bobbed her head up, down, and around me, breathing deep. "You reek of the stuff."

Sighing, I said, "You're going to be a lot of work, aren't you, Genny?"

"The best people are."

"Moving on. Were you born after Liam?"

"Nope, that honor went to Bane. They're six years apart. Then my parents went full speed on the baby-making again, pushing me out two years after Bane, then Sunny two years after that."

"Wow, you are a big family. I can sense how close you guys are, even though your door policy comes with an ass-kicking for your own brothers."

"They deserve it. You don't know the disrespect I dealt with. All because Liam let Tricky stay with me for a weekend, and we went on a little bike ride, and she let go of me for like a second, and maybe, sorta, she kinda flew off the back while I was going forty miles an hour."

My eyes bugged.

"It was *nothing*," she said. "She flew into a guy who was kind enough to break her fall. There wasn't a scratch on her. I'm telling you the little booger was laughing about it. Then here comes Liam saying I shouldn't be left alone with a hamster, let alone a human, and I'm never babysitting again. Can you believe that?"

*Yes, I can.*

"The fucking nerve of that guy! Refusing to let me watch my own niece. I'm great with kids, Feisty. Kids fucking love me."

"Oh, Genny." I linked our elbows. "I really like you too."

She winked. "Course you do."

"Are we getting close?"

"Very close, as it happens. There's a break in the trees up ahead. You'll see the heads first, don't freak out."

"You don't start a sentence like that if you don't want me to freak out."

"Sunny, we're almost there," she threw over her shoulder. "Just so you know, Feisty's in. If she can hold her own with me, those Backstreet Boys you call a gang are no sweat. But when you talk to Vito," she said, returning to me. "Make sure you pull the same move. Crowded bar, lots of witnesses."

"You think he'd hurt me?"

"I *know* he'd hurt you if he doesn't buy your story. He's a stupid, violent, loudmouth banger and that's what stupid, violent bangers do. He hangs out at Cooper's most Saturdays, you..."

Genny's voice faded. My distraction had nothing to do with a wish to get in a bad situation by not listening to her warnings. No, I lost focus on her, because through the trees, I saw heads.

Arm slipping free, I stumbled wide-eyed over the roots, stepping out onto a clearing. A scene both mesmerizing and wrong, I took in the rolling dips and flowered mounds blanketed in living green. It was a scene from a postcard, if not for random shallow craters in the earth, rimmed with dirt and charred grass.

On the far side of the clearing sat a cabin, and on the other side, a pumpkin patch grew up to and out into the tree line. Watching over it were six scarecrows in a row, each topped with creepily lifelike mannequin heads. They were silent sentries hung from their post, perched on bodies of straw, tracking my approach. I wasn't kidding. Each head was angled our way as if to clock intruders coming in.

I stepped back. "I would like to leave now."

"Seconded," Sienna said.

"Chill, guys," said Sunny. "Bane—"

*Fweeeeeet.*

High-pitched whistling pressed on my eardrums. I turned as a red streak cut across my vision.

*Boom!*

I hit the dirt screaming, and was showered in more dirt. A scarecrow sentry on the end was dust—reduced to smoldering remains at the bottom of a new crater.

"What was that?!" I shrieked.

Sienna and I were the only ones on the ground. Sunny and Genny helped us up, dusting us off. "That was Bane," they said in unison.

"Whoo! Did you see that?" A figure jumped off the cabin porch, wielding a bazooka. "Fucking nailed it at forty yards."

I darted between the siblings, peering over Sunny's shoulder. He was their brother, let them face the charging weapon-wielding loon who almost blew me up!

"What's this? Visiting? To what do I owe the pleasure?"

The assumed Bane swallowed the distance, and another feeling broke through shocked terror. The genes brewing in this family were ridiculous. It seemed no matter which of their fathers Adeline reproduced with, they weren't capable of having children anywhere short of beautiful.

Sweat glistened on Bane's bare chest, accentuating the bumps and divots of his tightly honed body. Oh shit, all the things I could say about his body. His skin was penny copper—both from a life in the sun and genetics. He opted to shave his head, but for the unobstructed view it gave me of his Greek nose, lopsided smile, and thick brows, I determined this was the wisest hair decision anyone ever made.

"Little sis, baby bro, get the hell over here."

My shields left me behind, going up to greet, hug, and slap backs with their brother.

"Wicked aim," Sunny congratulated. "Nailed it."

"You like?" Bane rubbed the bazooka like a fond pet. "Put this baby together myself. Won't tell you what a bitch it was getting the parts out here—won't tell you now, anyway. I see you brought guests." Unprotected, Bane latched on me and Sienna. "A present, by chance? It's been weeks since I've known the touch of a woman."

"Nah," Genny said. "Milady's squeamish about sex. Oops, I said the s-word. Don't pass out from all the blood rushing to your cheeks."

*Seriously, what sins did I commit?*

"What the hell were you doing with that thing?" I snapped. "You almost blew us up."

"Almost is the difference between having something to be mad about, and complaining for no reason."

"You—"

He passed the weapon off to Genny and pumped my hand. "Good to meet you, I'm Bane. What's your name?"

Sunny tucked a flyaway behind my ear. "This, brother, is Mrs. Bellisario."

I whipped around, brows flying to my hairline, and Sunny gasped. "Did I say that? Oh my gosh, Angel, I didn't want you to find out this way." He sucked in a deep breath, and let it out slow. "The truth is... I'm psychic too. I've known our future since the day we met."

"Really?" Sienna breathed.

"No, not really!" I pointed behind Bane. "Over there, now."

Smirking, he retreated, holding his arms up in surrender. A joke because giving up was not among his skill set.

"Back to introductions," Bane said. "You are?"

"Kenzie—"

"And you?"

"Sienna, nice—"

"Kenzie and Sienna, cute names. Not like Bane. Sure, in Hawaiian it means long-awaited child, but I've suspected they chose it for the back-handed meaning—getting back at me for putting Mom through twenty-four hours of labor. Long-awaited for real."

I made to agree, but he was already moving on.

"You're covered in dirt. Did I get you in the blast? You're welcome to use my shower. I'll dig up a change of clothes for you and toss yours in the wash."

"Thank—"

"But I know you didn't come all the way out here to use my shower. Especially since, though it's lovely to meet you, Kenzie and Sienna, I don't do visitors. Fewer people to worry about walking in the blast zone. Why'd you bring them out here, Gen, and did you at least bring provisions from the outside world? Food? Beer? Porn?"

"The day I pick out my brother's porn is the day our family has officially gotten too close."

Bane tossed a grin her way, flashing blinding pearly whites. "Too true, but I'd have taken that over two reasons to pack up and move again. What—"

Lurching forward, I clapped a hand over his mouth. "Damn, you're like a runaway train. No chance to jump in. Taking this from the top, *almost* getting blown up is a damn good reason to complain. It's lukewarm to meet you too. I think Bane's a great name and I like it even more knowing the meaning in Hawaiian.

"Ouch, your poor mom. You did get me in the blast, but I brought most of this dirt with me. That said, I'd kill for a shower, but I can wait until I get home. And we are here for a reason. Sunny will tell you all about it when he gets the chance."

"She found his off-switch in five minutes," Sunny said. "Why'd it take us years?"

Bane gently removed my hand. Underneath, amusement curved full lips. "There is no off-switch. Touch of a woman, remember? I stopped because I forgot how tiny and soft your hands are. I may have creamed my pants in the middle there."

"Wow."

He beamed. "Don't mind me, I'm harmless. I'm told I talk too much and too fast, but that's what happens when you're the son of an infamous semi-mute. I chattered at my father for hours to get a word or three out of him. Usually, it was 'for the love of God, let me sleep' and 'don't follow me into the bathroom!'"

I snorted, bursting out laughing.

"Oh, I got a laugh out of her. Cute one too."

"Do it again," Sunny said.

"Does she have a button I can press?"

"Yeah, I found it the other day." Sunny tickled my side, sending me half giggling, half squealing away from him.

"Let me try." Bane got the other side. I almost fell into a crater escaping them both.

"Now I see why you live all the way out here." I wagged my finger between the smirking brothers. "This is a court-ordered separation."

"Pretty much." Genny led me and Sienna toward the cabin. "Sunny will fill him in. Come on, there's food inside, and I could use a shower after that hike."

"How long are we going to be here?" I worried my lip, thinking of the tree I had to climb and the window waiting for me to slip through that night.

She glanced over her shoulder. The brothers were locked in conversation. "As long as it takes Sunny to convince Bane you're fit to do the job, and he has to help you do it."

Thirty minutes dragged into an hour, which turned into two. The setting sun cast its last rays through the cabin windows, turning my toes rosy pink and burnt orange. I wiggled them over the edge of the chair, basking in the mossy scent of Bane's sweater. Sienna and I broke down and grabbed showers following Genny.

I wasn't sure what I expected of the interior. It defied my expectations all the same. The place wasn't so much a home as it was a workman's shop. All sorts of machines I couldn't name claimed the available space not taken up by a single couch, small dining table, kitchen, and a television over the table saw.

I peeked into the master bedroom on the way to the bathroom. The room was sparse, though his queen-size bed was neatly made. My heart twinged seeing that bare room. From what Genny, Liam, and Sunny said, Bane chose to live out here. That didn't make it any less of a lonely existence. No wonder he talked a mile a minute when there was someone to speak to, and blew up creepy scarecrows for fun.

"Why did he move out here?" I asked Genny. She sat atop the kitchen counter, drinking coffee. "Was it just so he could blow things up in peace?"

"Bane goes into the city to keep an eye on Waterford and the men working for him. The main racket in that borough is weapons manufacturing—the illegal kind. It's both an easy gig and a deadly one. The men get on with their business without being told. Late shipments mean late payments. But if one of them gets it into their head they'd do a better job running things than Bane..."

"There's an arsenal conveniently at their fingertips," I finished.

"He used to move around the city. Now he moves around the woods, making weapons and blowing shit up in peace."

"And with him by my side, the Sons of Saint won't doubt Sunny chose me to step up in his place. Do your crews all know each other?"

"They know of each of us. We are the Merchants."

"—bad idea." Bane's voice came in ahead of him. "She runs away from a tickle. She's not ready."

The brothers entered the cabin. Bane went straight for the fridge and a bottled water. Sunny beelined for the couch, lifted my feet, and placed them on his lap. He started rubbing my arches. They were sore after ten miles, I didn't think about stopping him.

"Were you talking about me?" I spoke up.

"Only about you," Bane replied, "and your sister. Sunny told me the plan. It's not a bad one—except for the fact those guys will smell innocence on you like a coyote sniffs out a rabbit."

"I'm not some helpless little girl. I'm going to slap the next Merchant that makes me repeat it."

"Nothing to do with helplessness." Bane dropped on the rug, stretching out against the table saw. I followed his body down, cursing my thoughts. Even his feet were attractive. Bane boasted long, spindly toes covered in ink. The base of the castle depicted on his feet began at the toes and continued up, its spires climbing his ankles. "I don't doubt you're a strong woman, capable of handling yourself, but I don't have to tell you the everyday asshole is nothing like a banger willing to put a bullet between your eyes for looking at them wrong."

I flicked to Sunny. "*Would* any of your guys put a bullet in my head for looking at them wrong?"

"I didn't put 'looking for short-tempered, homicidal sociopath' on the job flyer, lollipop lips. My guys are good guys. They don't act without a reason, but..."

I didn't like that pause, or the hesitation that flashed across his face. "But what, Sunny?"

"But thinking that you're an impostor trying to fool them and take over the crew is a reason, so, yeah, it'd be best if they didn't doubt you." Sunny gestured to his brother. "Bane'll help you with that part, I'll help you with the details. If you know everything about my guys from their favorite sandwich to their favorite weapon, along with everything you know about me, they'll figure we had to be close."

Bane did the nodding in my place since I didn't agree. I didn't say anything.

Our eyes met at the same time. Mine panicked, Sienna's placid. She wasn't concerned about what we just heard—Sunny's crew would kill if the sniff test came up suspicious. What would we do if they didn't believe me? One of them could pull a gun a lot faster than Sunny or Thatcher could bust in to save the day. And then, of course, what if they did believe me? If the Sons of Saint welcomed us with open arms, dropping their guards and giving me a peek into a traitorous mind, and the traitor looked back? Wouldn't he do exactly what Thatcher suggested, and snuff me out so I couldn't take what he tried to kill Sunny to get?

"Are you sure?" I asked, slicing in Bane and Sunny's conversation. "Are you sure you can teach us enough that they'll buy the ruse?"

Sunny took my hand. "I wouldn't have asked you to do this if I wasn't sure."

Just like that, my panic vanished. Sunny promised to protect me. I believed him.

"You guys can spend the night here, Kenzie, Sienna," said Bane. "I'll give you my bed."

"Glad that's settled." Genny hopped off the counter. "I've got to get back, and it's a long walk."

"You've got to go back and tell Bugsy you're moving out of Harlow," Sunny stated. "You too, Bane. Till we get this guy, you're living in the compound."

"Aww," Genny cooed. "Look at you, worried about your big brother and sissy. Adorable, but we can take care of ourselves. I'm not ditching my girls."

"I'd wager a bet this guy has a better chance of tracking me down at Fairfield where the whole city knows the Merchants live, compared to the cabin out in Nowhere, Elmshire Woods," Bane said.

Sunny stood, expression smoothing into the one that threw me—grave. "I'm glad you're both comfy, tucked up with your toys and bikers—the replacement family—but did you ever think maybe your niece, who was almost killed and knows it, would feel safer if her family was around her. Neither of you even fucking knew until I told you!

"If I had bled out in the trash and Liam and Tricky got in that car, you would've heard about our deaths on the news, and then called our mother to explain why you were the last to know."

Genny looked away, jaw clenched.

"Both of you, get your heads out of your asses. We're at war," Sunny roared. "Pick a side. Either you're a Cardinal and a Scourge, or you're a Merchant."

Sunny slammed out the door. Genny wasn't far behind him. If she went to have it out with him, or if she took off, I couldn't tell as the silence stretched between us.

I jumped when Bane clapped. "No point sitting around. Sienna, you're up first."

"Up first?" I repeated, standing with Sienna. "Up to do what?"

"I'm teaching you both to fight. The crash course." Bane folded his arms, popping corded muscles up and down his body. I forced myself to stay on his eyes. Whatever was happening between me and Sunny, developing a crush on another brother was sure to complicate it.

"We know how to fight. Sienna and I... went through a hard time when we were kids. The people in our neighborhood weren't compassionate about it. I came home bleeding three times. The fourth time, they went after Sienna. I made sure it was the last."

He hummed. "Respect. That story turned me on even more than those soft, calloused hands. But what kind of training are we talking about here and what kind of bullies?"

Bane dropped the *turned-on* comment so casually in the conversation, I almost addressed that instead of the important question. "Self-defense classes with my gym teacher. She saw the kids from school corner me, so she taught Sienna and me how to bend a wrist till they thought twice about touching us again."

"Good to know you have some of it down. I'm teaching Sienna basic self-defense. Throat punches, eye gouges, nose strikes, groin kicks. That sort of thing."

"Cool," Sienna said.

"Not cool." I stepped in front of her as she made for Bane. "My sister won't be gouging anyone's eyes out."

"We hope," he finished. "But if it goes south and her life's in danger, don't you want her to know how to put them down and make them *stay* down?"

"Of course, but—"

"There's nothing noble about dying or getting injured because you were too weak to win."

"I'm not saying—"

"I'll give you guys weapons—guns, knives, bazookas—whatever you want, but if your attacker gets it off you, you need to know how to fight them off."

"I agree—"

"If you agree, why are we still talking? Let's do it."

"Agh," I cried. "You're an extremely frustrating man."

Bane barked a laugh. "So I've been told. Seriously, if you want to take your chances, that's up to you." He backed away, arms out like *what can I do?* "I won't force you. That said, when I leave you to the Sons of Saint, the two of you will have to watch the other's back. You learned to fight to protect your sister once. Why wouldn't you do it again?"

Folding my arms, I ate all the distance he put between us. "Not a runaway train, you're a snake charmer. You also happen to be right," I added grudgingly. "It can't hurt to learn a few moves, but you get why I don't like the thought that we'd need them. Because it means we failed."

Sobering, Bane said, "You won't. I get the impression that's not something you do, Mackenzie."

"Then Sunny didn't tell you my history, or where he found me."

"He did. I know what you survived the last eight months, and the point is, you survived. What you should be saying to yourself now is if you made it through that, you can make it through anything. Keep saying it, Kenzie, until you believe it."

I stood there long after Bane and Sienna grabbed mats and went out the back. So long I was roused by a tap on the shoulder.

"Let's do this, mon chéri," Sunny said. "We have to leave before it gets dark."

"You're really leaving me here?"

A crooked smile graced his handsome face. All traces of the angry, passionate Sole gone. "This is the safest place in the world—second only to the compound. Bane won't let anything happen to you."

I bit my lip, penning in a silly response. *That's not what I mean, Sunny. I meant, are you really going to leave me here... without you?*

"I know he won't," I replied with the sane, non-clingy response. "Ready when you are."

Sunny and I pushed the limits of sunlight, going over every member of his crew from their weaknesses, their strengths, their habits, and the little things only Sunny would know. Through the entire conversation, only one thing surprised me.

"Your crew is half women?"

He clutched his chest like my surprise offended him. "I'm an equal opportunity employer, Angel. If my sweet, sainted mother has taught me anything, it's that ladies can fillet a dude just as well as any man."

"Then why are you called the Sons of Saint?"

"'Cause the People of Saint didn't have the same ring to it."

I inclined my head. "I'll give you that."

Genny stuck her head in. "Sunny, smooch her goodbye and move your ass. I'm leaving in five minutes whether you're behind me or not."

Sunny, of course, obeyed her and kissed me on the cheek. "See you tomorrow."

My chest fluttered under the impression his lips left behind. Would I go so far as to call it poison? I don't know. What did you call it when someone burrowed so deep inside, your heart raced, pulse jumped, and breath quickened under their command?

"Tomorrow."

After they left, I went out back to watch Bane and Sienna spar.

"Right in the palm, as hard as you can."

Sienna didn't hold back. She reeled her elbow and struck, striking his hand dead center.

"Nice." Bane shook out his wrist, bouncing on the balls of his feet. "You're a natural. Perfect stance, strong follow-through. How does a ho learn to fight like that on the streets? Did your pimp teach you a few moves to fight off the choky johns?"

"What did you say?!" I propelled off the deck, flying at him. "Fucking asshole!"

"Wait—"

"Sis, no!"

I jumped and Sienna caught me, hauling me back. My punch swung inches from his nose. "Don't you ever speak to her that way!"

"Kenzie, it's okay." She forced me to look at her. "Bane didn't mean it. He was teaching me. It's all for the act." She had to repeat it twice for it to penetrate.

"The act? What are you talking about?"

Bane poked his head over her shoulder. "Apologies. That was confusing to walk into without a heads-up. To pull this off, it's not just knowing how to fight. It's about the right attitude."

My chest heaved, pumped by the residual need to punch his face in. "How does calling my sister a whore teach her the right attitude?"

"Like I said, I believe you're both strong, tough women, but you're not dealing with everyday assholes. Those guys are law-abiding. They know the limit, and for their own sake, they don't go past it. The world you're in now doesn't know rules or consequences.

"There's only so much I can teach you. You're not going to become different people overnight. The best actors can fake it, but they draw on something to get them in the mind of their character, so this is what you do." Bane cupped my cheeks, beating back my flash of surprise as the intensity in his gaze burned me. "Think of that guy who bumps into you on the street, knocks your bag on the ground, then keeps walking without an apology.

"Think of the stranger you overheard saying something nasty about the Black guy sitting in the corner of the café, minding his own business. Think of the jerk who cuts you off, and mean kids in school who bullied you."

Those events, each of them I lived, roared through my mind.

"When shit like that happens, the rage flares up and centuries of honed warrior instinct shifts you into fight mode—your fists are already balled up before you can think. But then," Bane said, "something else interrupts. It's the centuries of polite society distilled and drilled into your brain since you could walk. You can't punch a racist asshole or they'll call the cops on you. You can't rip out that bully's hair and break her nose against the locker, or you'll be suspended. You can't call that jerk who almost knocked you down a cunt-sucking asshole, or you're the crazy lady shouting at people in the street.

"It's that compulsion to blend in civilized society which makes you un-ball your fist, walk away, and take the high road... that's what will give you away faster than a name slip or shifty eyes." I tensed in his hold. "You have to go with nature, Kenzie. When your fist balls, swing. When the acid drips onto your tongue, burn everyone who dared talk back. Vito, the Sons of Saint, they're going to test you, and if you hesitate to address disrespect, they'll never do a thing you say. They certainly won't see you as boss."

Slowly, I nodded. "I understand. You mean just like now when I sprung to tear your limbs off without hesitation. I have to be in that mode every second that I'm playing this part."

"Can you do it?"

I looked to my sister. "I can do it. I'll imagine every barb, threat, or hit is aimed at Sienna, not me. If I do, I won't pause a second to knock out a bitch," I said. "But let my sister have a break. We haven't eaten yet and I scoped out your pantry, fully stocked.

"How about you get some food going while we spar?" I asked Sienna.

"Okay. Any requests?"

Bane took hold of my hips and positioned my stance on the mat. "I have chicken thawing in the fridge and potatoes in the pantry. I was planning to roast them up."

"Say no more, roast chicken, veggies, and potatoes coming up."

"I saw through that," Bane said after the door swung shut. He folded my fingers in, curling them on my palm. "You said you understood, but you still sent her away so I couldn't lob insults at her anymore. They're going to see that too."

We were so close, heat radiated off him, warming my skin and chilled fingers. "See what?"

"That she's your weakness."

I stiffened. "And it'd be the last stupid act they committed if they tried to get to me through her."

Bane stepped back, raising his palms. "Strike in the center. Throw your weight into it."

We worked through the moves—each one taught again, then again, then five more times until he was certain the stance, strike, and power ingrained in my muscles. For some reason, Bane didn't toss insults at me between hits. Maybe he believed having Sienna as motivation was all I needed.

"Practice every night," Bane said, dropping down on the mat. "Sunny will spar with you. He learned from the best. He won't let you get rusty."

Roast chicken and my sister's humming floated through the screen door, beckoning me into the warmth. I found myself sitting at his side.

"Who's the best?" I asked. "You?"

"Nah." Bane turned his face to the starless sky, grin playing on his lips. "My dad. He trained as a boxer. Could've gone all the way, but a life of crime called to him." Bane laughed at his joke.

"You say dad like you don't have four of them."

"No, when I say dad, I always mean mine. Baris Alexander." He turned to me. "Don't get me wrong, they're all my fathers. They taught me everything. They raised me. But I had to share my other fathers with my brothers and sisters. I shared my mom with everyone. Baris is the one who's... just mine." Bane pulled a face. "I sound like an ass, don't I?"

"No," I said quickly, laying a hand on his knee. "You don't. I know you love your family. But we all need that person, don't we? The one we feel closest to. The one we know we can tell everything, and they'll understand. Sienna was always that person for me." I laughed. "When we were little, we invented a secret language, and at night, she'd sneak under my covers and we'd tell each other stories only we understood. We didn't have a word for everything, so we'd make up something and sprinkle in gibberish."

"That's sweet," Bane replied. His deep voice was calmer than I ever heard it—words tickling my ear softly, instead of bowling me over. I found myself lying down next to him—letting those words travel a shorter distance. "My father couldn't always speak to me, so he left notes for me to find. The day of my first boxing match, I found a note cheering me on in my glove. Even though he sat still and silent the entire match, I knew inside he was shouting louder than everyone else."

"That's sweeter." Shifting, I traced his face, moving over his sharp cheekbones' bumps and dips. "Can I ask you something?"

"Why do I live out in the middle of nowhere with scarecrows for company?"

"Yeah. Why do you?"

"Sunny or Genny didn't tell you?"

I lifted my shoulder. "Genny said you don't have to worry about your men killing you and taking over if you're out here, but that's not it, is it? Why bother with the killing part when you're never around? Whoever runs things when you're not there, is the de facto boss anyway."

He chuckled. "Sunny was right about you. You're perceptive."

"So, what's the real reason?"

"The real reason," he repeated slowly. "If you didn't think less of me before, you will if I tell you the truth."

"No." I said it, and meant it. "I won't."

He turned his neck, studying me with the same closeness. The silence stretched between us and I accepted he wouldn't answer.

"I live out here because in these woods I'm not tempted... to care."

I was supposed to say something. I should've said something, but nothing came to my lips as his words sunk in. Bane didn't need me to. He kept speaking, pushing my heart further and further down.

"Years ago, I made a choice to give up love, marriage, children, friends. It's a lot easier to keep that promise when none are around me."

"Why?" I rasped. "Why make such a promise?"

"Should I tell you the truth again?"

I nodded.

"Will it make you cry?"

Resting my hand on his wrist, I nodded.

"When I was nine, my parents took us to the park. Despite what people say about my family, my folks did everything to give us a normal childhood. They shielded us from the truth of what they did, and filled our lives with pancake breakfasts, Christmas parties, soccer practice, and everything they wanted from the childhoods they didn't have.

"When the guy snatched me off the playground, hissing in my ear that my parents would find nothing but pieces of me, I didn't know why."

"Oh my gosh, Bane, were you—?" My throat bobbed hard. "What did he do?"

"Nothing. Never got the chance," he said. "My dad saw him duck behind the hedges with me and chased him down. Dad ripped me out of his arms and... he didn't pause or think of me standing there. Roaring, he snapped his neck in two, killing him in front of me. That was the first time I saw my dad lose control—let alone hurt someone."

"I'm sorry. I can't imagine how traumatic that was for you."

"It was, but not in the way you're thinking. After he killed him and the mist cleared, Dad broke down. He hugged me—apologizing, crying, speaking more words than he had in a week. Guilt racked him for letting me witness him kill. For making me the target of bloodthirsty killers. In one afternoon, my blissful childhood was over, and he blamed himself.

"That's how he remembers that day, but you want to know what I remember when I look back?"

"What?" I whispered.

"That's the day love broke my father. He broke his vow because of love for his son. He destroyed my world because he loved his son. He apologized for being who I needed him to be, for saving me, because he loved me. That was the day I realized that I made the strongest man I know... weak."

Bane held my gaze, trapping it under a darkening sky. He touched my cheek—a light, gentle graze, collecting my tears.

"I promised that day I'd never do that to him, my mother, or my fathers again. To my brothers, sisters, nieces, or nephews. I trained hard. I turned my body into a weapon, then I mastered all the others out there. I wasn't going to be that helpless, clueless child. My death would not be used to destroy my family. Over the years, my promise grew to include a wife, girlfriend, or child.

"Arms dealers have a short life expectancy. How can I have a kid knowing I'll likely never see them graduate? How can I ask the woman I love to sit at home late at night, wondering if I walked out the door that day for the last time? And don't let me forget the danger they'd have to live with every day. Liam was forced to take Tricky out of school. Her normal childhood ended at four. At least I got five extra years.

"That's the real reason, Kenzie. It's why monks live on top of mountains, and I live in a cabin in the woods. Why surround yourself with all the things you can't have?"

"Bane, you can." I surged over, palming his cheek. "It doesn't have to be this way. You have to know that. Genny told me your oldest sisters are out of the life. They have families and normal lives. You can too."

He was shaking his head before I finished. "This is who I am. Polite society was never meant for me. I was born to punch first."

"I don't believe you." My voice rose. "None of this is as set in stone as you've convinced yourself it is. *I live a dangerous life, so I'm going to get killed or get my family killed.* No, Bane. No one's life is guaranteed. No one has the picture-perfect family that's promised to reach old age together. It's a messy, frightening, crazy world but you find people who'll be by your side, walking through it together. That's how it works."

"I know you don't understand—"

"I do understand. You're not the only one who was ripped out of a blissful childhood. I know that love destroys you." Tears soaked my face. "It's been killing me for nine years."

Bane sat up. "Kenzie, I didn't mean to upset you. Let's just go inside, eat dinner, watch a movie—"

"No," I said, grasping his arms. "We're telling the truth tonight, Bane, even if we think less of each other. So, this is the truth—when I was fourteen, my mother shot my father in the heart. She's currently serving a fifteen-year sentence in Cinco Pen for murder."

"Kenzie—"

"No, please. Let me say this." The plea came out as a sob. He quieted. "You have to believe me, Bane. I didn't know. Didn't *see*. I loved my father. He was funny and goofy and loving. He'd pick us up from school and surprise us with ice cream cones, or drive us to the movie theater. He never raised his voice, spanked us, or sent us to bed without dinner. For fourteen years, I thought I had the best dad in the world. It wasn't until Mom killed him that I saw the monster."

Bane pulled me closer to him, rubbing my arms to warm me, but he didn't interrupt.

Taking a deep breath, my story came out. "My mom and dad seemed like a normal couple. He went to work. She stayed home, taking care of us and the house. Mom had so much on her plate, he had me help out and pick up groceries at the corner store. When Mom was busy cleaning, he picked us up from school. Mom was tired after a long day, so Daddy would help us with our homework."

My eyes fluttered shut, unable to spend another second drowning in his. "Even when he pulled out the timer, setting the minutes she could use the bathroom or shower, Dad had an explanation for that too. *It's the four of us and one bathroom, we want to make sure everyone gets equal time.*"

"And I believed that like a little fool. I swallowed all of my father's *logical* explanations for isolating my mother. For cutting her off from her friends, never letting her leave the house alone, making her go to bed and wake up when he ordered, for only allowing her three minutes to pee. Mom didn't speak against him, Dad never lost his charming smile, and I just didn't *see* it. I didn't see that my home... was a cage."

I didn't carry on for a long time. Bane was patient, letting us sit in silence until I was ready to break it.

"A couple weeks after my fourteenth birthday, Dad and I were at the kitchen table going over my homework while Mom made dinner. I got up, saying I had to use the bathroom, and for the first time, he pulled out the timer and told me to be back in three minutes. I was washing my hands when I heard the gunshot."

"Kenzie, I'm so sorry."

"She didn't try to get away with it. Mom called the police herself. She held up her hands to be cuffed. I screamed and cried and demanded to know why she did it. She didn't say a word to me until they escorted her out the door. Mom turned to me and said, 'You're free now.'"

Shaking myself, I wiped my face on my borrowed sleeve, breaking his hold. "I can't say why I'm sharing this with someone I just met. A horny hermit man in the woods who almost blew me up." We both cracked a smile.

"Except that... my dad was the first," I admitted. "He was the first man to fool me into believing he was anything but a monster. Men have been fooling me ever since, and it's no wonder. I've always been a fool—oblivious to what's going on right in front of me."

"Don't say that," Bane said. His force blew me back. "You were a kid, Mackenzie. Kids believe in the worlds their parents create for them."

"I've told myself that and a host of excuses and platitudes over the years. I've repeated all the positive psychobabble from the therapists, and some days, I believe it. Other days, I count up all the mistakes I made in my life and with the men I chose, and all the same thoughts cross my mind, Bane. Wouldn't it make sense to swear off love and dating? Couldn't I have told Sienna to figure out her own life instead of stretching myself out so thin, I couldn't support either of us anymore and we ended up on the street? Why continue visiting my mother in prison when she reminds me of everything I wish to forget? Love and family have taken so much from me, why don't I say no more?"

He leaned back, sighing as he looked away. "You choose not to and now I have to do the same? I appreciate how difficult it was to share your story, but we live different lives."

"I didn't choose, Bane." I gently turned him to face me. "I'm single, and since my last, I've rejected every guy that comes my way. I haven't seen my mother for months. When we had spare change, Sienna was the one who called the prison to talk to her. I was too ashamed. Still am. As for supporting Sienna and giving my sister her life back, I can't even do that for myself.

"Eventually, I will have to make a choice to put my faith in someone, face the mother who gave her freedom to give me mine, and keep a promise to my sister to give her everything my parents couldn't. I want to believe I'll have the courage to choose love, and even though you're a horny wild man in the woods who I just met today, I want to believe you will too." I lifted my shoulders. "'Cause it seems to me if we don't, then they both win. My dad succeeds in trapping me in a loveless cage, and your kidnapper achieved his goal—ripping you away from your family."

Bane whispered something. I thought it was "too perceptive" but he lifted his head, grinning, and I decided I imagined it.

"You've given me a lot to think about. For what it's worth, even though you're a random woman who trespassed on my property and tried to break my nose... I hope you choose love too." Getting to his feet, Bane held out a hand for me. "Come on. That's all the soul baring two strangers should do for one night. There's something I want to show you." Bane pulled me up and wiped my face, teasing a giggle out of me as he tickled my nose. "You're not afraid of spiders, are you?"

"No," I drew out. "Why?"

"Because I'm going to show you the stars."

*SUNNY*

"I already ate, Bethy." I made for my room, Fuller on my heels. "Tell Shonda to wrap it up. Her leftovers are just as good for breakfast."

"Are you sure you're alright, Sole? You look pale. Come here, let me—"

I gently grasped her wrist, stopping it short of my forehead. "I'm fine. Just tired. It's been a long day of being dead. What I need is a hot shower, change of clothes, and a scotch."

Her lips pursed. The woman swore I was developing a drinking problem.

"I'm bringing you a plate all the same. You shouldn't be drinking on an empty stomach."

See?

I bowed deeply. "Yes, Mommy Fuller."

"Silly boy." She walked away, shaking her head, but damned if I didn't hear fondness lace the reprimand. What mattered was she walked off, and didn't see me grimace straightening up. I went into my room, shut and locked the door. Shedding the smile I wore all day, agony scrunched my forehead—ratcheting up as I peeled off my soiled clothes.

"Dammit, Gen."

The fake shout during our fake fight was louder than I intended, since the pain was real. Between her wrenching, cycling through Cinco, and trekking ten miles back and forth through the woods. It was safe to say I went against doctor's orders.

*"What's the damage?"*

*"The infection has cleared up and your scar is healing nicely."*

*"That's great. So why do you look like you're about to tell me I'm stage four?"*

*Bending over, Hendrix retrieved a folder from her bag. "There's something else we have to discuss."*

*I tried to sit up. Hendrix guided me back down, taking a seat on the edge of my mattress. "Sunny, I'm afraid the fall damaged more than your liver. There's a fracture in your vertebrae here." She tapped a spot below my neck.*

Slowly, I made my way over to the nightstand. My knife case lay there waiting for me—leather smooth on my palm, bowie knife fitted to my grip. The target hung beside the closet a mere two yards away. Impossible to miss, I mastered two yards when I was seven.

*"It's too soon to say how this will affect you. For now, you're on bed rest. I'll prescribe you some pain meds, and you'll use a wheelchair. If your symptoms don't improve or get worse, let me know right away."*

*"What's worse?"*

*"Severe pain."*

I raised the knife, pain rippling up my spine. Reeling back, I let it loose as a shudder jerked my arm.

*"Numbness. Muscle spasms."*

My aim went wide, bouncing the blade off my door. It lay on the carpet miles from where it should be.

*"It's very important that you let me know if you experience any of the above. It'll mean surgery, but it would be necessary to stop the compression getting worse."*

*"What happens if I get the surgery?"*

*She hesitated—a pause that told me all I needed to know. "Months of recovery," she finally said. "Rehab. Physical therapy. But I have every reason to believe you'll make a full recovery."*

Hendrix went on to say more. I tuned the rest out. Like I said, the pause told me everything.

I sunk onto my chaise—opposite direction of the pain pills I'd been double and triple dosing for a week. I'd head in that direction eventually—that's where the scotch was.

I didn't have a drinking problem. This would be my second of the week, including the few sips of beer I had at Genny's bar. I didn't have a pill problem either. I loathed the stuff—hated having to take it, then take it again when one dose didn't make a dent in the pain.

What I had was a war to win. A family to protect. And a promise to keep.

Kenzie couldn't know that the true reason I needed her to chase my would-be killer down while I played dead was because—

"I can't do it myself." The knife burned a hole in my carpet. "I can't defend myself. I can't win a pretend fight against my sister."

I can't protect my crew, business, or family on my own, and if I get that surgery, I'll be no use to Kenzie. I told her I'd protect her—be there whenever and wherever she needed me.

"I won't let her down."

Dragging myself up, I downed the pills, put away two fingers of scotch, and accepted a plate of Shonda's famous chicken and gnocchi with a smile.

Setting the food on the nightstand, I picked up the knife, lining it up to the target at one and a half yards.

I'd do this all night if I had to. I wouldn't stop until my promise was kept.

*MACKENZIE*

Bane led me deeper and deeper into the woods.

I had a tight hold on his left hand and the other held the flashlight, warning the critters of Elmshire that we were coming. Bane certainly seemed sure of himself and where he was going. He hadn't stopped talking since we set off. All the same, a thought occurred to me.

"Why did I agree to tramp through the woods with a perfect stranger? For all I know, you're leading me to the open grave where you dump your victims."

"I haven't descended that deep into the *madman in the woods* stereotype."

"You did tell me you were taking me to see the stars." I glanced up at the light-polluted sky. "There's no chance of that this close to the city."

"Guess you're going to have to trust me. Careful up ahead," he said. "There are low branches."

I studied him in the scant light. Bane said it nicely, but I heard the slight reproach earlier, reminding me I didn't know what was better for his life than he did. He had a point.

What he did was illegal, dangerous, and prone to making enemies. Any semi-sensible criminal would realize they chased death or incarceration, and that kind of thing messed a kid up—ask me how I know. Bane was trying to be responsible. Not bringing children into this world who might grow up without him. Not leaving a wife alone to raise those children while dodging nosy-neighbor questions about the supposed legitimate businessman she married.

Anyone else would applaud him for the sacrifice, rather than spill her life's greatest tragedy and reveal more about herself than she ever intended.

"I hope it didn't come across like I was judging you," I blurted. "I understand why you made the choices you did. I really do."

Bane peered at me over his shoulder. "You weren't judging me, you were sad for me. You care about my happiness and we just met. It was sweet, Kenzie. You're sweet." He sighed. "Which is unfortunate."

"Why?" I drew out. "Because now you have to dump me in the grave?"

He laughed. "Because dammit, I'm starting to like you. I planned to introduce you to Sunny's gang and return to my cabin. Now you've got me worried you won't make it through to find the guy who deserves you, make it right with your mom, or build a new life with your sister. Now you've got me invested." Bane tossed me a wry look. "This is why I don't have visitors."

My lips tugged up. The thought that knowing me for a few hours scuffed that vow he built around his heart, pleased me more than it should.

"Does this mean you'll move into the Fairfield with us until this is over? There are twenty-seven floors. I bet there's room for you."

"It means I'll stay close by to make sure you, Sienna, Tricky, and my family are safe."

I swatted his backside. I was getting comfortable—fast. "That's what I said. Don't be such a guy, spinning my words like you thought of it on your own. Say 'yes, Kenzie.' 'You're right, Kenzie.' 'We're in this together, Kenzie.'"

"If I do, will you smack my ass again?"

"How about a kick up the ass?"

"I might be into that. I don't know." He sighed mournfully. "It's been so long."

"How long are we talking?"

"Oh? I thought sex talk made you blush."

"We're talking about *not* having sex. There's nothing scandalous about a dry spell."

"True." Bane suddenly snapped me to his side. I circled his shoulders as he lifted me around the waist, helping me over a fallen log. "Five weeks, four days, and eighteen hours for me. What do you got?"

"You won't handle it when I tell you." What was happening? There was some kind of magic in Bane's free-flowing stream of chatter. All his talk made me comfortable doing the same.

"Now you have to," he replied.

"Are you ready for this? Five months—going on six."

"Six— You're kidding?" he cried. "Oh, Kenzie, you poor thing." Bane hugged me tight. "Brave little soldier, you know true celibacy. You give hope to us all."

Giggling, my fingers skittered up his side. Bane shot away from me, howling. "Whoops, I found your button too."

Grinning, we reached for each other at the same time, holding hands during the dark forest walk. I stopped caring about where the mad woodsman was taking me, and wished we wouldn't get there soon.

"It's too bad we can't help each other out," Bane spoke up. "End my dry spell. End your hellish torment."

I chose my words carefully. "Why can't we? I don't have a boyfriend. You'll never have a girlfriend. We're free to do what we want."

"I'd have said the same thing an hour and a half ago, but it's too late now. I like you, Mackenzie Blaine. Like you more and more each second I know you. And if there's one rule you follow when you swear off relationships, it's don't get involved with people you like."

*Talkative, blunt, open, honest. What was with these Merchant boys? Every one of them insisted on being like no man I ever met.*

"Over there." Bane pointed with the flashlight. "It's up ahead."

The glow lit upon a strange opening in the trees where branches entangled, twisting in and around themselves, and sparing a small opening between the trunks—forming a natural entrance. Bane and I ducked our heads, stepping inside. The torch pierced the gloom, lighting our surroundings.

I screamed. Seizing Bane, I climbed up his body, strangling his neck and waist, wrapping myself around him. "Oh my god, oh my god, oh my god! Bane!"

Everywhere you turned, covering each branch, twig, and leaf of the hollow, were thick, clinging spiderwebs.

"Whoa." Bane wobbled on his feet. "Kenzie, it's okay."

"It's not okay!" I shrieked. "Why would you bring me here?!"

"You said you weren't afraid of spiders!"

"That one spider crawling up my drain—sure." I barely recognized that high-pitched screeching as coming from me. "Not a fucking colony!"

"Kenzie, it's okay, I swear," he wheezed. My hold on his neck was pretty tight. "Trust me, just look. The spiders are gone. They... abandoned this spot a long time ago, leaving behind their webs."

It took more coaxing to peel my face from his neck. Half whimpering, I raised my eyes, following the light where it landed. Web after web, no spiders.

"See," Bane soothed, stroking my back. "It can be a jolt stepping in a dark hole full of webs, so I asked if you're afraid of them, but I promise you, none are here."

"O-okay."

"Want me to put you down—?"

"No!" I clung tighter.

"Stupid question. Don't know why I said it." Bane encircled me instead, holding me close. "I'm sorry, Kenzie. After everything you told me, I wanted to make you smile. All I did was scare the shit out of you."

"It was a sweet thought, Bane." Our cheeks glued together—closer to him was farther from the webs. "But I go for funny movies and stand-up, not sticky death traps."

"It wasn't the webs I wanted you to see. Well, it was, but— Look."

The hollow lit up as if someone flicked a switch, bathing us in glowing fairy lights. I gasped, my head falling back, taking it all in and making no sense of it. What was I looking at?

"When it rains, droplets collect on the webs," Bane replied. I hadn't noticed I spoke the question out loud. "The hollow is protected by the trees. The raindrops are slower to dry, and if you know a guy who can position mirrors in the right places at the right angles, then this is an incredible place to visit at night—"

"—to see the stars." I laughed—a bright, wonderous sound at the beauty of nature, and one clever man. Silken strings carried their prizes—tiny drops reflecting one thin light beam into thousands of refracted spotlights. They twinkled like the starry sky I watched on television. It was beautiful and haunting and strange. It was perfect.

"It's incredible, Bane." I kissed his cheek, tasting the salty sweetness of him on my lips. "Thank you."

"I'm happy you like it. I—"

Something touched my shoulder. "What was that?! Bane, it's a spider, get it off!"

"Okay, time to go." Bane rushed us both out. Only after confirming five times that what fell on me was water, not a living creature, did I calm down. What I didn't do was let him put me down. My hands and legs would not unlock. I put it down to experiencing the most terrifying and thrilling moments of my life at the same time. Forget fight or flight, my body went with freeze.

Bane was soothing, stroking my hair. He didn't voice a complaint about carrying a grown woman for twenty minutes through the forest.

"Your heart's beating so fast, it's drumming a beat on my chest."

"You can thank yourself," I said. "Next time, say webs. Hundreds and hundreds of webs."

"There won't be a next time with anyone else. You're the only person I've shown that to."

"Really?" I looked at him in surprise. "Why?"

He smiled. "Not many people visit me. Those that do, I didn't think they'd appreciate it—webs, mirrors, and rain. But you..." Bane grasped my chin between two fingers. "I'm glad it made you laugh, if only for a little while. You were born to laugh, Mackenzie. It's the sweetest sound man could never replicate. It almost made me believe I could make a different choice."

Ducking down, I buried my face in his neck. Bane was right, this was a problem.

I liked him too.

# Chapter Seven

The next morning, Bane packed an obscene number of weapons—and only weapons—loaded them into a cart, and pulled it behind on our trek out of the woods. Thatcher waited for us at the mile marker with his Jeep and two guards. Sienna ran up and hugged him. When she found time to become best friends with the head of security, I had no idea.

"Here's the deal," Bane said. He reclined against the car door—and therefore was unaware of how many times I stole glances at him.

*Real great, Blaine. Develop a crush on a hermit who's sworn off relationships. On top of the crush on a single dad who believes you're too young for him. On top of the sweet, devilish, sexy guy who'll lose interest fast when he finds out you're fantasizing about all of his brothers.*

Guilt sobered me. Even if I got to a place I felt comfortable dating, what would it be like dating Sunny and being around his brothers all the time? The night before while I slept in Bane's bed, breathing in his woody autumn smell, I had a wild thought about Sunny's mother and her men. Bane, Liam, and Sole knew a poly relationship could work, they'd be more understanding of the idea than most men.

A wild thought, immediately killed by Bane's confession. He had to share his mother and fathers which drove a need to bond exclusively with his biological dad. If he ever gave up his vow of singleness, why would he do it for a love he'd have to share too? Why would Sole or Liam for that matter? I didn't have a reason to believe they wanted that kind of relationship either.

*So choose. Choose the man who chooses you.*

Sienna roused me. "Kenzie, are you listening?"

"What? Sorry, no. I missed it."

"I said," Bane repeated. "We're stopping by the compound first. Change, eat, conceal all the weapons you like on your body. Then, we're heading out."

"Alright. I'm ready."

"Remember what I told you," he said. "You too, Sienna. First thought, first impulse. Don't hesitate, take shit, or break eye contact first."

I repeated his instructions to myself during the ride, the trip up the elevator to Sunny's suite, and while I changed out of Bane's borrowed clothes into my new persona. When Sienna and I came out, a man stood before Sunny's front door. I almost didn't recognize him.

Gone was Bane's oil-stained jeans and inked chest. Polished loafers hid the castles on his feet and a suit dipped in midnight clung to his body. He opted to leave the tie on the rack. Bane's dark-blue shirt buttoned partway, giving a glimpse to those who could look but not touch.

*I'm the only one who can't touch. Bane's fair game to the women he has no feelings for.*

Bane accepted a gun from Liam, sliding it in his back pocket. Sunny tossed him a knife and it landed on his palm, flipped nimbly through his fingers, and disappeared in the sheath concealed under his jacket. I was the designer—had the degree to prove it. But I could lock myself in a room for a week sketching, and never come up with a look for Bane as scorching as the one before me.

Sole and Liam fell in beside him, the three of them going over last-minute details. Differing heights, builds, looks, and personalities, but each had managed to do it while I wasn't looking—fill me with their poison.

Right then, I knew why I was risking myself... and it wasn't for money.

"Angel, you cool?"

"Fine." It came out more as a croak but was the best I could do. "Let's go."

"Like the attitude," Bane said, holding open the door. "After you."

I hesitated, flicking between Sunny and Liam. Now seemed like the time for them to say something reassuring.

Sunny kissed my cheek. "You've got this. Remember what we talked about."

Liam said nothing—simply pressed a kiss to my knuckles, shook Sienna's hand, and watched us walk on. Bane led us down into the parking garage. A red Range Rover sat in the back, beeping its welcome.

"Sir," said one of the guards. "Let us escort you."

"No need, Coates. I'm all the security they need."

A bold statement. One I shouldn't agree with, but deep down, I felt safe with Bane. His commitment to sparing a potential love from pain let me know he wouldn't give any less in protecting me and Sienna.

He drove out of the Fairfield, setting the course for Sunny's office. If I thought we'd make the drive in silence, I was wrong.

"See that bakery? They make the best apple Danish pastries you've ever tasted. Top-three date night: grab a couple of those bad boys and do the lovers' walk in Harmony Park. And over there..."

I saw through Bane's chatter. The time we spent together the night before helped me see a lot about Bane. At first, I pegged him as a stir-crazy nut, high on having someone to talk to. Then, I figured he loved the sound of his voice so much, he didn't care to hear anyone else's.

Bane was neither of those things. He listened when it was time to listen. He showed understanding and compassion when it was needed. But he also talked over fears that had to be squashed. And he waxed on about nonsense when you needed to take your mind off your nerves, and breathe.

"Thanks, Bane," I said, "but I'm okay. I'm not nervous."

"Who said you were? I was talking about Trapp Tower."

I hid my smile. "Course you were."

"Look, Kenzie, Sienna. There it is."

Leaning forward, I peered out at Sunny's *office*. "You're kidding me. It's... It's..."

"An arcade," Sienna said.

Yes. Despite my brain telling me I couldn't be seeing what I was looking at, my eyes didn't lie. A three-story Funhouse Arcade loomed at the end of the street. The Funhouse franchise went out of business years ago. Why wasn't I surprised that when the time came to buy up an old building to house his operation, Sunny went with this one?

Bane parked beside a row of cars, each more luxury and expensive than the last. He held open the door for us, and the new Sienna and Mackenzie stepped out.

Sienna's flowy dresses and flowered hair bows didn't make the trip out of Sunny's. The woman who dropped her high-heeled boots on the ground followed them with slim legs wrapped in leather. The black bodysuit top fit her like a second skin, transforming my kid sister from fun-loving psychic to vision-wielding badass. Her change was much more profound than mine.

Ripped jean shorts were my go-to on park days. The embroidered boots with flames climbing my ankles were one of my Jasmine Boutique buys, and the pink off-the-shoulder top I sewed out of chiffon, balanced the razor edge of cute and sexy. The one thing I truly needed for this show was my phoenix jacket—made in the last few months of my pregnancy and completed the day before I gave birth to my baby girl.

I was reborn into a new person the day I had Laurel. As I stepped into the arcade, I would be new again.

Inside, rows of unplugged games awaited us. Sienna's heels sunk in the swirly, multicolored carpet as we checked out the orange walls and an old concession stand. This place had everything it needed if the Funhouse company people ever scrounged up the money to reopen the place. What it didn't have, was a single person around.

"This is the right place, isn't it?" Sienna asked. "Could they have packed up and moved since Sunny disappeared?"

"This is the right place," I said. I fixed on the revolving security camera hanging over the air hockey table. "Don't need those in a twice-abandoned building."

"This way." Bane strode over to the concession stand, flipped the counter up, and made for the door in the back. Together we passed through from the sad shrine of former afternoon fun, and into a criminal's paradise.

My eyes bugged taking it in at once. Sunny told me exactly what the Sons of Saint got up to, but hearing it was nothing compared to seeing it.

*"I run every racket. I'm in every business, Angel. If there's an underground operation in North Quay, I'm in charge of it and I get the largest cut. In exchange, those operations are allowed to survive my notice."*

I understood what it meant to be in every racket much better than before I walked through the door. The arcade games were cleared away, leaving an open, warehouse-type space with two loft floors above. The whole thing was clearly soundproofed since I didn't hear a sound from the dozens of people talking, counting, cataloging, and working.

To our left, two women wearing gloves handled priceless antiques, pulling them out of crates bearing foreign airport codes. On my other side, a rack of weapons sat opposite a shelf of ammo, and in the middle, three tatted-up guys were taking them down and checking them. A woman at a desk placed under a spotlight lamp, carefully counting out a pile of what looked to be diamonds. Priceless paintings next to the soda machine. A printing press by the bathroom.

All of this was just on the bottom floor. What was happening on the second and third I was curious to find out, but it'd have to wait.

Sienna and I held still as the tatted gentleman finished checking their guns were kill-ready and loaded, then aimed them at our heads. The conversation stopped. The work stopped as every eye, and weapon, fixed on us.

"This is quite a greeting," Bane said good-naturedly. "I put on a suit and none of you recognize me? I'll give you a hint. I made those weapons that you're going to point at the floor. Now."

"It's Bane."

"Alexander."

"Sunny's brother."

His name bounced around the crowd. One after the other, they dropped their weapons.

"Alexander." A spiky-haired blond guy with a ring through his eyebrow pushed ahead of the pack. "What are you doing here? Where's Sunny?"

"That's what I'm doing here, Ryker."

*Ryker.* The name summoned the information. *Ryker's Sunny's right hand. Keeps an eye on the operation in-house while Sunny tracks the street gangs, making sure everyone behaves as they should.* Ryker was also cute in a pissed-off, leather-vest-wearing, face-tatted-biker way.

Bane treaded the semicircle. "You've been trying to reach Sunny for almost two weeks, and you haven't heard back. I bet you assumed the worst. Unfortunately, your assumptions are true. Sunny is dead."

"No, he can't be."

"That's a lie!"

"Not Sunny."

I looked around at the crushed, furious, broken expressions. Sunny said he and his crew were close, and gazing at them, I felt the loss of their boss. *If one of them is faking their sadness, I can't tell. Yet.*

"How can he be dead?" demanded a woman with purple hair and a tight white halter dress. Athena. Sunny said I'd know her by the hair. *That she oozes sex appeal from her pouty, purple lips and tree-bark heavy-lidded eyes would also be a good description.*

"It's not true," Athena cried.

"It's true," Bane said. "He was taken and thrown off an overpass. Someone found and tried to get him help, but there was no ID on him. When he died, they didn't know who to call. Eventually, we tracked him down and found out what happened."

Ryker swore foully. "Who did this?!"

"The family will take care of that."

"Like fuck!" Chin-length brown hair, stacks on stacks of muscles, tight body shirt, and a faint scar on his chin. Sunny's enforcer, Makai, shoved Ryker aside. "He's our boss! We want in on this. It's our right to take this shit's head and hang it over Main Street."

"Oooh, the right?" Bane repeated. "Should you be talking to me about your rights to avenge my brother when this went down right here in North Quay? Should we be talking about your rights, Makai, when it's your job to watch his back, and you were fuck knows where when he was snatched off the street and left to die like trash under an overpass?"

The veins popped in Makai's forehead. He did not mistake Bane's light tone for what that comment was.

"Should we talk about your rights on the day I made funeral arrangements for my youngest brother?" Bane got in his face. "Should we be talking about you at all?"

Ryker pushed Makai back. "He's hot, Bane. We all are. Sunny was our boss. We've been looking for him since he disappeared. When you find the guy who took him out, you've got the Sons of Saint behind you, waiting to tear him apart."

"Such a sweet offer," he mocked, "but I don't need you behind me. What I need is for you to listen up. All of you." Bane strolled over to us, placing his hands on our shoulders. "Sunny's gone and SOS needs a new boss. Say hello to her."

Chin high, I stepped forward, face placid as their expressions shifted from grief to something else. "Hello, everyone. I'm Mrs. Bellisario." I flashed the huge, shiny rock on my finger.

Silence spread through the room. Athena broke it.

"Are you kidding me? Bane, who the fuck is this?"

"She just told you. This is Sunny's wife, Mackenzie."

"He's not married!"

"Recent development," he said. "If Sunny didn't get around to telling you, that's not my problem. Sunny's business, and North Quay, stay in the family. She's family. Sunny trusted her. She's in charge."

"But—"

Bane plowed on. "I'm certain you didn't take advantage of the cat being away, and got up to shit you shouldn't."

Ryker replied, "Of course not—"

"Good, then the books are in order, the money's adding up, shipments are going out on time, and collections are prompt. I want Mackenzie and her sister, Sienna, up to speed on the whole operation by nightfall. She's taking Sunny's cut and Sienna gets eight percent."

"Eight percent?" Ryker turned bulging, raging eyes on my sister. "Who the fuck is she to get that much?"

"That's how much you get, is it not, Ryker? Seeing as she's taking your job, she gets your salary."

Ryker's lips peeled back from his teeth. I may have to use those eye gouges and groin kicks sooner than expected.

"This isn't right," Makai said. "Sunny wouldn't do this. He wouldn't—"

"Also," Bane carried on, "I want three guards assigned to each of them. So I'll know exactly who to hold responsible if something happens to my beloved sister-in-law or her sister." It's incredible how he was doing that—dropping threats so easily like candy on Halloween. Makai, Ryker, and Athena kept trying, and failing, to get a word in. "Never liked that Sunny chose this place. It's too out of the way, and too easy to surround. You should consider a change of venue while we're hunting down Sunny's killer. He might not stop at Sunny and go after his business—"

"For fuck's sake," Makai growled, "do you ever shut up—?"

Bane punched him dead in the mouth. Makai flew into Athena and the man I thought was Xander, taking them both down with him.

"No," Bane lofted, "but it looks like you do."

My fingers curled behind my back. Strike first, hard, and fast. I didn't think I'd get a demonstration so soon, or that Bane would look so sexy doing it. *Since when are mad woodsmen my type?*

"Anyone else got something to say?" Bane challenged. "What about you, Makai?"

He swiped the blood off his chin, gaze burning for revenge, mouth silent.

"You do have something to say. I believe I told you all to say hello."

A few half-hearted hellos went up while Athena glared defiantly at Bane, then at me.

*That's my cue.*

I smirked. "Don't look so confused. We haven't gotten to the freaky part yet, Athena. Ryker, Makai, Boone, Olive, Trinity, Koda, Xander." I rattled off their names, rippling hackles down their backs. "The rest of you, get back to work."

They didn't do it fast, but they turned. Bane said I was the new boss. *I* said I was the new boss. What could they say?

"No one fucking move," Makai barked, shoving onto his feet. "We don't know you, bitch. You don't give us orders."

*"Makai's a hothead," Sunny said, resuming my spine-melting foot rub. "Loud, brash, doesn't always think before he speaks. But if ten guys ambush me in an alley, and they have, Makai's the one I want next to me throwing punches."*

Bane's warning not to look away first or accept disrespect rang in my ear. I saw him in action, but looking at the mass of muscle in front of me, if I hit Makai too, I'd break my knuckles on his chin.

My reply was calm—almost bored. "As a matter of fact, I do. Sunny and I were seeing each other in secret. He didn't want his enemies to know about me. We got married a month ago in a private ceremony with only the family. His wishes were that I take over if anything happened to him, keep the business running and the home safe. That's what he called this place—a home. Your home.

"I will do right by my husband and see that his legacy continues on, so you either get behind me"—I glared a hole in Makai—"or get the fuck out."

I was proud of myself. I delivered that entire speech and my voice didn't shake once. The same couldn't be said for my banging heart.

Makai and Ryker shared a look. "You buying this?" Makai asked.

"Hmm." Ryker circled me. "No, I'm not. Secret wives? Surprise new boss? This isn't Sunny. No... none of this smells right." Ryker whirled on Bane. "He's not really dead, is he. Sunny was taken, but they haven't killed him. They're holding him hostage and forcing you to plant this *fake*—"

The fake was me.

"—and her silent sidekick, so they can finish the job they started months ago—taking apart the Sons of Saint." He leveled a gun between my eyes. "Who are you really?"

*"They won't kill you without a reason, but believing you're an impostor is a reason."*

Bane was quiet behind me. It wasn't him they were doubting, it was me. If I was going to earn their trust, now was the time.

I chose my words carefully. "When Sunny was six, he fell in a koi pond while leaning over to feed them. He thought it was so funny he climbed out and jumped in again. His first kiss was Oakley Morgan. She ran up and smooched him out of nowhere, then ran off giggling. He had a massive crush on her, so he wasn't complaining.

"They went to different high schools after that, but randomly met up again at a party. Oakley ended up being his first kiss, and the first girl he had sex with."

The gun lowered a fraction.

"Sunny loves dirty jokes, Jolly Ranchers, and a collection of knives his father gave him on his eighteenth birthday. But you, Ryker, love Maggie Robertson." Ryker reeled back. "Even though she's married... to your brother. Sounds bad, but you were in love with her first, and your brother knew that. Didn't stop him asking her out, and when they got serious, you kept your mouth shut—staying out of the way."

"How did you know that?" he gritted.

"How do you think? Sunny told me. He told me everything about you, how you all met— Athena: strip club. Makai: a different strip club. Xander: your father tried to trade your life to keep his dirty business. Now, does first kisses and unrequited love sound like something a hostage shares or a husband?" I got in Ryker's face. "You better say the right answer this time, because what kind of weak-ass bitch did you think my Sunny was that he'd let anyone keep him like a fucking pet, and walk in here and take over the gang?"

His gun fell the rest of the way to his side. Ryker studied me—the shrewd, calculating right hand Sunny said he was. And to give him props, Ryker picked me out as a fake. Let's hope his perceptiveness fell short of mine.

Ryker lifted his chin, eyes narrowing. "Even if I believe you were fucking Sunny, or that he up and decided to marry you in secret, why should I believe he picked you to take over? Sunny messed around with everything else, but he was serious about the Sons. He'd never name a random who didn't have a clue about our gang."

"Right," Athena echoed. "Sunny knew we wouldn't put up with this."

"And you know only a Merchant can run this borough," I shot back. "That's me, sweetheart. The Sons of Saint are mine, and this isn't a democracy. Everyone but the eight I named, back to work."

No one moved. Looking around at the still crew, Athena grinned, arms folded. "You know what? I have a better idea." Her hips swayed carrying her to me. "What do you all think about the Sons of Saint becoming a democracy?"

"Hell yeah."

"I'm not taking orders from that chick."

"Don't even know her ass."

"I say we vote," Athena shouted. "We decide who runs the crew and the borough, and that'll have to be good enough for Big Brother Bane—unless he wants to lose the crew and the whole business entirely."

Where was Big Brother Bane? Leaning against the wall, even farther away, looking bored.

*Feel that? That nauseated feeling?* I imagined Sunny saying. *That's the balance of power shifting.*

Oh, yeah. I felt it.

I glanced at Sienna. Her eyes widened a fraction, mentally screaming, *Do something!*

Bane *and* Sunny warned her that she couldn't interfere or stick up for me if the crew turned. If they didn't respect me at the start, they'd respect me even less if my little sister came to my rescue. I was the boss, they either learned to do what I said when I said it, or I run out with my tail between my legs before the shooting started.

"Cut the shit, Athena," Ryker snapped. "We're not voting."

*What? Is Ryker throwing his weight behind me?*

"She's right about one thing, this isn't a democracy," he continued. "This is about Sunny and respecting his memory. The guy told me everything. He trusted *me*, and it's me he'd want to take over in his place."

"Don't get carried away," Makai said. "Sunny trusted me just as much as you. We talked about what to do if anything happened to him, and he said there was no one better than me to run the Sons of Saint."

Athena scoffed. "Funny how no one else was there to hear that conversation. I run the largest, and most profitable, part of the operation. Why should either of you step over me?"

I raised my brows at the three of them. Sunny's plan was becoming less of a Hail Mary and more a genius stroke. His supposed body was barely cold and these three were fighting over who got the crown. *Maybe one of them paid a bald man to help them take it, and if they did, Thatcher was right that they weren't about to let me bust in and ruin the plan.*

*But which one of the three, 'cause they're about to get everything they want unless I snatch control.*

"Raise your hands," Athena said, "if you'll follow me."

Hands crept toward the ceiling.

*Do it now, Kenzie!*

Wild, scorching energy flooded my veins, propelling me forward. Snatching Athena's purple mane, I kicked the back of her legs. She swung and struck me in the mouth. Blood filled my mouth as I dropped her screaming to the ground. Her cry cut off with a choke as my blade pressed to her neck.

"Go ahead and vote," I said, flashing a smirk so Sunny, I wished he was there to see it. "I kill winner."

Twin barrels pointed at my face. "Let her go," Ryker said.

Someone flashed out of the corner of my eye. Sienna kicked Athena's hand, sending the knife she tried to conceal flying.

I smiled at my sister. "Thank you." For Ryker and Makai, "Go on, shoot me. I'm certain I'll *slice* on the way down, taking at least one of you traitors with me." I twisted her hair, stomach twisting with it when Athena screamed.

"Traitor?" said Makai. "We're not—"

"Save it! I'm more certain now than when I came in. Sunny's dead, do you hear me? Dead! Some lowlife piece of shit killed my husband, and instead of respecting his choice for boss, you three are snapping and snarling at each other to step over his corpse onto the throne."

"That's not true." Ryker's hand shook. "I'm not—"

"You're pathetic," I spat. "Some best friend you turned out to be."

His gun shook harder.

"The only thing that matters right now is Sunny and avenging his death. His family may not want you involved, but you were his family too. You want to make this right for Sunny just as much as I do... or at least I thought you did. Maybe what you really want are the Sons of Saint and this borough. Maybe you killed Sunny to get it."

"Fuck you!" Makai's spittle dotted my cheek. Real, quavering emotion crept into his voice. "We loved Sunny. He was our brother."

"Then stop wasting time. Ryker, Makai, Boone, Olive, Trinity, Koda, and Xander, we're going to Sunny's office where I'll tell you all I know about Sunny's attack and the person behind it. We're coming up with a plan to find this bastard by the end of the week. The man who killed my Sunny doesn't get to live longer than that.

"The rest of you, *get back to work*." It was a miracle, or it seemed like one. The crowd peeled off and went back to their stations, resuming cleaning their guns, counting diamonds, and prepping antiques without back talk or questions. And Makai and Ryker, they lowered their guns.

"This doesn't mean I believe you are who you say you are," Ryker warned, "but I'll throw in with anyone who wants that motherfucker dead." He turned away. "For now."

I released Athena, tossing her away from me. Guilt tore me as she hit the floor. She had every reason not to trust me and want to protect her crew from a random flashing rings, demanding they hand over their business and money. Plus, Sunny liked her. He said she was smart, funny, and badass, and the two of us were meant to be friends.

*I did what I had to do to earn everyone's respect. At least it's done now. I won't have to pull a knife on anyone ever again.*

Athena straightened—her hair wild and sticking up. She leaned as I passed, lips brushing on my ear.

"Just so you know, your *husband* was fucking me up until the night he disappeared. Did he tell you that?"

I stiffened. *No, he did not.*

"I'm so glad you're here, boss. Let's go get our Sunny's killer." She blew past, slamming into Sunny's office, though I took her name off the list of invitees.

*Almost,* I corrected. *I earned almost everyone's respect. Athena was going to be a problem.*

"Are you okay?" Sienna whispered.

"Fine." My mouth was aching. I already felt my lips swelling. "I'll throw up later."

"Nicely done." Bane stroked the back of my hand. "Sunny was right about you. You're one of a kind."

"And you were even less of a help than I knew you'd be. They were talking mutiny, and you just hung out in the back."

"Had to. Once you got going, I couldn't let them see my semi."

"Again, Bane, wow."

"You're almost there, Kenzie. Get them talking about the night Sunny was thrown and all that led up to it. If Bald Man's accomplice is in that room, eventually he or she will slip up."

Bane trailed us to the office door. "I'm heading out," he called inside. "You all play nice. Especially you—Athena, Makai, Ryker." Bane's voice changed. "If anything happens to them, I'll start with the three of you first."

That was not in the script. Actually, I was pretty sure saying something like that went against Bane's code—never reveal you care. Don't expose a weakness.

But everyone heard it as my blasted cheeks heated. Bane cared, and he'd kill anyone that hurt me.

He shut the door and I recovered quickly, putting my bitch-boss mask back on. Sunny's office—*my* office—claimed a few of the arcade games. They lined the walls, a mishmash of color clashing against the blue, red, and orange carpet. In the middle of the room sat his desk and the leather, high-backed chair, I reclined in it under the watchful eyes of the wary leaders of his crew.

Sunny ran a full-scale criminal enterprise. Eight different rackets within one gang, under one boss, and that boss was me. For as long as Sunny was away, I wasn't just playing at being the boss, he expected me to run the gang for real.

*"You don't know the kind of sweet, green cash my crew brings in daily, but you'll find out. If the traitor is one of my guys and he takes over, he'll have more than enough to launch a full attack on every Merchant. Law-abiding soccer moms would turn hit woman for the cash reward he could put on Liam, Genny, Bane, and my parents' heads. You're running the show now, Yummy Mummy."* That knee-weakening grin flashed in my mind. *"No pressure."*

"I'm running the show now." Sienna lay out on my desk, adopting Genny's pose better than I ever could. "While we're working out how to find Sunny's killer, I want you, Koda—" I pointed at the slim, hottish guy wearing wire-frame glasses and a flaming goat tattoo on his neck—hard to miss. "To get me the books. All of them. Logs on the shipments that went out and came in since Sunny was taken. Get me the ledger, the roster, the collection schedule, and let everyone out there know I'll be speaking to each of them—today."

"Yes, boss."

"Yes, boss." Leaning back, I gifted them a bleeding-red smile. "Has a nice ring to it."

*BANE*

I sat atop the car hood, basking in the setting sun. Out of the woods, the afternoon air came with car exhaust, cigarette smoke, and gasoline. After stopping by Waterford and in on my Scourges, I ditched the monkey suit and returned for Sienna and Kenzie.

*Kenzie.*

The sight of her dropping Athena—one of the toughest women in Sunny's gang—played on a loop. Any fantasy I entertained about hooking up with her, rolling around on a mat sans clothes, her clinging to me as tight as she did the night before while I plowed her, making her scream louder than a damn spider—

All those thoughts were pushed down and buried. Mackenzie was dangerous. I guessed it during her snarky first greeting. Sensed it as she told me her story, tears soaking her sun-kissed cheeks. And I confirmed it as she lashed out without hesitation or mercy. Brutality and compassion in one beautiful package. If there was such a thing as soulmates, Mackenzie Blaine would be mine.

The sisters trudged outside, making for me and the car.

*That's why when this is over, I'm going back to my cabin and you're returning to wherever tempting young fashion designers who can make a girl scream come from.*

"How'd it go?" I asked.

Kenzie grunted in my direction. She looked exhausted.

"Went great," Sienna said. She waited to spill the rest till we were in the car. "Kenzie got everything Sunny asked for. From what we could tell, all the money's accounted for and shipments went in and out without a hiccup."

"Did they give you any more trouble?" I directed the question at Kenzie, but she was resting on the window, eyes closed. I wasn't sure if she heard.

"Not trouble exactly," Sienna admitted. "Ryker challenged everything she said. Why did she want to do this? Or what was she doing with that? Makai just sat there glaring at her like he was trying to telepathically explode her head, while Athena did the opposite. She was the Cheshire cat, grinning and winking at her through the whole meeting."

"Unsettling enough," Kenzie's side of the car spoke up, "but wait until you hear what happened after the meeting ended and Ryker gave me a tour. I went back to the office to grab something and Athena and Makai were still inside—alone. They stopped talking the minute I walked in and made excuses to leave."

"Interesting," I said. "Did they give anything away when you discussed Sunny's murder?"

"No. I watched Xander during the part about Laser, the club Sunny went to that night. He didn't so much as twitch. I told them the Good Samaritan who rescued Sunny saw the person on the bridge. They all denied knowing any pale hit men like the guy I described, but I assume hit men don't make a lot of friends, so hearing no was to be expected.

"Then I turned it on them, asking who they thought had the means and motive to kill Sunny. Makai and Ryker both said leaders of gangs the Sons have put down. Athena said the husband of one of the many women he was sleeping with—because she wants a slap," Kenzie hissed. "And here's something interesting, Olive said Luca Adams."

"Should I know who that is?"

"Luca is a particularly loathsome pimp," Sienna spoke up. "He manipulates women into working for him. When that doesn't work, he forces them."

A growl leaked through my teeth. "Where is he?"

"Liam and Sunny are working on that," she replied. "Sunny said a friend asked him to shut Luca down. Maybe Olive was that friend."

I filed Luca Adams away to be dealt with at my earliest opportunity. Forget North Quay not being my borough, that kind of shit didn't go down in any borough.

"I spoke to everyone in that arcade," Kenzie continued. "They named dozens of enemies the Merchants collected over the years. A few of them from before Sunny was born. The only thing I'm sure of right now is something's going on with Makai and Athena."

*Let's see if those powers of perception do more than pick me apart.*

"Sunny knows them best. Tell him all that and he'll have more to say about it."

"After I do, I'm throwing myself in a hot shower, then hitting my bed running. No wonder you live in the woods." She stroked my arm. "Even though this is your world and *strike first* is your default setting, it must be draining to remain on high alert twenty-four seven."

There she goes again—empathizing with me, trying to comfort me. My life through her eyes had to be pretty bleak. A fact I should find patronizing, but damned if all I was thinking about were those soft hands, and how long I'd last if they were stroking another appendage.

I didn't confirm or deny the effect it had on me, and Kenzie soon removed her hand. I both mourned the loss and was thankful for it. The Alexander men believed in keeping vows. I had to put distance between me and her—emotional distance at the very least.

Picking out a random landmark, I launched into its history for the duration of the ride. If I was talking, I wasn't thinking about the burning handprint she left on my skin.

Kenzie fell asleep halfway there. I didn't let Sienna wake her when we returned to the Fairfield. Reaching in, I lifted her in my arms. She was like a sack of feathers. Eight months living on the streets would do that to you. What it didn't do was make her a smidge less beautiful.

*You've lived a life harder than mine. Harder than most people,* I thought, gazing down at her. *How did you hang on to kindness, compassion, or hope?*

"You can do it."

I raised my head. "Do what?"

"Make a different choice. Have everything you think you don't deserve."

"Mackenzie told you," I replied, voice flat.

"She didn't tell me anything, and I didn't have a vision either. My sister isn't the only observant person around here. I see the way you look at her, and then shake your head like you're chasing away a stupid thought. Let me guess: *I can't abandon my self-imposed exile for this woman I just met, nor can I ask her to hide in exile with me. It just can't work. There are no good choices.*"

I observed her, silently adjusting my opinion of the youngest Blaine. She was one to watch too.

She lifted her shoulders. "If there are no good choices, toss them and pick different ones. I want my sister to be happy. It's too soon to say if you're good enough for her, but if you are, it'd be great for once if good men ran to her, instead of running away. Not like the life she's lived, where every slimy, creeping slug of a man chases her down."

"There are plenty of good men out there happy and willing to give your sister everything she deserves. That guy is not me."

"Why not?"

"Because I'm not a good man."

The reply ended the conversation.

Mackenzie stirred as I carried her into her room, placing her on the bed. She blinked up at me—eyes wide, beautiful, and trusting. I turned to go.

"Thank you for what you said today." I stopped in my tracks. "You weren't supposed to show that you gave a crap about me, but you warned Athena, Ryker, and Makai off anyway."

"No problem," I lofted, and tried to leave again. Tried to keep the same breezy tone. I failed at both attempts. Shifting to face Mackenzie, I adopted calm, serious, and open—all I fought not to be. "You know... I can teach you."

"Teach me? Teach me what?"

I traced the edge of her split lip, stopping the breath in her chest. "To fight, Mackenzie. I can turn you into someone no one will talk back to. No one but the stupidest fool would threaten you. They'll think twice before hitting you, or taking away what's yours. I can teach you, Kenzie... to be a Merchant."

She reached for me—so slow I could've stopped her. Kenzie cupped my cheek.

"If I say yes," she whispered, "will you let me teach you too?"

Gently, I drew away, chancing the barest kiss on her fingertips as I pulled back. I shut the door behind me, fearing I started the countdown to impending disaster.

*MACKENZIE*

Sunny dug into the spot between my shoulder blades, rippling pleasure and pain down my spine. Between my nap, Shonda's cooking, and Sunny's after-dinner massage, I felt like me again.

"Caught Athena and Makai huddled in a corner, whispering," he repeated. "What would those two be up to?"

"What could they be up to?"

He moved up to my shoulders. We were in his bedroom, me relaxing on the chaise while I relayed my day.

"Makai is my enforcer. Athena's my smash-and-grabber."

Sunny explained the term to me the night before. Athena led the group of women who broke into armored cars, robbed the occasional house, and raided the odd safe-deposit box. Smash in and grab.

He swore they weren't on a crusade of mindless theft. The opposite, Athena recovered paintings, jewelry or documents from soulless rich bags who took from those who couldn't fight back. Like a sweet couple who sold a gold bracelet gifted by their grandmother to pay for a medical treatment for their daughter. It came out later the bracelet was ten times more valuable than Maxwell Gold Company quoted, and when they tried to get the bracelet back, they were told to fork over twenty grand or crack their asses on the tough shit.

Athena and her girls raided the place, got back the bracelet and other pieces the schemers got by taking advantage of desperate people. All were returned to them.

Hearing that story made me like Athena. Hearing she screwed Sunny up to a few weeks ago on the other hand...

"Who knows what they're up to, if anything," Sunny continued, unaware of my churning thoughts. "Could be innocent. *They* could be innocent."

"Left that up to you," I mumbled.

"What?"

I spun on him. "Is there a reason you didn't include that you and Athena were sleeping together in the dossier?"

Understanding dawned. "Threw that in your face, didn't she?"

"Yes," I snapped. "Do you have any idea how ridiculous it was spouting that I was your true, hidden love, while that woman smirked at me, acting like *I* was the clueless fool that didn't know my man was cheating on me?"

"Hmm. Must've sucked."

"Damn right! You should have told— Is this funny to you?"

"No," he said, grinning wider, "I'm just really liking this side of you, Mrs. Bellisario." Sunny sinfully rolled the title on his tongue. "Jeal-ous."

"I am not jealous."

"The green-eyed incubus of envy has got you, baby."

"I have a knife."

He howled, tears streaming down his face. "Athena and I weren't close to serious. We hooked up when we were bored and our clothes happened to be off at the same time. If she made it seem like anything else, it was to rile you up. Which worked," he said, risking another kick up the backside. "Here's my question: how much did you love wearing that ring and telling people you're Mrs. Bellisario? Told you I see the future."

I glanced over his shoulder at the clock. "If you're really a psychic, you'd know what I'm going to do to you if you keep teasing me."

"Cuff me to the bedpost, ride me, rear when I buck." He tapped his forehead. "I've got a clear picture of that vision."

My knees pressed together as the vision passed to me. Sunny wouldn't let up until his kisses, flirting, touches, and teasing finished their work—tearing down my defenses. I had a feeling he wouldn't stop after that either.

I checked the clock again. *I have to leave soon to get as much time as I can with Laurel.*

"Something wrong?"

"What?" I tore away.

"You keep looking at the time. Somewhere you need to be?"

"No— I mean, it's getting late and I wanted to catch Tricky before her bedtime. See the look on her face when I give her the jacket."

"Let's go now." Sunny laced his fingers with mine, coming with me upstairs. I thought about pulling away a hundred times during the ride up. Despite his explanation, it didn't sit right that he didn't say there was more than friendship between him and Athena. He told me everything from her style of fighting to her go-to meal when they ordered Chinese, but the fact he knew the face she made when she came just slipped his mind?

*You're hiding something from me.* The thought was a stone in my stomach. *Just when I thought I finally found you—the man I could trust.*

Sunny rubbed the back of his neck, wincing.

"Are you okay?"

He started. Sunny didn't peek me watching him. "Oh, yeah, I'm fine. It's nothing."

"Is it still uncomfortable for you sleeping on your back?" I automatically rubbed the spot. "Is here where it's bothering you?"

"Yes, but it's not a big deal. It just twinged for a second."

"It's your pillows. They raise your head too high. They make special ones for that. I'll buy you some."

"Thanks." He pulled away and pressed the call box for Liam. I studied him, confused.

"Are you sure you're okay?"

"I'm sure." Liam came on the intercom and that was the end of the conversation. I resolved to get him the pillow anyway. Why did men insist on acting like nothing got to them? Instead of toughing it out, he could let me help him.

We walked into Liam's place and found we weren't the only ones wanting to visit with Tricky. Bane held her, smooching her cheek while Genny got her from the other side. She giggled under their kiss onslaught.

Liam sat in his armchair, my present sitting at his feet. To anyone else, he was another handsome, expressionless man typing on his phone. But to me, he radiated contentment at having his daughter home with him. Every other second, he glanced up, eyes shining on Tricky.

"Are you sure you're okay, Booger?" Genny asked.

"I'm okay, 'cause if anyone messes with me, my aunty Genny will kick their ass!" she cried, throwing two punches.

"Damn straight." Genny high-fived her as Liam pinched the bridge of his nose, sighing audibly.

"What about your uncle Bane?" Bane asked.

"You'll kick them twice!"

Bane shook his head at Liam. "This girl's going far, bro, I'm telling ya."

"Kenzie." Tricky looked so happy to see me, I had a flash of Laurel's toothless smile as I climbed in the window, and almost teared up. How did I love this little girl so much already? "Uncle Sunny." She pointed at her cheeks. "You kiss me too."

Laughing, we obeyed our orders.

"Guess what?" Bane said. "I'm moving in right upstairs, Tricky. What do you think about that?"

Her mouth formed a tiny "o" of surprise, eyes huge. "Really?"

"Really, really."

"Yay," she squealed, bouncing in his hold. "Aunty Genny, you are too?"

Genny's smile faded. She flicked between Sunny, Tricky, and Liam. "No," she finally said. Genny lifted her out of Bane's arms and onto the floor. She kneeled in front of her. "I won't be upstairs, but I'm never far from you, Tricky. Here." Genevieve placed a phone in her small hands. "If anything happens—if Daddy gets himself in trouble and needs me to save him again, just press one and I'll be there."

They hugged tight. "You too."

I didn't know who she was talking to until my phone came flying at me. I yelped, fumbling to catch it. When did she get it out of my pocket?

"I put my number in there."

"'Cause you'll kick butt if anyone messes with me too?"

"Nah. It's so you can let me know when we're doing this threesome." She popped a kiss on my lips, pulling a surprised squawk out of me. What was with these Merchants dropping kisses on every unsuspecting mouth they came across?! And why a threesome? Who for the love of all that's good, would be the third?

She saluted the boys. "Until I grace you with my presence again, good-bye, my brothers." She blew out the door, leaving us in the bewildered, head-clouded state that was the true gift following the grace of her presence.

"Elizabeth," Liam said. "Kenzie has something for you."

I looked at the clock in the middle of presenting her gift. *Nearly eight twenty. If I grabbed a cab now, I'd get there just after Charlie put her down for the night.*

I caught Sunny looking at me and quickly fixed on Tricky. "Here you are, love. I hope it's perfect."

Tricky gasped, pulling it out. "Wow. Daddy, look. Daddy, look." She jumped up and down, showing off her missing teeth, rushing to put the jacket on. "It's so pretty. Thank you." She threw her arms around my neck, knocking me on my butt.

I squeezed her back, kissing her on the forehead. "You are so welcome. Have Daddy take a picture of you with your new phone."

Elizabeth loved that idea. I backed toward the door as the photo shoot commenced. "I'm tired," I told Sunny. "I'm going to hit it early. Bye, guys," I said, raising my voice. "See you in the morning."

I sped out of the apartment into the elevator. After a long, stressful day where I embedded myself in a criminal organization, and therefore broke my biggest rule, what I needed more than anything was to hold my daughter—reassure myself that I still could.

*Don't break the law.* Eight months on the street, I never gave in to the temptation to steal a bag of chips from the corner store or run a dime bag from one street corner to the next. If I was arrested, that'd be all the ammo Charlie needed to prove me an unfit mother and win custody of Laurel for good.

Eight months, I followed the rules. Two weeks with the Merchant Princes, and I broke every single one.

"Right here," I told the cab driver. He let me out five houses down from her window, and I crept up, peering through as Charlie sat down with her popcorn bowl. I didn't waste a minute pulling out my new knife and scaling the tree.

Laurel paused mid-nibble on her toes, blinking up at me. Tension easing, I lifted the window, slipping inside.

"Da!"

I laughed softly, settling her in my arms. "Very close, baby. Off by just one letter. Try Ma. Mama."

"Da." She gazed at me like I was a curious thing, spouting strange sounds. I made faces at her, laughing as she laughed at me—her two tiny little teeth brightening her smile. Laurel tried gnawing on her fist, so I sat down to nurse. While she ate, I told her about my day.

"His name is Ryker. His dad was a member of the Kravet crime family. That's how he and Sunny met. While their fathers worked out terms, the two boys were sent to play outside. They didn't see each other that often when they were little, then the two ended up running across each other at high school orientation. Sunny's siblings were older than him and had their own friends, while Ryker knew what it was like to live a double life. Sunny said they were meant to be brothers.

"Imagine that, huh?" I stroked her curls. "Those two go off and build an empire together, and here your mom is, she doesn't speak to a single friend she had in high school. Although, it didn't help that by my first day of orientation, everyone in my neighborhood knew what Grandma did to Grandpa," I whispered.

"Some people thought she was a crazed lunatic who just snapped. They knew my dad as a sweet man and involved father, while Mom never went to parties, PTA meetings, school plays, or games. And when she did, she stood there quietly and never talked to anyone. Then I walked into school, quiet and not talking to anyone, and my classmates jumped all over me. They said crazy was genetic and I would end up like Mom—locked away."

Laurel let out a long, rumbling sigh like she knew the woes of the world. Smiling, I let her grab on to my finger.

"Those who did believe the truth of what Dad did to her were even worse. I'd see it in their eyes, baby—the judgment. *Why didn't I say something? Why didn't I get my mother help? I was old enough to understand what he was doing to her was wrong, yet I happily skipped around the neighborhood? What was wrong with me?*'

"Some people only thought it, Laurel. Others said it." I leaned back on the glider, gently rocking her. "I know what you're thinking. Why is Mommy telling you such a sad story tonight? It's because for the last nine years, that day has been my first thought when I wake up. There're questions that I've asked myself in each quiet moment.

"Were there signs and I ignored them, refusing to believe my dad wasn't a good man? Was there something I could've done to help her? Was there really no way out for me and Sienna for our mom to believe that final act was the only way to free us? Why didn't she take us and leave instead of taking away our mother and father on the same day?

"Then there was a new question on my mind. It popped up about nine months ago." I gazed down at her, meeting those green, staring eyes. "If it was to protect you, would I do anything different?"

Laurel popped off, having had her fill. "Da. Baaa baa."

I nodded along to her string of babble, mmh-hhhing and cooing in the right places.

"That's a very good point, my love." I settled my baby on my knee, patting her back. "I told you all of this because... because—" My eyes filled. "Because today I finally... answered the questions. My mother was caged for fifteen years, and I was in my own type of prison for eight months. We both followed the rules for the sake of our children—never fighting back or stepping out of line, because if I stole those chips or picked a pocket, I would have done that for me, not for you. Me with a record and no parental rights did not help you. And Mom...

"I see now how smart Dad was. How insidious. The abuse was emotional, manipulative, and Sienna and I were set up as the accomplices. If Mom divorced him, he'd fight for split custody and win. Why wouldn't he when there weren't any bruises on us? We were cleaned, clothed, fed, happy little daddy's girls. We would've told the judge we wanted to live with him. And if Mom took us and ran, the police would have hunted her down as a kidnapper, returned us to Dad, and tossed her in prison. Either way, we ended up alone with him.

"So she endured him for us, and when she finally acted, that was for us too. That's not to say what she did was right, but her reasons... weren't wrong. I can say that now, give my mother that understanding, because today all the things I did, were for you. When this is over, we won't have to worry about that bald man coming after us. We'll be safe, and I'll finally be able to start over with you and Aunty Sienna. How does that sound?"

Laurel burped. I took that as a good sign.

"I'm gonna get you out of this place," I cooed. Drawing my legs up, I rested her against my thighs, tickling her nose with mine. She giggled and waved her chubby fists. "You're gonna have your own room with two drawers full of clothes Mommy made just for you. You'll be the best-dressed baby in the whole borough."

"Da, da, da."

"Mama," I said. "Ma—"

A thud sounded on the other side of the door. "Laurel?"

My heart cannonballed into my throat.

"Is someone in there?"

Picking her up, my mind clouded in panic. I grabbed the chair arm and shoved it in front of the doorway, ripping a scream from Charlie when the knob smacked into it.

"Laurel?! Who's in there?! What are you doing?!"

Laurel burst into wails. Rushing across the room, I peppered her face with salty kisses—my breaths shallow and ragged as I placed her in the crib.

*I have to get out! She can't see me—*

Charlie rammed the door, screeching the glider across the hardwood. "What are you doing to her?!" Laurel's screams ratcheted to deafening.

Seizing the window frame, I propelled myself out, jumping for the branch. My calves struck the wood, and I missed.

"Ahhh!"

I tumbled through the air, striking the ground front-first. The impact boomed through my body—ripping air out of my lungs, blinding the world in pain.

"Ma— Mackenzie?" Charlie's cry penetrated. "Mackenzie Blaine! You stay right there," she screeched. "I'm calling the police."

*My jacket. The phoenix. She knows it's me. She'll tell the police. I have to go,* my mind shouted. *Get up. Run!*

I crawled across the lawn, face soaked and crying harder as Laurel's sobs rang in my ears. Pushing myself up on shaky knees, I took a step and fell.

Her front door banged open. "Don't move! How dare you break into my house!"

I shoved up, swallowing the pain, and ran into the street.

*Beeeeep!*

Whipping around, my vision bled white in the headlights. Squealing tires rang through the street—the last sound I heard before the impact threw me off my feet.

# Chapter Eight

"Kenzie!"

A hard body slammed into me, knocking me off my feet. We landed hard on the sidewalk, the shouts of Charlie, the neighbors, and the driver waking up the whole neighborhood, but none as loud as Sunny's.

Falling on top of him, my face was in his, watching it crumple in agony.

"Sunny, what—? Are you okay?"

"My b-back," he forced.

"What are you doing here?"

"Stupid girl," shouted the driver. "What were you doing in the middle of the road?"

"We... have to go."

"But—" Sirens lit the street.

"We have to go now!" Sunny lifted me and ran. He cut through two houses, sprinting across their lawns. I breathed out, but not in. The shock wore off and summoned the pain of Laurel, Charlie, the fall. I didn't move or speak as Sunny saved me, leaving the sirens fading in the distance.

We hit club street. The noise, sounds, and smells battered me, and all I wished to do was sink into a hole where I wouldn't be found. I frightened my daughter. Abandoned her screaming in her crib while I fled like a criminal into the dark.

"Whoa, dude." Someone laughed nastily. "Where are they handing out the cute drunk chicks? I'll take one home."

I finally looked up at Sunny. "Stop," I croaked. "Sunny, stop. Put me down."

He stumbled into Club Heaven's alley and set me down. I peeled off my jacket as he slumped on the brick, panting.

"What were you doing there?" My voice sounded dead to my own ears. "Did you follow me?"

Sweat beaded on his forehead. "Fucking right, I followed you. You were acting weird all evening, then you said you were going to sleep and took off. I overheard you and Sienna talking about a place you shouldn't go, but do anyway. I'm guessing we just came from there."

I shut my eyes, hugging myself. "Thank you for saving me. The car would've hit me if you hadn't pushed me out of the way in time, so... thanks."

"That's it?" Sunny asked. "That's all you have to say."

"We should get going—"

"What were you doing, Kenzie? I saw you." Two fingers grasped my chin—gently, but firmly, making me look at him. "You broke into that woman's house. Why?"

"It's complicated."

"So uncomplicate it. Tell me the truth."

My heart thudded in my ears, amazing me that it still beat. It felt like a dead thing in my chest. "You wouldn't understand."

"Try me."

"It's nothing, Sunny. When I was kicked out of my apartment, Luca sold all my stuff. That woman bought a necklace that belonged to my mother, and I tried to get it back. She caught me. End of story."

Sunny's face shuttered closed.

"That's it," I said, voice growing smaller. "Really."

"You're lying." It wasn't an accusation. Sunny spoke it as a simple statement of fact. "You don't want to tell me, and you don't have to."

My eyes swam. "Sunny."

"It's none of my business. All that matters is you're okay." He said all the right things, and with each, the dead thing shrunk—withering inside my rib cage. "I'm just glad you're okay."

"Sunny, please."

He said all the right things, but he didn't smile. He didn't grin or call me a silly pet name. The silver sun in his orbs, brightening at the sight of me, went out. Sunny gave me his back. "Let's go home."

"My daughter," I sobbed, sinking to my knees. "She has my daughter, Laurel. She's nine months old." Silence filled the alley. "Sunny? Say something, please."

"Pie."

I goggled at him. "What?"

"Pie," he repeated. "I know a place that's open late. Serves the best strawberry pie you ever tasted."

"But..."

"That's what we need right now." Sunny lifted me in his arms again. "Pie."

SUNNY SLID ME ANOTHER piece of pie. He was right, it was the best damn thing I ever tasted.

"I was an intern at Caddell House," I began. "Me and Lyla. The two of us graduated Cinco University the same year with the same degree, and got two of the eight coveted internships. Lyla never liked me in school. She thought my designs were bargain basement and hers haute couture. She was kind enough to tell me every chance she got.

"When I ended up at Caddell House with her..." I whistled. "She was pissed. Lyla shouted at me when I walked in the first day, demanding to know what the hell I was doing there. That day kicked off a rivalry I had no fucking interest in."

Sunny sat opposite me in the booth, eating silently. We had our privacy in the back of the cute little shop. The other two patrons flirted with each other in the opposite corner. Just me, Sunny, and pie.

"Every day, Lyla was relentless. Coming after me for my clothes, shoes, hair, designs, lunch. That bitch breathed malice. I ignored her—keeping my head in my work and out of the drama. Those were not fun days for me. The only one who made it bearable was my boss, Damien Frost." I paused, wishing the story could end there.

"He took me under his wing. Eight interns, but it was me he'd stay late with to bounce ideas. Damien was Lyla's opposite. In her eyes, I did everything wrong. In his, I was perfect. My designs were fresh. My style fun and unique. Damien talked me up to the other senior designers, even invited me to lunch with them. When it came time to fill the open junior designer spot, he wrote me a glowing recommendation. Looking back, I never stood a chance."

"You fell for him."

"Fell hard," I stated. "Heart-shaped eyes, doodling-Mrs. Frost-in-my-journal hard. How could I not? He was sweet, supportive, handsome, older, and mature. Twenty-two and naive against his thirty-five and experienced. We started sleeping together three weeks after I was promoted."

"What changed?" he asked.

"Talia Barker."

"Caddell's creative director." Of course Sunny knew who she was. The woman supplied his wardrobe.

I nodded all the same. "Talia fit the ballbusting, take-no-shit, doesn't-care-if-she-makes-you-cry stereotype, but if you impressed her, she gave credit where credit was due. Have you ever heard of the Phenomenal Five?"

"No. What is it?"

"The top five Cinco fashion houses choose five of their best designers to compete in the competition. It's open to everyone from the senior designers to the interns. Once the twenty-five are chosen, the creative directors vote for the top ten. The top six through ten get a spread in Cinco Couture magazine as up-and-comers.

"The Phenomenal Five have their designs featured on the cover and get a runway show during Cinco Fashion Week. Everyone wanted to be one of the five, Sunny, and Lyla was going to be. So when Talia sought me out specifically and said in front of everyone that she expected to see my submission by the end of the week, Lyla and her harpy crew wanted my head. It burned her up that Talia even knew I existed, let alone threw her version of public support behind me becoming one of the five.

"It was even weirder because around that time, Talia was in rare form, snapping and cutting down anyone that brought her a dress with a loose string or a button out of alignment. Her favorite, Damien, got the brunt of it. Supporting me and not him was just another slap in his face. But she truly loved my work, said I'd go further than Caddell House one day. Me, Lyla, and three of her crew passed the first round."

"What happened then?"

"What happened then," I whispered, cutting pieces of my pie that didn't make it to my lips. "What happened is I threw up for five straight mornings in a row. I was tired, achy, and my period was late. I told Damien I was pregnant, stupidly believing he'd think it was good news."

"Where does that shit live?" Sunny growled. "You haven't finished, and I already know I'm going to find him when this is over."

I laid my hands on his. "Damien is basically unreachable these days. You see, the reason Talia was furious with him and taking it out on everyone was because she suspected him of cheating."

"Cheating? They were together?"

"Yep," I drew out. "They kept the relationship a secret. Talia didn't want her sex life a topic of discussion at work, and Damien... well, it was easier to trick foolish little designers into bed when they didn't know you were engaged."

"Engaged? The fucking shit-sucking, micro-dick cunt. Should've been a jizz stain on his mommy's mattress."

His tirade tugged the corner of my lips. "Pretty sure I said the same thing when he told me about him and Talia, followed by denying Laurel was his. He'd have nothing to do with my kid, and if I opened my mouth, he'd have me fired. Damien had a lot to lose. If Talia found out that not only were the rumors true, but he also knocked up a junior designer, he'd lose everything. She was one of the biggest names in Cinco fashion with an even bigger eight-figure trust fund. While Damien was a thirty-five-year-old marketing undergrad from Ohio who made sixty thousand a year. With millions on the line, he decided he wouldn't leave it to chance, and teamed up with Lyla to destroy me."

"Lyla," Sunny said. "Was he sleeping with her too?"

"I don't know," I replied honestly. "Maybe they were, or maybe Lyla was just waiting for her moment and Damien stepped up at the perfect time. About a week after I told Damien I was pregnant, Talia called me into her office—Damien and Lyla were both there. Talia said she knew the truth. The designs I submitted were stolen and passed off as my own. I was out of the Phenomenal Five, and out of Caddell House."

"They convinced her you faked your designs? How could they do that?"

"It was easy, Sunny. That's the worst part—how easy it was to destroy my life. Gotta give Lyla credit though. She thought of everything," I spat. "Lyla dug up my old college roommate and paid her to say she created the Phenomenal Five designs. She didn't stop there, Courtney told them she sketched everything in the portfolio I submitted for the Caddell internship."

Sunny just looked at me, eyes huge in disbelief.

"Courtney spun a whole story of two fashion majors sharing a dorm, and the one who wasn't quite good enough. *I* paid her to sketch my portfolio, and ever since I started, I asked her help fixing and tweaking my designs to make them Caddell-worthy. When I hired her again two months earlier, offering to pay a thousand dollars for new sketches, she did it because she needed the money, but when she saw her work was chosen as one of the Phenom finalists, she *couldn't keep silent anymore.*"

"Kenzie, that's insane. Why in the fuck would Barker believe her? You sketched those designs yourself. Hang around you for longer than an hour, and I'll catch you with your head over a sketchpad. How could she watch you design that line and then swallow her bullshit?"

"She didn't see me design my portfolio or the Phenom line. The drafting, the samples, the rejects, the maybes—all of it I did at home because I didn't put it past Lyla to sabotage me. Isn't that ironic?"

"So Talia fired you," he said softly. "Just like that."

"No. It was when Courtney revealed my drafts, samples, and maybes for my line and my old portfolio that she believed her. '*How could she have gotten her hands on these if they were locked up in my apartment like I claimed? Why would she have kept year-old discarded sketches of an old roommate?*' My story didn't make any sense, Talia said. She ordered me to get out before security threw me out. I was a stain on Caddell's good name.

"I snapped back that my story made sense when you factored in that Lyla was a jealous bitch and I was carrying Damien's love child." I scoffed. "Talia did not take that well. I was a liar and a thief, and if she ever saw me again, she'd make me regret ever hearing the name Caddell. Security threw me out on my ass, and five months later, Talia and Damien got married and she received a huge promotion. She's head of design at Caddell House New York. Last I heard, the darling couple are planning to adopt a son."

"I'm so sorry, Kenzie." Sunny squeezed my fingers. "If it makes you feel any better... I have a private plane and New York is a three-hour flight. Damien doesn't have to make it through the night."

I laughed mirthlessly. Sunny didn't.

Smile fading, I gazed into his quicksilver eyes, and didn't see the sun. *He's kidding, isn't he?*

"No," I said, just in case. "That's not necessary. Damien Frost is a loathsome cockroach and I pray someone dips his balls in honey and turns him into a piñata for bears, but still, he gave me the greatest gift. What I want most of all is for the kind, sweet man I used to know to reappear, so my daughter can know her father."

"That sperm donor isn't her father. A real father wouldn't give her up for all the money in every trust fund." Sunny tipped my chin, preventing me from looking away. "My dad used to say: Money is easy. There's always money to make, find, or steal. You can't say the same about family. When they're gone, you can't steal them back. So never get so seduced by the game you forget what's important. Dollar bills won't sing your children to sleep, or blow you."

I snorted, clapping a hand over my mouth to smother a laugh. "That started so profound."

"Yeah, well, my old man's one of a kind."

"But not wrong."

Sunny shook his head. "All of this is wrong. They can't get away with what they've done."

"They have gotten away with it, Sunny. Talia burned me. She warned every fashion house in a three-state radius that I was a thieving, cheating liar. No one would hire me. They wouldn't even let me past reception, so for months, I tried to clear my name.

"It took me a while, but I finally figured out how Lyla did it. Back at Cinco U, she heard I was applying for the Caddell internship too. She must've paid Courtney to make copies of my designs and get her hands on my drafts. She was probably planning to get the edge over me by peeking at my concepts, then designing something better. Then we both got the internship and that was that. When Damien teamed up with her to drive me out, she thought what almost worked before would work now. Damien still had a key to my place. It was easy for them to get all my drafts and samples, and give them to Courtney for her big performance.

"I tracked Courtney down two months after, and maybe because she felt some guilt for ruining a pregnant woman, she admitted it went down exactly how I said, but if I told anyone she said that, she'd deny it. She is now a junior designer at Caddell House—the job they promised her on top of the money. She wouldn't ruin her shot to save me, so there went my last chance to prove I did nothing wrong."

"Not necessarily." Sunny fished out his phone. "Courtney. What's her last name? Don't worry, I'll find out."

I blinked at him typing something out. "Sunny, what—?"

"Keep going," he said, his smile putting me at ease. "I'm listening."

Warning bells clanged that I should find out exactly why he wanted to know Courtney's name. But there was time to do that later. Once I started telling my story, I found I couldn't stop.

"You can guess what happened. I was jobless, pregnant, and packing a degree in the one industry that would have nothing to do with me. I took a job working as a waitress, but my pregnancy was rough. I couldn't keep anything down. Threw up more food than I put in my mouth. Eventually I got dehydrated, ended up in the hospital, and my boss fired me.

"Medical bills piled up—I was drowning. Sienna dropped out of school and got a job to try and help, but by the time Laurel came, I was broke, in debt, and living in Luca's apartment building. After that monster peeled off his flesh mask, I got my baby and my sister away from him, but of course... there was nowhere to go."

"So, you had to give Laurel up."

"No. Never," I said firmly. "I went to an old foster mom. She cared for us after our mom went away. Diana was good to us. I asked her to take care of Laurel until I got back on my feet, and she wanted to help me. She felt terrible for saying no, but she was already fostering three children under three, and a newborn in addition was too much for her.

"She recommended a friend of hers, *Charlie*." I spat the name. "Said she was a licensed foster too, who wasn't caring for any children at the time.

She was free to devote all her time to Laurel. The three of us sat down and talked, agreeing to an arrangement where Laurel would sleep safely with a roof over her head, and I'd come to see, feed, and be with her every day. For the first few months, everything was fine. Then Charlie lost her fucking mind."

"Ah. All that screaming and shouting for the police tonight wasn't for show."

I shook my head. "I think she got attached to Laurel. Just fell in love with my sweet baby girl. I could understand that. I could even understand she bonded and it was hard for her to think of letting go, but nothing excuses her stopping me on the doorstep and warning never to come back to her house again.

"She dug into my past—the accusations that got me booted from Caddell House and what happened between my parents. Charlie screamed in my face, banging on that I was criminal scum on a crash course to track marks and a pimp. She wouldn't let Laurel go down with me."

"Let her?" Sunny repeated, brows snapping together. "What does that mean?"

"She said..." I swallowed and tried again. "She said if I ever came back, she'd lie to the police and tell them she found Laurel abandoned in an alley and left to die. I was a dangerous, homeless, unstable thief and the courts would lock me up for child endangerment and award her, a foster mother with a spotless record, custody of Laurel."

A low, vicious tone leaked into his voice. "Is that what she said." Sunny typed something else in his phone. "Was it a setup from the beginning? Diana and Charlie taking advantage of you?"

"No, Diana had no idea. When I told her, she was horrified. She drove straight over to Charlie's and they got in a screaming match right there on the porch. Diana promised her that if she tried making up those lies about me, she'd stand by my side and tell the truth.

"Charlie shot back if we went to court, Laurel would be taken away from both of us while social services sorted it out. She'd end up in foster care—the good kind or the bad kind—we wouldn't know until it was too late. And after all that, I'd stand up before the judge with no home, money, or job, and they'd give Laurel to someone else anyway." Tears ran down my cheeks. "That's how I got here, Sunny. Sneaking in windows to see my baby because if I took her and ran, I'd subject her to the hell of running from Digger and sketching out a half-life on scraps. But if I fought, the blackmailing kidnapper trying to steal her from me would get exactly what she wanted."

A growing pit in my throat—always there and always choking—tugged the tether to a woman possibly awake on that cold night, looking back on the steps that brought her here.

*Yes, I do, Mom. I understand.*

"Well," I said as the silence stretched past comfortable. "That's the truth, Sunny—all of it. I'm sorry I lied and hid it from you. It's hard to talk about e-even now. It's hard to admit that I'm failing my daughter, again and again... every day."

Still, Sunny didn't speak. He simply observed me, my soaked cheeks and chin reflected in his eyes.

"Say something, please."

"You know why I didn't tell you about Athena."

My mouth opened and closed. *Athena? How was she important right now?*

"It wasn't because I was trying to hide it, though I bet that's what you thought," he continued. "Deep, dark complicated feelings for her that tear me up when I think about my feelings for you? Nah. I didn't tell you we slept together because I honestly didn't think it was important. I don't pack a shred of romantic feeling for her, and she doesn't for me. I can say the same of the other women, in and out of my crew, that I've hooked up with.

"Sex isn't all that serious to me, Angel. It's a fun thing to do, like bungee-jumping, partying, and going a hundred and fifty on the back roads. I've always been that guy," he said, leaning across the table, dabbing my tears with his napkin. "Life's fun and I'm going to have as much of it till I die.

"A motto that makes for an interesting life, but doesn't convince people you're a serious person. Most think I don't know when to stop playing around or when it's time to stop laughing, but that's never been true. I know what's real, Angel, and when I find it, I don't let go."

"What... are you saying?"

"I'm saying it's you, baby. I take *you* seriously. Your smile, your laugh, the way you bite your lip when you're nervous, and hide your grin when I say something dirty. There's nothing more real to me than the millions of moments that fill your day—making you happy or stealing your tears. It's been my God-given mandate on this earth since about three—two seconds after we met, to give everything I have if it means you're still smiling."

I was not smiling then. Sunny warped in the wetness clinging on my lids. They spilled as a sob escaped me, forced out as his sweet, loving words filled me.

"And now that I finally know what you want more than security deposits and three-quarters of a million dollars, I'm going to get it for you." Sunny got to his feet, snapping my head up. "Let's go, sugar lips. There's a guy I've got to get out of bed."

"Go where? What guy?"

"My obscenely expensive, never-lost-a-case lawyer." Sunny tugged me out of the restaurant. "We're getting your daughter back."

"WHY THE FUCK WOULD you even say that, Sloane? You don't have any other cases. You don't have other clients. This case is your first priority. It's your life."

"What is he saying?" I asked.

Sunny paced the length of his bedroom, which meant I was pacing his bedroom. I was half a step behind him, straining to hear the nasally man on the other end.

"Because my retainer single-handedly funded both your beach houses."

"Did he say he can't do it?" I hopped up, getting my ear closer to the phone. Why was Sunny so tall!

"No, I'm not Laurel's father. Not yet," Sunny added. "Will be as soon as I get her mom to sign the marriage license."

*For the love of Jolly Ranchers, this guy.*

"I want her away from that woman and home with Kenzie by the end of the week. Then you make it happen!"

"Sunny?"

"No, her parental rights weren't taken away. She—"

I tackled Sunny.

"Holy shit!"

We collapsed in a heap on his bed. Straddling him, I pinned his shoulders down. "Put it on speaker."

He put his hands up in surrender. "Yes, ma'am."

Eric Sloane's voice filled the room. "—make this easier. How did the child come to be in the custody of Charlie Mayberry?"

"I fell on hard times and she agreed to take care of Laurel until I got on my feet," I replied. "Then, she decided she wasn't giving her back."

"Would I be speaking to Laurel's mother?"

"Yes, I'm her mother, and I never signed away my rights, nor were they terminated. Social services didn't place Laurel with her. At this point, she's basically a kidnapper."

"Why haven't you involved the police?"

"She threatened to tell them horrible lies about me. That I abused and abandoned Laurel, and she was the hero who saved her. At the time I was broke and homeless. I didn't have the means to fight her, and if I was willing to risk my daughter in the system, I wouldn't have gone to Charlie in the first place."

"I see." The *click-click-clack* of keys sounded on the other end. "The picture is becoming dreadfully clear."

"Can you do anything?"

"Oh, yes, Miss Blaine. I can do a lot with this. Wait for me to call you," he said. "I should have more information by end of day."

I placed a hand over my racing heart as Sunny ended the call. "That's good, right? He can get her back?"

"He *will* get her back."

"What do I do? How do I help? How do I make this go faster?" I shot rapid-fire questions at him. "And what about last night? I broke into her house. She'll have told the police everything by now. They're probably looking for me."

"Burglars that sneak in to feed and burp babies, and then skip off without taking anything, aren't high on their manhunt list."

"Charlie will change that. She refuses to give Laurel up, Sunny. That woman has actually convinced herself she's Laurel's rightful mother."

"Course she's obsessed." Sunny snuck a hand under my blouse, drawing slow circles above my tailbone. Goose bumps rippled under his touch. "Everyone who meets you wants a piece of you. Some take it too far."

I groaned. "Just tell me I'll get her back."

"You'll get Laurel back."

My tension might've eased, if not for Sunny's touch tightening my muscles.

"Soooo," he said. "Does Laurel look like me?"

"Why in the world would she?"

He shrugged. "Because I've rewritten our history. We actually met a year and a half ago at a club. I was drunk off my ass, and you were the naughty vixen who took me in the back for a ride. I stumbled home unaware we met, and you strode off with prime Bellisario seed and didn't know."

I laughed. "That's a nice story. I almost wish it was the real one." Climbing off, I swooped and kissed Sunny—a brush of the lips that was over as soon as it started. "Thank you, Sunny. No matter what happens... thank you."

"She'll be home soon, Angel. Trust me."

"I do."

I was almost to the door. "Kenzie, wait."

"What's wrong?"

"Seeing as you're feeling me hard right now." Sunny hopped off the bed and jerked his chin at it. "You, me, shall we...?" He thrust his hips, hands grabbing on an imaginary Kenzie as he drilled her from the back. I slammed the door on Sunny's raucous laughter.

"Ridiculous man," I muttered between titters. I got my bedroom door closed before my happy, light giggles escaped. Sliding down to the floor, I cupped my heart again.

*"It's been my God-given mandate on this earth since about three—two seconds after we met, to give everything I have if it means you're still smiling."*

To say I was feeling him was the understatement of the millennium. His beautiful speech. The hours he spent all night, then half the morning, dragging his lawyer out of bed to fight for my daughter. It shocked me that there was ever a time I wondered if Sole was a man I could trust. Or how I scared myself wondering if he was another Damien in disguise—charming, kind, and supportive when he wanted something, and a beast if I got in his way.

Sole was nothing like Damien, or Luca, or my father. He respected me—looked at me and saw a strong, smart, fierce woman even when I didn't see her in myself. Fuck yes, I wanted Sunny in every way possible. The fears and excuses in our way were fading fast.

Sunny better get ready.

"YOU CAN'T DO THIS."

"Step aside, ma'am."

"No!" Charlie shoved on the wood, fighting to slam the door in their face. "You can't take her. Laurel belongs here."

Clearing his throat, Sloane plucked the warrant from the officer and stuck it through the doorjamb. "According to this, we can take her. Ms. Mayberry, I represent Laurel Blaine's mother, she—"

"She's a druggie and a thief! You're not putting Laurel in the hands of that whore!"

Sienna gripped my hand harder. I had a vision of my own—seeing her tear across the sidewalk and rip Charlie's head off. I grasped her shoulder in case, holding her back. Sunny's arm slid around us both.

Sunny was out and he shouldn't be—he risked too much standing in the open in broad daylight with two cops, but he took that risk in a blond wig and tanning lotion which veered his sun-blessed skin into orange-blessed. For me, he was here.

"Whore?" Sloane in action was even better than the efficient, no-nonsense man I spoke to on the phone. He told me I'd have my daughter in my arms within twenty-four hours. Watching him then, I shortened the timeline. "One in the many lies Miss Bellisario warned us you've leveled against her. She has a spotless record. No arrests or convictions for drugs, solicitation, neglect, or abuse. Miss Blaine is Laurel's mother, and she will be taking her home now."

"She never wanted her! That monster dumped her in the alley behind my house. I found Laurel next to the trash."

It was me who had to be held back. For her to speak such a filthy lie eroded my self-control. Sloane instructed me to wait on the sidewalk and let him handle it, but if he didn't shut that woman up quick, all bets were off.

"Stand aside!" the officer barked. "Now. If I have to tell you again, we're taking you in for obstruction and kidnapping."

"Kidnapping?" she cried. "But I—"

Her break in concentration gave him the chance to move her out of the way. Officer Guzman stormed the place. Charlie made to go after him and his partner stopped her, drawing her out onto the lawn.

"This is all a horrible misunderstanding." Charlie's ruddy cheeks paled sallow. "I did not kidnap that baby. I rescued her. I did the right thing."

"If that was the case," Sloane replied, "you would've contacted the police and social services the night you found an abandoned baby on your doorstep. As a foster mother, you know the proper procedure, so explain why there's no record of Laurel's official placement in your care?"

A wicked smile twisted my mouth as she stumbled over her answer. Whatever Sunny paid Sloane, it was not enough.

"Someone made a mistake," Charlie said. "The paperwork was lost."

"Hmm. A more accurate view of events is Miss Blaine asked for your help when she fell on hard times, because she's a good mother who wanted Laurel safe and healthy. When the time came for you to return the child to Miss Blaine, you refused because you'd grown attached and determined you'd make a better mother."

"Lies." Charlie folded her arms, her glare burning me where I stood. "It's all lies. She has the maternal instinct of an alley cat. I will fight this, for Laurel's sake. My baby deserves better than that woman."

Officer Woods looked his nose down on her. "Miss Blaine is willing to not press charges if you stop making this difficult. That's a very generous offer since the alternative carries the maximum sentence of life imprisonment."

"She's not pressing charges?! Why on earth would she? It's me who dealt with harassment, threats, stalking." She leveled a finger on me. "The other night, she broke into my home. I filed a police report and told them exactly who to look for. How does that fit into her *spotless record*?"

Officer Woods flicked to me. "Is this true, Miss Blaine?"

"What night are we talking about?"

"You know! Don't play innocent."

"Which night, Ms. Mayberry?" Woods repeated.

"Two nights ago around nine thirty. I went upstairs to check on the baby, and she jumped out the window, scaring poor Laurel. She probably came here to steal money for drugs."

"That bitch is pushing it," Sienna gritted.

"She's a desperate animal backed into a corner. It's her last chance to get a few strikes in before I go for the throat in three, two, one..." I raised my voice. "Two nights ago at nine thirty? I was nowhere near here. Tony and I were at Rocco's Pie and Creamery from eight o'clock until midnight."

"That's right," Sunny replied smoothly. "My lady and I were getting our strawberry pie on. We were there the whole time—didn't leave once."

"Liar! She broke into my home."

Woods fixed on us. "Will the other patrons or employees be able to confirm this?"

"No reason they wouldn't. The owner, Rocco, served us himself. I'm sure he remembers a handsome couple like us."

Charlie was shouting, cursing, and carrying on. Right then I understood why Sloane ordered me to stand there in my bow tie dress and heels—the appearance of calm, classy, and collected while the kidnapper ranted on the front lawn, tearing any bit of her credibility to shreds. The maternal, mother-bear side of me hated Charlie Mayberry in every corner of her soul. Confusedly, it was also the same side that didn't wish to see her thrown in prison.

Despite what she put me through, my daughter was a healthy, happy nine-month-old and that was due to Charlie. She took care of Laurel when I needed her—if only she hadn't gotten unclear about the fact it wouldn't be forever.

"All right, Ms. Mayberry," Officer Woods said. "Officers are assigned to your case. I'm certain they're following up on every avenue, including Miss Blaine's whereabouts that night."

"Rocco's," Sunny called.

My head rested on his arm. Sunny's office was an arcade, and his go-to alibi was a pie shop. Dear old Rocco owed Sunny a favor, or ten. When he needed an alibi, Rocco swore up and down Sunny was there at whatever time he said.

"But as you know, Miss Blaine is innocent until proven guilty. Your accusations aren't cause to take a child from her mother, and leave her with someone who doesn't have a right to her."

"Please, listen. This isn't about me. It's about what's best for—"

"Laurel."

My baby's curly chestnut crown poked above Charlie's head. Wrapped in a pink blanket and matching hair bow, Officer Guzman carried her out. I stepped toward her, then I was running. "Laurel!"

Sprinting to her, arms out, Laurel immediately reached for me, twisting out of the stranger's hold. I snuggled her to my chest—breathing in her powdery baby smell, and burst into tears.

Charlie, Sloane, the officers, and the nosy neighbors peeking over their porches all faded.

"It's over, Laurel," I whispered. "We're together, and Mommy will never let you go again."

LAUREL BLINKED UP AT us from her car seat. We showered her in praise and kisses from both sides, swinging her head back and forth.

"It's been so long, baby girl." Sienna kissed her fist and Laurel tried to grab her mouth for the trouble. "How's Aunty's favorite niece?"

"Oh, Sunny," I said, "you said she'd be with me by the end of the week and I still can't believe it. We have to stop at Green Mart. I don't have anything for her. She doesn't have a place to sleep."

"Mind if we stop at home first?" Sunny posed as chauffeur, sliding in and out of Leighbridge noonday traffic. "Grab something to eat, show Laurel her new home, and Liam can tell you where the baby stores are around here. He might also have some stuff he saved from Tricky, so that'll shorten your list."

"That's a great idea. Isn't that a great idea, Laurel?" I was cheesing so hard my face hurt. Laurel mimicked the grin, laughing with me. My heart filled to burst.

Fuller, Shonda, and all the staff dropped what they were doing the second we came inside. Bane, Liam, and Tricky were right behind them.

"She's so cute." Tricky jumped up and down, fingers wiggling at her. "Can I kiss the baby?"

"Sure you can. Laurel loves smooches."

Tricky popped a little peck on her nose. "Hello. You're my new sister."

"Lizzie, no," Liam said quickly. "She's not your sister."

"But you said I could have one?"

"Yes, but—" Clearing his throat, he flicked to me and back to her just as fast. "I didn't say that one was Mackenzie's daughter."

Elizabeth scrunched up her face, either 'cause she was confused or she thought he was.

Bending down, Liam presented Laurel a finger, and shook her hand. "It's nice to meet you, Laurel. I'm honored to share our home with you. I hope you're"—he drifted up, our gaze locking—"very happy here."

"Da."

"See?" Elizabeth cried.

Liam whisked her away, likely giving it another shot at explaining family dynamics.

"The kid's frickin' adorable," Bane said. "Good job."

I laughed—lighter and freer than I had in months. "Thank you. I worked hard to get her just right."

"Look at this precious love," Fuller said, shedding ten layers of ingrained sternness and revealing the soft woman underneath. "It's wonderful having another baby in the house."

"I promise Laurel won't make extra work for any of you."

Fuller waved that away. "Don't be silly. We're here for the three of you, whatever you need. Especially you," she sang to Laurel. "Aunty Bethy is more than happy to be there for you."

Laurel kicked her feet, gurgling and babbling her thanks.

"Yeah, Kenzie," Shona said. "Truth is, we were waiting for the day Sunny walked in with a former one-night stand and their raven-haired love child. Leave it to him to go about it creatively."

"I like to keep you on your toes, Shonda." Sunny tossed his wig at the coffee table and put his arm around me. "Before you go, can I show you something?"

"Sure. It won't take long, will it?"

"Not long at all."

Sunny's hand was warm on my back, leading us past my and Sienna's rooms to the double doors at the end of the hall. Twisting the knob, he let it swing inward. I gasped, and Laurel grabbed my jaw—tiny fingers curling around my bottom lip.

That was fine, my mouth wouldn't close anyway.

A white crib tucked against the wall, draped in the featherlight wings of the pink canopy. A gray glider and fuzzy pink ottoman sat beside it, beckoning me to put my feet up and relax with my baby. Above our heads, gold-painted steel butterflies flew to the ceiling. But none of that was what made me tear up. Covering the entire wall sharing Laurel's crib, were dozens of painted lilies.

Suddenly, Liam and Bane were there, stepping in behind Sunny, sharing in my surprise.

"I hope you like it." Sunny rubbed the back of his neck, lifting his shoulders. "You're a designer, you probably had your own vision. If you don't like it, we can get rid of it."

"I dug up all of Lizzie's baby things," Liam said. "This was her crib. What I didn't have—the changing table, dresser, and bookshelf—Bane bought and spent all night putting together."

"The three of us stayed up all night," Bane added. "Sunny and Liam painted the lilies."

"Elizabeth loved the fairies, and Sunny swore you'd love these," Liam said. "Though my artist skills are still lacking, so not quite an even trade."

Laurel freed me. "Sunny, Liam, Bane, it's incredible. I don't know how to... Thank you so much." I smiled at Laurel. "We love it."

Bane whipped a piece of paper from his pocket. "Alright, I've still got a couple things to get off Fuller's list. Baby in the compound again, so we're going babyproof crazy. Write down what else you need. I'll grab Shonda and knock this shopping list out in two hours."

"You don't have to, Bane. Truly, you guys have done so much for me. I'll put her down for a nap, then I'll go out and pick up the rest."

"Mackenzie."

Fire licked my cheeks. I couldn't help it. Liam had this power of saying my name like a naughty sex act. *His voice should come with a warning label.*

Liam grasped my waist and the fire raged into an inferno. "You and Laurel have spent too long apart. You finally have her in your arms again, it's our pleasure to be your errand boys, so you can spend all day right here—just the two of you. The first day of the new life you're starting together." He guided me onto the glider and put my feet up. Sunny was right behind him covering us with a blanket.

Bane bowed deeply. "Your princes are at your beck and call, miladies."

"My princes?" I teased.

"Our mother calls us that," Liam said. "The princes of Cinco City. Her being the queen, naturally."

"All women are."

Sunny chuckled. "Mom will like you. Yeah, that was our tag for a while—Cinco City Princes."

"Then we became the Savage Princes," Bane mused, "after a certain brother on a specific boat with a particular match and tub of gasoline."

"A youthful indiscretion," Liam lofted. "Henrik taunted me. Said I was too chicken to go through with it."

"Bear said the same thing the night you scaled the balconies buttnaked," Sunny said. The brothers strolled out, leaving me to my imagination. "You want to get Liam Hunt to do something, tell him he can't."

"I like to believe I've changed in the last decade."

Bane thumped his back. "You do like to believe that, brother."

Liam's laugh echoed in the hall.

"Savage Princes." Sunny's voice carried back to me. "Always thought that had a nice ring to it."

SIENNA AND I SPENT the whole day with Laurel—learning her habits and quirks I missed outside the stolen hour or two during Charlie's *Grey's Anatomy* marathon. Bath time: She loved it. Laurel squealed and splashed in the tub, showing off both her teeth. Diaper changes: My girl whipped and rolled like a ninja, trying to get away. Sienna had to distract her with videos on her phone. Nap time: Only if I held her until she fell asleep—which I did, soaking in each precious second with her.

Around us, the guys babyproofed, built, and set up the final things we needed. I watched them as they ducked in and out of the room, their whole day devoted to creating a comfortable space for a baby they met that day and her mother they've known for a few weeks.

That night, I laid Laurel down to sleep, murmuring how much I loved her. She looked so peaceful in Lizzie's old crib, sleeping under a field of lilies. I turned on the baby monitor and slipped out, tiptoeing to my room.

"—not long," I heard Sunny say.

"Have you been feeling alright?"

Fuller and Sunny stood just around the corner, their conversation filtering into the hallway.

"Are you sure you've recovered fully after the fall?"

"Feeling fantastic, Mama Fuller, and that's a word we don't use enough. Fantastic, incredible, tremendous, outstanding—all words that describe me."

"You would tell me if it was otherwise, wouldn't you?"

I went inside my room, stepped out of my clothes, and took a quick shower. I heard Sunny coming down the hall as I did up the last button, admiring myself in the mirror. *Damn, I'm good.*

Movement flickered out of the corner of my eye. "I'm off to bed, Angel. As always, the open invitation to join me..." Sunny stopped dead, and reversed backward to my doorway. "Still... stands..."

He stared at me, expression frozen taking me in. The right reaction considering I was standing in the middle of the room wearing nothing but a purple lace bustier with matching garter and thong.

"Hello."

I laughed softly. "Hi. Want to know a secret?"

"Yes, please."

Turning, I gifted Sunny a view from all sides. "I don't buy underwear or lingerie."

"Fantastic policy." His knuckles were white, gripping the knob and closing us in. "I never liked underwear. Hate the fucking stuff. Get rid of yours right now, I won't blame you."

"I don't buy lingerie," I said, slinking toward him. Sunny tensed. His vein's pumping heat called to me, trumpeting the blood rushing south. "Because I prefer to make my own. Something so intimate should be personal—tailored to the one you're taking it off for."

Sunny moved as I moved, dropping to his knees before me. Hunger ravaged his eyes, sending a shiver up my back. I forgot how delicious it felt to be looked at like this. I forgot so many things, then Sunny fell into my life.

He grasped my waist, fingers slipping under my thong's band—holding me still.

"Some lovers want to unwrap their present," I continued. Turning, my ass wiggled in his face, ripping a hiss through his teeth. "See how I designed the back?" Or maybe he didn't. I wasn't sure Sunny made it higher than my ass. "I weaved the ribbons through metal buckles—each one has to be unlatched, then the lace pulled out, and underneath you'd unzip me."

Sunny grunted angrily—those little buckles, ribbons, and zips now his enemy.

"But other lovers," I continued, facing him, "can't stand to wait. They want it *hard*, *dirty*, and *right now*." Chest heaving, his eyes darkened with each word.

"So here's the secret, Sunny." I backed away till the back of my knees bumped the mattress. "It would take you ten minutes to get me out of this bustier, unless you popped the hidden clasp right here." My finger trailed between my breasts. "As for me, I don't want to wait another ten minutes to—" I pumped my hips like he did the other day in his room.

"You, me, shall we...?"

Sunny launched at me. I went down squealing, hardly hitting the sheets before my top sprang apart. Sunny was a wild beast flinging the corset across the room, tearing off my garters, and ripping down my thong. In his frenzy, I couldn't get at him to return the favor. Between breaths I lay naked beneath him, shuddering in wake of his naked lust.

He flattened his palm against my chest, slowly running down my stomach, the tiny patch of hair crowning my middle, and over my thighs. "You are... the most beautiful woman there ever was, or will be."

My lip suffered between my teeth, stopping my moan. It wasn't dirty talk or normal teasing, so why was damp slickening my folds? Every word from his lips made me feel sexy and wanted.

"Tell me nine-month-olds sleep through the night."

"They do."

"Good." Sunny trapped my gaze, holding it as he tore his shirt, flinging it over his shoulder. "Because I'm not letting you out of this room until morning."

"I—"

Sunny swallowed what would've been my agreement with a kiss. Our lips clashed with the force of flint striking steel, throwing off sparks. Kissing Sunny was so many things, and poison wasn't one of them. His kisses were life, fire, passion, and excitement. They ignited my blood—switching on nerve endings I didn't know I had.

We were out of control, rolling and wrestling on the bed. I shoved his pants down with my foot, and he grasped it and flipped me over, pinning my wrists to the mattress. I felt him everywhere. Against my fingertips, tangled with my tongue, bobbing between my thighs. He was everywhere—except inside of me.

"Want to know a secret?" Raven locks tickled my cheek, then chin, following his sizzling trail of kisses on my neck.

"Yes," I breathed.

"Your wings are hidden from me, Angel. Locked up tighter than the back of that corset, and there's only one way for me to set you free." Sunny kissed me slow and thorough, leaving me dazed. "But I won't stop at one. Tonight I'll learn every way to make you fly."

My lower belly throbbed—sounding a warning that if he wasn't inside me soon, I'd explode.

Sunny descended on my breasts, flicking my right nipple to a stiff peak. I moaned so loud I probably woke Sienna and the whole house. Sunny did promise loud hot sex with the bonus of making everyone uncomfortable.

My tortured pebble disappeared between his teeth. He sucked and reared back, surprise decorating my juices dotting his mouth. "Whoa. That's new."

"I'm sorry. I should've warned you."

"No," he broke in. "Don't apologize for anything about you, Kenzie. Though I'll tell the truth..." His tongue skimmed his lips, collecting the droplets of milk. "That's not bad."

Locking eyes with me, he bent and swirled around my nub as he pinched the other. "It's not fair how fucking sweet you taste. Every part of you is addictive." Sunny nipped and sucked my breasts—only the heated skin. He practically dared me to beg him to take the peak. "Should I have another taste, baby?"

"Uh," I cried, back arching off the bed. "Fucking hell, Sunny."

Why was this so hot? The idea of him drinking from me was so illicit—forbidden. I didn't want him to know how much I wanted it. Couldn't bear for Sunny to make me say.

"Say it, Angel."

My voice was barely a whimper. "Sunny, please."

"Taste you? Oh, I will." His nose glided past my belly button and tickled my crown. He slipped past my folds, and I melted into the sheets.

Sunny licked my pussy as doggedly as he pursued me—not letting up though I moaned, screamed, begged, and at one point, flipped and crawled away. "Oh no, Angel, we're not playing chase anymore." Sunny hooked around my thighs, lifting and pressing my face into the sheets, and resumed tongue-fucking the shit out of me.

"Ah, yes," I cried. "Right there! Right—"

I jerked—body just about bending in half. My orgasm exploded through me and leveled all in its wake. My core the impact zone, and my weak limbs, panting breath, and dripping sex the clinging survivors of the devastation.

Sunny turned me on my back. My arms and legs snaked around him as we shared another kiss. "Why the hell did I wait so long for this?" I asked.

"I believe you were going for gold in the 'How Blue Can Sunny's Balls Get?' Olympics," he replied, making me giggle. "Want to see if you won?"

"Yes, I do."

Sunny tugged off the final layer between me and him. My breath caught taking in the size of him. The running stereotype is cocky, brash guys like Sunny talk big because they don't carry big. I was pleased to say that stereotype didn't apply to him in any way. Sole Bellisario's cock was a long, thick sword with a cut tip. I thanked fate for childbirth, 'cause that's the only reason he'd fit.

My pulse sped up as I crouched before him. "Hmm. They don't look blue."

"Are you sure?" he replied huskily, tangling in my hair. "Check again."

Ducking between his legs, I licked his balls. He grunted—fisting my hair tighter. "Fuck, Kenzie!"

*You haven't yet, but you will.*

"They're definitely not blue. This means I didn't win." I smirked at him while I traced the underside of his cock. "Can I go for gold in another category?"

"Holy hell, woman, you better not have plans for the next seventy-plus years. 'Cause you're mine."

I swallowed him to the hilt. A grand total of two boyfriends—both of them escaped demons from hell—left me worried my experience didn't compare to a man who admitted sex was so commonplace for him, it didn't need mentioning. Sunny's shower of praise and filthy promises as my head bobbed between his legs rid me of the last traces of insecurity.

Sunny strangled my headboard. "You're fucking incredible, Kenzie."

"Angel." I licked the precum gathering on his tip. "I love being your Angel."

He tipped off the bed.

"Sunny?" Scrambling to help, I watched him tear his pocket off getting a condom. He rolled it on, and molten pools met mine.

I scrambled away, one more chase in me. A vise closed on my ankle. Sunny growled low in his chest—a primal, shivery sound that confirmed what we both knew. I was never getting away from him again.

Sunny draped over me, his weight warm, safe, and protective as he pushed inside. I groaned and he captured my lips, tasting every fevered noise I made to his pumping.

It was ten times more amazing than my dull imaginings. Sunny inside me was like coming home. He filled me past my limit, rolling my eyes up in my head.

Pulling out, hard thrust in. Pull out slow. Hard thrust fucking in. Over and over again he nailed that spot. Sunny had me choking on my damn moans. I forgot how to breathe around the same time I lost the ability for speech.

Bucking and writhing underneath him, begging for more, and Sunny was there—holding me and whispering in my ear.

"S-Sole," I cried.

"Come for me, Angel."

The dam broke. I came so hard black spots danced in my vision. Sunny was a beast behind me, shuddering against my body as he filled the condom with prime Bellisario seed. A wild thought came to me that I wished it was me he filled. That I felt him explode inside me like he felt me.

*Going condom-free is a discussion for later in the relationship. Don't want to scare the guy.*

"Damn, girl." Sunny lay on me, squishing me into the sheets. I loved his weight on me too much for me to move him. "We're even better at that than I knew we'd be."

"That was me out of practice," I teased. "Just wait until I get the hang of this again."

"If it's practice you need..."

That kicked off a sex marathon the likes of which put all other sex marathons to shame. Sunny swore to find all the Kenzie buttons, switches, and cheat codes to make me *fly*. I came so many times I lost count. Toward the end of the night, I was definitely flying high on something.

Sunny and I crashed in a sweaty, tangled pile of sheets and limbs. Something stirred me from sleep in the early hours of the morning.

A distressed sound broke the peace, dragging me out of sleep. *Laurel?*

I snapped awake, rolling toward the baby monitor. Laurel's cries poured out of the machine.

"Shh, it's okay. I've got you."

*Sunny?*

My eyes adjusted to the dark, confirming Sunny wasn't next to me.

"We don't want to wake Mommy." Laurel faded as she was carried away.

I dressed quickly in the dark, tugging a T-shirt over my head and slipping Sunny's boxers on. Silently, I tiptoed into the hall, following my cranky baby.

"You must be hungry," Sunny said. "Not to worry, principessa. I'm all over it."

Peering around the wall, I was treated to the view of a bare-chested Sunny, bouncing and soothing Laurel with one hand while the other prepared her bottle. He was a whiz filling the bottle, measuring the formula, and mixing it together. The whole time Laurel fussed and fidgeted, making angry sounds.

"Yes, ma'am. Picking up the pace." He made like he was heading for the microwave, and I opened my mouth to stop him. Sunny veered for the sink and held the bottle under warm water.

*Why am I surprised? The only one who beats me out for number one girl in his life is Elizabeth. Of course he knows how to care for a baby.*

"Powdered milk. Are you really into this stuff? I'm just saying, I've tried the real thing, and this can't compare." He gave Laurel her bottle. She drank noisily, sucking it down fast. "Seems you like it just fine."

Sunny ducked in the fridge, pulling out a beer. A fuzzy, fluttering feeling warmed my heart seeing him drop a kiss on her curls. "All right, you've got your bottle and I've got mine. As soon as you're asleep, I get to slide back in bed with Mommy. For now, since we're both up, we might as well get some work done."

He settled on the couch, Laurel secure in the crook of his arm. The other balanced his laptop on his knee. I took that opportunity to step out.

"Sunny?"

"Oh, hey. Sorry, I tried not to wake you."

"I'm afraid Laurel had other plans." I took my baby in my arms, snuggling her against my chest. She was holding pretty tight to that bottle, so I let her keep it, giving my boobs a break. "What are you working on?"

Sighing, he carded his fingers through his hair. "I'm going over the numbers and reports you got from my crew for the fifth time."

"Is something wrong with them? I went over it, everything seemed to add up."

"It does, baby, that's the problem."

It did something to my insides hearing him call me baby, but I was getting distracted. "It's a problem that everything's accounted for?"

"It is and it isn't. So far, no one's taken advantage of my *death* and stuck their hands in the pot. No money skimmed off the top. No back-alley deals. And no one named themselves King of the Saints, seizing control of the gang. If killing me wasn't a bid to take my throne, what the hell has all this been for?"

A terrible thought turned my stomach. I held Laurel closer. "What if it stops and ends there, Sunny? He just wanted you dead. You and Liam, and maybe Genny and Bane too. He played games with you for a while—attacking your business, making sure you knew you had an enemy you couldn't see or fight... then he struck."

Sunny nodded, fixing off in the distance. "Then we've hit the problem, Angel. He could be anyone or anywhere. If we can't find a money trail or a rat to lead us to him, then we won't stop him before he tries again."

"Don't say that." I ran my fingers through his hair, massaging his scalp. "I'm not done yet. So far no one in your crew's stepped out of line, but I have a feeling... Something isn't right, Sunny. Did you ever tell Makai that he would run the Sons of Saint if anything happened to you?"

His brows snapped together. "Makai? No. Too much of a hothead. Guy's got a shorter fuse than a birthday candle. He leads the Saints and they'll be at war with half the gangs of Cinco in a week."

"That's not what he told everyone when he, Ryker, and Athena tried to oust me. He was on the edge of tearing up, saying you had a private heart-to-heart and tapped him to rise in place of the king."

Sunny barked a laugh. "Course he did, the self-serving bastard," he said fondly. "Gotta love that guy. He's got a temper, but he ain't stupid."

"You don't care that he lied?"

"Oh, I didn't say that." Humor drained out of his tone. "Makai, Ryker, and Athena know that none of them could step up to lead the Saints. We own North Quay. It's a Merchant borough and a Merchant gang. They couldn't keep what isn't theirs. Bane, Genny, or Liam would've made sure of that."

"My showing up threw a kink in someone's plans," I said. "Maybe it has something to do with the attacks, maybe not, but those three did not care about anyone's wife—let alone yours. Give me more time to find out why. There's still Vito to talk to. Any day now, Genny will text me, letting me know he's at Cooper's waiting to be duped." I slid my foot up his calf. "I've got my bitch-boss act down, baby. He won't know what hit him."

"Hmm. I'd like to see that. Does she make an appearance in a lace thong?"

"She likes to make her appearances naked," I purred, leaning in as he bent.

Laurel's bottle smacked him in the face. It bounced off his nose, rolled off his knee and thudded under the coffee table. "Da."

He blinked. "Ow."

Snorting, I clapped over my mouth, trapping my guffaws.

"Uh, was that a warning? Mommy's boobs are mine?"

"No," I said, propping my little troublemaker up to burp. "It's another quirk Sienna and I discovered. Laurel likes to throw her bottles after she's done with them. You just happened to be in the firing zone."

With Laurel missile-free, he chanced a kiss. "I meant to ask this sooner. Do you still want to do this? I didn't know when I asked you to dangle yourself out there to draw in this guy that you had a kid. Liam's mercenary idea is starting to look attractive."

"You know it's too late for that. What is he or she going to do? Announce they're your second long-lost spouse? I have an in. They're listening to me. I'm picking up things. I can see this through, Sunny."

"I know you can." He laced our fingers, dropping kisses on my knuckles.

Low lamplight played with his locks, burnishing them a dusky orange. He smiled—not a grin or a smirk—and crinkles lined his stormy eyes. Sole was simply breathtaking. To stare at him too long was an act of blasphemy. To get too close broke laws. Someone so beautiful could not be real. But he was real, and he was mine.

"Tonight was amazing," I whispered. "I know there's a lot we have to talk about, but that had to be said. Most incredible night of my life."

He winked. "I aim to please. But what do you mean we have a lot to talk about?"

I worried my lip.

"Uh-oh," Sunny said. "You're about to say something I don't want to hear."

"Don't pretend you have me all figured out," I replied, poking him. "It's just since Damien and Luca, I promised myself I'd do things differently with the next guy. Damien strung me along, never making promises or committing because it turned out the scum was engaged. While Luca was a collection of snakes that formed a humanoid body and learned to walk and talk." Sunny snorted. "This time, I want us to be clear from the beginning about what we want. Are we casual, serious, or casual hoping to be serious? Think about it and then—"

"Serious." There wasn't a moment's pause.

"Sunny, wait. Committing to me means committing to Laurel. You're twenty-five years old and you only found out this week that the woman you're into has a kid. Take some time to consider if this is what you really want."

"Okay, I will." Sunny gazed off in the distance. "Done. We're serious. You were mine from the second your tent broke my fall, and I've known Laurel for a day and I already love her." He pulled me close, laying my head on his shoulder. "I won't run out on you, Kenzie."

Eyes stinging, I squeezed them shut. "I know," I rasped. "You were mine from the day you fell on my tent too."

We were quiet for a while—the only sound Laurel's coos and soft hums.

"There's something else we should talk about," Sunny spoke up.

"What?"

"The way you look at Liam and Bane."

I froze. I cycled through a half dozen emotions: surprise, panic, guilt, regret, sadness, and fear. What did Sunny think? We had an amazing night together. I felt closer to him than ever. Tell me our perfect night doesn't end here.

"What do you mean?" I stalled.

"Angel, it's okay." Sunny's smile let me know it truly was. "I don't know how far it's gone with you three—"

"It hasn't," I said quickly. "I promise we haven't done anything."

"I believe you. I just want to say this and it can be the only time we ever talk about this, if that's what you want. Unlike other guys, I'm cool with poly relationships. I know they can work. I've never been in one, but I've also never cared that much about the person I was with to call it poly when they were screwing other people and I was too.

"You and I are real, and if Bane or Liam make you feel even a fraction of how happy I want you to be, then you don't have to worry about me."

I kissed him. "Why are you so amazing?"

That grin curled his mouth, ringing the alarm bells. "It's pretty easy. I can be the sweet, cool, accepting boyfriend all day long because Liam doesn't date women under thirty and Bane doesn't date at all. Feel whatever it is you feel for them, baby, 'cause I'm the one who's going to keep you."

I gaped at him. "Are you telling me you didn't mean anything you just said?"

"I'm saying we won't find out."

"You— You are such a—"

"I'm all of the above, Angel. I understand if this means the bitch boss will want her revenge," he said, backing away. "In that case, she should know the handcuffs are in the bottom-left drawer."

Irritation and lust battled for dominance. Sunny crooked his finger and lust kicked irritation's ass.

I placed Laurel in her crib, my girl drifting off immediately.

Outside, Sunny raced me to the bedroom. Unfortunately, or fortunately, he got to the handcuffs first.

"WE WON'T BE GONE LONG." I kissed Laurel's chubby cheek, then kissed her five more times. The baby munched on her breakfast, blissfully unconcerned by my fussing. "If something's wrong or she needs me, call and I'll come right back."

"Kenzie, we'll be fine, dear." Fuller laid out toys for Laurel in preparation for her after-breakfast free-play. Bethany had a full day planned for my nine-month-old. "Adeline hired me on as extra help around the time Liam turned six and developed a deep-seated desire to maim himself. Whenever they turned their back, he was either in something he shouldn't or throwing himself off of it." We laughed. "Trust me, the Redgrave babies and Tricky have thrown everything at me. This sweet little girl and I will be just fine."

"And I'll be here." Sunny came out of the kitchen and set his breakfast beside Laurel. "The two of us got plans too. This one has a good arm, and it's never too early to learn knife-throwing."

"I know you're kidding and I still had two heart attacks during that sentence."

Sunny drew me in, tongue bidding entrance. I sighed into his deep, soul-melting kiss.

"One more thing," Sunny began. "I was going to tell you when he came up, but I hated to ruin your good mood. Liam's searching hard for Digger. It's what he does when he's not here with Tricky. Kenzie, Digger's business is bigger than we thought. Bigger and more organized. It turns out Luca Adams isn't his real name."

"What? Who is he?"

"We have no idea. This fake life he's set up is good, Angel. Very good. It held up when I looked into him the first time, believing he was a low-level pimp. Liam dug deeper and that's when it all fell apart. Adams popped out of nowhere six years ago, but who or where he was before that is a mystery. We can't find records of any properties or buildings under his name, and we can't find him. He went into hiding after soiling himself in that old factory."

"So, what do we do now? Does Liam need me to help? I'll tell him everything I know about Digger—where he took me and the people he talked to."

"Do it, honey buns. Catch him when you come back tonight, before he leaves for work. It's personal now," Sunny forced through clenched teeth. "If I could be out there hunting him down, I would. Best I can do is ride a laptop, searching for a digital trace of him. Bane has the Scourges on this too. We will find him," he said, stroking my palm. "You get first shot when we do."

Rage welled in my rib cage. Sunny gave Digger the chance to do the right thing. Set his captives free and get out of the business with his head intact. He could've done the right thing, and going by Liam, Bane, and Sunny's strengthening crusade, his answer was no.

*Get comfortable in whatever hole you're hiding in, Digger, because I'm going to bury you in it.*

"Ready?"

Sienna stood by the door, dressed head to toe in leather. The two of us were returning to the arcade—alone. Well, alone except for the security guards driving us there and back. A lunatic was out there planting car bombs. The Merchants learned their lesson on leaving their cars outside unattended.

"I'm ready."

I kissed Laurel half a dozen more times. "I'll see you soon, baby girl. Be good for Sunny and Ms. Fuller." She let out a string of babble that I translated as goodbye, she loved me, and she'd be good.

Down in the parking garage, Coates and Wexler waved us into a black, tinted truck. Sienna and I talked in the back seat while we headed out of Leighbridge.

"What are you going to do about Athena?" she asked. "She'll keep challenging you, and considering your new *change in status* with Sunny, her taunts are gonna hit home."

"Maybe she and I can come to an understanding. Putting a knife to her throat every time she goes too far will get old fast."

She eyed me. "I had a vision last night."

"Good or bad?" I smiled lopsidedly. "Do you have good ones these days?"

"Last night's was kind of both. You, me, and Sunny were in the woods. We were searching for something, and excited because we were close. I turned to tell you it was just up ahead, and you were gone. Vanished like you were never there. I spun to Sunny and he was gone too. I searched for both of you... until I disappeared."

"What do you think it means?"

She tilted her head, thinking—the move was all Mom. "I think it means the answers we're looking for are within reach, but if we don't figure it out fast, we never will." Sienna blew out a breath. "Again, not very helpful. What's the point of this gift if it isn't useful when it matters?"

"At least you're not getting visions of my death."

"Nope, just visions of you fighting a war you're not winning."

"They're warnings, Si, and those are far from useless. Without the sign saying *danger: sharp curve ahead,* we'd fly off the cliff." I laughed mirthlessly. "You warned me about Damien—said there was an edge to his smile and lies in his eyes. Did I listen?"

"The only thing that rotted shithead did right in his life was Laurel. I hope he's sitting in that New York mansion drinking himself to death toasting his loveless marriage."

I hugged her arm, resting my head on her shoulder. "Your insults are always so much better than mine. Did you hear about Luca?"

"Bane told me this morning."

"Bane did?"

Her head bobbed against my forehead. "He's training me to fight, Kenzie. You should see his place. Bane keeps an apartment here too, and he turned one of the bedrooms into a dojo, and the other into a workshop. Plus, his rare-weapons collection is insane."

I tried for casual. "Sounds like you two are getting close. Did he tell you that he doesn't date and hookups are all he's looking for?"

"What?" She cracked up. "Oh my gosh, no. He's pushing thirty, Kenzie, and I'm not legal—his words. The guy basically dubbed me his little sister, and real talk, older men are your thing, not mine."

"They're not my thing," I cried.

"Admit it. You love all that experience and that they know their way around an orgasm. Although, I bet *Sunny* is teaching you the wonders of men your age."

"It's official: we're too close."

She threw her arms around me. "Yes, and I love it."

The arcade loomed ahead, signaling the return of my tough-boss mask. "Almost there."

"One more thing," Sienna said, chewing her lip. I wasn't the only one with that habit. "What do you think about visiting Mom this week or next? She's asking for you."

"Yeah," I said softly. "I'd like to see her. Finally, I get to tell her good news."

"We'll have a million pictures of Laurel to show her."

"Two million. I can't stop myself. My girl could be a baby model. Every face she makes is adorable."

Gushing over Laurel shifted me out of bitch-boss mode. I re-summoned the persona as I marched past the forgotten games, slamming into headquarters.

Sunny's people were machines. Eight o'clock in the morning and they were loading, unloading, cataloging, and counting bills without a hitch. They were also surprised to see me.

"Boss." Trinity ran up, shooting in front of me as I made for my office. She grabbed my arm. "Boss, wait—"

I snatched her hand off, bending the wrist back. "No."

Sienna burst into the office, swinging the door into the wall. I came in as they jumped up—their chairs tipping and crashing to the floor.

"Athena. Makai," I drawled, voice calm. "I didn't know we had a meeting. Hope I'm not late."

The two glanced at each other, then ping-ponged to the chair in front of me. Slowly, it swiveled.

"Right on time. I was just... leaving..."

Our eyes bugged in unison.

"Kenzie?"

"River."

# Chapter Nine

"River, what the hell are you doing here?" I blurted.

"You're asking me that?" He sprang up, circling me and Sienna like he was confirming we weren't holograms. "What are you doing here?"

"You two know each other." Makai pulled his gun. "How?"

"Put that away before you hurt yourself," I snapped.

He bounded across the distance, training his gun on my face. Athena's set River and Sienna in its sights.

"How?" Makai hissed.

"What's going on in here?"

Ah yes, because this is what the situation needed: Ryker.

Sunny's right hand coolly surveyed the situation as though early morning standoffs were as common as Saturday morning cartoons. "Makai?"

"These two know each other," the enforcer replied. "They're hiding something."

"That's fucking rich," I said. "You didn't walk in on me having a secret meeting in your office."

Ryker cocked a brow. "What meeting?"

"How do you know her?" Athena barked.

I opened my mouth. "We are—"

"Not you." Makai's muzzle dug into my temple. "Delaney was clearly surprised to see you here, which means you haven't fed him the bullshit yet. I want to hear from him first. Let's see what he comes up with."

I gritted my teeth. Sunny had Makai pegged. He was a hothead, but he wasn't stupid.

"Will everybody relax?" The corners of River's eyes crinkled with that charming smile. "This is a misunderstanding. Mackenzie asked me for help after Sunny was thrown off that overpass. We're old friends, she knows I

259

have connections. I was sorry to hear those connections didn't help, and Sunny died anyway."

I could've kissed the crap out of that duplicitous double-talker. His gift for telling the truth without saying anything at all was magnificent.

"The woman who found Sunny and got him help," I said to Makai, but looked at River. "She was homeless. No one knows the homeless of Cinco like River. I hoped if we tracked her down, she might have more to tell us. The best she could do was that the killer is older, white, and bald." I narrowed on Makai. "All of which I told you. Now put the gun down before I make you eat it."

"All right, easy." Makai holstered it. "Can't be too careful."

"Your turn. What were the three of you doing in here?"

"I'd like to know that as well," Ryker said.

"I had a proposition for them," River replied. "I heard the Sons of Saint were having problems moving merchandise. Their trucks are getting hijacked en route."

"Who told you that?" Ryker demanded, advancing on him.

Shrugging, River flashed me a wink. "One hears things. Anyway, I offered to help find the people behind it... for a price, of course."

"Offer rejected." Ryker pinned Athena and Makai with a glare. "Sunny was clear: we don't work with you, and they know that. Why the fuck did you let him in here?"

"He said he had information about Sunny," Athena said. "We had to hear him out. We rejected his offer too, Ryker. Chill."

River and I locked eyes through their entire talk. "You three are cute," I said, "but I make the decisions here. All of you go, I'll hear River's offer."

Ryker didn't move. "What else do you need to hear? Sunny refused to work with the Rat King, that should be enough for you."

"Your boss told you to leave. That should be enough for you."

He made a harsh noise in his throat. Took me a second to realize it was a laugh. "Whatever you say, *boss*." Ryker brushed against me, walking past. "When you two are done, we'll talk. There's something you should know."

Makai, Athena, and Ryker filed out. Sienna was last to go, saying she'd keep an eye on things outside. It was just me and River.

"You ass."

He laughed—mirth racking his body and dreads dancing above his golden eyes. River was homeless, and if you knew what to look for, you'd see it. If you didn't, he was another gorgeous man wearing too many layers and scuffed shoes. But what set him apart were those layers were clean and dirt never touched his crown. Even then, his devastating smile struck me—though I wished to punch it in.

"Nice to see you again too. I've been looking for you, you know. Heard Digger caught up to you, then you and he disappeared. I was worried."

"I bet you were. In between working out how to use Sunny's death in your favor. I knew you two had history." River came toward me and I moved back, keeping our distance. "You tried to trade him to repay your favor—"

"Which you still owe me."

"Now I find out he didn't want you anywhere near his business. What the hell are you doing coming here?"

"I told you." River shot around the desk, coming for me. "Came to offer my assistance."

"You came to make use of him being out of the way. Why? What was up between the two of you? How—?"

River snagged my belt loop. Towing me in, he lifted me onto the desk, wrapping me in a hug. "I missed you, Kenzie. You look good—happy, healthy. I'm glad."

Against my will, I softened, molding my body to his. "I missed you too. How are you? Is everyone okay? Are they getting enough to eat?"

"They're as good as can be expected. We've taken over the warehouses in the Bayside District, so at least we've all got a roof over our heads."

"If you guys need anything, tell me. I can help now—repay what the crew did for me and Sienna. You don't have to steal anymore."

"Oh, yeah? You're going to be my sugar mama? I could get real used to that."

"Behave," I said, poking his chest. Though I didn't let go.

River was warm, familiar, and gentle. He was protection when I had none. A home when I lost mine. I never trusted him for a single second, but I also never doubted he'd be there if I needed him.

"What was the story between you and Sunny?" I heard myself say. "Why wouldn't he work with you?"

"Ask him. He tells the story like a tragicomedy."

"I can't ask him. Sunny passed away."

River laughed, his fingers light and teasing in my hair. "Come on, Kenzie. I know he's not dead."

My mind went blank. "What? Why would you think—?"

"The city is still standing, isn't it? If Adeline Redgrave and St. John Bellisario's kid were murdered, they'd burn all of Cinco down to get his killer—fuck the collateral damage. They damn well wouldn't be chilling up in their retirement home in the Hamptons while Liam Hunt, Genevieve Hunt, and Bane Alexander continue on, business as usual."

My jaw worked but nothing came out. Sunny and Bane told me what to do if people questioned Sunny's death. They didn't tell me what to say when they flat-out knew it wasn't true.

"Sole's kicking back in the compound, isn't he? Hoping that playing dead will help flush out his killer." He rubbed my back. "Not a bad plan, but how did you get involved? And why isn't his crew in on it? I felt them out and they have no idea he's still knocking around... unless..." River snapped his fingers. "Sole doesn't trust them. All those warehouse raids and hijacked trucks, he thinks he has a mole."

"No."

"No," River repeated with a laugh. "That's all you have to say? No?"

"Sunny is dead, River. I brought him to his family on his final day, and to thank me, they gave me and Sienna a place to live. In exchange, they asked me to help them find his killer. They figured this would be the best place to do it."

"Whatever you say." I could tell he wasn't buying an ounce of the bullshit I was slinging. "You still owe me that favor."

I shook him off. "I swear, if you—"

"Let me take you to dinner."

My rant died on my tongue. "Dinner?"

"Yeah, dinner," he said, brushing my hair behind my ear. "Even before you disappeared, it's been a long time since we sat and talked. I like to think we're friends underneath your disapproval."

"We are," I replied without hesitation.

"I also like to think we're insanely attracted to each other and a bed away from rolling in the sheets."

Face heating, I did not have a quick answer for that.

"So, let me take you out." He kissed my hand, gazing at me over my knuckles. "We'll catch up, have fun, no pressure. What do you say?"

"That's all you want? Just to spend time with me?"

"That's all I ever wanted."

Shivers climbed my spine. It might've been a line, but damn if it didn't set off bubbles in my stomach. "Okay," I murmured. "Sounds fun."

He tipped my chin. My breath came in short bursts as his lips erased the distance.

River's mouth painted mine—light as a brushstroke caressing me, and sweeping up to press a kiss on my forehead. He drew back and I stopped him, my hand on his neck, bringing him back to me.

The door banged open. "Oh, damn. You two are those kinds of friends. Looks like Sunny wasn't the only one fucking around," Athena crowed. "Wifey was too."

Bane's advice wasn't perfect, since my first reaction was to jump out of my skin, pushing River away. I slowed my heart, keeping an even voice as I replied, "Looks like it. Did you need something, Athena?" I flicked over River's shoulder to Ryker coming in the room, noting our positions. "Apparently Sunny had an open-door policy."

"Relax, *boss*." I wondered if Athena was capable of saying my title without mocking. "We wanted to know if you two made a deal. Or if our friend the Rat King really has information that'll lead us to Sunny's killer."

"My information wasn't good enough," River replied, sliding out of my reach. "No deal was made. But I'll have my people ask around. Who knows, they might come up with something valuable that'll finally bring on a new alliance between our crews."

"That'll never happen, Rat King," Ryker said.

"Why do you call him that?" Fury burned the question. "Because he and his crew are homeless? Sunny should've warned me his right hand was a judgmental, privileged jackass."

Whistling, Ryker smirked. "Yeah, he should've. But in this case, I'm not being my usual self. The Rat King is River Delaney's street name. A rat on its own is weak, but hundreds of thousands of rats banding together to swarm is unstoppable. This guy runs the largest crew in all of Cinco City, stretching into almost every borough, and that they're homeless is just the bonus."

My frown faded turning on River, seeing that charming smile twist.

"They're everywhere, watching everything, spying on everyone, and most of the city doesn't see them—or want to. The reason none of the Merchant gangs have taken Rockchapel is because the largest population of homeless in the city live there, and they all obey their Rat King. River ordered his people to run them out if they tried, and after enough sabotage and disappearances, the Merchants got the hint." Ryker raised a brow at my shock. "I'm surprised you didn't know, seeing as you're friends. River Delaney is one of the most dangerous men in Cinco City."

A thousand replies shot to my mind—all going unvoiced as River bowed and kissed my hand. "That's my cue. Goodbye, Kenzie. I'll pick you up here at seven next Friday night."

River swept out of the room. Sense returned to me and I hopped off the desk, hurrying to catch him and demand an explanation.

Ryker's arm shot out, stopping me in my tracks. "One minute, boss. There's something I have to tell you. It's important. Life or death."

Torn, I watched River get farther away, fighting with myself. *You're going out with him next week. I'll get all the answers I'm looking for then. River won't get away without giving me an explanation.*

"Okay," I said. "What is it?"

"Athena, give us the room." Ryker waited, then faced me full on. "What I have to tell you is this: I don't trust you. You're lying through your ass and have been since the second you walked in here."

"Ryker—"

"I will find out why you want Sunny's crew and what you did to him," he whispered, nose bumping mine. Icy blue pools surged up, sweeping me under and drowning me in the depths. "When I do, I'll blow your brains out." He stepped back, the first smile I'd seen on him stretching his lips. "Just wanted to make that clear, boss.

"Oh, and we've got another shipment of counterfeits going out this afternoon. You need to approve the crew and alternative routes."

"Thank you, Ryker," I said lightly. "I'll be right there."

He saluted me. Heading out, our eyes didn't break till the door shut.

SUNNY'S LAUGHTER BOOMED in my ear. "Ryker said that? Ha ha, that's my boy right there, baby. Watching my back even when I'm dead."

"I'm glad you're thrilled the bonds of brotherhood are holding up," I deadpanned, "but where does that leave me? I am lying to him. What happens when he figures it out?"

Sienna, our guards, and I neared the compound. The conversation could've waited till I was home, but his best friend's plan to assassinate me was pressing news.

"He won't. If he distrusts you that much, he'll be too busy checking and re-checking every decision you make in regards to the Saints. Going over the books every night. Running requests through him first. You don't have anything to worry about there since you're not working to sabotage the crew. That's what he'll figure out, and then he'll ease up."

I relaxed. "You're right. Once he sees I'm not a threat to what he cares about, he'll stop resting his hand on his gun when I walk into a room."

"You almost home? I've got bottles of honey and whipped cream with your name on it."

Desire heated my arousal, making me cross my legs. "Be there in ten minutes. I just have to stop by Liam's first."

Inside the Fairfield, I rode the elevator up to Liam's floor and buzzed to be let in. Tricky answered and opened the doors with the code she somehow got her hands on. She ran into the hall to meet me, decked out in a pink, yellow, and purple unicorn bathing suit. I picked her up and spun her.

"Look at you. I love your suit."

"Thank you. Are you coming with us?" She clapped, bouncing in my hold. "And Laurel too?"

"Where are you going?"

I entered their apartment as Liam came into the living room. My mouth went dry.

His bare, sculpted chest was first to drag my attention, revealing Japanese characters tattooed along the *V* leading down into his swim trunks. He bent to put the cooler on the floor beside the kitchen table, and the shorts inched down, showing his—

I flicked away, fixing on a photo of him and Elizabeth in London. That was the man I needed to see—a loving father who's not interested in me. Anything else is torture.

"Liam."

"Hey, Mackenzie." He tossed Tricky a knowing look. "Your visits are always a reminder to change the code."

"I came because—"

"What are you doing right now? You busy?"

"I, uh, no, I'm not busy. My next stop was downstairs to spend time with Sunny and snuggle Laurel."

"Bring her along." Liam picked his swim shirt off the couch, tugging it on to cries from the heavens. "I'm taking Elizabeth to Sunshine Water Park. Some other kids from her playgroup are going too. She's been cooped up too long, and you have too," he said. "Your days shouldn't all be about finding him."

"That does sound like fun," I said, smiling at Tricky. "But I don't know if Laurel's ready for a water park."

"They have an area for small children. Afterward, we're eating out at McDoodle's." Liam grasped my waist—apparently unaware of his lethal power over women because my heart raced dangerously. "Come on," he said, giving me a little shake. "You two have been apart for so long. Start making some happy memories with her."

"All right." The words were out of my mouth before sense could stop me. "Give me twenty minutes to get us dressed and pack her things."

He grinned—so wide and genuine it pinched the air from my lungs. "Perfect. We'll be here."

Tricky came with me, giggling and exclaiming about all the fun we would have. I listened in a daze.

*I'll bet anything he does know his power over me. He got a yes out of me so easily, I don't know how it happened and I was there.*

Sunny was cool about postponing our honey and cream date. "Either way, you'll be in my bed tonight." He kissed me hard, curling my toes in my boots. "Have fun."

"I will," I purred, "and I will."

Downstairs, we packed into another Rolls-Royce and set off. Sunshine Water Park was a fixture of the Leighbridge community—which meant it wasn't a rinky-dink floating Band-Aid parade. My eyes widened taking it all in.

Families in designer swimsuits crossed our paths with nannies trailing behind, carrying the towels, food, and kids. A glance at the map sketched out raft rides, wave pools, a lazy river, three kid play areas, and a splash pool. All over there were places to stretch out on lawn chairs and soak in the sun.

Liam led the way to the Pelican Café where the playgroup kids and parents were waiting. Strike that—the playgroup moms were waiting. Four beautiful swimsuit models waved and called us over—each lifting their bikini-clad boobs a little higher as Liam approached.

Their kids, three little girls and one boy, ran up and hugged Tricky. Looked to me Liam was doing a great job getting her out and socializing with kids her age even with homeschooling.

"Afternoon, ladies." The incorrigible man pecked kisses on each of their giggling cheeks. "Thank you for inviting us."

"No, thank you for coming," said one of the moms. "Who's your friend?"

Liam grasped the small of my back, searing his touch on my skin. "This is Mackenzie and her daughter, Laurel. Mackenzie, this is Brooke, Zuri, Noelle, and Molly."

"Oh my goodness," Molly cooed. "Look at this little doll. Mackenzie, she's adorable."

"And she's your first, isn't she?" Brooke asked.

"Yes, she is."

"I can tell. You still have that new-mom panic in your eyes."

"I do?" I laughed. "Probably because Laurel cried the entire car ride here."

"Next time, bring along a sound machine or drive with the windows down. My Bronson loved listening to the sounds of the city—calmed him right down."

"Great tip, thank you."

Zuri squeezed Liam's arm. "Would you be a dear and take the kids to the fun zone? We'll get the snacks and meet you there. And it'll give us a chance to get to know our newest members."

"No problem." The eager five grabbed his hands, shouting off everything they wanted to do as they carried him away.

I thought at first they sent him away to size me up, but Brooke, Zuri, Noelle, and Molly turned out to be sweet, kind wells of information. They gave me tips for Laurel and insight into what I had to look forward to. Laurel was her happy self, pointing and waving at the new sights.

"Are you doing homeschool or traditional preschool?" asked Noelle.

We strode around the park—the four of them gorgeous strutting Amazons and me in a floppy hat with sunblock smeared on my nose. They did nothing but tell me how great I looked post-baby, but I admit I felt like a short, awkward waif next to them.

"I'm leaning toward preschool," I said, "for the socializing."

"Goddard School, Greenacres, and Newbridge are the best in the city," Zuri said. "My kids went to Newbridge. Get Laurel's name on the list now. If they give you any trouble, tell Donna I recommended you."

I thanked her. "Hey, should we meet up with Liam now? He has his hands full with five kids."

Brooke flapped a hand. "Liam's wonderful. Honestly, I wish my husband was half as involved as he is, or even a fraction as helpful. The playgroup was his idea, and he's been a godsend offering to pick up all the kids from school so they can play, or taking them out for lunch and letting us ladies have a spa day. I'm telling you, if I wasn't already married..."

She didn't have to fill in the blanks. The other women were nodding along with her.

*I wonder if they'd be as eager to leave their husbands if they knew he was a part of a criminal syndicate and he personally oversaw the organized crime of Leighbridge.*

*Since he looks that damn good and is amazing with kids on top of it,* another voice said, *I'm pretty sure none of that will slow them down while they're signing the divorce papers.*

Despite Liam's willingness to wrangle the kids on their own, we made our way to the kiddie fun zone. Liam chased Lizzie and the kids around a fake shipwreck, popping out behind things and roaring. The kids "fought the kraken," shooting him with water guns. A fun game, but not a Laurel game.

I carried my bundle of chub to the baby splash pool. The water barely covered her thighs and she freaked out, squealing and kicking happily like she did in the tub. I floated her toys around her—content simply watching her have fun.

"Don't move." Liam appeared out of nowhere, holding his phone on us. "Quick, Mackenzie, while she's smiling."

I obeyed, letting him snap a couple of us smiling, then more of me kissing her cheek and holding her.

Shoot done, he dropped his phone on his chair and came back to us. The serious, dignified man lay on his stomach and made little waves with his hands, floating Laurel's ducks to her. She shrieked as she grabbed her captives—babbling at full speed and tossing them around.

"Thank you for this," I said, resting my chin on his shoulder. It wasn't meant to be an intimate move, though my skin tingled doing it. Mostly I wanted to play too. "You were right. Making these memories with her is everything."

"These are the times, when Lizzie is running around happy with her friends, that I don't feel like a complete failure as a father. If she grows up and resents how restrictive I've made her life, at least I can look back and remember the times she enjoyed herself."

"Liam, Elizabeth looks at you like you're Superman, Spider-Man, and Iron Man rolled into one and made out of ice cream. She could never resent you."

"See, I would've said Batman or Wolverine. Darker origin stories."

"Do you have a dark origin story?" I asked. "We've talked a little, but I'm realizing there's so much I still don't know about you."

"I didn't, to be honest." That's what Liam promised me—honesty. "My life was charmed. Private schools, chauffeurs, unlimited bank account, and parents who made time for me every day. Mom cooked my favorite breakfast in the mornings and Dads helped me with homework. I didn't want for anything—especially their love and attention.

"I know that now and I knew it then, even so, I'm ashamed to say I did resent them at times. I hated the bodyguards who followed me around. Hated having to carry a weapon everywhere since sixteen, and I wasn't too pleased with the girlfriend in senior year who used me to get access to the compound and steal information about my parents' business. I couldn't trust anyone or have a moment's privacy, and my folks got the blame."

"Your rebellious phase was catastrophic, wasn't it?"

His laugh was richly smooth, and ended up getting Laurel to laugh along.

"Catastrophic is putting it mildly."

I rubbed his arm. "I can't say what the future holds or how Elizabeth will feel about it, but I know this much. If she does become resentful or starts acting out, she'll have a father who understands how she feels and will listen when she needs to talk. That makes all the difference, Liam."

Liam laid his hand over mine. "You're wise for twenty-three. Wise, compassionate, and insightful. How did that happen?"

I considered my answer. "I grew up faster than most kids. The year I was supposed to be shopping for training bras and giggling over posters of One Direction, I spent watching my mother sit on trial for murder and dealt with bullies daily. You have a lot of time to think about the childhood you want, when you're standing outside it. You spend even more time wishing for understanding and compassion, until the day you accept it has to start with you."

A soft smile hung on his mouth as he kissed my fingertips. "Why can't you be seven years older?"

"I tried," I said, sighing. "The owners of the time machine refused to let me go back and engineer an earlier meeting for my parents. So rude."

He laughed, shaking me on top of him. "You make me laugh, Mackenzie Blaine." Liam looked away. "You make me wish things were different."

*"I can be the sweet, cool, accepting boyfriend all day long because Liam doesn't date women under thirty and Bane doesn't date at all."*

A wild emotion gripped me. "Why do things have to be different, Liam? They're right just the way they are. Who cares that you're twelve years older than me? We're both adults."

Liam's teeth ground. I sensed his promise to be honest warring with the reserved gentleman who didn't enjoy hurting people he cared for. "It just wouldn't work."

"Why?" I pressed. "Give your reasons, so I can tell you why they're bull-shit."

He chuckled. "There you go again, saying exactly what's on your mind."

"Now it's your turn."

Shifting, he gazed over my head. I followed his line of sight to Lizzie climbing the jungle gym. "Giselle was twenty-three."

*Giselle. Elizabeth's mom.*

"She was excited about the baby at first... when it meant a wealthy baby daddy who'd shower her in cars, shopping, and trips. Then Elizabeth came, and it got too real for her. She was young and beautiful, and had a lot of life left to live. Nipple cream, baby carriers, and spit-up didn't factor into a glamorous life."

I was quiet for a minute, respectful of what he'd been through and the cost of sharing it with me. "Liam, we haven't known each other long, but at the very least, you know I'm not another fresh-from-college, looking-for-a-good-time twentysomething. I have Laurel, and I had Sienna to look after before my daughter came along. My life has always been... real... and I'm not looking to run away."

"That's just my point." Liam pushed up, sliding me off his back. "You never got a childhood, and you won't get to experience your twenties the way others will—the way I did. You were forced to grow up fast, and now you're asking why I won't be a part of it. Are you looking to be a twenty-four-year-old stepmother? Is your life's dream to be in your thirties with a resentful teenager who hates you just a bit extra because you're here and her mother isn't? All of that with the burden of thirty-five years' worth of my issues."

"Liam—"

He held up his hand, silencing me better than a shout.

"We're at different places in our life, Mackenzie. It wouldn't work."

"I don't believe that," I said, picking up Laurel.

"I do. We're friends." An air of finality hung over us as he squeezed my hand. "I hope we always are."

I said nothing, and he walked away. What was I supposed to do? Beg, plead, and humiliate myself even more? Or worse, tell him I wanted to remain friends too when that was furthest from the truth.

Laurel whined, rubbing her eyes.

"It's okay, baby girl." I rested her head on my shoulder. "Let's get dry and take our nap."

I found the playgroup moms and grabbed a lawn chair. Laurel had her fun, but she was clearly ready to wind down. After I changed her into dry clothes, she fell asleep on my chest and napped until it was time to leave.

Liam and I didn't say much on the drive—a fact that wasn't noticeable over Tricky's excited chatter. We didn't speak at all at McDoodle's. Liam busied himself with Elizabeth while I spoke to the other moms. Back at the compound, we strode side by side out of the parking garage.

"I didn't get a chance to tell you the reason I came over," I began. "Sunny mentioned you were having trouble hunting down Luca. I was with him for a few months. I know some of his friends and where he likes to go. Maybe I can narrow the search down."

"Anything you know would help. I can't act on the information tonight, but stop by in the morning. We'll talk then."

"Okay."

"Good evening."

Our awkward goodbye left us free to part ways at the elevators.

I thought about what Liam said during dinner, while putting Laurel to bed, and in the middle of movie night. I might've kept obsessing if Sunny hadn't pulled me into his room and showed me the many additional uses for whipped cream and honey.

A sticky, thoroughly fucked mess lay beside him that night. Too sticky to get comfortable and fall asleep. Every time I flipped, the glued-on bedsheet tried to come with me. Slipping out of his bed, I took the baby monitor with me, crept across the hall to my room and climbed in the shower.

I didn't notice thoughts of Liam following me inside, but as I stood under the spray, there they were.

I both understood his reasons and was pissed off by them. I wasn't some fun-loving, unattached airhead who couldn't think past the next party. I didn't *want* to be one either. Obviously, I wished some things had gone differently and my mother wasn't in jail for murder. Ditto wishing Luca Adams was never born. But never for a second did I regret becoming a young mom, or that tough circumstances strengthened my relationship with Sienna.

Like I told Liam, I had a lot of time to think about the life I wanted, and in my dream future, I was safe, healthy, and surrounded by people who loved me. If among those people were a grumpy teenage Elizabeth and her hot, stubborn father, that was more than fine with me.

*I should tell him. Give him a dose of honesty in return. At least if I get it all out and he still says no, I won't look back later and regret not fighting for us to have a chance.*

Mind made up, I wrapped myself in a towel and made for the phone on my nightstand. I blew out a long breath, and let it all spill out.

**Me: When I was eight, I turned a corner without seeing the dog tied to the pole. It snapped at me, coming so close I felt its hot breath on my face. For years after, I wouldn't go near a dog. Big or small, fluffy or short-haired, docile or sleeping. At that point, the fear was more real than the actual experience. It didn't matter that the leash did what it was supposed to do, all that I could think about was almost.**

**I've let fear control me in the same way in other instances in my life. A fear of how a man could hurt me was enough to avoid a guy who could love me. The fear of standing out was enough to keep me silent and small while people like Lyla Dawson stepped on me.**

**Maybe that's why I'm so drawn to you, because that's one of the ways we're alike. Liam, the universe, just like the leash, did its job. It stopped Giselle from getting too close and so enmeshed in your lives—that if she ran two, five, or ten years later, she would've left ten times the devastation in her wake. All Elizabeth's known her whole life is a father who loves her, instead of a mother who resents being tied down.**

I don't mean to downplay the pain of Giselle leaving you and Elizabeth. The fear of another woman abandoning your daughter is real, but at some point, it's not about age, life experience, or maturity. Because when you're saying no to someone who makes you laugh and hears what you can't say, then it's not about protecting Tricky, it's about protecting your heart.

I want to promise you that we'll have a perfect life and the perfect relationship to go with it, but I can't. What I can promise is I'll never look at you and see a rich baby daddy or dream about the Chanel bags you'll buy me.

I'll look at you, Liam, and see the man splashing in the pool with Laurel, pretending to be a kraken, blending unicorn smoothies for Lizzie, painting lilies in the nursery, and yes, the man whose gaze bites with sub-zero cold when he plans revenge against everyone who hurts the people he loves. You're rage, vengeance, passion, kindness, and protectiveness, and when you're mine, I won't let you go.

I typed the final period, panting like a marathon runner. So much for not begging him to be with me. This text left my soul bare, and if he rejected me again, the scars he'd leave on it would last two lifetimes.

*But it's true. This is real. This is me.*

Biting my lip, my fingers flew across the screen again.

But since you're also an incredibly stubborn man, why don't I make it easier for you to leave the gentleman at the door? You can't resist a challenge when someone says you can't, so how about this...?

You're too scared to put me on my knees and make me swallow every thick, throbbing inch of you.

You can't strum my clit till it sings, plunge inside my pussy, and fuck me till I come screaming on your fingers.

I bet you've never been near an asshole, let alone teased it with a rim job. You won't have the balls to go near mine.

And as for binding my wrists with your tie, bending me over the couch, and stretching me with that big cock... you couldn't find my pussy with a map and a flashlight.

You can't put a hitch in my step that makes me moan Liam Hunt with every lovely ache, so maybe you're right, we shouldn't even try.

I giggled, throwing myself back on the sheets. Writing that second half felt insanely good. Of course I would never in a million years send it, all the same, it was great holding nothing back—privately, in my room, where no one else but me would read it. Imagining the look on Liam's face was sweet enough to tempt me, but no.

"Erase, erase." I highlighted the entire second half. "Era—"

"Ah! Babababababa."

Jerking, the phone slipped through my fingers and smacked me full in the face. Laurel's baby talk poured out the speakers—the soundtrack to my jumping up, scrambling for my phone.

"No," I whispered. "No, no, no."

*Sent.*

The whole message. *Both* halves winged through digital space to Liam's cell phone.

"This can't be happening."

*LIAM*

My nightstand vibrated. Peeling an eye open, I threw the covers off. Blue light pierced the gloom, confirming I had a text message.

Late-night messages were common when you owned a string of underground nightclubs, and were in charge of the underground activities that went down while everyone danced above. I checked the screen.

*Mackenzie?*

I hesitated—my finger hovering above open. It pained me turning her down the second time. Even harder than the first. She may not see it now, but what I did was for the best. The two of us were at different points in our lives. Mackenzie was better off with a guy like Sole who still had years of adventure in him—including creating a new, young family. A man twelve years her senior with a six-year-old and more issues than a magazine rack wasn't what she needed as she started a new life with Laurel.

*I should delete this*, I thought. No doubt it was what Mackenzie promised: a string of unfiltered explanations to why my reasons were bullshit. Why make it worse for us and continue dragging it out? I said my piece. We were nothing more than friends.

*She heard what I had to say. Perhaps the least I could do was hear her out too. My answer won't change, and we can each leave it be knowing we said our piece.*

I hit open.

Differing emotions tumbled through me as I read her message: confusion over the dog story, pain at the life she lived, fury toward those who stole her smile, and splintering in my chest as I read her promises to the man she saw in me.

Then I read the bottom half of her message.

**Mackenzie: ...make me swallow every thick, throbbing inch of you...**

My eyes bulged on the first line and grew wider as I read. Who knew this woman had such a dirty imagination and the mouth to go with it? And to accompany her messages with taunts at my inadequacy. The sheets wrinkled in my fists.

**Mackenzie: ...binding my wrists with your tie, bending me over the couch, and stretching me with that big cock... you couldn't find my pussy with a map and a flashlight.**

*I can't find your pussy, can I?*

The old Liam—young, brash, daring to prove himself—rose from the depths, bringing his savagery and arrogance with him. But he didn't come alone. Lust flooded my veins, rushing down and engorging my cock.

Mackenzie formed in my mind as irresistible as her strutting around dripping wet in that bikini—unaware of the eyes following her wherever she went, including mine. I felt her pressed against me, breasts plump and firm on my back, hand stroking my arm. Mine slipped under my waistband, gripping my cock.

**"...strum my clit till it sings..."**

I spread Fantasy Mackenzie on the kitchen table, her pussy wet and dripping for me. My thumb worked her clit, flicking and rolling the bundle of nerves while she moaned beneath me, taking back every word.

**"...plunge inside my pussy, and fuck me till I come screaming on your fingers..."**

My dick twitched, a living thing in my strangled, jerky hold. I picked up the pace imagining the feel of her warm and tight squeezing down on my fingers.

**"...make me moan Liam Hunt with every lovely ache..."**

And she was—moaning and screaming my name while I gripped her ankles, pumping inside her sweet, cum-hungry hole.

I grunted, burying my face in the pillow. The pressure built to a fever pitch, jacked to the limit by my furious tugs, and burst free. Hot, sticky ropes wet my boxers, leaving me panting under the sheets.

"Holy shit," I breathed. I haven't had a fantasy, or a tug, that satisfying in a long time. Heaven help me if I ever got my hands on the real thing. I'd fill her till my balls were shriveled raisins, then collapse into a coma—another casualty of a mind-blowing fuck.

"Liam?"

I shut off the phone, tossing it on the nightstand as the other side of the bed stirred.

"Are you awake, baby?" Hendrix snaked an arm around my waist. "Ready for round three?"

"No, get some sleep." I turned on my side, facing myself and my mess away from her. "Sorry I woke you."

She drifted off in minutes. Alone in the dark with the message I read five more times and jacked off to twice, I confirmed all my predictions.

Mackenzie Blaine was trouble sent to upset the carefully balanced world I created, and she awoke a long-forgotten side of me that ached to return the favor.

# Chapter Ten

M*ackenzie*
"Oh, Laurel, you'll never know what you've done to Mommy."

The baby kicked in her high chair, contentedly putting away her banana, yogurt, and whole wheat mini-pancakes breakfast.

"Da."

"It absolutely is a disaster," I said under my breath. "He wasn't supposed to read the whole thing. Now I'm supposed to meet Liam in twenty minutes to tell him everything I know about Adams. If finding that doo-doo head wasn't vital, I'd hide under my sheets and never come out until Liam retires and moves out to the Hamptons. I mean, what do I say to him? How do I look him in the eye?"

"Doo," she drew out, forming a cute little "o" with her yogurt-covered mouth. "Dooo."

"Thank you for confirming Mommy can't swear around you anymore. You're picking up a lot of new things, aren't you, baby girl? Like Sunny's mischievous side."

My phone buzzed, shooting my heart in a corner to hide. Was that Liam? My phone fell radio silent after it attacked my face and ruined any chance of me and Liam. All morning, I shifted between willing my cell to buzz with a reply, and staying silent so I didn't have to face rejection for the third time.

*I will anyway when I go upstairs. Unless this is a call asking me to do this over the phone, so he can maintain his distance from the creepy, obsessed woman sexting him in the middle of the night.*

The buzzing got more insistent, urging me to pick up the call. I checked the screen and relaxed.

"Hello?"

"Sup, Feisty, heard you got your kid back."

I blew kisses at Laurel. "I did. Are you coming over to meet her?"

"You're coming to me. Swinging by Harlow at least," Genny replied. "Vito will be at Cooper's tonight. This is your chance."

The phone shifted to the crook of my shoulder. I continued feeding Laurel, growing serious. "How do you know he'll be there?"

"Heard it from a reliable source who asked another reliable source. A friend of Vito's is getting married and the bachelor party starts at Cooper's, bounces around half a dozen strip clubs, and ends in a brothel knowing that guy. Your best bet is to catch him at the bar before he gets too blissed-out drunk and the guys lead him off all over the borough."

I nodded along. "Tonight at Cooper's. Is nine o'clock too early?"

"Nine is good, but I'd come earlier and stake the place out. Remember, you need him to think you're running a hostile takeover of North Quay, and if he wants in, he has to prove he's a serious threat against the Merchants."

"I can do that. I know what to say to this guy."

"Bring the little one for backup. It's always a good idea to avoid Vito outnumbering you. You'll see it when you meet him. Stand in the same room long enough and you need twelve showers and a chemical peel."

"FGH," someone called through the speakers. "We've got company. Two punks on bikes drove past the bar three times in the last thirty minutes. I think they're scoping us out."

"Bring their asses in here. Make them feel comfortable."

I winced. Genny flung her brother around the room as welcome, and that was her going easy. I didn't want to think what she'd do to a couple supposed spies.

"How is everything going at Barbarella's?" I asked. "I was freaked when this guy came after Liam so soon after Sunny, but it looks like he's gone quiet."

"I'm not too sure," Genevieve admitted. "Haven't seen a bald guy hanging around, but the other night..."

I sat up straighter. "What? What is it?"

"It's most likely nothing. My place isn't as secure as the Fairfield. Nowhere in the city is, but I haven't slacked. I hooked up motion sensors and alarms everywhere you can think of, including the building across that has the best sniper angle to take me out."

"Sniper angle? Are you serious?"

"Dead serious, Feisty. My aunt is an expert at these things. She taught me that despite what people think, snipers don't shoot from just anywhere. Movement, wind speed, distance, light, temperature, etc., are all taken into account. Once you know where your target will be, the work begins. I judged from every window in my house, and the best spot is a sixteen-story building across from me—the twelfth floor. If he pops me while I'm knocking back a beer in front of the television, lights out. Exactly why I bought out that apartment, and the one above and below.

"I didn't really think anyone would try to take me out this way. My enemies like the straightforward approach, but you know, if a security expert tells you to lock your windows at night, you lock the damn windows. Aunt Gianna told me to buy out those apartments, so I did.

"They're mine, Kenzie. No one else has a reason to step foot in there... so tell me why the other night, the motion sensors went off on the twelfth floor."

"Someone was in your apartment?"

"Yes."

My mind spun. *Was it him?*

"I beat it over there the minute I got the alert, but nothing. The lock was picked and the dust disturbed, but no sign of the guy."

"No cameras?"

"No, and I'm fucking kicking myself for it. I only rigged the place with motion sensors. At the time, I didn't see the need to deck out three apartments I wasn't going to use. Now my ass gets the picture: always listen to your aunt."

"But, Genny, I— You don't really think he went up there with a sniper rifle." My gaze snapped to the open curtains. "Couldn't there be another explanation? What if the building's super ducked into an apartment he knew was empty to have phone sex with his mistress?"

"Babe, I don't know what the fuck's going on. Maybe it has nothing to do with Sunny and Liam's would-be killer, but the timing is suspicious.

Think about it, Feisty. Put yourself in his head. You dumped Sole Bellisario off a bridge, and you're seen by a witness. Oh, shit, what do you do?

"Get smarter for the next one. Hire a guy to put a bomb in Liam's car, and then kill him. No witnesses. No one to point the finger. But wait— The car blows before Liam gets in, and you fucked that up too. Now Liam knows someone's after the family and he's warned us all to be careful.

"There are still three Merchants left in the city, and they're looking for me as hard as I'm gunning for them. I'm gonna take them out and I'll be sure this time. So why not grab a gun, a window, and kill the Merchant who isn't living safe in the Fairfield?"

I shuddered. Inside the killer's mind was a cold, vile place. "Why aren't you living safe in the Fairfield, Genny? You just said the timing is too suspicious. If this guy is following you home, planning his next attack, wouldn't you be safer here?"

"Hi, we obviously haven't met. My name is Genevieve Ava Hunt, member of the Merchant crime family, and founder of the Cardinals Motorcycle Club. If you're looking for Pansy-Ass Little-Bitch Hunt, member of the Spineless Cunts, and founder of the Runaway Club, you dialed the wrong number."

"You called me," I muttered.

"This shithead isn't running me out of my borough. Didn't work when the roided-up mob set the original Barbarella's on fire with me inside, and it ain't going to work now."

"Your stubbornness is your least attractive trait."

Gen barked a laugh. "I don't have unattractive traits, Feisty, that's why you're sporting a low-key girl-crush on me. But because I know how you and my bros worry, I've packed up and moved to one of my safe houses. It's a basement apartment. No windows, three ways out, and cameras clocking every corner and alleyway."

"That's something at least. Take care of yourself, Genny. This guy isn't going to win. He doesn't get an inch. He won't win even the smallest victory. The only prize he'll receive is a taste of the fear he gave Tricky that night at the restaurant."

"I've never agreed with anyone more."

Genny hung up by way of goodbye. My chat with FGH was over. *Now for my chat with Liam.*

I finished up feeding Laurel, then carried her into Sienna's room. My sister ate breakfast in her four-poster canopy bed with the television on low and silk robe snug and tight. To say she fully embraced her new life was an understatement.

"Do you mind looking after Laurel for me while I run upstairs? She just ate, so she's ready for Aunty-time."

"My favorite time of day," Sienna said, holding her arms out for the baby. "We'll find him, Kenzie. There's nowhere that rat can hide."

She said it, and I believed it. Digger would not get away with what he's done. We would find him, and when Sunny shoves a gun in his mouth, I won't stop what comes next.

I jerked to a stop as that vicious thought went through my mind. Slowly, I raised my head, beholding my reflection in the hallway mirror.

*So that's how it happens... that's how that look gets in your eyes.*

Shaking it off, I got in the elevator and hit the button for Liam's floor.

I wasn't changing. I'm still me. I'm still a person who chooses violence as the last resort. Luca Adams lied, manipulated, and tried to force me into prostitution. Even the pope wouldn't shed a tear if he died a slow, painful death. Wanting Adams to get what's owed him is normal.

*But unlike Damien, Lyla, Talia, Courtney, or the rest of them, this time I can do something. I can take Luca down alongside men who'll make sure he stays down for good.*

*Just how far am I willing to go?*

"Hello." Liam's voice caressed my ears, chasing dark, conflicted thoughts away, and replacing them with panicked, embarrassed ones.

"Liam, it—it's me. I'm here to—"

"Come in." The elevator slid open on the final word.

Hands wringing, my pulse revved the closer I got to his door. "Just apologize," I whispered. "Say you were working through your feelings and accidentally sent that text."

I knocked. No one answered and I tried the knob. *Open.*

Wood swinging in, Liam revealed inch by inch on his armchair, finger gliding around the coffee mug's rim. The curtains drew shut, casting shadows over his face, and he didn't move as I came in.

"Liam, I..." The apology stuck in my throat, burned up with my cheeks, neck, and palms. All of me flared hot with embarrassment. I made the biggest fool of myself. "Where's Lizzie?" I squeaked. *Maybe if I take the long way around, I'll make it to the apology.*

"She's out with Uncle Bane."

I waited for him to say more. Nothing came except a lifting brow and widening smirk. The floor opened up and swallowed me.

Liam read the text. Read every damn word, and he was more than pleased to let me stew in humiliation until I brought it up.

*So do it, Kenzie. Harpoon the elephant in the room.*

"Liam, about that text—"

"What text would that be?" he asked, drawing out the words. "Would it be the one you sent me in the middle of the night where you called me a coward, then dared me to do something about it?"

"I wouldn't... put it like that, exactly." I took a step, then two. Liam was a sculpted masterpiece stretched out in that chair—his Caddell pants molded to his calves, and shirt opened at the chest. His beauty crushed me... because it couldn't be mine. "It was one of those 'write an angry letter and don't send it' situations. I never meant for you to see it."

Liam crooked a brow. "So, you didn't mean what you said? You don't want me to strum your clit till it sings, bend you over my couch, or fuck your pussy—"

"Liam, stop," I cried, clapping my hands over my face. "I'm sorry, okay. If your goal is to humiliate me—mission accomplished. Can we forget this ever happened?"

"I don't think so." His deep baritone rolled out of his chest. "Kneel."

"Excuse me?"

"You heard me. Come over here. Kneel."

Confused, I slowly closed the distance. Stopping short of his armchair, I dropped to my knees as he got to his feet.

"Look at that." He tangled in my hair, leaning my head back. "I had no trouble getting you on your knees."

My mouth opened and nothing came out. *What did he just say? What is happening right now?*

"Want to know what your accidental text did to me, Miss Blaine?" Liam circled me, his hand dropping beneath my chin, and keeping my eyes on him all the while. "I didn't get a minute's sleep."

"Why?" I rasped.

"Because I'd close my eyes and one line of your message would pop in my head. Next thing I know my hand's in my boxers and I'm jacking off to the first, second, third, and fourth best tugs of my life."

A strangled noise escaped my lips. I couldn't have heard what I thought I did. It wasn't possible Liam Hunt confessed he spent the night masturbating to fantasies of me.

The air thickening with my arousal proved he did.

"So, now we have a problem, Mackenzie."

"We do?"

Liam's hand traveled down, slipping inside my iridescent cutout-back minidress, skimming the top of my bra cup. My breath trapped in my lungs. I would pass out—from his touch or lack of oxygen, either way, I would sink into dark bliss.

"Yes, we do. You're in my head now. Whispering filthy promises through your bee-stung lips. Teasing me in a dripping wet bikini. Crouching on your hands and knees, ass in the air—daring me to get a taste."

He traced a pattern between my chest.

*An X.* Liam's X branded above my heart, marking his next conquest.

"I can't get a thing done. Can't focus without drifting back to that text, and craving to prove I'll win your challenge. So, yes, we do have a problem, Mackenzie, 'cause I have to get you out of my system."

"Liam," I whispered.

He towered over me, dominating my world with Liam, Liam, Liam.

Then he disappeared.

My blood thrummed as he blindfolded me with his tie. A million awkward situations tormented me since that text pinged his phone, but this never crossed my mind.

I couldn't see him, though I felt Liam around me, stroking my throat, thudding the floor as he dropped, grasping my zipper. Liam peeled my dress off and sucked in a sharp intake of breath.

He unwittingly unwrapped another Kenzie Lingerie Creation. My recent change in relationship status with Sunny prompted an end to my granny panty days, and the return of lace thongs and sheer bodysuits. We hadn't been together long and Sunny managed to have me out of my clothes for more hours in the day than I was in them. I wanted Sunny to get a new treat every time he unzipped me, but that morning's treat was taken by Liam.

A blue bralette weaved in bright lilac roses twined around my breasts, drawing his eyes to my hardening nubs—its wanton need displayed for all to see through the sheer tulle. My boy shorts were no better—made of all tulle bearing only embroidery on the sides, they left nothing to the imagination.

"You are"—his tongue tasted my neck, making me gasp—"exquisite."

"No one has ever called me exquisite before."

I shook like a leaf—trembling down to my toes. Something about not seeing him or knowing what he'd do next left me helpless in the best way. He was well named as Liam Hunt.

I was his prey.

"Because you've been with boys before." My bra popped and fell to the floor with a soft sound, covered by my squeak. "A real man would've told you every day that you're a masterpiece."

"Ah!" Liam swept me into his arms. I had the brief sensation of being carried, then something cool pressed against my stomach.

*Leather.* Liam bent me over the couch, and ripped hours of painstaking, delicate work off my body. I had a second to register the cold air on my cheeks, before a firm swat zinged my left butt cheek.

"Liam," I cried.

"Won't have the balls to go near your ass, am I getting that right? Couldn't find your pussy with a map and a flashlight?" He stroked my lower lips, discovering their wet secret, and teased inside. "Looks like I found it."

Liam pushed two fingers through my entrance, burying to the knuckles. I moaned loud and deep from a primal, animalistic part of me. "Uhh, that feels so—"

*Thwack.*

"Ah!" The swat rocked me, squeezing me down on Liam's fingers. "Bastard."

He chuckled huskily. "You wanted to remember my name with every ache, so let's hear it."

"Liam." My back arched, giving him access, driving him deeper. "Liam."

"Fuck," he hissed.

The clink of his belt hardened my nipples. I reached for the blindfold.

"Don't you dare."

"Why? Liam, please, I want to see you."

"You don't get to see me. You'll imagine me. Tonight. While you're lying in bed spreading this sweet pussy, you'll fantasize about me gripping my cock and smiling with your juices on my lips, and it'll keep you up all night."

Frustration and desire dizzied me. "You are a cruel man."

I didn't know if he heard me. Liam spread me over the couch the same way I wrote in my text and slipped his tongue inside. I was lost.

Strings of unintelligible, panted nonsense dropped from my lips. I think I was begging. Pleading with Liam to take off the blindfold, let me see him, let me touch him, and my most fervent wish, to fuck the crap out of me.

My pleas didn't reach or slow him down. He ate me out to his heart's content—dipping to suck on the bundle of nerves. Bobbing up to gift me a new experience—swirling his tongue around my puckered hole.

I came once, then twice—toes digging in the leather and screaming Liam's name. All I had to picture the scene of me bent and at his mercy was his hand on my hip, and the *fap, fap, fap* of his fevered tugs. Even though I couldn't see what I was doing to him, I heard his strangled dick, rough grunts, and my name on his lips.

Liam smacked my ass mid-tongue fuck and I came hard, flopping off the couch and dropping headfirst toward the hardwood. Liam caught me and gently pulled me back—his shirt damp and sticking as he molded to me, pressing his mouth to my ear.

"I'm not afraid," he whispered, "when I'm with you." Then he stiffened, and warm wetness covered my thighs.

Liam held me for a long time, our bodies cooling, breaths slowing. I made to speak half a dozen times, but nothing seemed right for the moment, so I let it go. Was this an admission of something? A beginning? Asking too soon might remind Liam of his reasons for believing we're not a good idea. He knew how I felt. I was more open with him than I intended to be. The ball was in his court. If he was ready to move past fear and build something real with me, it was his turn to say.

His warmth disappeared from my back.

"Liam?"

Silence responded, broken by the sound of his zipper, then running water and a cool cloth wiping me clean. Liam even dressed me quietly. He didn't say a word until he removed the tie, gazing into my eyes as he replaced it—the unruffled, legitimate businessman once again.

"Luca Adams."

I blinked at him like he slipped into another language. "What?"

"You came to tell me what you know about Adams. Where he goes. What he does. Friends. Family." He gave me his back. "He's proving hard to find. At this time, any information—"

I grasped the back of his shirt, pulling him up short. "That's it? After what just happened, we're back to business as usual. There isn't anything you want to say to me?"

"Mackenzie."

"Liam," I said firmly. "You promised me the truth. No tricks, no lies... no leading me on. Just honesty."

He growled, tossing his head. "I told you the truth, Mackenzie, and it's the most honest thing I've said. More than I knew I could be. I can't say more, because I've said it all."

"*I'm not afraid when I'm with you.*"

"Oh," I said softly.

"Do you understand?"

I ducked my head, smiling so goofily, I didn't want him to see. "I understand."

"Good." Straightening, Liam got out of my hold and picked up his laptop. "Adams. He hasn't been by the apartment he owns since his last run-in with Sunny, and I haven't dug up other property in his name. Did he mention anywhere else? Did he take you there?"

My lip surrendered between my teeth, fighting me to smile. Being this close to him and sharing the intimate tour he took of my body did terrible things to my concentration. The man laid me out like a Christmas turkey while I've yet to see him out of a bathing suit.

*This is important, Kenzie. Focus on taking down Adams. Liam isn't going anywhere. I have no plans to leave his head, or his fantasies, so he'll have to spend a lifetime bending me over to get his fill.*

"There was the building Digger trapped me in when he grabbed me on Halloween. It's empty now," I warned. "After I escaped, I called the police and they raided the place. Luca isn't stupid enough to go back there."

"Not to that particular place, but he could own other buildings in the area. That's a good start."

Liam drained me of every bit of Luca-related information. If it helped put an end to the man and his business for good, I'd give him details of our lackluster sex life. Whatever it took.

Bane and Elizabeth returned by the time we finished up. Liam snatched the remains of my boy shorts off the floor as Lizzie's feet thundered down the hall. He stuffed them in his pocket, and didn't give them back.

Bane and I headed downstairs. Tricky had homeschooling, and I personally couldn't spend another second near Liam without jumping and tying him up, stealing a peek at what he denied me.

"Genny called earlier."

Bane strolled at my side, handsome in a pair of jeans and a fitted black tee. My eyes kept drifting to him. The man was a young Jason Momoa without the hair but ten times the devilish grin. Standing this close to him reduced me to a giggling teenage girl who saw a cute boy for the first time.

"What did she say?"

The question brought me back to reality. "Vito will be at Cooper's tonight. I'm going to see what he knows about the attacks on the Merchants."

"Want me to come?"

"You can't," I said, pushing the button for the elevator. "He has to think I'm betraying the Merchants. Won't work if one is waving at me from across the bar."

"I can manage more subtlety than that," he said with a chuckle. "Vito will never know I'm there. I'm not saying you can't do this on your own. Just offering to be close by in case you have to prove yourself again—violently."

*Good point. Vito will be surrounded by a bunch of drunk bachelor partiers willing to jump in on a bar fight.*

"If I do have to prove myself, you coming out to rescue me will blow my last chance to hell," I replied. We went in and I hit the button for Sunny's place. Bane pressed nine for his. "I want you there. Just promise me you won't act unless he's murdering me."

"Cross my heart and hope to die." He made the sign and flung it away. "But where are we on maiming? If he's just cutting off an appendage, can I keep drinking my beer?"

"Go away."

His cute, infectious laugh followed me onto the eleventh floor.

"Tonight at Cooper's," Bane confirmed. "And afterward, we'll go out just the two of us."

"Wait, what—"

"I'm thinking pastries and the walk in Harmony Park."

"B-but you said—"

"Eh, let's wait and see what we're in the mood for." Bane winked through the closing sliver. "Later, Kenzie."

I gaped with my metallic reflection. "And there goes another doo-doo head."

Eventually, I squashed the urge to chase him down and went inside. Heavenly smells wafted outside the kitchen courtesy of Shonda, and by the chattering, Sienna too. I peeked in on them, but Laurel wasn't there.

*Is she down for her nap already?*

Sticking my head inside the nursery, I confirmed Laurel wasn't in there either. I padded down the hall to Sunny's room.

"—trick is to stay relaxed and stand up straight." Sunny's voice filtered through the open door. "Right foot forward and throw."

I stuck my head in the room, and choked on a scream.

Sunny wore a bouncing Laurel in her baby carrier. His arm raised over his head, readying to throw the knife at its target. Laurel had her knife too. Gripped in her tiny fist, she nommed on the weapon's handle.

"Sunny, have you lost your mind?!"

He started, swinging around. "Whoa, baby, you scared me."

"I scared *you*?" I shrieked, rushing to Laurel. "What the hell are you doing letting her hold a knife?!"

"Rubber," he said, way too breezy for someone about to get their ass kicked. "Rubber knife, Angel. Rounded edges. These things couldn't hurt a butterfly."

Taking it from her confirmed what he said. I pressed the tip to my palm and it flattened on my skin. Laurel fussed for her new teething toy.

"Better than my old man," Sunny said. "Papa Sinjin strapped me to his chest, then went out and practiced with the real thing. Pretty sure I held a knife before I held a bottle."

"That cannot be true. Rubber or not," I said, willing air back in my lungs. "Let's agree to keep weapons—rubber, plastic, real, and fake—away from the baby."

"Fair enough. We'll wait till she's four to start training. That's when I started."

I was torn between happy he saw us together in four years, and seriously disturbed that he believed in those four years, he'd go out and fling knives with Laurel.

"We'll talk about this later. Much, much later." I nuzzled Laurel's cheek, murmuring to her to settle my baby. She was way more upset at losing her knife than I wanted her to be.

Calming, she grabbed a fistful of my hair. Tugging and playing with it occupied her. I glanced at Sunny while she held me captive.

I hooked up with his brother.

Sunny said it was okay, and in the same conversation, said he wasn't worried because Liam and I, or Bane and I, would never happen.

*Technically, we haven't happened. I sent an accidental sext, and Liam made me beg like a bitch in heat. We didn't have sex or talk relationship. What was there to tell Sunny?*

*The truth,* another voice said. *Just the truth.*

"Sunny, did you mean what you said about sharing me? The sweet bit at the beginning, and not the end where you ruined it."

He laughed. "Yeah, I meant it. I'm secure enough to share because I'm the only antidote for the poison working through your veins. Too long out of my bed and the symptoms start—heart palpitations, shakes, uncontrollable fantasizing, and nonstop masturbating. Forty-eight hours and you're jumping me for sweet relief."

I rolled my eyes, though he was giving a scarily accurate description of what it felt like going one hour without his arms around me and us tangled in the sheets—let alone forty-eight.

"Why?" he asked.

I chose my words with thought. "I do have feelings for Liam, Sunny, and I want to be honest about it. But how honest do you want me to be? If... something happens between us, do you want to know?"

"Don't give me the gory details, sweet cheeks. It's my older brother we're talking about, but you don't have to do some weird, sneaking-around thing with code names and signals."

I cracked a smile. "Good to know. I'll just say Liam and I are getting closer. I'm working on his younger-women hang-ups."

"You're the kind of woman you break all the rules for. Something tells me you won't have to work too hard on him." Sunny threw his knife. It smacked dead center on the flat end and slid off. "I'm sick of this apartment. I've read every book on my shelves and re-watched my favorite shows twice. Never die, Angel. It's boring as shit." Sunny gave Laurel a finger to hold. "Though I am enjoying my time with you, Mini Blaine. Don't get me wrong."

"I know this sucks, Sunny." I wrapped them both in a hug. "I'm meeting up with Vito tonight. Hopefully, he has the answers we're looking for."

"I hope he does. I can't keep this up forever. Too long and it'll get dangerous for you."

"Why would it be dangerous for me?"

Sunny sat in the chaise, Laurel tugged me along by the hair. "New boss, new blood," he said. "North Quay has other gangs. I let them exist as long as they know who they're working for. Once word gets around about *my wife,* they'll test the boundaries to see what they can get away with. The kind of test that isn't settled with a punch or hair-pulling. Knowing that going against the Merchants comes with a death sentence is what keeps them in line." He looked at me with hooded eyes. "You willing to reinforce the message?"

I said nothing. Just shook my head.

"I wouldn't want you to be in that position either. We need to know something about this enemy, and we need to know it soon." He kissed me. "Who's watching your back tonight? Want Coates on your tail? I can bust out the rags too."

"Bane and Sienna are coming. We'll be fine. I'm just going to talk to the guy, and we're not leaving the bar."

Vito Bernardi had the same policy. That night, Sienna and I rolled into Cooper's Bar and Grill at eight thirty, dressed in our finest badass gear. We parked ourselves in a booth next to the entrance and sipped on soda. Me because I was breastfeeding, and Sienna because the bartender carded her.

Nine o'clock passed. Then nine thirty. By ten, we worried the bachelor and his boys changed their minds about starting the party at Cooper's and went directly to the strip clubs. We were getting up to leave when shouting, laughing, and carrying-on bowled through the door. I spotted Vito at once.

Genny described him as a marriage between Satan's red, rotting asshole and the spitting image of his Gorgon mother—complete with hideous eyes that turned you to stone. Between her added commentary, I got out of her that Vito sported long, black hair, greenish-brown eyes, a snubbed nose, and a grin that showed off his crooked teeth. Oddly, the imperfect smile didn't mess up the one detail Genny left out, Vito Bernardi was smoking hot.

I clocked him at twenty-six—maybe twenty-seven, and he spent all those years being more handsome than one person could handle. Probably had a part in his character flaws.

The guys found a booth in the back, ordered a round of drinks, and began giving their livers a kicking. I sat for a solid twenty minutes, waiting for Vito to break away from the pack so I could talk to him. He was parked in the middle of the booth with three guys on either side of him. Extracting him would be obvious.

"I'm going for it anyway," Sienna called over the noise. "They're not going to stay here much longer with lap dances calling their names. I'll get him out into the alley. Wait for us there."

"Are you sure?"

"Yeah, it'll be fun." Damned if she didn't look like she was having fun too. "Bosses have minions to do their bidding. You can't go around summoning people on your own."

It took more coaxing, but she finally got me to leave and let her do her thing. I comforted myself that Bane was nearby watching.

Cooper's alley was as glamorous as the seedy, sticky-tabled dive I walked out of. As in, not at all.

Bags of garbage missed the dumpster and ended up a five-foot-high pile of stink in the corner. The bags shook as whatever critters lived in it feasted. Brick walls on three sides, all depicting the finest Cinco City street art had to offer. I posted up underneath a green squid forming the letters "BB" with its tentacles. Sienna came out minutes later.

"—damn good in those shorts, baby. Love to see them on my floor stained with jizz."

My hairs stood on end clocking that disgusting leer and the even more vile words aimed at my sister's backside. Twelve showers and a chemical peel? Vito didn't waste two seconds proving Genny right.

"Coming before I even get my pants off?" Sienna rebounded—Bane's master student. "Not a wise move, admitting to a girl you can't get to the finish line."

"Oh, I can fu—"

"Shut your fucking mouth," I snapped. Sienna could hold her own, but I wasn't about to watch the perv show when I had a job to do.

If anything, Vito's grin widened. "Easy, darling. I've got enough for the both of you." Vito snatched me to his chest. I flashed, grabbed his ear, and twisted.

"Ahh! Ah, fuck! Okay!" He got his hands off me. "Let go."

I shoved him back. "Better."

"Damn, what the hell do you two want?" The skeezy letch vanished fast, and the pissed letch took his place. "She said you had a proposal I'd be interested in. If it ain't your pussies, fuck off."

"Charming," I said dully. "Our pussies aren't on the table, Vito. I'm married."

"Then you can fuck off twice. Waste of my—?"

"Stop. Talking. Every word you utter gets me closer to changing my mind. Just listen," I began. "I am married— Or, I was married to a guy I think you've heard of. Sole Bellisario."

Vito's face shuttered closed. "Walk out of this alley now, or you and that hot piece of tail will be carried out. And you won't be looking as pretty as when you came in."

Disgust curled my lip. "You're talking, Vito. Didn't I tell you not to do that? Now your cut of the money dropped five percent."

"What mon—?"

"Ten percent."

Vito closed his mouth. I had a feeling he would at the magic word: money.

"As I was saying, I married Sole, and after his death, I inherited his money, cars, apartment, and the gang that goes with them."

Vito's eyes widened, the lone reaction to hearing Sunny was dead. It seemed word hadn't stretched this far into Harlow.

"I run the Sons of Saint and North Quay now, and it turns out, boss is a good color on me. The Merchants let me take over because I'm Sunny's wife, but it's obvious they don't trust me. They second-guess, or override, every decision I make. I can't leave the house without their guards tailing me. I get only half of Sunny's cut as boss. The rest is split between Genevieve, Liam, and Bane."

*What does this have to do with me?* read loud and clear on his face.

"I'm taking... steps," I said carefully, "to get out from under their control and run my crew, my way. I'm sure you know better than anyone that's no easy feat."

Vito's jaw clenched. "Yeah, you could say that."

I didn't clock him for talking, since he was also listening. "I'll get to the point. I'm looking for allies—discreetly. Once I make my move, I need friends at my back, and I hear you're a good friend to have in the fight against the Merchants."

"Is that what you heard?" he said, laced with sarcasm. "Who exactly is telling you shit about me? You think I'm falling for this? Coming up to me, saying you're Sunny's wife, and running his crew? My hard, tanned ass." He ripped something out of his pocket. A glint of silver, then the blade bit my throat. "Who are you really?" he hissed. "What do you want?"

Sienna surged forward. I threw up my hand, stopping her. I knew Vito wouldn't make this easy on me. My play was to remain calm and confident. Confidence fooled people better than lies.

"I told you who I am. Sunny and I kept our relationship a secret, but there's nothing to hide now. He's gone and someone had to step up in his place. You can ask around North Quay and everyone will tell you it's me."

"Then, you're one of them! You're trying to trick me." The knife shook on my neck. "Get me to admit—"

"Admit what? That you hate the Merchants and want the Cardinals out of Harlow? Everyone knows that, dumbass. Genevieve sure as hell knows it. Here I am giving you a chance to *do* something about it, instead of blowing hot air in her direction. Surprise: that's not working."

His eyes narrowed to slits. I heard the gears in his mind turning. Now to tip him in the right direction.

"Look, if you're not interested, say so. We'll stop wasting our time." I grasped his wrist and shoved the knife off. Vito didn't fight me. "I've been in charge for about a week, and I've counted up the money going into SOS's coffers. We're flush. So, I'm offering a sizable gratitude payment to whoever helps grab hold of the Saints for good—no Merchant interference. In addition, they'll be allowed to run their business in North Quay at a reduced fee."

"Generous," he spat. "But why would Sunny's wife do such a thing? Betray his family."

"Why wouldn't I?" My bitch-boss voice made me shiver. I based it on Lyla, and it was freakishly close. "I loved Sunny, not his family. Sunny treated me as an equal. His family treats me like another servant at their beck and call."

"They treat us all like servants. That bitch and her twisted family of freaks, believe they own Cinco and everyone in it. There are a lot of people who want them taken out, and they'd do it at any price."

"Are you one of those people?"

His expression gave nothing away. "Maybe. What are you offering?"

"It depends on what you offer, Bernardi. Weapons, explosives, information, money, friends with all of the above. The more you can offer me, the more I'll offer you."

Vito opened his mouth. Suddenly, he shook his head, backing away. "Nah, you have to prove yourself first. Once I know you're legit, then I'll tell you what I have to offer."

"*You* have to prove yourself worth it." Folding my arms, I stared him down. "I'm not jumping through your hoops, only to find out you're barely a scratch on Genny's paint job."

"I'm more than a scratch!"

"Then give me a taste."

Vito bared his teeth, growling. Not nearly as menacing as he wanted it to be. I got that look from Ryker and Makai whenever they laid eyes on me, and with them, I believed they wanted to kill me.

"Six months ago," he finally said. "One of Hunt's warehouses went up in flames. Police decided it was another meth lab explosion."

"Yeah. What about it?"

"Let's just say the cops got a few things wrong." A nasty smile flashed his crooked teeth. "I know what really happened, how, by who, and how to pull it off again. Enough of their business goes up in flames, and the Merchants will be too busy trying to keep their hold on their own boroughs, they won't bother with North Quay. How much is that worth?"

"That's worth a lot, Bernardi. That's name-your-price information."

His smile widened. "Excellent. Now, it's your turn. Three weeks ago, the Sons of Saint busted into my friend's shop. He ran a side business, making a little extra for his family. You'd think Sunny would have some sympathy, and you'd be wrong.

"He emptied his safe, took the cash, and stole all his merchandise. Among the haul was a bag of three-carat diamonds worth seven million dollars."

I flashed to the woman at her station, examining the sparkling prize.

"If you're really Sunny's widow," Vito continued, "running the Sons of Saint, and willing to strike a hard blow against the Merchants, you won't have a problem getting those diamonds back and handing them to me. I mean, you are *the boss*. His crew can't stop you. If you can't get me those diamonds, it's obvious you ain't running shit. You're not in a position to take anyone down."

"Done."

His smirk twitched. "What?"

"Done. You want the diamonds, they're yours." I laughed. "Wow, for a second I thought you'd ask me to do something difficult."

"I—"

"Let's meet back here tomorrow. Same place, same time."

Vito blinked rapidly—looking between me and Sienna like he was checking the women who dropped out of the sky, offering to hand him his enemies and seven million in diamonds on a platter were real.

"When I hand those diamonds over, I want a name, how your friend covered his tracks pulling off the explosion, and where I can find him. He and I are going to do a lot of business together."

"Not just him," Vito said. "My crew is small, but we're strong. We've taken chunks out of Cardinals' Empire, and Hunt hasn't been able to stop us."

I stuck my hand out. "Then, we have a deal."

He hesitated, then shook. "Deal."

Vito backed toward the door. "I've got a party to get back to and dollar bills to stuff down a G-string, so we'll have to pick up where we left off later." Vito reached for Sienna's hand, who smoothly slid away. "Like the ones who play hardest to get. You go down fighting, just makes it more fun for—"

Sienna spun, kicking the back of his leg.

"Ah!" Vito flew back and landed hard on his ass—the thud resounding through the alley. "Bitch!"

"Our deal doesn't come with a free pass for disrespect," said my sister. "Last warning."

I swear I was buying out a trophy shop and giving them all to her.

"See you tomorrow," I sang, the two of us striding off. A string of curses, insults, and oaths were our goodbye. Didn't matter as long as he showed up the next night with a name.

"Do you think this is it?" Sienna asked. We hit the sidewalk and left Cooper's on a quick march. The bar was located on another red-light street, and almost every alley we looked down had another shady deal going on. "Is Vito about to give us the guy who attacked Sunny and started this all?"

"I don't know. Though he is about to tell us who murdered Frenchie and her friends. If he's been strutting around free all this time, he won't be after tomorrow. That's still a win."

"Assuming you deliver the diamonds," Bane announced, falling in step with us.

I whipped around. "Where did you come from? And where were you listening?"

"From a good spot to jump in and break his neck when he pulled the knife on you." Temper leached into the answer. "But you were incredible, Kenzie. And you, Sienna. Handled him without a problem."

"What can we say?" Sienna returned. "Sunny hired a couple of pros."

"Who might fail," I said as what I agreed to sunk in. "What if I can't get the diamonds? I have no clue where they are or if they're still in the arcade. If I go in there demanding seven million' worth of jewels, so I can seal a deal with a Merchant enemy, Ryker will hand me a bullet in the brain instead."

"You'll need Sunny on this one." Bane drew ahead to the street corner and waved down a cab. "He'll know what his crew does with a score."

Bane was right. I dialed Sunny as we climbed in, and vaguely explained the situation, mindful of the whistling cabbie.

"He knows who caused all the trouble for your sister six months ago, but he won't tell us unless he gets something in return. Three weeks ago, his friend lent you something. He wants it back."

"What's the something? I stole a lot of shit three weeks ago. Cough when I say it. Vintage Porsche Roadster, a Cézanne, a Penfolds Grange Hermitage 1951..."

My mouth fell open at the list of screamingly expensive items Sunny's gang helped themselves to. Ryker gave me an inventory list along with the shipment information, but it was written with general descriptors: French painting, vintage car, 1951 bottle of wine.

*Holy hell, how rich is this man?*

"—diamonds."

I coughed.

"The diamonds?" Sunny repeated. "Athena recovered those in a smash-and-grab job. The guy, Ira Hansen, was a slumlord, running a drug business on the side. He hoarded hundreds of thousands while his tenants lived without heat, working locks, or electricity. Naturally, that scum and Vito are good buddies.

"Athena raided the place, emptied it of everything we could fence, and split the money between the tenants. After we took our fee, of course," Sunny added. "Your boy doesn't run a charity."

"Of course."

"I have no idea how he got his hands on those diamonds. Each one is worth about thirty-five thousand dollars. They're big-time for a wannabe drug kingpin like Ira. My guess is he stole or blackmailed some rich bag for them.

"I'm telling you all of this because unless Ryker and the guys are changing the rules in my absence, the diamonds should still be in the arcade."

"They wouldn't have sold them? I can't say what happened to them since I saw them the other day."

"We don't know where they came from—only that they don't belong to Ira. For all we know, he did blackmail them off an innocent person, or murdered a jeweler to get those diamonds. Until we know how hot a score is, and the possible blowback if we sell them, they're kept in the safe. Like I said, that's where they'll be unless Ryker is making up his own rules."

"What safe?"

"The one in our office." Sunny said this like I was pretending not to know what he meant.

"I don't know about any safe in our office."

"Really?" He chuckled. "Ryker, the cagey prick. Course he didn't tell you. There's a fortune stashed away in there. Not to worry, Angel. I'll tell you where it is and how to get in. Step one is vitally important."

"Okay," I said, gripping the phone. "What do I do?"

"First: come home, proceed to take off all of your clothes, and ride my dick till it pops like a piñata. The rest of the instructions will follow."

"Goodbye."

I hung up on his guffaws. Sole Bellisario was incorrigible. I was also starting to believe he was psychic. The man predicted I'd fall for him, let him worship my body every night, and he'd put a ring on my finger. He was three for three while I was still figuring out how he and the Merchants became my whole world so fast.

"Stop at 411 Dunston Street," Bane said. "Sienna, you cool if we drop you off? Kenzie and I have plans."

The elevator ride that morning crashed into my musings. The most insufferable and one of the sexiest men on the planet wanted to take me out after swearing we'd neither date nor hook up. I blame Vito for distracting me from the gnawed-lip fretting I was supposed to do that day to prepare.

"Yeah, drop me off," Sienna replied. "I'll grab a car and head back out. I'm supposed to meet up with friends tonight."

"You are? Who?"

"Marty, Nathan, Samara, and Destiny."

"Guys from River's crew," I said. "Sienna, I told you what Ryker said about River and his *gang*. This changes things. No wonder it always felt off between me and River—like I didn't know the whole story. We don't know what the four of them have done for him."

"I know what they've done for us. Samara brought us to River when we hadn't eaten in a week and I had that cut that got infected. Destiny shared food, coats, and blankets with us. Marty saved me from Digger's guy. Whatever they do for him, they're our friends." She gave me a look. "River's our friend too, despite all he's hidden from us."

"I know. I just—"

"River?" Bane broke in. "As in River Delaney?"

I twisted to him. "Yes. Do you know him?"

"Not a lot of guys out there named River," he said simply. "I know the Rat King."

"It's weird hearing him called that. We were with his crew for months and nobody said the words rat or king." I blew out a breath. "Part of me thinks Ryker is messing with me."

"Ryker doesn't have a sense of humor. Whatever he told you about Delaney is true, but it's not a surprise you never heard his crew mention the name. It was given to him. He didn't choose it for himself, and as you can tell, it's not a term of endearment." Bane gazed out the window, watching the city zip by. "Few of us get to decide what we're called. What we become known for decides that. My dad, the unstoppable street fighter, became Brutal. Sole's known in the streets by another name too."

"Isn't it Sunny?"

The corner of his lip curled up. "Far from it, my friend. His name is Demone."

"Demone? As in demon?" I laughed. "That doesn't suit him at all. Do they call him that because he shuts down rivals or helps himself to the majority of their profits?"

"Something like that."

"What's yours?"

"Bane."

"A cause of great distress. It works." I shook my head, getting back to Sienna and the point. "Si, I know they were there for us when no one else was, but people don't keep secrets for no reason. A *group of people* for sure don't hide that they're a gang unless they're up to something innocent witnesses shouldn't know about. Just promise me you'll be careful."

"I promise, but trust me, we lived with them for months. If there was darkness in their hearts, I would've sensed it. I mean, yeah, we knew they stole and picked pockets to survive on the streets, but if they were just another gang looking out for themselves and what they could get, they would not have taken in two empty bellies, on top of other homeless people River brings in from the cold every day. River isn't some greedy kingpin, counting his cash stacks while his people die for him. If he didn't give away more than he kept, he wouldn't be homeless too."

Sighing, I kissed her cheek. "You're right. I know there's a good, kind side to him. It's just easy to forget—buried under his half-truths and backhanded trades."

The cab turned the corner, coming up on the Fairfield. Sienna hugged us both bye and climbed out.

A soft statement came from Bane's side of the cab. "That's how he does it, you know. River."

"Does what?"

"Gets so many people to follow him. It's how the Rat King amassed an army rivaling the size of the old Kings. Everyone in his crew is just a little bit in love with him.

"Columbia Street," he told the driver. "After-Hours Fresh."

"What's with this veil of secrecy?" I grasped Bane's chin, making him face me. "I asked River what's the deal between him and Sunny, and he says to ask Sunny. I ask Sunny, and he tells me to ask River. So, now I'm asking you. Why won't Sunny do business with him?"

Bane grinned. "It's just you and me and an incoming surprise, and you want to talk about old history right now?"

"I really, really do."

"Fair enough. It's pretty simple." He flicked to the back of the driver's head. "We'll discuss it later."

It's then the panic came back, reminding me Bane asked me out for reasons unknown. We were quiet on the drive, soaking in the city lights and soft Bollywood music drifting from the speakers. It's odd to say about a nonstop talker like Bane Alexander, but he was one of the few people I could sit with and enjoy peaceful silence.

The cabbie let us out before a trendy, carnival-themed bakery dubbed After-Hours Fresh.

"My mother's a chef."

Bane helped me out and rested his hand on the small of my back like it was a normal, everyday thing. My drying mouth and prickly skin said otherwise. Why did every touch from Bane make it seem like I was feeling for the first time?

"She knows where to find the best of everything, in every borough, and in every cuisine. Some of them are places you'd never think of."

"What will we find here?" I drifted closer, bumping against his side. Bane didn't draw away.

"This place is a treasure trove. Best funnel cake, candy apples, cotton candy lemonade, kettle corn, and nachos. They're only open at night and everything's made fresh to order—hence the name."

"Sounds delicious."

"Yeah? 'Cause we'll get something else if you'd like it better. Serious, all the bests. Try me."

"Cotton candy lemonade and nachos. Can't think of anything else I'd like more."

We chimed the bell going into the colorful, clown-painted restaurant. While we waited in line, I tossed him the most difficult and random meals I could come up with.

"Baked Alaska."

"Chelsea's Café in Waterford."

"Ooh, fresh sushi."

Bane gave me a look. "Rockchapel Fish Market. Come on, Blaine. Don't go easy on me."

"Okay, okay," I said, laughing. "Masala dosa."

"Alright, she's bringing her good stuff now. I'm going to have to say... Flavor of India, Leighbridge."

"This one is really going to stump you."

Bane paused to give our order. "Lay it on me."

"First, I want to know what I win."

"What do you want?"

"A tattoo." It was out of my mouth so fast, I surprised myself. Though once I said it, nothing else would do. "Whoever did yours is a true artist. I want their name. What I have in mind is intricate."

"The name of my tattoo artist—done. What do I get if I win?"

"Nicer outfits for your scarecrow sentries."

Bane smiled. His tone was soft and caressing as he replied, "What if I want something else?"

I licked suddenly dry lips. "Name it."

He accepted our food, holding my lemonade up to me. Gaze locked, my lips wrapped around the straw. Tangy sweetness delighted my taste buds, and a stray, dirty vision overcame of my mouth swallowing Bane—his hand on the back of my head as he burst.

Bane's grin widened like he plucked the mind movie from my head and watched it start to finish—twice.

I took the drink and nachos from him, face burning. Bane paid for us and we made our way down Orchard Street.

"I want one of Kenzie's creations," Bane said. "Tricky wants us to be matching, but I don't think I'd pull off a purple unicorn jacket." I giggled at the image. "A jacket in whatever you choose. I trust you."

I loved hearing him say he trusted me more than I'd admit. "Agreed. Here it is... fugu."

Bane sucked in a sharp breath. "You evil, devious woman," he said over my cracking up. "Choosing a delicacy banned in all fifty states. Wow. If it was anyone else, game would go to you, but..."

"No. Don't tell me you know a place that serves the best fugu."

"Genji's Steak House. There's a secret restaurant through the back door of the main restaurant. He serves many illegal dishes. Haggis, beluga caviar, shark fin soup, horse meat, and when you're done, wash it down with absinthe."

I shook my head, smiling up at the starless sky. "You've lived a very different life from me, Alexander. I'm realizing that the longer I'm with you guys. How much I've missed, and how much more I'll get to experience."

"Anything at the top of the list?"

"Visiting the places on Sunny's map."

We strolled, ate, talked, and laughed. I was so caught up in just being with him, I didn't pay attention to where we were going until we hit grass.

"Harmony Park," I said. "You were serious. You're... taking me on the lovers' walk?"

"Yep. There's something I want to show you."

Bane moved and I didn't.

"What's wrong?" he asked, taking my hand. "It'll close in twenty minutes."

"Bane, is this a date?"

His crooked, heart-stopping grin kick-started my heart. "Course not," he replied, crushing said heart under his boot and tossing it in the trash with our food cartons. "I don't date. You know that."

"Are you serious?"

He frowned. "What's wrong? You look upset."

"Oh, do I?" I snapped, eyes stinging. "You said food and the Harmony walk are top-three date-night ideas. What was I supposed to think?"

"Ah, I see how that's confusing. I'm sorry, I didn't mean to give you the wrong idea. Hey," he whispered when I didn't speak. His touch was gentle drying my eyes. "I am sorry. Tell me how to make it up to you."

"You don't have to make it up to me. Just tell me what we're doing here. Why did you invite me out?"

"Why? I didn't know I needed a reason." Bane traveled down, rubbing my chilled arms. "I wanted to talk to you, eat with you, hang out with you. Because I thought we were friends."

I dropped my head, racked with shame. Of course he did. Sitting, talking, and opening up are what we did. It always came easy between us—so easy, he was honest from the first day that he wouldn't date or sleep with me. I was the stupid one, reading into a sweet offer to take me out and have fun.

"We are." I raised my head, giving a genuine smile. "Course we're friends. Sorry. I'm as rusty with the friends thing as I am with the dating thing. My social skills have been abandoned on a desert island without food or water for eight months. Spoiler alert: they're dead."

Bane laughed. Good, I was trying to make him laugh. It chased away the awkward silence coming to kill us.

"I'm sorry, Kenzie. I should've been clear." He swept out a hand. "Still want to go?"

I hesitated. "Going on a lovers' walk isn't something friends do."

"I promise there's a vitally important reason that we need to go on this walk. There just is no other way."

"Vitally important?" My good mood crept back. "We talking life or death?"

"At least. May also impact future events. We can't predict all the ramifications. I just know we've got to go into that park."

"When you put it like that..."

Chuckling, we picked up our feet. If he noticed that I didn't walk as close or he realized that I noted his hand wasn't on my back anymore, neither of us commented on it.

"Good evening." A woman sat at a fold-up table, handing out tickets. Behind her, an arch proclaimed Harmony's Lovers' Walk. I'd never been, though I heard of it, and wanted to ever since. No surprise that the last two assholes I dated weren't the romantic types who took me out for moonlit walks.

The two of us ambled along the paved path, letting other couples pass us. Fairy lights twined in the trees, and tucked between us, flickering light displays of hearts, dancing couples, flowers, and the artist's imaginings put a soft smile on my face. This place was beautiful. What cruel irony to have finally found the man who wished to share it with me, but *me* was the last thing he wished for.

"So, tell me about River," I spoke up. "What's the story?"

Bane cleared his throat. "Sunny and River built it up. The story's not that interesting, to be honest. You've got a sense of how Sunny's business runs."

I nodded.

"Unlike other organizations, we don't make our money through traditional revenue streams. I manufacture weapons and sell them legitimately through shell companies. Other men in my line of work sell to war-torn countries and organized crime. Our business wasn't built by preying on the helpless. It never was."

"Where do Sunny and River come in?"

"Sunny has the same principle. He steals from thieves. He collects protection money—protection from himself—from gangs instead of the sweet couple running the mom-and-pop. But that's a smaller pool of targets. Gets even smaller when River and his crew go after the same people.

"River's screwed us on smash-and-grabs. Either by leaving anonymous tips that someone was about to rob them, or intercepting routes and codes to get there and steal it first. He's delayed our shipments, stolen potential clients from us, and all around has become a massive anal-tearing dick in the ass."

"River has?" I cried. "But— But he— We can't be talking about the same guy."

"River Delaney—tall, dark, and homeless. He's the same guy."

"You said *us*. He goes after all the Merchants."

"Sunny, Genny, and me. It's harder for him to get to Liam. Leighbridge is a wealthy borough. Not as many homeless people there, and they stand out like sore thumbs when they do. His crew doesn't have the presence there to do Liam damage, but the rest of us, he's relentless."

"But why?"

Bane sighed. "Another old grudge passed down to the next generation. My mother and his mother got in an... argument. My mom won that argument, and his didn't take it well. Ever since, he's had his fun proving how difficult he can make our lives."

I turned that over in my mind. "I'm not suggesting this at all, but... why have you guys put up with it? If he's cost you that much trouble and money, isn't it the nature of legitimate businessmen to settle a threat harshly?"

He drifted closer. Somehow, his hand found its way above my belt again. "Normally, yes. In River's case, he's bulletproof. Everything he takes from us, he gives to his people. Poor, sick, addicted, abandoned. He lives on the streets himself, even though he's stolen enough to set up in his own penthouse. Keeps none of it, Kenzie, and as a result, he's done more for the homeless of Cinco City than all the charities and food drives combined."

"If you shut him down, you leave all those people with nothing," I said softly.

"We're not monsters. And River isn't a monster—though I wouldn't bring his name up around Genny. He hasn't hurt, killed, or gotten any of our people arrested. As much as we dislike losing money to him, we can stomach the reason. The main beef is the guy can't be trusted. His first fucking word was a lie. We've tried brokering peace twice, and he double-crossed us."

"Hard to argue with why Sunny won't work with him. River shocks me once again, but honestly, I was expecting the story to be juicier. Like River stole his first love or they're fraternal brothers separated at birth. One was raised by the evil parent, the other by the good. Now they're locked in an eternal battle of the soul, when what they truly want is a hug from their brother."

Bane laughed so hard he wheezed. "Top-notch storytelling, Kenzie. I'm selling you my life rights. How will you spin the tale of the mad woodsman?"

"First of all, stolen. Mad Woodsman is so the title." I spread out my hands. "For you, we open on a rabbit jumping through the forest—sweet and innocent, nibbling on a leaf as the predator"—I clapped—"strikes. The symbol for your loss of innocence. Then fade to black— Bam! Fight scene."

Bane was crying. His laughter bounded through the trees, teasing giggles out of me, it was that infectious.

"Hold up, we're almost there." Bane clapped his hands over my eyes. "You can't see it yet. Keep walking, I've got you."

"You're not going to walk me into a tree, are you?"

"Nope, even though you ended my movie with me going actually insane and marrying a pine cone."

"It's unexpected," I said, tittering. "The audience won't see it coming."

Bane was warmth on my back. He engulfed me in the heady scent of pine needles and brandy. As he led me through a dark world, my eyes welled and I prayed he didn't notice. Why did it feel so right with someone who wanted no part of me? I thought love was done tormenting me. Looked like her hunt for my tears wasn't over.

*I have Sunny. I have the beginning of something with Liam. A friendship with Bane—a man who listens to my pain, then chases it away—can be enough for me.*

"Ready?"

"I'm ready."

Bane fell away. My vision cleared, and I gasped. Starlight lanterns clung to the branches, delighting in blues, purples, and whites. I spun and the glowing colors swirled with me, painting the sky hazy.

"It's beautiful." I ran up to him, hands grasping his outstretched palms so naturally. "This was the vitally important thing I had to see?" I asked with a joyful laugh.

"What can I say? I've taken up the mission of showing you the stars, Mackenzie Blaine. Wherever they might be."

My chest welled, bursting with all the things I wanted to say. *Thank you. I want to be with you. Fuck your vow. I see stars whenever I'm with you.*

Bane's expression changed. "Mackenzie..."

A hard force thumped my back, propelling me at Bane. He caught me—securing my waist and his arm around my back, holding me to his chest.

"Oops," chimed some tipsy yuppie. He and his girlfriend staggered off. "Sorry about that."

I barely heard him. Our lips hovered centimeters away, his heightened pants tickling me. "Bane," I whispered.

We moved at the same time.

His mouth crashed on mine, tongues battling in a clash that drew moans from us both. Starlight swirled around us—bright, shining beams exploding around me. And anchoring me to the ground: Bane.

We kissed fiercely. Ferociously. Weeks of self-imposed exile brought him to the tipping point, and Bane didn't hold back.

He tangled in my hair, cupped my ass, wrapped my leg around him, dipped me under the stars. Wolf whistles pierced the night and I didn't care. All that existed was him.

Bane grasped my face, tearing away. His chest rolled with ragged pants. "Kenzie, I'm sorry. I shouldn't have—"

"Ugh! Shut up." Grabbing the back of his neck, I crushed our lips together.

Bane forgot his excuses. He swept me up and pressed me against a tree. He didn't break away again.

# Chapter Eleven

"Call when you're in," Sunny said. "I'll tell you what to do."

"How bad will it be if Ryker finds me digging around in the safe?"

"Pretty sure he told you, dimples."

*Oh yeah. Death.*

"You can't explain why you need the diamonds without getting into the rest of it. We're close, Angel. Vito could lead us to the man behind all of this, and the last thing we need is Ryker slowing you down."

The sun beat a retreat across the sky, abandoning Cinco to streetlights, lightning bugs, and the late-night revelers. I stood outside the arcade, prepping for the world's easiest heist. Didn't get much simpler than the owner telling you where to look and handing over the code. Easy, but that didn't mean I needed an audience. This late, Sunny said most of them were gone, leaving the guards on standby. Ryker would be off doing whatever prickly seconds-in-command do.

"Okay. I'll call you back in a minute."

"Wish Mommy luck, Laurel."

"Da," my baby cried right on cue.

I fought to keep the smile off my face walking in. Serious bitch boss on a serious job to take down a serious guy. So what I was flying high on the sexy make-out session Bane and I had in Harmony Park, then in the back seat of the car, then in the elevator up. I wanted to take it back to his place, but Laurel and her nightly bedtime routine called my name.

I had my baby back, Sunny was an incredible boyfriend in and out of bed, Liam's punishment heated me up whenever I thought about it, Bane dumped his vow, and we were closer than ever to finding out who tried to kill Liam and Sunny.

Putting on a pissed-off mask was harder than ever these days.

Inside, the guards greeted me at the concession stand. "Boys."

"Boss," they replied.

"I forgot something," I said, compelled to give a reason. "Won't be here long. Everything as it should be?"

"Yes," Orlando said. "No trouble."

"Good."

I passed by them, moving into the back room. Most of the hustle thinned out, leaving half a dozen people going about their work. One of them was Athena.

"Oh, hello, *boss*." She hopped off the couch she was riding with three other women on her team. Each one as dangerous, muscular, and gorgeous as her. Sunny wasn't messing around when he said he surrounded himself with beauty. "Dropping in on us? What's wrong? You don't trust us?"

My teeth gritted. Oh look, there's my pissed-off mask. "Course I trust you, Athena," I said, tilting my head. "Why wouldn't I? Unless... are you planning another secret meeting with a rival of the Merchants?"

The smirk wiped off her face. Behind her, two of her girls stood up. "Secret meeting? What is she talking about, Athena?"

"It wasn't like that," she snapped. "He approached us for a deal. All we did was listen. Final decision goes to you obviously, *boss*."

Erasing the distance between us, our chests bonked with neither one backing down. "Do it again," I whispered. "Please. Say my title like that again, so you can find out what'll happen."

Her eyes flashed. Fists balling, I felt their ache to bury in my stomach.

"Sunny told me about you," I said. "Went on about how strong, smart, funny you are. That you're the best at what you do."

She blinked, glare fading. "He said that?"

"Yeah, he did. Sunny swore I would like you. Seemed to believe we're destined to be friends." I softened. "I get that I came out of nowhere, popping up the day you find out your boss died. I don't blame you for not trusting me, but if you believe anything, believe this. I'll do whatever it takes to find the bastard that attacked Sunny. He was the first guy in, well... ever, to treat me like I was worth anything. He didn't deserve to go out the way he did, and someone's going to pay for it.

"Tell me right now, Athena. Are we doing this together or aren't we? 'Cause I've got no time to be fighting you in the middle of this war. What's it going to be?"

Athena studied me for a long time, either searching for the trick in my words or deciding whether or not to punch me after all.

She clicked her tongue, flipping her hair over her shoulder. "I'm not who you need to worry about. We want the same thing, boss."

*Boss.* No mocking added.

"As long as we do, we're good." She went back to her girls.

Bane's advice was good, but sometimes, the straightforward approach worked too.

I continued on to Sunny's office, dialing him on the click of the latch.

"I'm here. Where do I go?"

"Go to the bookshelf. Third row from the top. It's behind Native Son." I rushed over, taking Sunny's desk chair with me. He was tall enough to reach the shelf without help, I was not.

Climbing up, I lit on Native Son.

"There's a switch," Sunny continued. "Flip it and the wet bar swings open."

"Seriously? That's so cool."

I did as he instructed and, as promised, soft creaks pierced the silence. The wet bar swung away from the wall, revealing a chest-high opening. I ducked inside and stood up within a small room. A steel door faced me, and by its side, a metal keypad.

"You in, Angel?"

"I'm in. What do I do?"

"There are two codes and a passphrase. First code: 14738."

I typed it in, and heard the faint sound of the bolt disengaging.

"Press and hold zero, then say: All that we see or seem is but a dream within a dream."

I recited it word for word—my reward another disengaged lock.

"Oooh, Edgar Allan Poe. Very literary, baby."

"You like that? There's more where that came from," Sunny said. "I was an English major. Can quote that Shakespeare shit and Poe stuff all day. Whatever gets your thong off."

I giggled. "You were not."

"58274," he said, "and I was. Always knew I was going into the family business, so it didn't matter what I majored in. English sounded cool, so I went with that."

I typed in the final code, pulse humming as the door swung in. This may not be a heist in the traditional blood-pumping, one-step-ahead-of-the-cops sense, still, it was pretty damn thrilling.

"Wow."

When Sunny said safe, he misspoke. Vault was the accurate description, and treasure trove the one I went with. Five metal racks stacked four shelves high claimed the space rivaling the size of Sunny's office. Everywhere I looked, an item worth four times my life looked back at me.

"I don't know where Ryker put it," Sunny said, "so you'll have to look around."

"I'll find it." I started with the rack in front of me, skimming the neat labels for "Diamonds: Seven million dollars."

"How's Laurel?" I asked.

"Bathed, changed, and playing the piano with her feet. Fuller bought her a tummy-time toy that lets her play music when she kicks. Afterward we're chilling until you come home."

"You're so amazing with her, Sunny."

"This surprises you? I excel in all areas, baby."

I heaved a sigh.

"Totally nailing this stepdad thing, so whenever you're ready to make this official, let me know."

"Oh?" I moved to the second rack. "What if I said I'd hop a plane with you to Vegas tonight?"

"I'd say wear something slutty underneath your wedding dress 'cause the only thing better than a Vegas wedding is a Vegas honeymoon."

My toes curled thinking of what we'd get up to in a Bellagio suite, and him carrying me over the threshold inside one.

"I never wanted to get married," I confessed. "Seeing what my mom went through with my father... Putting a ring on her finger convinced the man she was his property. I was terrified of stepping inside another cage."

"Was?" Sunny said gently.

"Yeah." A smile stretched across my lips for more reasons than one. I took down the blue velvet pouch, spilling the diamonds on my palm. "Was."

My prize disappeared in my pocket. "I've got it, Sunny. I'm going to meet Vito now."

"Where's Sienna? Don't meet him alone."

"I'm not. Sienna is catching a ride with Bane and meeting me there, while Bane does his invisibility trick. I don't put a double cross past Vito. It occurred to me that with seven million dollars in his hand, he could knock me out and take off."

"Coates and Wexler should go with you too. They'll be discrete."

"We can't risk it. It's too much of a risk having Bane hang around too. Whoever attacked you was watching close enough to know when your guards were around, and the one night you went out alone. If they're hooked up with Vito and watching me just as closely, discretion in this case is you staying home." I ducked out of the hidden compartment. "I've got to go. I'll call you when it's done, and I'll have a name."

We said our goodbyes and hung up. Climbing on top of the chair, I flicked the switch—sliding Native Son and the wet bar into their rightful place.

"Wasn't expecting you this late."

I jerked and nearly toppled off the chair. Grabbing the leather, it swung around, pointing me straight at Ryker.

"Me?" I jumped off, hoping just how bad a fright he gave me wasn't written on my face. *Oh no, did he see the wet bar move? Did Ryker notice the book I put back on the shelf?*

"What are you doing here?" I asked. I resisted flicking to the wet bar and giving myself away. "I thought we discussed the open-door policy. It doesn't exist."

"Orlando called." Ryker stepped farther in the room, letting the door shut us in. "Said the boss stopped by to make sure everything was okay."

"Huh." I moved, inching toward the door. I had to catch a thirty-five-minute ride to Harlow where Vito was waiting. I didn't have time for this. "So, you rushed over here to check on me? You've got to get yourself a life, man."

Ryker chuckled, and my insides curdled. He smiled for the second time. Why did that not feel good for me?

"Where is it?"

I tensed. "Where's what?"

"Orlando said you forgot something. Where is it?" he asked slowly.

"I thought I forgot one of the inventory sheets." I was proud of myself for the quick answer. "I was missing a page and thought I left it here, but it seems I didn't. Probably is at home mixed with the wrong papers." Turning, I cast a look at the bookshelf. "While I was here, I gave Sunny's books a look. An impressive collection I expect from an English major. Did you study the same thing?"

Ryker narrowed on me—gazed fixed, steady, and hard. I waited for a reply, none came.

"Well, lovely talking with you as always." Brushing past him, the diamonds were an anvil in my pocket. "Go to a club, Ryker. Meet a girl, or guy. Go back to their place and bang some of that stress out of you." I saluted him. "See you tomorrow."

"Good night, boss."

I kept my head up, strolling through the warehouse like I owned the place—because I did.

I caught the first cab that rolled up, ringing up Sienna in the car.

"Did you get it?" she asked by way of hello.

"Got it. Where are you and Bane?"

"Ten minutes from Cooper's. Are you sure we can pull this off? Vito isn't a choirboy to begin with and we're about to walk in with seven million reasons for him to betray us."

"I've got it worked out. Just remember what we talked about."

"This could all be over tonight, Kenzie."

"What will you do if it is?"

"I believe a bookstore is my reward. Although, this tough-girl, beating-jackasses-up thing is fun. What about you? Moving into the compound permanently and becoming a mob wife? I admit, wealth and power look good on you."

"It's weird to think about. I know what he does. I'm *doing* what he does, but everything I've learned about good, bad, right, and wrong goes out the window when I'm with the guys. All I see is the man who fought to get my daughter back, painted fairies with me, and took me to see the stars. They're not guys you walk away from—legitimate day jobs or not."

"Kenzie, you dated a bunch of guys who pretended to be good and turned out rotten. The natural move was to fall for men who are as bad as it gets, with golden hearts on the inside."

"So, you don't think I'm crazy?"

"Remember when I told Sunny that he had a long, interesting life ahead of him that isn't meant to be cut short by hairless assassins?"

"Yeah, I remember."

"Well, that's true... as long as he's with you. That's why the visions stopped. As dangerous as the Merchants, their life, and their enemies are, you're safest when you're with them." Sienna clicked her tongue. "I couldn't tell you this earlier, of course, because you've got a mile-long stubborn streak and would've ditched Sunny just to prove me wrong."

"That's not true," I cried.

"It is. Thankfully the forces that govern my gift had everything under control."

"It's so comforting to know I never had any control over my life." I checked the street signs. "I've got to go, Sienna. See you in a bit."

"See ya."

The cab dropped me off directly in front of Cooper's. Sunday night, the crowd thinned out, leaving a few patrons clinging to the last hours of the weekend and a couple guys at the bar drowning their sorrows. Sienna waved to me from her booth toward the middle and beneath the television. She got up and left, and I sat down.

A few people filed in and out of the bar while I waited. I stayed glued to my seat, going over my speech backward and forward. Vito arrived ten minutes late, strutting in at nine forty. Two guys came in behind him and peeled off, taking up stools near the entrance. From the pointed looks in my direction, I figured they were with him.

"Mackenzie Blaine." Vito sat down, smirking away. "That's your name, isn't it?"

"Yep, and it wasn't a secret. So why do you look proud of yourself?"

He put his arms up. "I'm cool. It's just nice to know who I'm doing business with. According to what I dug up, you worked some fancy-ass fashion job, then vanished off the face of the earth. What happened?"

"Met a guy and it didn't work out. Met another guy and it went even worse. If you want to have story time, you first. I heard your grandfather was a King."

Something flashed in his eyes—gone as quickly as it came. "My father, his father, and his father's father were Kings. They were the oldest gang in this city. The Kings were unstoppable." He leaned across the table. "Here's what Sunny—what all the Merchants—left out of the history lesson. When they took over, they gave the gangs a choice. Work for us and you keep your money, territory, and your lives. Work for us, and we won't hunt you down like dogs. They got a choice, Blaine... except for the Kings.

"The Merchants obliterated them. Whoever wasn't killed was arrested. Whoever escaped death and jail was stripped of the little dignity they had left. My grandfather was killed. My father was arrested. And my mother and I stood on the front lawn as the repo men carried our life away."

"I'm sorry," I replied. And a part of me meant it.

Whatever happened back then, one thing was certain, the Merchants didn't take over the Cinco underground by asking nicely. Blood was spilled. Lives ruined. Families destroyed. Children still weep over their father's grave—even if he chose a life of crime.

"Don't be," Vito hissed. "It made me stronger. It taught me the lesson my father tried to teach me. Whatever you want in this life, take it. Or someone else will take it from you."

I thought of Lyla, Damien, Luca, Charlie, Courtney, Talia. "This world isn't for the meek. It never was."

He nodded firmly. "I've got a right to hate the Merchants. Before we do this"—a faint click sounded under the table—"convince me you do too. 'Cause right now you dropping out of nowhere to throw a bunch of money on my lap isn't smelling right."

I blinked lazily. "If you wanted to test me, couldn't you have done that last night? I've got what you asked for. I'm here to make a deal."

The muzzle bit into my knee. "Answer the question."

*Think of something, Kenzie. Give him a version of the truth.*

"You looked into me, so you know I left Caddell House under a cloud."

"Yeah, and?"

"I was set up," I replied. "Framed. I was bullied for months, but kept my head down and did good work. What did it get me? Thrown out on my ass and burned in the fashion world. No one would hire me, and I was forced to move out of my apartment, into a shithole."

The gun fell off my leg. "What happened?"

"I got involved with a guy. He was the 'even worse' that I mentioned. Long story short: he forced me into prostitution."

"Forced—?"

"Rape, Bernardi. When I refused, he locked me in a room and sent enough guys in that I eventually said yes."

"Wow. That's messed up."

I inclined my head. "I got away from him—got free. Then I found out that Sunny Bellisario paid Adams a visit before he ever got his hands on me. Sunny knew what he was doing, and instead of shutting him down, he gave Adams a slap on the wrist and sent him on his way. Sunny ain't responsible for all the shit that happened to me, but he's responsible for enough.

"The Merchants appointed themselves judge, jury, and executioner of the underground. No one fucking asked them to, but Sole made it his job to protect the women of North Quay from men like Adams. If he won't do the job right, he and his whole damn family can go."

He bobbed his head hard. "That's what I'm saying, thank you. So marrying Sunny and taking over the gang was a long con?"

"Started out that way, then things got blurry. What can I say? I've never had the best taste in men. But whatever feelings I started to have for him didn't matter. I was taking him and the Merchants down either way."

"Did you kill him?"

"No, that wasn't me. Don't have a clue who did it, but Sunny had enemies. Becoming a young widow wasn't a surprise, and with him out of the way, taking out the rest of them gets a whole lot easier. So, are we doing this or what?"

"We're doing it," he said. "Show me the diamonds."

"Uh-uh. The gun. Hand it to me under the table."

Vito scoffed. "You've got the diamonds. I could've shot you and taken them at any time."

"That's exactly why I don't have all the diamonds," I said to his falling face. "They're waiting nearby to be brought in at my signal. After you've given me the name and it checks out. Oh— and after your boys at the bar find another place to be tonight, then the diamonds are yours."

"How do I know the diamonds are nearby? For all I fucking know, you'll take the name and run."

"Why would I do that, Vito? I want to work with you. That's a lot easier when everyone trusts each other. You make the first move."

He flicked from me, to his friends, to the door, and back to me. There was a soft thud as the gun landed next to me.

"Now my turn." I fished the pouch out of my pocket and slid it across the table. "Five out of the twenty. You get the rest after I get the name."

Vito snatched it up. Caring little for secrecy, he dumped them on his palm, squinting at them. Wasn't sure what he saw, but he nodded at me and tucked them in his jacket.

"It's Grant. Lochlan Grant. He's a loan shark based in North Quay."

"Why is a loan shark blowing up warehouses?"

"Because he moved in on Harlow. Grant had to start up a side business because Sunny's seventy percent cut doesn't leave much for the essentials. He had a few people in Harlow who owed him, and when one woman didn't pay up, his boys taught her a lesson. Grant had no idea she was a Cardinal.

"FGH beat his ass in the street, in front of his wife and daughter. The man spat his teeth on the sidewalk."

"Then he hit the warehouse and didn't take credit for it? Why?"

Smiling, Vito tapped his nose. "Long game, baby. Hunt is always in that bar surrounded by fifty insane bitches packing .45s. Going at her headfirst won't work, so he hit her where it hurts."

"That was six months ago. What's he done since?"

If anything, his smirk widened. "Trust me, he has plans. Grant's got something for all of them."

"How did he get his hands on the stuff to blow the warehouse?"

"Everyone's got friends, baby."

That was so close to what I told Genny and Sunny, I shivered.

"Friends that are a helluva lot easier to make when you say you're looking to take the Merchants down a few pegs. Every gang, loan shark, and crime family in Waterford, Leighbridge, North Quay, and Harlow are chafing under their rules. We want the chains around our necks gone. That's how I know he'll be very interested in what you've got to say."

"Lochlan Grant." Eyes on Vito, I dialed Sienna and gave her the name.

"I'll call you back in five minutes," she said.

Sienna called back in four.

"Grant checks out, sis. Thatcher didn't have to look up the name. He's a loan shark like Vito said, and earlier this year, Genny taught him a painful lesson. Turns out, he got loud with Sunny after that. Threatened to stop paying him his cut, so Sunny sent Makai to change his mind."

I whistled. "That'll cause a grudge. All right, we're good here. Bring the stuff." To Vito, I said, "Send your boys out."

Vito jerked his head at them. They filed out, and minutes later, Sienna came in.

"Pleasure doing business with you." It was Vito's superpower turning a simple sentence into the foulest catcall. "Here's my number." He put the card in Sienna's hand. "Call me when it's time to get serious. Or, you know, just call me."

Growling, he snapped his teeth at her, blowing kisses on the way out.

"Ugh. Somehow, Genny *down*played how disgusting that man is."

I hugged her to me. "Let's get out of here. I'm due for twelve showers, and Sunny's going to take them with me. Not a bad tradeoff."

"Hold on," she said. "Let me text our invisible friend that we pulled it off and he can bring the car around back."

Sienna and I made for the back door, saying goodbye to Cooper's and my double life. Lochlan Grant was the guy we wanted. Working to keep Sunny rich and then, when he branches out, Genny kicks his ass and humiliates him in front of his family. The cherry on top, he tries to get out from under the Merchants' hold and gets his ass kicked for that too. Hatred like that boils until you think if the Merchants won't set you free, you'll free the world of the Merchants. Oh yeah, Thatcher needed to speak to Lochlan Grant.

The two of us stepped out into the alley.

I asked Sienna, "Did Thatcher say if Grant is b—?"

"Don't move."

Hands seized me from behind, hauling me off my feet and away from Sienna. Any thought of screaming fled as the muzzle dug into my temple.

"I knew it," he hissed. "I fucking knew it!"

My eyes bugged, but Sienna said it for me. "Ryker? What the hell are you doing?!"

"Catching you two traitors the fuck out is what I'm doing. I heard everything."

"Ryk—"

Ryker snaked around my throat. His arm was a band on my windpipe. "Shut up! Say another word and I paint the brick with your brains."

"Ryker, calm down," Sienna shrieked. She threw her hands up, tears spilling over. "It's not what you think. You have it all wrong."

"I have it wrong?" He shook me. "I knew when I saw you pawing around on that shelf that you knew about the vault. You stole the diamonds, and when I followed you to get them back, I found you sitting there, waiting. So I waited too. It was even worse than I thought.

"You targeted Sunny. Tricked him!" Emotion ravaged his words. "I bet you convinced him to keep your relationship a secret to stop the crew looking up the truth about you. All so you could get revenge for something Sunny had nothing to do with!"

"R-Ryker," I rasped. My nails raked his arm. "Lis-ten..."

"He would've stopped Adams if he'd known the truth. You should've known that. If you spent more than ten minutes with Sunny, you'd know he hates men like Adams. He would've hunted him down for—"

Sienna rushed him and Ryker whipped the gun on her, skidding her to a hard stop. She tripped and hit the concrete.

"Sienna!"

"All of this to get back at his family—take down the Merchants." Ryker shook against my throat. "For that, you killed him."

"I didn't!" *Bane! Where are you?!*

"Liar," he hissed, pressing the gun deeper. "You get tangled up in his life and then he just happens to be killed by someone else, just in time for you to infiltrate the crew and steal for Vito Bernardi."

"No, Ryker, you... have to listen to me! You don't understand!"

He cocked the hammer. "This is for my friend."

"No!"

"Sunny isn't dead!" Sienna shot up and grabbed him, fighting to tug me free. "Let her go!"

"What? But you—"

"It's true," I cried. "He's not dead. But... someone did try to... kill him. This was a plan, Sunny's plan, to draw them out. I swear, Ryker."

"You're lying."

"Talk to him yourself! My phone— It's under the name Trouble. Call him. Ask him!"

"Get me to drop my hand so you can get free? Nice try, bitch."

"I'll do it." Sienna scrambled for the phone.

"Hey! Drop it!"

"Or you'll what?" Furious, tear-filled pools burned him. "Kill us both? If you do, Sunny will kill you. This isn't a trick. What kind of scam involves calling a dead man? He doesn't answer and you kill us anyway. Sunny is alive. Let me prove it to you."

He growled, clenching me tighter. Black spots danced in my vision.

"Put it on speaker."

Sienna smashed her fingers on the buttons and held it up as it rang.

"Sienna?" Sole's unmistaken baritone poured through the speakers. "Everything okay?"

Ryker's gun hand flopped at our sides. "Sunny?" he breathed. "How—?"

In a breath, Ryker was gone. His arm flew off my neck and the rest of him with it. Roaring, Bane clamped his throat and tossed him across the alley. Ryker crashed into the brick, collapsing to the ground in a still, bleeding heap.

"SO IT WAS ALL SUNNY'S idea?" Ryker winced, pressing a dishcloth packed with ice against his head. "Why didn't he tell us? Tell me at least."

The four of us sat in Bosco's Diner—the best place to get chicken and waffles, according to Bane. I'd give him that, they were pretty damn good.

"No one outside the family knew," I croaked. My voice had yet to recover from my throttling. "Hard to play dead when everyone and their brother knows the truth."

"Nah, that's not it." Ryker leaned back in his seat, that familiar scowl returning. "He suspected one of us, didn't he? Even me. The smug, shit-eating bastard."

"He didn't actually," I replied. "Sunny refused to believe you guys had anything to do with it, but it made more sense to be sure. Especially since he was drugged the night he went to Laser to check out the connection between Xander and the owner."

Ryker made a noise in his throat. "Yeah, well, I guess I'm a smug, shit-eating bastard... because I checked Xander out too. I checked out everyone in the crew when Sunny went missing without a word."

"You did?" I pushed my waffles aside. "Did you find anything? Is anyone in the crew connected to a guy named Lochlan Grant?"

"Lochlan Grant. You and Vito were talking about him. What's he got to do with this?"

"You first," Bane barked. He hadn't forgiven him for my sore throat and Sienna's scraped knees. "Sunny's kidnapping went down at Laser. He suspected the owner of running a bootlegging operation with Xander getting a cut."

Ryker shook his head, then stopped, grimacing. "Nah. Xander's clean. He's hooked up with the owner all right, but not because they're cheating Sunny. It's because they're cheating on the owner's wife. They're fucking."

My brows blew up my forehead. "Are you sure?"

"Yep. Didn't catch him with more cash than he should've, but a friend of mine clocked a recurring charge at the Lotus Inn. Xander meets him at the club, and then they duck out and go to the hotel. All of my people are clean."

"Are you certain? Sunny has almost forty people in his crew. How do you know every one of them is trustworthy?"

"I know." His tone clanged the bell of finality. "I checked them twice and I checked you twenty times. If I suspected any of them for betraying Sunny, I wouldn't have hesitated any longer than I did with you."

"Fair enough."

Sienna brought the conversation back around. "Are we saying it's just coincidence that Sunny was taken at Laser?"

"Not a coincidence," Bane said. "He was watched. Followed. What was special about that night wasn't where he went, it's that Sunny went there alone. Whoever was tailing him saw their chance and struck."

"Maybe Grant," Sienna said. "Is he bald? White?"

Ryker spoke up. "White, yes. Bald, no. Full head of salt-and-pepper hair. Again, what does he have to do with this?"

"Everything. Possibly," I added. "You know what's been going on. Your routes hijacked. Your warehouses raided. Genny, Liam, and Bane dealt with sabotage attacks too. This enemy hates the Merchants—all of them. Sunny stayed dead so I could find out why. That's what you heard between me and Vito. He definitely fits the suspect list. The guy despises the Merchants for what happened to his family. We figured he'd have friends who felt the same. With him pointing us in the right direction, we'll narrow it down to who brought Sunny up to that overpass."

"I get it," Ryker said, "but Lochlan? I overheard you guys talking about the warehouse blown up in Harlow. If Vito's got you convinced Grant did it, the guy's putting you on. Lochlan is small-time. He doesn't have the balls to do it himself or the money to hire someone else."

I gave him a serious look. "Genny beat him in front of his family. You grow balls after something like that. And you can't be sure he doesn't have money. He moved his business into Harlow, and only got caught because he sent his boys after the wrong Cardinal. Isn't it possible he could've set up shop in another borough? Like the one the Merchants haven't taken over."

"Rockchapel," Ryker, Bane, and Sienna said.

"Lochlan Grant is where we start. At the very least, Thatcher needs to talk to him about the *friend* who gave him explosives. Two Hunts and two bombs? Now that isn't a coincidence."

Pushing his plate aside, Ryker dropped his makeshift ice pack on the table. "Vito's information better be worth something, because Sunny's vacation is over. Tell his ass to show up at the arcade tomorrow—better yet, I'll tell him." Ryker got to his feet.

"Wait," I said. "Sunny can't reveal himself until we're sure Grant is a part of this and he gives up his bald pal. If it's not Grant, I'll get more names out of Vito. I'll make him give me info on his crew. He seems to think they're a threat to the Merchants."

"If they're not, they will be. Blaine, you just handed the enemy seven million fucking dollars. He could hire two dozen hit men with that kind of money. More than enough for each member of the family. Sunny's getting his ass back to work, because no matter what, I'm stealing those diamonds back tomorrow before he has time to fence them. Vito will think you double-crossed him and you won't get another word out of him."

"But—"

"Am I wrong, Bane?" he demanded.

Bane gazed at me and shook his head. "He's not wrong, Kenzie. We have to get those diamonds back. As it is, I had three of my men follow him after he left Cooper's. He doesn't get to keep his prize."

"Why did you let me give it to him, then? Why did Sunny?"

He smiled crookedly. "Don't you know? Sunny risked it because Vito chose a simple, nonviolent test to prove yourself. He could've asked you to bring him Genny's head in a bag or deliver a *special package* to the Fairfield. We weren't going to risk you and Sienna getting hurt, or asked to do something you couldn't."

My chest cracked open. "Oh." *They chanced their enemy becoming too powerful to stop, to protect me.*

Sienna got up too. She put her arm around me, squeezing me tight as we trudged home. "Let's hope Grant is the guy we're looking for. I don't know about you, but I'm ready to hang up my badass double life."

Bane drove us to the Fairfield, dropping Ryker off at a nice-looking apartment building on the way.

I was bone-tired. The only thing on my mind was a shower, hot tea, and snuggling with Laurel. The elevator pushed us out on Sunny's floor. Bane stopped me stepping off with Sienna.

"Kenzie, can I talk to you for a minute?"

"Sure." I reached for him as the doors closed.

Bane slid out of reach. "Wait."

"What's wrong?"

"Kenzie, I..."

My smile melted seeing the expression on his face. "Bane, don't do this," I whispered.

"I already did it. I swore I wouldn't fall for anyone. I won't saddle a woman I love with this life."

"You're not saddling me with anything. Bane, why can't you see that this isn't a life you force on anyone, it's one they choose. They choose to be with you. *I* choose to be with you knowing what you do and how dangerous it is. Living with you, marrying you, having kids with you. It's my choice. If I'm willing to risk the future, why won't you?"

"Because you don't understand the risk!" he burst out. "A couple weeks playing a role doesn't prepare you for what this life is like. If Vito asked you to prove yourself through blood, could you do it? Innocent blood, of course not, but it doesn't mean he gets to walk free. It doesn't mean blood doesn't get spilled.

"Could you torture him to find the bomber that almost killed Tricky? Can you break bones to maintain fear? Can you demand half the contents in a man's safe while he's on his knees begging and pleading that he needs the money for his family? Can you do what it takes to be the monster that monsters are afraid of?

"Can you love a man that does?"

"Bane, that's not you," I forced past the lump in my throat. "You're not a monster. You—"

"And that you believe that"—he gently cupped my face—"is all the answer I need. I am a monster, Kenzie. Never tried to be anything else. Never wanted to be. You're searching for goodness in me because that's all there is in you.

"One day, you'll come face-to-face with the real me, and that goodness won't bear it. It'll torture you—torn between right and wrong—until you either hate me or push your morals so far down you won't be you anymore. I can't stand those choices, so I'm making one. You and I will not happen, Kenzie."

Bane slashed my chest open.

"Ever."

My heart was torn out—still beating in his fist.

"Last night was a mistake."

He squeezed tighter, tighter, tighter.

"My mistake, not yours. I shouldn't have taken you to the park or pretended we could be just friends."

My heart slipped through his grasp, smacking the floor.

"From now on, we should keep our distance. Make it easier on both of us. When this is done, I'll go back to the woods and we'll forget this happened."

Bane ground it under his boot, smearing my blissful happiness of just a moment ago across the tile.

"It's for the best anyway. Even if I was willing to break my vow, you're with Sunny. I couldn't share a woman with my brother."

Bane pressed *open*, stepping out of the elevator. "I'm sorry, Makenzie. If things were different, I... Damn, you make me wish things were different."

The doors slid shut, hiding me as I slid to the floor, crying on the remains of my smashed heart.

# Chapter Twelve

"Kenzie? Kenzie, are you listening?"

I blinked, eyes coming into focus. Sienna gave me a strange look.

"What's up with you?" she asked. "Your energy is different this week. Darker. Heavier. Did something happen?"

Looking away, I fixed on Laurel and her tummy-time toy. The piano was a huge hit. She lay there kicking and shrieking along with the *bong, bong, bong*, thrilled by all the noise she was making. I could never look at her and be sad, that time was no different.

My frown smoothed out, taking thoughts of Bane with it. "Only what was meant to happen."

Sienna stretched out on the sofa, resting her head on my lap. I silently thanked her for not asking more questions.

"Morning, Liam. Morning, Elizabeth." Fuller let them in and accepted a huge hug from Tricky. "Did you have breakfast yet?"

"Daddy made French toast and bacon."

"Yum. Laurel is about to have her breakfast. Do you want to join us?"

Did she want to? Tricky raced to the kitchen and plucked Laurel's breakfast off Shonda. I was ninety-nine percent sure Elizabeth hitched a ride down here for Laurel—forget that the rest of us were here. It was too adorable how much she loved my daughter. The other day, she proposed a list of matching-outfit ideas for the two of them, and what else did I have to do these days but sew and take care of my baby?

In the four days since Vito gave up Grant and Bane rejected me in the elevator, Sole Bellisario rose from the dead. With him running the gang again, there was nothing more for me to do.

Picking up Laurel, I carried her to the high chair and got her ready for breakfast. I would have fed her, but Fuller, Shonda, and the ladies loved to help out. Actually, they insisted on it. There was nothing I could do. Everyone loved my Laurel, I just had to share.

"Sienna, Mackenzie," Liam said. "When you have a moment, can I see you in Sole's room?"

"I'll be right there."

I peppered Laurel's face with kisses, then left her in the hands of Fuller and Tricky. Liam and Sunny were mid heated conversation when we came in.

"Everything okay?" I asked.

"No." Sunny pulled me onto his lap. Liam looked at us and flicked away. "Thatcher can't find Lochlan Grant."

"Can't find him?" Sienna repeated. "What does that mean? Did Vito lie to us?"

"On the contrary," Liam said. "It's looking more and more like his information was good. Grant packed up his house, wife, and kid, and moved. Their mail was forwarded to a PO box in Rockchapel."

"So he is there," I said. "Out of Merchant reach."

"That's what he thinks." Sunny stroked my thigh, zinging electricity beneath the tender skin. "One of his guys hands over his payments. The payments haven't stopped, so Ryker didn't have to look into him until his name came up in your talk with Vito. Grant moved, and he didn't want me to know about it."

Liam chimed in. "That, on top of the PO box, on top of the phony information used to open the PO box confirms Grant doesn't want to be found. That's reason enough to pick him up for a chat."

"How? You said the information behind the PO box is fake. Are Ryker, Makai, and the guys going to ask around Rockchapel?" I put that to Sunny. "See if a new loan shark blew into the borough."

"Can't," he said through gritted teeth. "Rockchapel belongs to the Rat King. He finds out we're looking for someone on his turf, he'll send his people to lie, trick, and lead us off course. Just to be an insufferable asshat."

"The answer is obvious, then, isn't it?" Sienna asked. By the blank looks Sunny and Liam gave her, it wasn't obvious to them. "Ask River to find

Grant. Find him, tail him, see if he left to get away from the Merchants, or if he left to plot against you guys."

"Impossible," Sunny said. "I told you. River will fuck me over just because he can. Just because it's me asking."

"So, don't ask." Sienna grinned at me. "Kenzie will. River will do it if it comes from her. Fucking over Kenzie will not help him achieve his ultimate goal of getting in her pants. You can always rely on River to put his own interests first."

"Sienna!" I hissed. "I keep telling you it's not like that. We're friends."

She rolled her eyes. "Yeah, whatever. I'm telling you, River and his crew are our best bet. It's worth a try." Sienna rubbed her temple, forehead wrinkling. "I feel something coming. I don't know what or when yet, but he's frustrated. He didn't get Liam. Genny moved out of her place, and now he knows Sunny's alive. He will strike again—soon."

"But you don't know who he is," Liam said. "Not even if it's Grant."

"I only have a name. I'd have to meet Grant. Read his energy and get a sense of if it matches the darkness I'm feeling."

"More reason to track this guy down," I said. "Listen, I'll ask River if it'll bring us any closer to catching this guy. My sister is right about one thing—the attacker just found out that every attempt to hurt the Merchants has failed. That's when you get frustrated, and when you're frustrated, you're reckless."

Sunny shrugged. "Beg a favor off the King if you want. Since I know this one will come with a price tag, make him agree to conditions."

With Sunny's green light, Sienna and I didn't waste a minute. We changed into sneakers, jeans, and simple tees. Our luck had changed, and we'd be a pair of assholes to rub our old friends' noses in it.

Sienna flagged down a cab in front of the Fairfield and gave directions to the empty warehouse by the North Quay docks. Marty popped out of nowhere as we stepped out. He always did that back in the day when we lived with River's people. Watching, waiting, listening. I should've put together that he was more than paranoid. Marty was River's second.

"What's this? Come back to visit your lowly chums."

"Came back to do this." I kissed his cheek. "And yeah, if we could talk to River, that'd be cool too."

He laughed. "River floats. No pun intended. He's in Waterford today, recruiting. Should be back before lunch. You hanging around?"

"How about lunch on us?"

"How about yes."

"We'll grab Cugino's. Breadsticks, pasta, salad."

"Sweetie, quit at yes. You've got my mouth watering over here. I'll send Mellow and Nathan to help you. We've got twenty-four."

*Twenty-four.* Twenty-four people taking shelter in the warehouse. Twenty-four mouths to feed.

"Did people leave?" I asked. "The crew cracked fifty when we were with you guys."

"Nah. I meant there are twenty-four in this warehouse," he said, pointing to the run-down building behind him. "There are more filling up the next three over."

"Okay, then ask Stevie, Lennon, Ameer, Yosef, and Bruno to come too. We'll need more hands."

The hostess fell over herself hearing the large order we placed. We kicked back for an hour and a half, catching up while they cooked and boxed everything. By the time we returned and passed out the food, River came back with a young boy and girl trailing behind him, making themselves as small as possible in their ratty sneakers and torn, dirty clothes.

"Guys, this is Jamie and Annabelle," he announced. "Say hi."

"Hey."

"What's up?"

"Good to meet you."

"Over here," Millie called. "We've got extra clothes and sleeping bags. Help yourself."

"Looks like we've got Italian too," said River. "My sugar mama comes through."

Sienna waggled her brows at me from over her mushroom risotto. "Sugar mama."

I pointedly turned my back on her. Taking River's hand, I tugged him outside.

"Come to deliver the good news?" River posted up against the wall, arms folded.

"What news?"

"Sole Bellisario has risen from the dead."

"Is there anything you don't know?"

"I don't know where you want to go to dinner this Friday."

I bit my lip. "About dinner."

"You changed your mind. Sunny poisoned you against me already."

"No. I was going to ask if we could make it the three of us. You, me, and Laurel. She's cooped up inside all the time. Plus, this is a great chance for you to meet her."

"I'd love to meet her. Let's make it ten o'clock. We'll have brunch in the park."

"Perfect."

I bumped against his arms till he let me in. River encircled me, resting his chin on my crown. I couldn't stop myself. I loved his hugs. Loved how warm and safe they made me feel. "Since you brought it up, if Sunny did poison me against you, you'd have yourself to blame since you let Bane and Sunny give me their version of events instead of explaining yourself."

"Did they tell you I was a double-dealing liar who sabotaged them every chance I get because of a grudge stretching back to our folks?"

"To put it nicely."

"Huh. Then, you don't need my version of events. That pretty much sums it up."

"Men," I muttered, pulling a laugh out of him.

"What have I done to let down my sex now?"

"Forever with these pissing contests. I hope you can set the war aside for a few days. I came because we need help."

"We. You're a 'we' with the Merchants now."

"I'm definitely a 'we' with Sunny. I'd like to 'we' with Liam, and Genny has this powerful ability to make everyone want to 'we' her. River, they helped me get Laurel back, and gave us a home. I owe them more than I can repay."

"I'm glad they were there for you. Truly, I am. It's taken decades, but they've finally put a point in their column—by making you happy." Golden, smoldering pools enveloped me, carrying me down, down, down. My knees shook as River brushed his lips over mine. "So ask me now," he whispered, "while I might say yes."

*Right, obviously. I'm here to ask for River's help, not make out with Sunny's rival. He said he would share me, but I wonder if River makes the list.*

My senses returned. "We think we're close to finding the person who attacked Sunny. Looks like he disappeared into Rockchapel, and I'm told that's your turf. We need you to track this guy down. If it's him, we can end this threat against the Merchants once and for all."

"And why would I concern myself with their threats? What's in it for me?"

"Why?" I grasped his jaw, making sure he saw my expression. "Because if you know everything, then you also know someone paid off a valet to put a bomb in Liam's car. His six-year-old daughter and I were seconds away from hopping inside when it blew. I can still feel the heat on my face, River. Hear her screaming. Do you want to see the marks her nails made on my neck—?"

"Kenzie, stop." River put my hand down, stopping me from pulling away my collar. "No, I didn't know about that. I'm guessing it happened in Leighbridge. Word from that borough doesn't reach me. If it did"—River's tone dropped dangerously—"I'd have found the fucker myself. Who is this guy? Where in Rockchapel could he be?"

"His name is Lochlan Grant." I told him the information I got from Vito, Ryker, and Sunny. "They don't know where he could be, but he's a loan shark. People have to know about him to do business. If you ask around, he has to turn up."

"I'll find him."

"What do you want in exchange?"

"Oooh." River shuddered in mock ecstasy. "My favorite question. Say it again."

Rolling my eyes, I said, "What would you like in exchange, O Granter of Favors?"

"See, now that's a good title. Loving it better than Rat King."

"Can't believe I ran with you for months and didn't hear the title. It's hard not to feel duped, River."

"You weren't tricked. Outsiders call me the Rat King. They say I'm a gang leader because a Black man with dreads looking after any group of people has to be a banger. I don't see us that way." He jerked his chin at the warehouse. "My people don't see us that way. We're a family. The only family we've got after ours died, abandoned, or lost us. All I've ever tried to do is look after people no one gives a damn about. Yes, sometimes we break the rules to survive, but that's what it is, Kenzie—survival. I've never stolen or tricked just because I can, or because it's easy. I wonder if your Merchant friends can say the same."

"Maybe they can't." The confession forced out of me. "But is it nobility that makes you snatch jobs out from under Sunny or hit his shipments? Kinda seems like you do that because you can."

River smirked. "Touché. But I wouldn't count my war with the Merchants. Stealing from thieves doesn't rate too high on the mortal-sins list. Why should I feel bad for taking from them and giving to my people?"

"You're a regular old Robin Hood."

"What I am was born out of necessity. The world needs men like me, as Sunny just found out. So, you mentioned price." I didn't like the look on his face. "I'll find Lochlan Grant. Where he lives, where he shops, what time he goes to the bathroom and if it's number one or two. In exchange, I get the diamonds."

"What?" I pulled away "How—?"

"Assume I know everything, Kenzie. It's easier that way. Ira Hansen is part of the reason my family has grown. He's a slum lord, did you know?"

I nodded.

"His apartments were a step below unlivable, but that didn't stop him jacking up the rent and tossing people out when they couldn't pay. I was planning to bust him—days away in fact. But Athena and her girls got him first. I applaud them for paying back the tenants, but that didn't help the people Hansen already evicted," River said, gesturing to the run-down, shabby home for dozens of people. "Those diamonds would go a long way toward getting those people their lives back. One of my guys heard Vito bragging about them a few nights ago. Next thing we hear, Vito's raging about a double cross and the diamonds are back with the Sons of Saint. I know Sunny has them. I get the diamonds or no deal."

"The Merchants stole them back because they weren't about to give an enemy the keys to an empire. Why would they agree to this?"

"A handful of diamonds is a small price to pay to end this threat. If Grant is behind Sunny and Liam's attacks, he's gotten closer to taking them out than anyone ever has. They're worried... or we wouldn't be having this conversation."

"Okay. I'll tell Sunny. Let him decide." I eyed him. "But if he says no, would you really do nothing? He could be the bomber who almost killed me."

"I didn't say I wouldn't find this guy. If he tried to hurt you, there's nowhere in any borough he can hide from me." His tone plummeted the temperature. "Without those diamonds, I won't find him for Sunny, but I will find him."

He kissed my cheek. "Either way, I'll take care of it. Sunny's answer decides if he gets a crack at him. Don't block the next unknown caller that rings your phone. If I find this guy, it's a waste of time you coming all the way out here, and I'm not setting foot in the Fairfield. I'll get my hands on a phone today. What's your number?"

I rattled off the number, secretly surprised that he'd do this for me—diamonds or no.

Sienna wasn't. "Right. Just like it'll be a surprise when he finally flips you off your feet and drops his pants. *It just happened, Sienna*," she mocked. "*I wasn't expecting it. Oh no, what if he doesn't call me?*"

"You're a mean person, you know that?"

She cracked up. The top of the street loomed ahead. After enjoying lunch and catching up with our old friends, it was time to go home. As soon as I got back, I was feeding Laurel and holding my baby as she napped. Sunny usually came in around that time to massage my shoulders and recite proof of his degree. Though he was back at work, he returned home in time to continue our routine. I wouldn't miss it.

"Believe it or not, I'm not this bashful, clueless girl who pretends she doesn't know when a man is interested in her," I said. "I keep denying anything will happen between me and River because it can't, Si. Not like this. Not when I still don't know who he is. It's hard enough making a relationship work when both parties are honest." Bane flashed through my mind, leaving the pain behind. "I won't make a go of it when I know he's lying."

"What's left to know?" Sienna linked our arms. "You know he's a king-pin with a generous streak who gives the Merchants a run for their money."

"It's just a feeling but... there's more to the story. Sunny speaks about River with more anger than the guy who tried to kill him."

Sienna spun on me. "You don't think that River is the one behind this?"

"No," I said automatically. "I don't know everything about him, but I know that."

"He asked you to give him Sunny when he found out that's who he got the doctor for. Ryker said River sabotages and hits their shipments all the time."

"By now, Sunny would've considered him. He wouldn't let me ask River for help if he thought the man was trying to kill his family."

"River doesn't want them dead, but he doesn't want them in business either. What happened between his mom and theirs to stir such specific hatred?"

"That's a question I'm starting to think I'll never get an answer to."

We flagged down a ride and hitched it to the Fairfield. Up in the apartment, Laurel was changed, tired, and ready for her boob and nap. Sunny rubbed my shoulders while I fed her.

"River said he'd do it for the diamonds."

His hands paused for a second. "Hmm. These diamonds are popular. I don't know where they came from or how Hansen pocketed them. I'm starting to think I'm the only one."

"What are you saying? Vito and River know where the diamonds really came from and somehow that's important?"

"It's the same thing again, Angel. Vito could've asked you to prove you hate the Merchants by murdering us in our beds, but instead, he asked for the diamonds. River could've exploited me for a lot more and stretched the pain out longer, but again, he asks for the diamonds. There has to be a reason."

"Seven million dollars isn't reason enough?"

"Let me put it this way. If you kidnapped an heiress and held her for ransom, would you demand a hundred bucks from her millionaire father, or drain the guy of every dollar you know he's got? When you have leverage, you use it. Vito and River had leverage, but they basically asked for the equivalent of a C-note."

When Sunny put it like that, it was hard to argue with him. I've gone over his books myself and accounted for the money he makes in a week. I've been inside the vault of stashed treasures, just sitting there collecting dust. If you can afford to let seven million in diamonds sit on a shelf waiting for its owner, you can afford to pay out much more to a clever rival who knows when he has you over a barrel.

*So why didn't River ask for more?*

"Does that mean you're not agreeing to his terms?" I asked. Laurel was slowing down, drifting off to sleep. "River said without the diamonds, he'll find Grant, but you won't get a piece of him."

"Bastard."

Laurel was fast asleep, so I let the bad language go.

"Can't have that. River knowing more about my enemy than I do? We're not playing that game at all. He can have them," Sunny announced. "I'll ask Sienna to pass on the news."

"Why not me?"

"Because I plan to have you in a tub within the next"—he made a show of checking his watch—"ten minutes."

After settling Laurel in her crib, I let Sunny lead me out. He didn't turn right toward his room. We snuck up a floor, ducking into the pink apartment.

"Ah, so you meant this tub."

Sunny peeled off his clothes, raising the temperature a hundred degrees. "The filthy things I'm going to do to you in that tub are on my bucket list, Angel. Take it from a formerly dead man, no time like the present." Sunny reached for me.

"Nope," I said, dancing away. "In the tub, Bellisario. I've got a few things to get off my bucket list too."

Sunny backed toward the tub, eyes peeled on me, while he felt for the switch. The jets turned on as my jeans pooled around my ankles.

I wore another set of showstopping lingerie. A plunging lace crotchless teddy. I made this one after Liam tore my last creation to shreds. For Sunny, I made it blue.

"In the tub, Trouble."

Sunny lowered himself into the water, not taking his attention off me for a minute. We were alike in so many ways. One of them that I fantasized about the things I wanted him to do to me in that tub since the first time we jumped in it. We had the same dirty mind—Sunny was just more vocal about it.

*And I'm more visual.*

Climbing up the small steps, I stopped on the top and slowly twisted before Sunny, giving him the three-sixty view of all the lace. What can I say? A designer likes to have her work admired.

High above the world on my platform, I did my striptease—slowly popping each button and dropping a strap. Sunny's hand disappeared in the water. His grunts told me what it was doing.

My legs dipped in and spread. I hung my ass over the rim, leaning back to give Sunny a clear sign of what I wanted next. He descended.

Sole took his time tasting me, his head bobbing between my legs as he got his fill. A small "eep" slipped out as he pushed two fingers inside, working in and out.

It was a warm night and warmer water, and neither chased away the goose bumps popping on my skin. Being with Sunny was like sticking my finger in a socket. Deadly, mind-bending, most would say unwise, but I've never felt more alive than when his electricity runs through my veins—bringing me into his world of adrenaline and living for the moment.

My orgasm ripped through me—proof that my comparison to electricity wasn't far off. I sank into the water with Sunny, my arms draped over his shoulders as we kissed. A tongue-clashing, heated kiss tinged with the taste of me. We broke apart grinning at each other.

"You know," I began, "during our many sex marathons, there is one position we haven't gotten to yet."

"We needed the right setup." He patted the tub. "Here it is. Now, take me."

I giggled. Pushing him back, I climbed on Sunny's lap, sheathing him to the hilt. I didn't worry about the lack of condom. Sunny and I talked about it. I told him I was on the pill. He said he was rich and could afford babies, and ours would be adorable, so bring them on. In every way, Sole Bellisario was like no guy I ever met.

I rocked on top of him, bouncing fast on the balls of my feet, then slowed down—taking as much of him as I could, and withdrawing to the tip. Sunny captured my nipple as I bucked on my bronco, scraping them between his teeth and zinging the sweetest balance of pleasure and pain to my core.

My climax peaked over the horizon, the pressure building fast.

Sunny shot out of the water. I shrieked, all of a sudden finding myself facedown and gripping the rim. "This is why we can't get through cowgirl. I ride you for ten seconds and you lose control, flip me down, and fuck the mess out of me."

"You won't be complaining in a second."

Looking at him over my shoulder, I lazily licked my lips, topping it with a blown kiss. "I'm not complaining now."

"This is why we can't have these things, baby. Every day and in every way, you beg to be fucked."

Sunny lifted my thighs, his grip loose for the jets and bubbles to carry me. Turned out we would experience a new position. This was my first time having sex while floating.

He started pumping—hard, fast, and literally wet. I locked my elbows, pushing back on each thrust, driving him deeper. Moans, grunts, cries, and sloshing water became our soundtrack, and when I finally came, I brought him with me—the two of us tipping off the edge.

Sunny gathered me in his arms, my back to him as he nibbled on my ear, holding me as I came down.

"I'm really glad you crashed on my tent, Sole."

"It was meant to be. On the worst day of your life, that's when angels appear."

"AH, BACK AGAIN SO SOON?"

I sashayed over the threshold, twirling on the welcome mat. Isla clapped.

"Gorgeous, darling. Satin bubble skirt dress with Peter Pan collar. Came out even better than I knew it would. Good thing too. I won't have to throw you out this time."

"I've come to fill your coffers, Isla. I told you this was the start of a long and beautiful relationship."

She laughed. "What can I get you?"

"A few friends of mine need new coats, jackets, and sweaters for the winter," I said, thinking of River's crew. "Warmth and function over style."

"Love, you know better. One need never be sacrificed for the other."

I inclined my head. "True. It's a big job, so I'll take half your stock of faux leather, fleece, and wool."

"Seems you were right. This is the start of a long, beautiful friendship."

While Isla rang up the fabric, Sienna and I looked through her collection of buttons, snaps, zippers, and thread. She knew nothing about designing. Didn't mean she couldn't pick what she liked and reject what she didn't.

*Not enough for seventy-five jackets. Coates and Wexler are waiting outside. Our next stop is North Quay to pick up more from my usual places.*

My phone went off in my purse.

"Hello?"

"Kenzie, it's me. Where are you?"

"River?" I glanced at Isla and crossed the room, moving out of distance. "Did you find Grant?"

"I did. You were right that he was hiding out in Rockchapel, and correct that he didn't change professions. Had my people ask around about a new loan shark and they came up with the name Amos Jefferson. I tracked him down myself. Jefferson is Grant."

"Cute," I said. "Changing it to another president's name. I heard that disguises are useless because one way or another, we turn them into self-portraits."

"Interesting thought with some truth behind it, but we'll save the human behavior debate for later. Where are you?" Urgency laced the question.

"You need to get to Banana Tree Café now. I've got a phone, but it's ancient. No camera. You have to come out here and see for yourself."

"Okay, I'll call Sunny—"

"No. Just you."

"Why? If this is about Grant, Sunny needs to know. He agreed to give you the diamonds, River, you can't cut him out."

"I hope you're arguing with me on the way to the car. Sunny can't know until there's something to know. Only you can tell me if there is. Trust me, Kenzie."

I hesitated for no more than a second. River lied and hid things from me all the time, but never after he included "trust me" in the sentence. He asked for trust when I could depend on it.

"All right, I'm on my way." I hung up. "Isla, you have the card on file. Charge it and ship the orders, please. I have to go."

"Bye, darling."

"What's up?" my sister asked.

"We have to get to Rockchapel. River has something I need to see."

Coates and Wexler were ever-alert silent figures in the front seat. I climbed in, asking them to head to Banana Tree.

Leighbridge and Rockchapel were on opposite ends of Cinco City, and may as well have been on different planets. The designer stores, sports cars, stretching skyscrapers, and champagne problems were replaced by mom-and-pop corner stores, bars on the windows, packed buses, and whiskey problems.

I lived in North Quay my whole life, and that was the only borough I knew. Leighbridge was too rich for a middle-class girl like me. Harlow was too dangerous. Rockchapel lacked the interests of a girl who liked fashion, music, and picnics in the park. Waterford was where the older couples and retirees spent their nest egg.

In the short time since I moved in with Sunny, I accepted I knew even less about my city than I thought I did. The Merchants controlled the fates of almost everyone, and I thought of them as a children's bogeyman story. A battle raged behind the scenes for the control of the criminal world, and the only battle I knew was with a self-entitled rich girl who couldn't stand to be beaten.

*"Can you do what it takes to be the monster that monsters are afraid of?"*

By no means did I live an easy life, but standing there in that elevator while Bane ripped my heart to confetti, he made me see a fact I never noticed.

I was a victim of my father's abuse. A victim of Lyla's scheming and Damien's lies. I was that psychopath Digger's victim and then I was another poor soul on the streets. All my life, I was someone to be pitied, saved, or supported. Even if others understood my desire for revenge, they didn't judge me for not taking it. If anything, refusing to let Lyla get to me and all the rest I let pass was seen as a sign of strength.

But what if it wasn't?

What if I was Genny and a loan shark beat one of the women under my protection for coming up short? What if I was Sunny and he refused to give me my cut? What if I'm Liam and my valet puts a bomb in my car? What if fear was how I protected myself and my family... and there was no room for victims in the equation?

My mother picked up a gun to save me. Could I? Lyla stole, lied, and cheated to get rid of a rival. Could I? Damien sabotaged and manipulated to protect his future. Could I?

Those were questions I didn't have to answer then or now, yet I looked in Bane's eyes and said I understood enough to make a choice. What did a victim know of loving a monster? When it got too real—when I witnessed him commit an act I never could—wasn't I destined to do what Liam predicted I would?

Run.

A dark, heavy mood gathered around me, hanging rain clouds over my head. *What did I know about choice? I don't think I've made a single decision about my path. My life is just something that happened to me.*

I swiped a stray tear away as we rounded the corner, pulling up to the curb before Banana Tree. I got a glimpse of the woman Bane must see when he looked at me, and it wasn't a flattering sight.

"I don't think we'll be long," I said. "Maybe twenty minutes? If it's longer, I'll let you know."

Wexler brushed that away. "Take your time."

Sienna and I stepped inside Banana Tree. The café stood out on the Rockchapel street. Two stories of yellow tables, painted bananas on the walls, mini potted trees as centerpieces, and twenty out of the twenty-five items on the menu included banana. What on earth was so urgent in a place like this?

I dialed River. "I'm here. Where are you?"

"Upstairs. Table by the window."

"He's upstairs," I told Sienna.

We climbed the steps and found River where he promised—peering out the floor-to-ceiling window to the street down below.

"River, what's going on? What's the emergency?"

"You asked me to find Lochlan Grant and I did," he replied as we sat down, "because you thought he might have something to do with Sunny's attack."

"Yeah?" Sienna prompted.

"Then I should up my price." River drifted back to the window, taking our gaze with him. "Because I just answered that question."

I followed his line of sight to the street over from the one where we parked. Another café claimed the view—charming with its purple and white awning, and Parisian bistro chairs. Sitting at one was a man with dark, salt-sprinkled hair and a thick build wedged inside a simple sweater and slacks. He sipped tea from a dainty cup, his plate of food ignored while he chatted with the man across from him.

Roaring pressed on my ears, muffling the café noise. *Pale, bald, mid-forties to early fifties, frigid blue eyes.*

"It's him," I whispered. "He's the man on the bridge. He tried to kill Sunny."

"I'm calling him," Sienna said, fishing out her phone.

"I can't believe it's him. Just sitting there." Watching him then, more details filled in the brief memory of that night. Even sitting, he towered Lochlan horizontally and vertically. No wonder he was able to haul Sunny away and toss him off an overpass. The man looked like he could lift a truck.

From across the way, I noted the thin slash of a mouth and wide nose. I had to believe Sunny, Genny, or Liam would've remembered crossing paths with him before the attacks. *Anyone would remember coming face-to-face with that dead-eyed, sharklike mask.*

"Grant knows him," I said, stating the obvious. "They're sipping tea like old chums. He is behind this. Why didn't you want Sunny here?"

"I wanted you to confirm it was him first, Kenzie. For you to be absolutely sure." River was more serious than I'd ever seen him. "Before you sentenced those men to death."

I reeled back. "River, what— Why would you say that?"

His jaw was stiff. "You're too smart for me to buy the naive act. What did you think Sunny was going to do to the man who pitched him off a bridge? Or Liam to the guy who nearly killed his daughter?"

"I—" My brain stalled.

"They were never going to see the inside of a courtroom. I know this. *You know this.*" The accusation was a stab in the chest. "What happens from this point on is out of our control."

"That's not true," I said when I found my voice. "I understand that some men become monsters to fight them. But I also know Sunny, Liam, Bane, and Genny. They do what they have to do, but they're open to other ways. They'll listen to me. I'll convince Sunny this doesn't have to end in blood."

"I'd love to sit in on that talk, if you don't mind. It'll be deeply satisfying to witness the moment you find out who Sole Bellisario truly is."

"He's a good man who treats me with respect. Liam is a loving father. And Bane spends his time looking for ways to make me smile." *Or he used to.*

"What can I say about the *Rat King*? Everything I learned about you was from someone else."

The mood shifted considerably. River and I switched between watching Grant and the mystery man and trading scowls. It was a relief when Sunny arrived. He'd bring sense to the situation. I wasn't naive. I knew the Sons of Saint weren't a Girl Scout club and illegal activity was the theme of Sunny's birthday parties growing up. He wasn't a saint, but River would never make me believe he was a cold-blooded killer.

Sunny gripped my thigh, leaning over me. "Is that him, Angel?"

"It's him."

"Talia Barker was a fool for believing that second-rate doodler could match your skill." He fixed on the assassin, his expression giving nothing away. "Your sketch was spot-on."

"What do we do now?" I asked Sunny but looked at River.

"We— Wait, look. Did you see that?"

"I saw." Sienna pressed against the glass. "Grant passed him a note."

I looked just as it disappeared into his jacket pocket. "Anyone else thinking that's not his grocery list?"

"He is a hired gun," Sunny said. "Maybe he works for Grant. Maybe they met over a tray of scones. Either way, we need to read that note. Delaney, will it cost me another seven million for a lift?"

River winked. "This one is on the house. All this intrigue has me curious." He left the restaurant and Sunny claimed his seat, attention glued on the man who nearly ended his life.

"Sunny?"

"Angel."

"What are you planning to do to them?"

Sunny didn't look away. "What do you want me to do to them?"

I wet my lips, swallowing hard. There was a strange tone in his voice. River's warning banged in my head. "I want you to turn them over to the cops. I'm a witness. I'll tell everyone who'll listen what that man did to you. He won't get away with it, Sunny. Let's call the police."

"Okay, that's what I'll do."

"Really?"

He faced me, and Sunny smiled. "Of course. Whatever you want, pillow cheeks. Though, I'd prefer to speak to him first. Grant and his accomplice. I'd love to know how they got around my security, hit my routes, found my stash warehouses, if they're the ones who killed the valet, bombed Liam's car, and killed Genny's people."

"The police have interrogators."

"I do a more thorough job."

"Sunny—"

"I really must insist on that condition," he said smoothly, voice low. "The police are welcome to them afterward."

"Guys, look," Sienna broke in. "They're getting up."

I dropped the conversation. *For now.*

The two men rose from the table and shook hands. Baldy dropped a bill on the plate, climbed off the patio deck, and turned as River crashed into him.

A solid oak of a man, the hit merely rocked him on his feet. River apologized profusely, and from the looks of it, the guy said nothing. Straightening his jacket, he sidestepped River and walked on.

River stopped a distance away, we assumed to read the note. He glanced across the street, nodded at someone, and crossed. Marty and River met in the middle and paper changed hands. Marty jogged after Baldy to drop the note back in his pocket. He'd never know it went missing.

"My policy on stealing hasn't changed," I said, "but that was cool."

"If that's what gets you going, baby, we can have a little 'bring your girl to work' day."

Five minutes later, River came up the stairs. "West Twenty-Third Street. Number 19. Nine p.m.

"That's in Harlow," River said. "Warehouse District. That was a shady part of town. The Kings used to hold their underground fights there. We're talking fights to the death."

"Oh my goodness," I breathed. "I'm starting to think your parents shutting them down was a good thing."

"No question it is," Sunny said. "After they were evicted, the warehouses returned to their normal function. During the day, workers do their thing hauling product and checking inventory. At night, they're locked up. Genny doesn't stash anything there because there are too many people and constant foot traffic."

"Which makes it a good place for her enemies to get up to something under her nose," Sienna said. "She doesn't have a reason to go out there."

"How do we know that's what the note means? *Getting up to shit at nine o'clock.* An address and a time doesn't tell us anything."

"It tells us almost everything," Sunny said. "Grant didn't give him the note to pass on to Nana. Our bald friend will be at this place at this time. The only thing we don't know is if it's tonight, tomorrow, or another night. I'll be there every night until he shows up. Then I'll take him."

"Sunny, what if that's the time and place for the weekly meeting of the assassins' club? Whatever a guy like him is doing in an empty warehouse at night can't be good."

"What if Marty follows him instead?" Sienna spoke up. "See where he goes. Where he lives. You could have your chat with him there."

Sunny and River answered at once.

"Not a good idea."

"Wouldn't do that."

"A killer's home is the last place you want to ambush him," Sunny explained. "Because he's the only one in the room who knows where all the weapons are hidden."

"Good point," Sienna muttered.

"And anyone following him is at risk if he notices," River added. "It's not worth it. Sunny's right on this one. The smarter play is to let this guy come to him."

"Let's go." Sunny took my hand. "We don't have a lot of time to get ready for tonight. Delaney, you held up your end, I'll hold up mine. Be at the arcade tomorrow morning."

River stopped me with a hand on the arm. "And I'll see you Friday morning." He said it like a statement, but it was a question.

Should I go out with him on Friday? Why stay in this pattern any longer where he refuses to open up and I disappoint myself waiting for something to change?

He stroked the soft, sensitive flesh of my elbow. "I want to tell you everything, Kenzie. I honestly do. When the time is right, I will. I just don't know when that'll be. I don't get to decide. Does that make sense?"

My mother and all the things I hadn't told River about my past floated between us. "Yes," I said. "I guess it does."

"Don't give up on me yet."

His smile was so wide and beautiful, my knees went weak. "Friday," I said, unable to stop myself. "We'll meet you at the park."

"I'll meet you at the Fairfield and we'll walk together," River corrected. "Years on the streets haven't pounded all the manners out of me yet."

"Friday." I fell into his hug. He made it so impossible to stay mad at him.

I finally tore myself away and met up with Sunny and Sienna downstairs.

"Sunny, are you sure about this?" I kept my voice low. "The only thing we know about this guy is he's a killer. He's not someone you meet alone in an empty warehouse."

"I won't be alone. For one night only, the Savage Princes get the band back together. Looks like you'll get to see us in action even sooner than you thought."

# Chapter Thirteen

S*unny*
    "We sure about this?" Bane loaded the magazine, aiming the gun at his television.

His apartment was hands down the best in the compound. Antique weapons covered every spare inch of wall. Our parents built the collection, then gifted it to Bane when they moved. It expanded with his buys, and soon, with his own creations—creating a paradise of swords, hammers, bows, arrows, guns, rifles, and a scimitar. With that for decoration, we forgave him the single table, chair, couch, and one full bed in a four-bedroom apartment.

"You didn't read the note, Delaney did," Bane said. "He could've lied about what it said. Wouldn't be the first time he's sent us in the wrong direction."

"He didn't lie." My fingers skimmed the knife collection, the now constant pain in my back twisting my muscles as I concealed them on my body.

"How can you be sure?" Liam stood still in the middle of the room. He didn't put half the wall on his hip, or do more than slip an item from his locked nightstand to his pocket. Our oldest brother had a specific fighting style that clearly served him well. He was alive. The men that tried to kill him were not.

Hundred percent success rate.

"Because Mackenzie Blaine trapped him under her spell long before she met any of us."

Both of my brothers avoided my eyes. *Interesting.*

"She almost died in that blast with Tricky," I continued. "River wouldn't ruin our chance to beat that shit into a smear just to mess with us."

Liam nodded, accepting this. "I'll take lead."

"Why? Because our sweet, sainted mother—let the heavens bless her—shoved you out before us?"

"Precisely."

"When you going to stop pulling that card?"

"When it's removed from my deck. In other words, after I'm dead."

"Doesn't matter who takes lead," Bane broke in. "The plan is always the same. Liam in the front, me in the back, you inside. I sent two of my men to babysit the place. It's not empty. The warehouse is owned by a rice company. The workers cleared out two hours ago. Bobby says no one in or out since."

"Why's this guy visiting an empty rice warehouse at night?" Liam asked.

"An excellent question," I replied. "We'll ask him that after 'why did you throw me off a fucking bridge?' and 'did you try to blow up my brother and niece?'"

Liam bared his teeth. "At that point, I'll take over the questioning."

"You didn't recognize him, Sunny? You sure you've never seen this guy before?"

"I'm sure. I was sure when I saw Kenzie's sketch and I'm certain now. He's not a known player. Fuck knows where this guy came from. Grant could've hired him from out of town, ensuring we didn't see him coming."

"Lochlan Grant," Liam said. "Months of attacks, raids, hijackings, revenue loss, four deaths, and two attempted, all because of some two-bit loan shark who took one too many hits from Genny?"

"Vito claims I was the final push over the edge," I said. "Grant announced that he refused to give me my cut, so Makai and I kicked his ass. Then, I busted his safe, helped myself to two hundred grand, and said my cut was now eighty percent. After, I reminded him that he'd live with a few of his organs missing. If he made me come back, I'd cut him open and make my money through what I could sell."

I shrugged. "Apparently, this hurt his widdle feelings, the stupid-ass, oversensitive, shit-in-his-pants baby."

"A murder rampage does seem an extreme reaction to a beating, two hundred grand, and a threat you didn't go through with," Liam said. "Where is Grant?"

"Rockchapel. Delaney gave up the address, but the free pass is over. He won't let us into Rockchapel to pick him up. Says if we want him, we'll have to lure him out."

"If Grant is smart, and so far he has been," Bane said, "he wouldn't leave that borough for his mother's funeral."

"Let's test that theory." Liam swept out, leaving that statement hanging behind.

The three of us headed down in the elevator. Sienna and Mackenzie were waiting for us.

"We're coming with you," Kenzie said. "I'm not letting you go alone. He's tried to kill you and Liam already."

I pulled her in, kissing her forehead. "Wasn't planning on going alone. Bane's got two of his guys. Liam's invited Donaldson and Lindsay. Makai and Ryker are meeting us there. Too many people and we risk getting noticed, but he'll still be outnumbered."

"Even more so if Sienna and I go too."

"Okay."

"Really?"

"Sunny," Liam barked. "It's too dangerous."

"That's why we'll need a getaway driver. This thing goes sideways, we'll get out of there quick." I smiled at my girl—beyond pleased at the fact that she was *my* girl. "You up for it?"

"Yes. I am fully certified in driving getaway cars."

"Since when?" Bane asked.

"Since Xbox."

They laughed, then abruptly cut themselves off and looked anywhere but at each other.

*Also interesting.*

"Let's move," Liam said. "It's almost nine."

We broke apart in the garage—Liam and Bane going one way, Sienna and Mackenzie coming with me. I led them to my pride, my joy, the light in my eye: my Maserati Quattroporte GTS.

I hopped on the red leather seats, shivering just feeling her cradle my ass again. "I missed you, baby."

"You're not talking to me, are you?" Mackenzie's question slid in ahead of her.

"Nah. Fucked you an hour ago. Me and Masie been apart for weeks."

"Men and their cars. It borders on a fetish."

"She's just jealous," I whispered to Masie. "'Cause I loved you first."

I didn't have to see my lady to know she was rolling her eyes. Kicking Masie on, I pulled back on the gear and the movement stabbed spikes up my spine, gritting my teeth.

*Almost. It's almost over. Once I have him, my family's safe, and Mackenzie doesn't have to put herself out there anymore, then I'll lie around for weeks, rehabbing a useless arm. Tonight I need to throw.*

*I need to fight.*

Harlow Warehouse District was a ghost town that time of night—complete with whistling wind and tumbleweeds. No one had legitimate business here after the doors closed and everyone trudged home.

"That's why you have to stay out of sight." I parked beside Warehouse Sixteen on the far side. It gave her a view to Warehouse Nineteen's side entrance but was far enough that if shit went down, she had plenty of time to get away. "Leave me if you have to, Kenzie. I mean it." I raised my voice over her coming rejection. "You've got Sienna and Laurel to think about. I've asked you to do a lot of things for me, but never to give your life."

"Sunny, nothing's going to happen to you." She cupped my cheek. "Get in there, get this guy, and get out. I'll be waiting *right here*. Come back to me."

I kissed her palm, wishing more than anything that Baby Blaine wasn't in the back seat and I could do sinful things to this woman while Masie watched.

"If he's punctual, this'll be over soon. Stay in the car—doors locked, lights off, engine on." I bumped the dash. "Masie's a tank. Solid frame. Tougher than steel. She'll protect you, as long as you stay in the car. Do not open this door unless it's to let me in."

"Stay in the car. Got it."

I kissed her, lingering a second longer on her soft lips. I tossed Baby Blaine a salute in the back and ducked out. Makai and Ryker emerged from the shadows, falling in step with me.

"Scoped the whole place out," Makai said. "No one's here. We're good."

"The three of us inside," I said. "Liam's and Bane's people are watching the front and back. He does *not* get away from us."

"We shooting to kill?" Ryker asked, trailing a finger along his handle.

"I want him alive. He and I have a lot to talk about."

"Where we dumping the body?" Makai didn't carry weapons... of steel. He flexed his fists, rolling his neck—a purist fighter. "Potter's Field is getting full."

I peered over my shoulder to Masie and the beautiful passenger inside. I smiled in case she was watching me. "There won't be a body. When I'm done with him, the cops won't have a toe to tag. He's dust."

Grins stretched their faces, their eyes glinting malice in the moonlight. "It's good to have you back, boss."

I couldn't see where Liam and his people were, which was the point. Ryker busted the door's padlock. We filtered inside pitch-black darkness, sensing more than seeing the rising shelves. My vision adjusted on India Market Basmati Rice. The logo stamped on every cellophane-trapped box on the shelves.

"What's he coming here for?" Makai asked. "Is this place a front and it's not bags of rice in those boxes?"

"Check one," I ordered. "Ryker, make sure this place is empty. I'll look around. Grant told him to come here for a reason."

We split in different directions, me sinking deeper into the gloom. My penlight flicked on, sweeping the row. So far, that's all it was—rows and rows, stacks on stacks of rice. Ahead of me there should be a warehouse foreman's office. A faint squeak pierced the silence, alerting me Ryker was in the office.

A hand grasped my shoulder. I whipped around, my blade swinging.

Bane glanced the hit off his forearm. "Easy, it's us."

My light lit up Liam and Bane. "What are you doing? You're supposed to be outside."

"It's ten minutes to nine," Liam said. "We believe this guy almost killed my daughter. I'm not standing in the wind with my thumb up my ass."

I jerked a nod. "This way. I think I heard something."

*MACKENZIE*

Sienna climbed up front with me, moving me to the driver's seat. Tense silence blanketed the car as the clock ticked down to nine.

"They're going to be okay," I said because I had to. Putting it out there—a demand to the fates—eased my anxiety a fraction.

Sienna didn't agree, so I looked at her, glimpsing her wince. "What's wrong?"

"Nothing— I mean, it's not nothing, but..." Grimacing, she rubbed her temples. "Kenzie, I don't think... that we should be here."

"What? What are you talking about?"

"Something's wrong. All of it, wrong." Her voice rose, pants coming faster. "Today at the café... Why didn't he speak?"

"Why didn't he speak?" I cast around, torn between watching for the guys and trying to understand Sienna. "I don't know what that means. What are you trying to tell me?"

"The same vision," she burst out. "The same moment over and over—trying to tell me something. Grant and the killer at the café. Why didn't Grant tell him, Kenzie?"

"Tell him what—"

She flashed, grabbing my arms. "The guy was sitting right in front of him. They met to talk in the middle of the day at a busy restaurant. They didn't care about being seen together, so why did Grant give him a piece of paper with this time and address? Why didn't he just tell him where to go? Why didn't he text him?"

Air punched from my lungs, leeching the warmth from my body as the same moment shown in my mind with sudden sharp clarity.

"Because he wanted whoever was watching to see," I whispered through numb lips.

"It's a trap."

*SUNNY*

The three of us fell in line. Liam in the front, Bane bringing up the back, me in the middle—my ears cocked for that faint sound I heard after the office door creaked. It was something else that wasn't metal.

My head snapped up. "There it is again. It's coming from up ahead."

"I don't hear anything," Liam said.

"'Cause you're both old as shit. I'm at my peak, bro, and I'm telling you"—I raised my knife—"something or some*one* isn't as quiet as they're trying to be."

Liam drew his weapon, crouching lower on approach from the corners.

"Sunny, switch," Bane hissed.

"What?"

"You're carrying in your left hand."

I stiffened, flicking down to the metal glinting in my left. "I know. I've been training with my left. I can throw just as good."

"Now isn't the time for just as good. Stop messing around. Switch."

"Right." Cursing internally, I switched to my dominant hand. Of course Bane, the highly trained fighter and weapons expert, had to notice.

Needles stabbed my shoulder as I gripped. Lately that was all it took, a squeeze or a clench, and pain flooded me.

I pushed it aside, listening for him to make another sound. It was close—a couple of rows ahead of us. He must've slipped in during the day with the workers and hid while everyone left.

*Beep.*

"Over there." I shot out in front of Liam, pressing my back to the metal. Nodding at them, I counted *one, two, three* and whipped around the corner—knife pulled back to let fly.

Nothing.

"No one's there," Liam said.

*Beep.*

"I'm still hearing something." I frowned. "Boxes of rice don't make noise."

*Beep.*

"I heard it that time," Bane said.

"Me too." Liam stepped lightly, inching down the aisle. "What is that?"

He stopped in front of a stack of loose boxes piled on the bottom shelf. Bending down, we pushed them aside, listening to the beeping grow louder.

I tossed the final box on the floor, and my penlight fell on the display.

*Ten.*

*Nine.*

*Eight.*

"Bomb!" I bellowed. "It's a bomb! Get out!"

*MACKENZIE*

"It's a trap."

Sienna threw the door open, racing for the warehouse.

"Sienna, wait!" I tugged on my seat belt. It stuck fast. "Wait for me!"

I yanked on the nylon, stabbing the release. The belt refused to free me. Bellowing, I thrashed in the seat, throwing my weight against the jammed restraint.

Sienna was running straight at a trap that Sunny, Bane, and Liam were in the middle of springing. I had to get out. *Now!*

Giving up, I snatched the switchblade from my pocket. "Sorry, Masie." I held the edge to the belt.

*Boom!*

Percussive heat blew me against the seat, light exploding in my eyes. Dazed, the world came into focus on a single point.

Warehouse Nineteen burning.

"Sienna!"

Flames engulfed the bitter remains of the structure, devouring every splinter, beam, and person in its path.

"Sunny!" I slashed the belt, flinging it away. "Liam, Bane, p-please, no."

I threw myself on the door, and our eyes locked. Artic-blue orbs beheld me through the window, driving straight into my soul. The assassin snapped back faster than my racing heart skipped beats, and aimed.

Screams ripped from my throat. Throwing up my hands, I flung away already knowing it was too late.

*Bang! Bang! Bang!*

The shots ricocheted in my skull, loud as my screams, trumpeting the crackle of broken glass. Trembling, I lifted my head to the near splintered but still-intact glass. The windows were bulletproof.

Roaring, the hairless killer smashed the gun's butt on the window. My foot jerked, punching the gas. Masie raced off, thudding over something. His shouts became screams.

My face was soaked. Fear and adrenaline ravaged my lungs. I couldn't breathe. Couldn't stop the fire. Couldn't see Sienna, Sunny, Liam, or Bane.

I drove as close to the warehouse as the flames would let me and tumbled out of the car, weakened knees dropping me to the pavement. *Where is he?!* I looked back but there was no sign of him.

"Sienna?" Flames poured from the busted windows, eagerly consuming oxygen to grow, spread, destroy. "Sienna! Guys?!"

I had to get to them. It couldn't end this way. They had to be okay. They had to be!

Shrugging off my jacket, I held it over my head and rushed the door.

# Chapter Fourteen

"Kenzie, no!" A human missile knocked me off course.

We collapsed on the ground, Sienna strangling me. "I'm okay," she sobbed. "It's okay."

"The guys are in there! Get help! I have to get them out—"

"Kenzie?" Sunny appeared through the haze, stepping out from the other side of the smoldering rice factory. "Are you okay?"

He ran over to us, and behind him ran Bane, Liam, Makai, and Ryker.

"We got out, Kenzie." Sunny held me as I cried into his shoulder. "We got out in time."

"He's h-here," I croaked. "The bomber. The man who tried to kill you. He was right there, Sunny. He tried to shoot me through the window."

"Fuck! Spread out," Liam bellowed to the men escaping from the shadows and surrounding warehouses. "Find him! That son of a bitch doesn't get away."

He did get away.

They searched the entire district, looking inside every warehouse that wasn't locked. All they found were a set of tire tracks from a car that peeled off fast.

Sunny piled me and Sienna in his car, driving behind Liam and Bane for home. There was nothing more we could do.

"We were close to a side door," Sunny said. "Makai was by the front, and a back door was in the foreman's office for Ryker to get out. We got lucky, Kenzie. We should've died in there."

"Please." I blinked and tears spilled over my twitching lids. I was jumpy, stressed, and hadn't stopped crying in an hour. In that moment, I truly thought they were gone. My sister, my Sunny, Liam, and Bane. I didn't think anything could feel worse than my child's father ruining me and abandoning me to the streets. I didn't know a darker day could exist than the day my mother shot my father.

I was wrong.

"P-please, Sunny... I can't..."

"I'm sorry." Sunny reached behind, finding my hand where it squeezed Sienna's. "Just breathe, baby. We're almost home."

He said that, but a millennium passed—each second stretched into agony, and all I wanted was to go home, wash the soot from my skin, hold my daughter and never let go.

Soon the Fairfield rose over the horizon, a shiny beacon of safety and an end to a horrible night.

Sunny idled to a stop behind Bane's and Liam's cars, waiting for their parking garage security guard to confirm it was them and raise the gate.

"It'll be okay, Kenzie." Sienna hugged me close. "Tonight proved one thing we know is true."

I looked into her miraculously smiling face. How could she do that? "What?"

"As long as you four are together, nothing can touch you."

"Things can touch me," I said softly. "Tonight, he nearly did."

"Kenzie..." Sienna drifted off, looking at something over my head. "Hey, Sunny— Hey!"

A hard force slammed into the car, rocking it on the wheels. Something flashed out of the corner of my eye, thudding on the hood.

"What the fuck?" Sunny jumped out, pulling Sienna and me out with him.

Masie was a tank. The motorcycle hurled at the frame at full speed, and there wasn't a dent on her. The same couldn't be said for the mangled bike on the asphalt—Genny's pride and joy.

She gasped on the hood where the bike flung her. I clapped my hands over my mouth, rushing to her side. Genny's right leg bent at the wrong angle. A mask of blood covered her beautiful face, gushing from a wound on her forehead. Genny didn't believe in conservative clothes when tight and revealing worked just fine, so the bullet wound through her shoulder was obvious for all to see.

"Genny!" Liam slammed out of his car.

"F-found me," she rasped. I ripped off my jacket and pressed it to her wound. "Shot... me. I ran and he... chased..."

Genevieve's head dropped on the metal. She was gone.

*SUNNY*

Liam, Bane, Fuller, and I hopped on our feet as the door opened and Hendrix stepped out. She gestured for us to sit down.

"Genny's going to be okay. Eventually," she added. "Her leg and shoulder are in bad shape, but the bullet went straight through and the leg will heal. She'll have to rest and take it easy for the next several weeks. Two things she doesn't excel at."

"Can we see her?" Fuller asked.

"Yes. She's awake, but I did give her something to help her sleep. Keep it short."

Hendrix stepped in my path as I made for the door, letting the others go in ahead. "Rest and take it easy aren't traits you excel at either. What were you doing walking into exploding buildings last night, Sole? It hasn't been that long, your back still needs time."

"I'm fine. One hundred percent. Why would I sit on my ass and let my brothers go into danger alone? Everything's fine," I repeated, flashing her a smile.

Her eyes narrowed. "You would tell me if it wasn't, wouldn't you? This is serious, Sunny. There's risk of permanent damage."

"Actually, there isn't because I'm all healed up. I've got to see my sister." I kissed her cheek. "But you're still the hottest thing in scrubs, if I may say so."

"Again, you may not."

Sidestepping her, I went inside Genny's old room. It was just how she left it the day she announced she was moving to Harlow and starting a motorcycle club to rule her borough. The curious clash of pink and black shown throughout the room. Pink headboard, black satin sheets, pink fuzz around the television.

Genny reclined on the bed, her foot propped on a mound of pillows and arm in a sling.

"—impossible," she said. "No one knows about that place. Not even my Cardinals. I don't know how he found me."

"Did he follow you from Barbarella's?"

"Also impossible. I know how to lose a tail. Besides, on my bike, he couldn't follow me in traffic." Genny was pale and washed out, matching the white bandage on her forehead. "He was waiting, Liam. I walked outside and he didn't hesitate. Just rolled down the window and fired.

"People were running and screaming. I saw him get out of the car to make sure the job was done, so I ran to my bike. He rammed me driving out of the parking lot—sent me flying and jacked up my leg. But my girl's tough."

Her girl as in her bike. Beat to shit and it got her all the way from Harlow to Leighbridge. The makers of that damn thing deserved an award and an obscene cash prize.

"I got back on and drove here, losing him through the back alleys."

"Who is him?" Liam asked. "Was it Grant?"

She started to shake her head and thought better of it. "Wasn't Grant. I don't know who the fuck it was. He was a young guy though. Blond hair, brown eyes, about my age. I didn't clock much else with the gun to distract me."

"This was timed," Bane said. "Planned. In one night, they almost took all of us out. The bomb in the warehouse and Gen coming out of her safe house. But how?" Bane punched the wall. "How did he know where you were, Gen? How did Grant know you were watching him at the café? Or that someone would be along in a moment to lift that note?"

"Can't answer the first question," I said. "But I can answer the rest."

I THREW OPEN THE DOORS. "Where is he?"

Ryker climbed off the stairs. He didn't ask who I was talking about, just jerked his head at my office. "Waiting for you inside."

By waiting for me inside, he meant River was sitting at my desk—feet up and messing with my Newton's Cradle.

"Was it you?"

"You're going to have to be more specific," River drawled. "Was it me what?"

I shoved his feet off. Grabbing him by the collar, River was hauled smirking out of my chair and shoved against the bookshelf.

"The warehouse was a trap," I hissed. "Something was going to happen at nine all right. We were supposed to be blown up!"

"Well, as these are corporeal fists wrinkling my jacket and not ghostly ones, you escaped. I'm glad to see it." The smirk twitched for a second. "Are Kenzie and her sister okay?"

"Why don't you ask if my brothers are okay?" I slammed him again. "Why don't you ask about my sister?! They came for all four of us last night. Genny was shot coming out of her place. What did you do, River?"

He lifted a brow. "Me? What I did was track down the guy behind this and serve him up on a platter? And I didn't do it for free. Why don't you get your hands off me and give me the diamonds?"

Everything Sienna saw in her vision—everything I should've seen came back to me. "It was all too neat. You found Grant oddly fast. And the day you do, he happens to meet with the guy who tried to take me out, and then *happened* to pass him a note for you to lift. We all rush over there, and no one's in the way when they go after Genny. Did you make a deal, Delaney? Huh? Decided to get rid of the Merchants for good?"

River shoved me away. I drew my knife at the same time as him, both of us glowering over the blade's edge.

"Think, Bellisario," he snapped. "You've known me for too long to believe I'd pull such an obvious play. I thought that meet was legit same as you. Getting myself mixed up in bombings and shootings? What's the upside for me?"

"Your crew finally takes over Cinco City."

"My crew isn't the take-over-the-city type. You're the kings, and we're the tax collectors. We keep you honest. We keep you humble. If you're gone, whose trucks do I jack? Whose gang do I trick, undercut, and rob? Who's going to hand over seven million in diamonds to protect his little family?

Any other gang would've hunted and killed every homeless person they laid eyes on by now, but not the sainted Merchants—convincing themselves they're the good guys while they fish in rivers of blood."

"Fuck you."

River threw his head back laughing. "Fine, I guess I deserve that. But your accusations, you can shove those up your ass. If you don't believe anything else I say, then believe this, I'd never put Kenzie in danger, and I damn sure wouldn't work for a man who did. It's pretty much a fact now that Grant is behind this, and he almost killed Kenzie and Elizabeth. She's six years old, Sunny. I have a fucking conscience."

"Oh, please. You gonna act like you care about Tricky? If that's the case, why did we miss you at the last six birthday parties, Uncle River?"

"Why didn't I get an invite, nephew?"

I grinned widely. "We were going to put it in the mail, but—oops, you don't have an address."

"Very clever. Are we finished now? You got your shots in, shoved me around a little, blamed me for the problems in your life. You checked off all your boxes, so how about we get back to business?" He matched my smirk. "You know how much my dear sister hates it when we fight."

My lips curled. "River Redgrave. Mom's half, and only, brother. It always made me laugh when you spun that sob story of abandonment and persecution, swearing you'd have nothing to do with us or the Merchant legacy. But look at you."

River made a show of lifting his hands and checking himself out. "What am I supposed to be looking at?"

"The Rat King. One of the most feared shadow kings in the streets, running a gang twice the size of ours combined. You just couldn't help it, River. It's in your blood," I said, closing the distance. "Redgraves can't settle for mediocre.

"We have to be great."

My face reflected in expressionless pools. "I'll say this once: I had nothing to do with the warehouse bombing, or Gen's attack. These attacks are too coordinated, too perfect, too timed. The tips called into the police about your routes and stash houses, half of them I didn't know about. This is the work of someone who knows your organization and your family inside out. Your first instinct was right, Sunny. You have a mole."

"You're not going to throw suspicion on my people to deflect from yourself. Just because you weren't responsible for all of the attacks, doesn't mean you didn't take part in some of it. That meet was a setup, River. Grant knew we were watching."

"Because Grant is watching you! He's watching Liam, Bane, Genny, and after you sent Kenzie to talk to Vito and he gave up his name, he knew you were watching him too."

"Vito's a part of this," I said, lowering my knife.

"Why wouldn't he be? Now, there's a man who wants you dead. When he found out you weren't..."

"He gave up to Grant everything he told Kenzie."

"It's all right that you couldn't get there on your own." River dusted off his coat, returning his blade to the inside pocket. "We can now move past all this unpleasant business and get to my payment. Where are the diamonds?"

"What's the story behind them? Why's everyone so interested in these diamonds?"

"They're worth seven million dollars," he said like I was an idiot.

"So it wouldn't have anything to do with Kristoph Barrett's reward."

River stopped smiling.

"Ah, there it is." Laughing, I threw myself in my armchair. "You miss a lot of things when you're dead, but I'm back, baby, and I know the word on the street is the reward for their return is more than their worth. Apparently, Barrett signed an ironclad prenup. When he decided to leave his wife for his secretary, he wasn't about to walk away with nothing, so he quietly swapped out the diamonds from his wife's heirloom, the symphony of stars, with cheap fakes. The real diamonds were stashed at his girlfriend's place, an apartment building owned by..." I snapped my fingers, beaming at River for the answer.

"Ira Hansen.

"Ding, ding, ding! What does he win, folks?" I cracked up. "Anyway, he was so close to getting away with it when wifey tells him she's pregnant. What can he do? He could ditch his wife in a heartbeat, but not his kid. He dumps his girlfriend and she's so pissed, she flings the pouch out the window and Hansen helps himself.

"Barrett has to replace the diamonds or his future is divorce, custody battles, and seeing his kid every other weekend. It also has to be *those* diamonds because they're certified and marked with serial numbers. Whoever gets them back is looking at a ten-million-dollar payday. Barrett can afford to be generous since he's dipping into his wife's millions. What's ten million when she's worth six hundred million as long as he's married to her?"

River gave me a steady, flat look. "Kind of you to walk me through what I already know. If you're done, I'll take the diamonds now. We had a deal. For better or worse, you know who's trying to kill you and where they are. I held up my end. Hand them over."

"Hmm. No," I drew out. "No, I don't think I will."

"It's not wise to go back on a deal with me, Sole."

"I'm not going back on anything. See, what I'm going to do is collect that reward, give you the seven million we agreed, and pocket the three mil for myself. Everybody wins, right?"

River's face was chipped from stone.

"Huh. I'm giving you seven mill cash, and you don't look pleased. You wouldn't happen to be running a double play, would you? Got someone else who's interested in the diamonds? Another party who's offering a trade you don't want me to know about?"

"Are you going to give me the diamonds or not?"

"I am... but not today. I think I'll wait a month, maybe two, possibly six. Until Barrett's wife figures out the truth and whoever you promised the diamonds can't use them for leverage, blackmail, or whatever they're planning. Call it payback for the Dario *and* Kabir jobs. Not to mention all the money you've cost me the last three years."

River's expression changed, and my muscles tensed—trained to react whenever I saw that smile.

"Nicely done, Sole. I admit, I figured you'd find out what they're really worth and find a way to screw me and make a few million in the process. Normally, this latest betrayal would stir the bad blood between us, but since we've recently forged a new working relationship, it's time we put the past behind us."

"We don't have a working relationship."

"Oooh," he hissed. "Did Makai and Athena forget to mention it to you?"

Alarm bells rang in my head, chasing away my smugness. "What did you do?"

"What did *you* do, Sunny? You played dead and sent Mackenzie, a stranger, here to tell your people what to do while your organization was falling apart. They were trying to help, if that's any consolation."

"What did you *do*?" I barked.

"I agreed to let the Sons of Saint buy stash houses and set new routes through Rockchapel. My people will make sure you're not ambushed. Plus, I've long since worked out an arrangement with a few buddies on the force. If a tip comes in about a raid, they'll let me know first—giving you time to clear out."

"Kenzie said she walked in on your meeting. You didn't get a chance to arrange anything."

"Kenzie walked in on the final meeting—seconds after we shook hands on a deal made." He pulled a face. "Now that we're talking about her, don't mention that I lied. If I told her the truth, she would've told you, and I'd have missed this look on your face."

I had no doubt the fury etched in my sneer was a sight to behold. "They gave you the Cromwell bracelet."

He patted his jacket pocket, showing me the priceless antique prize as proof. I stole it over a year ago, and saved it for that day I was ready to ask a favor of one of the wealthiest men in Leighbridge.

"That they did, dear nephew. A bracelet that, we both know, is worth a lot more than ten million—especially to the right person. Gatlin was so happy to get it back, he handed over control of four of his soup kitchen-slash-shelters. Three of them in..." He snapped his fingers, grinning like a loon mimicking me. "Come on, we're doing a bit."

"Leighbridge," I forced through clenched teeth.

"Ding, ding, ding! What do I win, folks? I win shelter for my people in the one borough we couldn't penetrate. I win more territory than even the Merchants. Tell Liam it's his lucky day. I'm going to spend a lot more time with my oldest nephew." River made for the door, unwisely turning his back on me. "Sell the diamonds to Barrett, Sole, give me the seven mill and pocket the difference. My side deal for the diamonds was a backup plan to hedge my bets. Good thing Makai is more trustworthy than you."

I shot off my chair, rushing him. River twisted—arm up and knife to my throat as mine pressed to his liver.

"You lost fair and square, Sole. Let it go because I'd prefer not to be cut up for my date with Kenzie on Friday."

"Liam will drive you out. I don't care what favors you traded. You won't take Leighbridge."

"Another mystery in this never-ending dance between me and the Merchants: which one of us is right?" River pointedly dropped his knife, giving his back. He knew I wouldn't do it—kill him. I had committed many sins and would commit many more, but I couldn't kill my mother's brother.

"I do have a confession," River said, pausing at the door. "It does feel pretty good knowing I've built an empire bigger than the Merchants and, one day, I'll crush yours under the tattered shoes of people everyone wrote off.

"You may be right about our blood. Redgraves don't settle for less than greatness."

He slammed the door on my roar, ducking out as my blade buried in the wood where his head had been. Pain rippled up my spasming back as the price.

"Makai! Athena!"

*MACKENZIE*

My sewing machine hummed a steady melody in my ear, calming my racing mind. I heard talking and laughter on the other side of the door and made no move to join. I promised Bane a jacket in whatever style I chose. I should keep that promise, before I left.

A tear splashed on the thread, racing away from my scissors. Bullets splintering glass rang in my ears.

"—too cute," I heard Shonda say.

I couldn't stay here. In one night, I almost lost my sister, Sunny, Bane, and Liam. I was nearly killed by a monster. Laurel waited months to get her family back, and because I got tangled up in this fight, we almost left her alone.

I wanted to be with Sunny more than anything. I wanted to break down Liam's walls, and make Bane believe that love was more powerful than vows. But what about what I wanted for Laurel? She deserved a safe home that she trusted her mother would return to every day, and it was my job to provide it for her.

*I can't choose my heart over my daughter. I'm sorry, guys. I'm so sorry.*

I turned in my seat, landing on the diaper bag and suitcase open on my bed. It would take some time for me to find an apartment, and it would take money. I'd sell some of the dresses, pants, lingerie, and jackets I made. It'd be enough to keep us going in a hotel until I found a job. The guys would have to understand I wasn't leaving them because I wanted to.

*Sienna too. She'll want to stay, and she's old enough that I can't make the choice for her, but after the warehouse and Genny's crash landing, she can't believe we're safer with the Merchants—*

"—babies start walking?" Bane asked.

"Nine months is possible, but early," Liam replied. "Laurel has plenty of time."

*Laurel?*

"You don't know what you're talking about," Genny said. "See the look in her eyes? She's ready."

Pushing away from my station, I padded out in the hall, peering around the corner.

Looked like everyone in the Fairfield was packed in the living room. Liam, Tricky, Bane, Sienna, Shonda, Fuller, Thatcher, Genny, and Sunny's staff. They all gathered around fixed on the main event: Laurel.

My baby girl clung to the tabletop, keeping herself up on wobbly feet. She gazed curiously at her audience.

"I'm telling you, she's gonna do it," Genny said. Her leg propped up on the wheelchair. Arm bound to her chest, someone drew matching red birds on her cast, sling, and the bandage on her shoulder. "She's about to take her first step."

"Should we get Miss Blaine?" Thatcher asked.

Fuller clicked her tongue. "Interrupt her rest to get the same puzzled look Laurel is giving us right now? It's much too soon for her to walk. This is her pull-up-and-stand stage. She's testing out her legs."

"Lizzie started walking around ten months."

"I did, Daddy?"

"You're my little prodigy, baby girl." Liam kneeled before Laurel, holding out his hands. "Come on, Laurel, you can do it."

"Right over here, baby," Bane said, dropping down next to him. "You like me better than Liam anyway."

Laurel goggled at them both, letting loose a string of babble their way. Her tiny fists clung firm on the coffee table.

All of a sudden, they were all cooing and cheering on Laurel. Tears filled my eyes, and they had nothing to do with sadness.

"All right, let me at the bite-sized toe-nibbler." Genny wheeled between her brothers. "She just needs a little incentive."

My smile froze on my face, picturing Tricky flying off the back of a motorcycle. I did not want to know what Genevieve Hunt's idea of incentive was. Time to intervene.

I shot out as Genny fished out something wedged between her and the chair. "What do you think about this, Laurel?" Dangling from her fingers was a soft, pink stuffed octopus—its fuzzy tentacles dancing for Laurel. "This was mine when I was a baby. You want it, don't you?"

Laurel pointed right at it. "Ooh," she cried.

"You'll have to come over here and get it."

As if she heard and understood the challenge, Laurel let go of the table... and stood.

For half a second. Wobbling, my baby fell on her butt without taking a step. Far from discouraged, Laurel flipped over and crawled to Genny—little face determined as her cheerleaders rooted her on. She reached Genny's chair, pulled herself up, and grabbed a tentacle.

Bane cracked up. "She outsmarted you, sis. You didn't say she had to *walk* over here and get it."

"Damn. Outmaneuvered by an infant. This is a rough week for me." Smiling, Genny gifted Laurel her prize, tickling her cheek with a tentacle. Everyone clapped and hollered, sending Laurel into a squealing/giggling fit.

I picked her up, holding her close as I kissed her crown. "Good job, baby."

*What about what I wanted for Laurel?*

I looked around at all the people who loved her. Who fought for her to be here and kept her safe.

What I wanted was for Laurel to be happy, healthy, and surrounded by love.

*And isn't that exactly what she is?* another voice asked.

Sunny said it and maybe it was long past time I accepted it.

"This is home."

I WENT BACK TO MY ROOM and returned my suitcase and Laurel's diaper bag to where they belonged. Running away from the first real home I ever had wasn't the solution. I once lived the picket-fence, mom-and-dad, soccer-on-the-weekends life, and it ended with a bullet. What seemed perfect rarely was. This life with the Cinco City Princes was dangerous, but horrors happened to me long before I met them. If I were to face more, I'd rather do it with the men who made me believe in love, sex, laughter, and life again.

Friday morning, I dressed Laurel in a red floral romper and matching hat. She was the cutest little fashionista and I told her so while I tucked her in the baby carrier and hitched her diaper bag up my shoulder.

Sunny and Sienna were locked in conversation when I came out.

"—don't get to choose," she said. "I see what I see and feel what I feel, trusting that it's the right information at the right moment."

"Any other vibrations on Grant?"

"It's weird about Grant." Sienna massaged her temples. "I'm still seeing the same vision of the two of them at the café. The first time it was a warning, and I don't think that's changed. There's more to Grant and that assassin. More to what's going on here. I sense strongly that the revenge is tied to your father, Sunny. Did Grant and Sinjin ever get into it?"

Sunny shook his head. "Nah. Grant was a small-time loan shark when my folks were running things. He wasn't worth their notice. It was me who took a cut of his business and Genny who kicked his face in. Dad had nothing to do with it."

"We're missing something. *I'm* missing something. Worst thing is my visions will get murkier the more I get tangled up in this. I can't see my own future."

"What about River Delaney?" he asked, blowing my brows up my forehead. "You were around him for months. The universe must've had plenty to say about him."

"My River visions were interesting, though I didn't make much sense of them and River wasn't up for explaining."

"Lay 'em on me."

Sienna tucked her feet under her, comfy on the couch with a mug of Shonda's homemade herbal tea blend. Sienna would've come with me if I left, but she would've done it with tears in her eyes. She loved it here—surrounded by people who listened and treated her gift seriously.

"I'd see him standing on a battlefield as the lone survivor. Once I saw him in an airplane hurtling to earth. That one scared me, but he pointed out he didn't have money to fly anywhere, so that wasn't likely to happen. But I guess that's not technically true."

Sunny leaned in, half coming off the armchair. "Did you ever sense that hatred in him?"

Sienna didn't hesitate saying no. "I sensed darkness at the core of who he is. But that's not a surprise. Everyone has a dark seed in their soul. Some let it lie and others tend it to grow. River's may be more than a seed, but it's not fed on hatred. That much I know."

I cleared my throat. "I'm heading out now. We're meeting River for brunch."

"Laurel's going too?" Sienna asked. "I thought this was a date."

"It's brunch. Besides, I want him to meet Laurel. We're going to the park. It'll be fun." I drifted to Sunny. "We won't be out too long. Laurel's naptime rules our life."

"Have fun," he said simply.

I opened my mouth to say more, then decided not to press it. Sunny had been acting strangely since he came back from giving River the diamonds. I asked him what was wrong and he said things didn't go as planned. No other explanation.

I didn't understand the full history between River and the princes, but I was content to wait until they told me. The guys gave me space to share my history when I was ready. I'd do the same.

Sunny kissed us both goodbye and sent us off. Hopping on the elevator, I rode it all the way down to the parking garage. River said he'd wait for me up front. With the second bombing and Genny's attack outside her safe house, Thatcher increased security at the door. It was a bit awkward standing there with all those guys when I was fairly sure the Merchants classified River as a threat.

"You ready to meet River, baby?" Laurel and I passed into the garage, heading for the security gate. "He helped Mommy when I was first on the street. Gave me food and a safe place to sleep. I know he would've helped me take care of you too. There are a few women in River's crew with kids. He would've kept you safe, which makes it hard to be angry at him. Whatever seed of darkness he's nurturing in his soul, it's surrounded by kindness and generosity too."

"Miss Blaine?" Coates stuck his head out of the guard box. "Were you talking to me?"

"Oh no, I was talking to Laurel." I waved her chubby fist at him. "We're heading out. Can you open the gate, please?"

"Of course. I'm manning the gate today, but if you wait a few minutes, Wexler can escort you."

"No, that's okay. We won't need an escort."

Coates lowered his phone. "You're going out by yourself? That's not a good idea considering what's happened in the last week."

"Trust me, I'm staying away from darkened warehouses and bald men. We'll be fine. My friend is walking with us, then we're spending the morning in a park full of people."

"All right, let me get this up for you." Coates pressed the gate button. It rumbled up, clearing my way to the side alley and River. It was almost ten.

He was up front or would be soon, then the three of us would spend the morning talking and getting to know each other without pressure or expectation.

"Mommy can admit to you that she's excited," I murmured to Laurel. "Between the crew, Sienna, Marty, Nathan, and the Sons of Saint. River and I haven't gotten a chance to spend real time alone."

"Da."

"Yes, you're right. We're not alone today either. But the three of us is just as great as the two—"

Pain exploded in the back of my head. I crumpled—darkness rushing in before I hit the ground.

# Chapter Fifteen

*Sunny*

I climbed out of the shower, snagged a towel off the rack, and slung it around my waist. Wiping the fog off the mirror confirmed I looked as pissed as the smoldering pit in my chest.

Instead of sharing that shower with my girl, she was off with the opportunistic shithead who jumped on my fake death to con my people into a deal that gave him more power. Makai and Athena didn't know the significance of the Cromwell bracelet or what Sir Richard Gatlin would do to have it and complete his collection. River bested me—again. I was "dead" and out of the game, and I still managed to lose it.

Listening to Mackenzie's story about Lyla Dawson and her unrelenting hatred, I couldn't help draw lines to my rivalry with River. We had to work the same business, but we couldn't be in the same room without trying to destroy each other.

*Speaking of Dawson...*

I padded to my closet, dialing Ryker.

"What?"

"It's a pleasure to speak to you too, dear and oldest friend. How is your morning going? Anything I can do to make it a happier one."

"Fuck off."

I chuckled. Ryker had yet to forgive me for letting him think I was dead. Actually, he swore he'd never forgive me for thinking him a traitor, and I'd better stay alert because he was picking his moment to kick my ass.

Eleven years of friendship. Some brothers you make outside the womb.

"What do you got on Damien Frost, Lyla Dawson, and Courtney Hicks?"

Ryker got serious. "Frost is in New York. His official title with Caddell House New York is marketing director. From what I've seen, his actual job is spending his wife's money hiding his affairs," he said. "Lyla Dawson works as a junior designer in the original Caddell House. Courtney used to work there too, but she left two months ago. I'm working on tracking her down now."

"Find her."

"I will." He didn't doubt it, neither did I. "Who are these people? What are we going to do to them?"

"Angel will decide their punishment," I said, removing my Brioni suit off the rack. I didn't see myself wearing Caddell for a long while. "If it's not good enough, I have something planned for each of them. They'll go down... and they'll know why."

*Beep. Beep.*

"Hold on, Ryker. I've got another call."

*Thatcher* flashed on my screen. I switched over to him. "Thatcher."

"Listen to me!" burst out of the speaker. "I'm not leaving—"

"Enough," Thatcher barked. "Sole, we have a problem down here. Normally we'd throw him out, but considering who he is, I'm asking you what to do with him."

"Is that River? What the fuck does he want?"

"He's demanding to know where Miss Blaine is. Says they were supposed to go out together, but she never arrived—"

"She was taken! Sole, he took her— Get the fuck off me!"

My jacket hit the wet tile. "Taken? Thatcher, she was going down to meet him. She walked past me out the door saying they were getting brunch and she'd be back in a few hours. You're telling me she didn't make it downstairs?"

"Sole, I'm sure—"

"Let him in. I'll be down there in two minutes."

I hurriedly dried and dressed. I stepped out of the elevator with Sienna right behind me. Give River some credit, he made an effort to smarten himself for his date with my girls. The jackets-on coats-on sweaters thing was given up for one gray sweater, clean jeans, and shoes that still had some tread. He shoved a guard aside rushing me.

"Sunny, it was one of your guys. You have to find his ass and bring her back."

"That's preposterous," Thatcher said. "Not a single one of my men would lay a hand on her. She must've changed her mind about meeting you and went somewhere else. All of this ruckus while Miss Blaine sits in a café, drinking tea."

"She's not drinking tea, you pompous fuck!"

My jaw clenched. Shouting, cursing, and carrying on wasn't River. The guy preferred to stand there smirking at everybody, internally laughing at all the fools.

"What is it you think *one of my guys* did?"

He took a breath. I think it was the first since he started. "We were supposed to meet out front at ten. I was almost to the door when a black SUV sped out of the alley, coming this close to hitting me. I saw inside. It was for a second, but a woman was lying down in the back seat."

Sienna shoved in front of me. "How do you know it was Kenzie?"

"There was a baby strapped to her chest."

"Oh my— Sunny, she wouldn't do that," Sienna cried. "Drive with Laurel out of a car seat? She'd never put her at risk."

I grabbed River's collar. "Did you see who was driving?"

"No, but he drove out of your garage and now it's sitting open for anyone to fucking come in! Someone had to open the gate and hasn't come back to close it. It was one of your guys! So who's missing?!"

"Thatcher, who's working the gate today?"

"None of my men would—"

"Who's working the fucking gate?!"

Muscles popped in his neck. Thatcher forced out, "Coates."

"Find and bring him to me. If he's not in my face giving me an explanation in the next thirty minutes, the next call I put out on him is a hit. Pull up the security tapes in the garage," I ordered, already striding off to the garage entrance. "Call Kenzie and don't stop calling until someone picks up."

I threw open the door. It banged into the opposite wall, revealing that for the first time in his miserable life, my uncle wasn't a liar.

The gate was wide open, and no one was in the guard booth.

*MACKENZIE*

"—next time she was alone. Wexler was always with me..."

Colors faded in and out. Red... gray... black... and nothing.

"Cut it fucking close, didn't you?"

I lifted my head and pain spiked my skull, tearing a groan from my lips. *Where am I? What's going on?*

"Whatever, man. You wanted the girl, I got her. Give me my money."

The colors stopped whirling, forming a bland, textured picture. The floor. I was lying on a gray carpeted floor, and the red... was mine.

My head throbbed the memory of my last moments.

*Laurel? Where's my baby?*

"Lau... rel?"

"Baby? Hey, baby. I think she's waking up."

"It's about time. Get her up."

The room spun as rough hands hauled me to my feet. Bile lurched up my throat, threatening to eject as pain and dizziness tossed my stomach. I was tossed on something soft. Slowly, the room came into focus.

Coates backed away from me, his manhandling done. We looked to be in an office or back room. A dirty, disgusting room with a used condom lying at my feet. Grimacing, I shifted away and was treated to the rest of the horrible place.

A thin woman with straggly hair bent over a table, snorting lines of coke. Beside her sat two men cleaning and reassembling their weapons. Half-naked women covered the walls and an overturned trash bin served as the only decoration. What was I doing here?

I grabbed for Coates and found I couldn't. My hands were cuffed.

"Why am I here?" I rasped. "Where's Laurel?"

Coates stepped aside. Another couch sat on the other side of the table, and tummy down on it lay Laurel. She looked around—confused and distressed at the strange, dank surroundings.

"Laurel!" I jumped up and someone grabbed my shoulder, throwing me back down.

"Ah ah." A chilling, familiar voice slid in my ear. "You're not going any-where."

Luca moved in front of me and his two goons took his place, holding me down. He crouched just out of reach of my kick. "You have no idea the trouble you've caused me, Kenzie. It got too hot in New York—the feds were looking for me. So, I changed my name, came here, and rebuilt my business. Everything was going just fine... until you."

Luca's mouth twisted, marring what I once thought was a handsome face. I was blind before, because Luca Adams was the most hideous beast to ever crawl out of a womb.

"You sicced Sunny on me. I'm guessing he hooked up with street trash like you for the same reason I tried to turn you out. You're just so damn tasty."

Luca stroked my cheek. I snapped at the finger. "Don't fucking touch me," I growled. "I don't know why you brought me here, and I don't care because you're going to let us go right now."

Luca was laughing before I finished my sentence. "Aren't you adorable? Giving orders like you're in charge here. I'm not letting you go. Why would I do that when I tried so hard to find you? To save you." He smiled into my eyes. "Your friends, the Savage Princes, are marked for death. They've got-ten lucky once or twice, but it's only a matter of time before he brings the Fairfield down on their heads. You should thank me for negotiating a trade for your life in exchange for theirs.

"A trade you're lucky I made for you. I know the Merchants turned their eyes on me because of you. Sunny couldn't be fucked to check up on me after his first warning, but after the two of you attacked me in that fac-tory, their men have crawled the city looking for me. They interrogated my girls. They've gone after my clients. They've made it impossible to do busi-ness."

"Boo-fucking-hoo," I said to him, but fixed on Laurel. My only thought was to get her out of here and away from this beast. "Don't hold your breath waiting for me to cry for you, rapist pimp."

He slapped me across the face. "That was always your problem. Even when we were dating, you never knew when to shut up."

I spat on his cheek. It earned me another slap, leaving my face, head, and all of me aching.

Luca snapped his fingers and one of his guys gave him a cloth. Wiping his face, he continued, "Times like these I wonder why I fought for your life. Despite everything, I still believe you're going to make me a lot of money. Young, pretty, clean. You're prime stock, baby. I'll get years out of you, but not here." He got to his feet, dusting off his knees. "Even after the Savage Princes and that blonde harpy are dead, it'll take a while to dismantle their organization. Their manhunt is closing in, so we're leaving. Moving to Europe and starting over there."

"We?" I repeated. Dread climbed my spine.

"You're coming with me, of course. We fly out tonight. You're my reward for the pain and money you've cost me." Blood leached from my body with every word. "In exchange, Coates is going to put the battery back in his phone and turn it on. His bosses, the Savage Princes, will think they're so clever tracking his GPS to this place. But they won't find him or you. They'll find a dozen armed men who'll make damn sure they don't get away with it this time."

"Why?" My whisper was so strangled, I barely heard it. "Why are you doing this? You're insane, Luca. Why can't you just fuck off out of our lives?"

He blinked lazily. "I'm far from insane. I'm simply a businessman. I invested a lot in you, and I intend to see that investment pay out. As a bonus, he promised me I'll be the one to put a gun in Sunny's mouth and blow his brains over the room. This is a great day," he said, grinning. "If only you weren't so selfish, you'd be happy for me."

"You won't win."

Luca paused, turning away.

"My guys are going to find and tear you apart. You'll be nothing but a bloody urine stain on the carpet after they free me, and *I* finish you. This will be the worst day of your life."

"That's where you're wrong, sweetheart. Empty threats won't work. I've already won."

Snapping his fingers, his men tossed him a bag which Luca threw to Coates. "There's your money, and you don't get extra for bringing me that."

Luca gestured at Laurel. "What is wrong with you? What am I supposed to do with a kid?"

"What was I supposed to do?" Coates snapped. "I couldn't leave it there."

"You can't leave it here either. Get rid of it!"

"No! Laurel!" A hand slapped over my mouth, stuffing the gun rag inside. Screams muffled, I thrashed in their hold, kicking and flailing at Coates as he picked up my daughter, resigned. Laurel's face crumpled. Her cries ripped my heart in two.

"Where do I take her? I've got to get out of town."

"What the hell do I care?" Luca said. "Go. And leave your phone here."

Cursing, Coates flung the phone on the couch and stormed off.

I screamed—face soaked and fighting harder than ever. His thugs' nails scored my skin holding me down.

"Wait," Luca called. "I've got a better idea. Freya, you've been begging me for one of these. You take her."

The woman dubbed Freya wiped the coke off her nose. "Really, baby?"

"Yeah, she's yours. Name her whatever you want."

"Ah, thank you." She ran and kissed him. "Now we're a family."

Freya held her hands out for my daughter—almost falling over at the weight of her. The woman was high as clouds and barely keeping herself up. Laurel cried in earnest. Wailing, she reached for me.

Freya twisted so Laurel couldn't see me. "I'm your momma now."

"Fucking loud," Luca snapped. "Freya, get her out of here. Take her to the house and wait for me. I'll be there as soon as I finish up."

"Okay." Freya walked out with my daughter without sparing me so much as a glance. Laurel's sobs faded down the hall.

"Hmmh!" I shouted and thrashed. Breaking free, I made it all of a step. The brutes tackled me to the floor.

"Don, Louie, take this one to the factory and get her ready to ship with the other girls. If she puts up a fight, beat her but don't mess up her face."

"Yes, boss."

I fought. I kicked, headbutted, elbowed, and thrashed in their grip. The two men were dark-haired, tatted, and their eyes held only emptiness. Their expressions didn't move from blank as Don popped the trunk of a dirty sedan and Louie turned me to face him. Don's punch snapped my head around. Louie let me tumble into the trunk, enclosing me in darkness.

*SUNNY*

"I'm coming with you!"

"You can't," I said.

Bane and I emptied half his stash of weapons and ammo. Liam and River were silent figures impatiently waiting at the door.

"One night throwing punches at Bane doesn't make you a fighter, Sienna. You'll slow us down."

"We're talking about my sister and my niece!"

"We'll get her back." Bane clipped his gun in his holster. "Coates's phone just turned on. We've pinged his location to an old office building in a shipyard outside North Quay. We'll get them both back—safe. Trust us."

"I can't just sit here," she sobbed. "What if I have another vision? What if it's a trap?"

Bane grasped her shoulders, gently moving her to the side. "We know what we're doing. Keep your phone on. We'll call you in an hour when we're all driving back safe and sound. One hour, Sienna. Time me."

Her lips trembled. Everything in her screamed to save her family, but she ran at that blast and felt the fire singe her skin. The kind of enemy we were dealing with wasn't one she was prepared to face.

"One hour," she said, pinning us through. "Or I come after you and get them myself."

I strapped the last knife to my belt. "Let's go."

The four of us marched out of the apartment—air crackling around us.

Coates was a new hire. Put on the payroll when Sienna and Kenzie moved in at Thatcher's request that we hire more people instead of spreading security thinner. Was he working for Grant the whole time, or did the waste of skin snatch up a bribe at the first opportunity? Whatever it was, he kidnapped my girls from what should've been the safest place in the city—their home.

"Coates doesn't live to see morning."

Bane punched the elevator button. "Like that needs to be said. The alternative was never a fucking option."

"Dear uncle," I said, "you can go now. We've got it from here."

"Another thing that didn't need to be said, because it's not happening." River shoved in ahead. "You all know this is a trap, right? They took Kenzie and Laurel to make you go inside the next building they blow up."

"Yes, we know." Liam's tone was even. "Grant has obviously given up on subtlety."

"He'll be expecting the three of you. He won't expect me." River spun me around, making me face him. "The only thing that matters is getting them back."

The three of us traded looks. I trusted a car thief with Masie's keys more than I trusted River, but this was for Kenzie and Laurel—and the look in his eyes when he spoke about them was the same as mine.

"They won't be expecting him," Bane said. "It's a tactical advantage, and we can't turn those down right now."

"Whoever wants to tag along, can," I said. "Fuck an hour, we're getting our girls back in thirty minutes. Coates is dead in thirty-five. I lead."

Neither Bane, Liam, nor River argued with me.

"What's your plan?" Liam asked.

I took out my phone, fingers dialing mid-answer. "One phone call. That's all it takes."

We rushed out the doors, blowing past Thatcher and his shouts for us to wait. I trusted the man absolutely, but I no longer trusted the men standing behind him.

"Stay with them," I ordered over my shoulder. "Every guard on staff tonight. We don't know if Coates had an accomplice. If any one of them touches their phone to call their mommas, break their fingers. Gates does not know we're coming."

Thatcher nodded. "If there is another traitor in our midst, they'll be found by the end of the night."

Masie was off being repaired. That left her brother, my Range Rover Sentinel, to carry us to the outskirts of North Quay. Coates's GPS location piped directly to my phone, showing he was in the same place, not moving.

We rolled past the entrance to the shipyard, seeing the building clear through the fence. There were no men or guards posted outside. They wanted us to come right in.

"You know what to do." I killed the engine behind a shipping container, shielding the car from view. "If one of us reaches the girls first, get them out whatever happens. There might be another bomb."

We filed out of the car, splitting apart almost immediately. Bane went to the far side of the office. Liam went around the back while I approached the door. I didn't see where River went.

Scanning the ground, I spotted a rock nestled within overgrown weeds. I flung it at the door, its thud alerting everyone inside. Actually, my shout did that.

"Hey! I know you're in there, Coates!" I crept away from the entrance. "Come out now and—"

Gunfire opened on the door, shooting the knob clear off the wood—riddling it with holes. They didn't let up for a solid ten seconds, making sure whoever stood on that blue welcome mat was mist.

He opened the door to check, and Bane dropped him with a single bullet.

Bane blew in, springing into action as three men streamed past the reception desk. Watching my brother fight—as in a true fight to the death, and not sparring or target practice. Getting to witness the real thing was a treat I did not wish on anyone, because that meant they had done something very stupid and gotten in our way.

Bane dropped and swept the first one's legs. He hit the floor, Bane ended him with the stab to the chest, vaulted over his body, and shot the second as he landed on his feet. Spinning on his heels, he buried a blade longer and bigger than the ones I carried in the final man's thigh and punched his jaw as he screamed. He collapsed and Bane ripped his knife free, letting the severed femoral artery do the rest.

Possibly it was a son's drive to best his father. Whatever drove Bane to train so hard over the years, it honed him into a fighter deadly with or without a weapon in his hands. Bane fought with a knife, gun, grenade, club, and his fists—once, all at the same time.

I closed over my hilt, pain throbbing the right side of my back. *Not now! Not when Kenzie and Laurel need me.*

Listening, Bane peered down a dark hallway that branched off to two others. He gestured for us to move. We crept down the corridor, my knife up and at the—

"Agh!" A figure materialized out of the gloom, muzzle aimed at my skull. Silver glinted above his head.

He choked, gun clattering at his feet as his hands flew to the metal biting his neck. Liam was a silent, ruthless shadow crisscrossing the garrote and pulling harder, harder, harder. He fell to his knees and Liam let him go the rest of the way—flopping over dead.

"There's nothing that way," Liam said. "They must be in the room down that hall."

"It's unlikely there's a bomb," Bane added. We didn't let our voices carry. "All these men wouldn't be hanging around here if shit was about to blow up."

"Which means there's something else waiting in that room."

"Very good," a deep voice replied. Something hard dug into my back. "How about the four of us go and find out? Don't even think about it, Alexander. I'll put a hole in his lung faster than you can—"

A sharp, vicious *snap* sounded in my ear. The gun was gone, and so was my lingering question of if River was willing to kill. For Mackenzie, he was.

The guard and his broken neck littered the path. River stepped over him without blinking.

"That was the last one," River said. "They were likely planning to pick a few of us off before we walked through that door. I looked around. There's a small, blacked-out window but no other way inside. We have to walk in and spring whatever trap is waiting."

"Then I'm going first." I pushed through them, striding toward the door and, on the other side, my girls. "If I die, avenge me."

I kicked the wood off the hinges and blew in. A dozen men formed a semicircle, the guns in their hands getting bigger as I scanned the row and landed on the final man.

"Vito."

*MACKENZIE*

The trunk opened up, allowing air in the fetid, moldy space. I coughed and agony racked my jaw. Don didn't care an ounce about Luca's order not to hit my face.

They pulled me out of the trunk. I squinted at my surroundings.

Luca told them to get me ready to leave, but we weren't at an airstrip or dock. It looked like an old bed-and-breakfast. By the skyline and driving time, I knew we hadn't left Cinco far behind. We were thirty minutes out.

*Thirty minutes. That's how long my daughter's been in the hands of a sociopath's drug-addled mistress. I have to get out of here. I have to get to Laurel!*

They practically carried me up the steps. Inside, the lights flicked on and I got a proper look at them. Both dark-haired, tattooed, and sporting guns shoved through their waistbands, but Don boasted a scar above his right eye and when Louie sneered at me, two rows of cracked, brown rotting teeth turned my stomach.

"You deal with her," Louie said. "I'll start on the rest."

My feet skimmed the floral carpet. I was certain then that the place used to be a charming inn—complete with cream wallpaper, pastoral paintings, and doilies over the lanterns. I knew this because it was still there, albeit cracked, peeling, and covered in dust.

Don tossed me inside a small sitting room. "Take off your clothes," he ordered, closing us in. "Or I'll do it for you and..." He buried his nose in my hair, inhaling me. "Take my time."

His hands pawed my wrists, then the cuffs sprang open. I spun, elbow slicing up and smashing across his jaw. Grunting, he rocked to the side and that was the distraction I needed. I snatched the gun from his belt loop.

Ripping out my gag, I croaked, "Tell me where my daughter is."

Don straightened slowly, gazing down the barrel. He said nothing.

"Tell me where she is!"

He moved and I shot back—his swipe going wide. We circled till my back faced the door. Don sized me up and down and laughed.

"You're going to give me the keys and tell me where Laurel is, or I'll—"

"You'll what?" His guttural, wheezy laugh grated on my ears. "Shoot me? You can't even aim that thing. You're shaking like a leaf."

*"Could you torture him to find the bomber that almost killed Tricky?"*

Roaring pressed on my eardrums. Sweat collected on the small of my back. I was shaking. Shaking, throbbing, twitching, and panting so hard, I couldn't suck in a full breath before it was out. All I could hear—louder than his laughter—was my baby crying.

*"Can you break bones to maintain fear?"*

"This is your last chance—"

"Save it, bitch." Don cracked his knuckles. "A delicate, round-eyed little princess like you isn't going to shoot me."

*"Can you do what it takes to be the monster that monsters are afraid of?"*

"Put that down before you make me—"

A gunshot tore through the room.

"Ahh!" Howling, Don crashed against an armchair, clutching his ruined knee. I fired again, ripping through the other one.

Don flushed pale as paper, eyes rolling up in his skull. He bellowed—tears, snot, and blood gushing free.

I cried along with him. Panting, twitching, and sore body throbbing, but... not shaking. My hands were steady leveling the gun between his eyes.

"Tell me where Laurel is," I rasped, "or so help me, I will kill you."

"Wait! Wait, you d-don't have to do this!"

"You have three seconds."

"It's not me you want!"

"Three."

He tossed his head, sobbing. "I don't— I don't know! Luca didn't tell any of us where he really lives."

"Two."

"I swear I don't know!"

"One."

A hard hit struck my temple. I tipped, gun sliding out of my hand. Louie shoved me the rest of the way down.

"What is with this bitch?" He wrestled the cuffs back on. "Hey, man, you okay?"

"What the fuck does it look like?! Get me a doctor!"

Black crept into my vision.

"We'll lock this one up—chains, cuffs, restraints, cage. She won't see sunlight till Europe."

Darkness swallowed me whole.

I woke sometime later, though I couldn't tell the difference. Walls pressed in on me—pushing on my knees, touching my toes, pressing on my head's sore spot.

A box.

I was bound, gagged, and trapped in a box... and it was moving.

# Chapter Sixteen

S*unny*

"Vito."

The crooked-teeth scum grinned at me. "Good to see you, Sunny. You're looking good, man. Amazing what a little trip off a bridge does for your complexion."

I slid off him to Adams. He relaxed on the wall, foot propped on it, and arms folded. "Where are Mackenzie and Laurel?"

"Don't worry about them," he said, waving the question away. "I'll take good care of them. You should worry about yourself right now. You're not going to walk out of here."

"Twelve armed men against one guy? Everyone standing in a neat little row—just in case one of you cowers on the floor to suck your thumb, the other guy will step in." I laughed. "You two really are piss-your-pants afraid of me."

"Look around. Does anyone look afraid?" Luca moved in front of me. "I know you didn't come alone. Liam? Ba—?"

"Now!" I hit the floor, covering my head and ears. Bane and Liam tossed the flashbangs inside, exploding light and sound, triggering gun blasts and shouts from the stupid fools who thought twelve men were enough to take us.

Liam, Bane, and River rushed into the room—snatching guns while Adams's men were too disoriented to point them the right way up. They weren't alone.

Ryker, Makai, Athena, and Athena's team rushed in behind them. Ryker would always and forever be the only call I needed to make when shit was going down.

Makai and Ryker descended on Vito, ripping the gun out of his hand. Ryker kicked him across the face. He hit the floor and had to be lifted on his feet. Luca didn't try running or reaching for his weapon. The two guns Bane had leveled on his eyes kept him still against that wall, arms up. Moving down the row, Liam helped Athena's girls restrain the groaning men on the floor, securing their wrists with zip ties.

I stood up amid the clearing smoke, bearing down on Luca and Vito. "Well, that was the shortest ambush in criminal history. Not a surprise since that's the one thing I hear you excel at, Adams—finishing too quickly." Muscles ticced in his jaw. "Which one of you geniuses planned this? Where are you holding Mackenzie and her baby?"

Luca tossed his head back, laughing. "I wish you could see yourself, Sole. Chest puffed and strutting around, damned proud of yourself for curling up on the floor while your big brothers and stronger friends saved you. Your only contribution to ending the shortest ambush in history is a jizz crack. But we can always count on you for that," he said, grinning away. "Sole 'Sunny' Bellisario. The jokester. The *clown*. Taking over territory his daddies gave him, and running it like the weak little bitch he is—giving out second chances and refusing to kill unless you absolutely have to."

I grasped Bane's shoulder, silently moving him to the side.

"You had me in that factory, and you just let me go." He shook his head in mock disappointment. "Set me free to snatch up your little girlfriend and stash her away where I get to have my fun with her again... again... and again."

An emotion sludged through my veins—thick, cloying, and familiar.

"Mackenzie's already made me money. That pretty little white baby of hers will sell for a great price. Then Mackenzie will sell over and over until I toss that slut in the trash like a used condom. What are you going to do about it, Sunny? Aw, let me guess." He snapped his fingers. "Crack another joke, flounce around acting the fool, then get someone else here to do what you can't stomach and force the information out of me. Admit it. You're so predictable.

"I mean, the thought that—that we could be afraid of you," he wheezed. Adams howled till his eyes watered. Vito and his subdued men joined in. "*No one* is afraid of you! All of North Quay laughs behind your back. So, go ahead, clown. Put on another show for us, then excuse yourself so the big kids can talk."

I nodded along, lips pushed out. "Wow, Adams," I began, chuckling. "You've given me a lot to think about. There may even be some truth to what you say. I am the guy cracking jokes, chasing a good time, and waking up in the morning with a daily affirmation on my tongue. I can see how I may have gotten a certain reputation."

"As a pathetic fool who still has his momma's milk on his upper lip," he helpfully clarified.

"You see, here's the thing." I erased the distance between us step by step. "Reputations are tricky. Easily manipulated, shattered with a word, repaired with a single act. Anyone can be just about anything in the eyes of those who see only what you allow them to see. But if there's one thing I learned from my parents"—my smile, my laugh, my *sunny* personality leeched away—"it's the benefits of wearing a mask."

"You—"

My hand whipped out, burying my blade in his torso. Adams's eyes bugged, and the laughing stopped. He grasped the knife.

"I wouldn't do that," I sang. "I just severed something very important. Pull that knife out and you'll bleed to death in exactly seven seconds. Keep it in and you have time to stumble your way to a hospital. Maybe they save you, or maybe they won't. But those odds beat seven seconds."

Luca choked, jaw working. I patted his shoulder. "What everyone gets wrong is that I don't refuse to kill because I can't stomach it. I hold off because I tend to get carried away. But what can I say? Crazy's genetic. My father is proud to know that of all the Savage Princes"—I tugged a gun off Bane and shot Vito through the thigh—"I'm the worst one."

"Ahhh!" Vito collapsed, clutching his thigh.

I shrugged. "Ah, what the hell?" I shot three more guys—their screams echoing in the empty shipyard.

"Here's how it goes," I shouted over their noise. "Whoever tells me in the next ten seconds where Mackenzie and Laurel are, gets to live. For the rest of you, your prize is bleeding out on the floor to the last sound you'll ever hear—this clown laughing."

"The boss's house!"

"The hotel!"

The hired hands shouted me down, clawing over each other for their lives.

"You can't let me die," Vito half sobbed. "I know... things. I can help you!"

I advanced on him. "What exactly do you know? And be quick. If that bleeding isn't stopped, you're dead in five minutes."

"This wasn't about Blaine," he rushed out. "That was just to get you here. We—"

A hand gripped my shoulder. "W-wait." Luca ripped my sleeve, hanging on to keep himself up. "Help me. She's at... 152 Bayview Way. I swear." Blood dribbled down his cheek. "Help me... please."

Smiling, I said, "Of course." I ripped the blade out of his chest. The pure shock on his face was as good as sex.

Luca slid onto the floor. "You... said..."

"You hurt my girls." I kicked him away. "Should've known I was lying, dumbass."

He flopped flat out on his back, light dimming in his blackened soul, and whispered one final word.

"Demone."

"River, Bane," I said. "152 Bayview Way. I'm right behind you."

They didn't waste another second tearing out the door. I kneeled in front of Vito, my knife tip dripping Luca's blood on his pants. Pain washed him out, soaking his face and chest with sweat. "I believe you were in the middle of bargaining for your life by explaining why anyone would do something so stupid as to come after my girls."

"I have information too," shouted Athena's captive. The three goons were begging and carrying on, but I focused on Vito. He'd been at the heart of this since Genny's warehouse blew up six months before. I was very interested in what he had to say.

Vito licked his lips. "It... wasn't just me," he rasped. "All of us—me, Grant, Adams, and Snyder planned to get you four here to end you once and for all. We work for—"

"Bane," Liam said. "Why are you still here?"

I turned as my brother and River filed into the room, ready to fling the same question, until I saw their hands up. Shooting to my feet, I backed against the wall where the door concealed me from the person coming inside—their shotgun leading the way and pressed to my brother's head.

"Oh, dear." A deep, nasally voice filled the room, clear over the bellows of dying men. "It looks like we've come just in time."

The side of his bald head appeared past the wood.

"Snyder, look out," Vito cried.

Too late. I reared, knife set to fly straight and true to its path. As I released it, my muscles seized—spasms rolling down my arm and jerking my fingers. My knife buried in the door, missing him by centimeters.

Snyder spun and fired. I threw myself to the floor, showered in wood paneling.

"Ryker! Makai!" Even as I shouted— As my people raised their guns—they poured through the door, a never-ending stream of armed, shaved men. We were overwhelmed in seconds.

"On your knees," Snyder ordered. Five men jumped me, one of them, Lochlan Grant, wrestled me down at his feet. River, Bane, and Liam were lined up next to me, while Ryker and my people stood with their hands in the air, no less than three guns aimed at each of them.

"Brother Walker, Brother Blake, Brother Hawkins, and Brother Ramos." Snyder nodded at four of his men. Traveling down, I landed on the walking boot encasing his left foot. Kenzie said she heard him scream when she drove away. Apparently, it wasn't out of frustration. "Get our injured brothers medical attention and bury Brother Adams somewhere dignified. He gave his life for our cause."

I bore a hole in Grant's head—wishing against all the riches in my vault that I carved that man up for parts when I had the chance.

Snyder swept a smile around the room, his gaze leaving frost where it landed. "Let us not waste time, gentlemen. Finally after all of our work and effort, we take our first victory."

They cheered. Grant bellowing loudest of all.

"Aim," Snyder said.

They cocked their guns, his pressed to my forehead.

"Fi—"

"Stop," I bellowed. "Who the fuck are you people? What do you want?"

"Isn't it obvious?" Grant sneered. "Kill them!"

"Hold on." Snyder held up a hand. "It is a fair question and the final request of a marked man. I will grant it.

"We, Sole Bellisario, are the Brotherhood. A group of men bound in one purpose: to rid Cinco City of the Merchant plague. For years, you've corrupted and controlled our home—creating a kingdom with you on high and the people your serfs. It is our mandate— No, it is our right, to kill you, and all who help you maintain your subjugation. Your question is answered," he announced.

"Brothers, on my mark, aim—"

No, I would not die here while Mackenzie and Laurel were out there waiting for us. I promised her I'd be there.

I latched on to my last chance. "Grant put you up to this," I said quickly. "Whatever he's paying you people, I'll triple it. Let us go and—"

Snyder's high, gasping laugh stood my neck hairs on end. "Brother Grant? He is no more in charge here than you are, Sole. You cannot corrupt our purpose with bribes or empty promises. The one we serve has a higher vision for this city—one where we are finally free. It is our honor to hand down your executions, knowing we further that goal."

Liam said, "Who do you—?"

"Enough," Snyder barked. "Brothers, aim!

"Fire!"

Gunfire rang in the empty, starless night.

_If you'd like to read the next book in the series, Daughter of Deception, click here._[1]

---

1. _http://mybook.to/DaughterofDeception_

# Keep In Touch

Join Ruby's mailing list for news, teasers, and more: https://www.sub-
scribepage.com/rubyvincentpage
Join Ruby's Facebook Reader Group:
https://bit.ly/3bNuCOq

www.ingramcontent.com/pod-product-compliance
Lightning Source LLC
Chambersburg PA
CBHW031833310726
48972CB00005B/1262